Love in Full Bloom

By Leah Banicki

Book 5 of Wildflower Series
Published by Leah Banicki

© 2016, 2017 – Written by Leah Banicki

https://www.facebook.com/Leah.Banicki.Novelist

Acknowledgements

I am so thankful to the many sweet souls who have helped me along the way.

To Liz, Tamera and Leslie, your generosity and help was invaluable. Thank you from the bottom of my heart for all of your hard work!

To my family and friends, thank you for all of the understanding and patience. I know I can get a one track mind when I am working. Thank you for putting up with my crazy writer mode. I know it has to be annoying!

To all of my readers... you give me so much encouragement. All the notes and messages mean so very much to me. I plan on continuing with these characters as long as you allow me to.

God bless you all!

Chapter 1

Willamette Valley, Oregon
April 1852
Corinne Grant

Corinne Grant enjoyed the sound of the morning birdsong, certainly a sign of spring coming to the Willamette Valley. The sun was shining through the windows that still held frost in the corners of the glass, proving that the chill was still holding. She put her hand to her stomach, she missed the fullness of pregnancy still, that secret thrill she had when her child was inside her. The baby reminded her every day with swift kicks and movement; proof of her presence. She felt a bit silly but she missed the feeling.

Corinne bolted from bed, tied her dressing gown over her nightgown, put on a pair of thick wool socks, and padded to the next room. Her long brown hair swinging freely down her back.

The sounds of her daughter Trudie, cooing and gurgling, was a joyful reminder of her heartfelt pleasure in being a mother. Corinne enjoyed seeing her daughter change and grow. She had been a late Christmas gift, arriving on December 27th, 1851.

Doc Williams had declared it an easy birth, which always made Corinne laugh. Easy was not the word she would have used exactly, but the hours of hard work and struggle had brought forth the little angel that brought Corinne and Lucas so much joy.

Gertrude Rose Grant was born in the early morning and by the dinner hour had brought out scores of visitors. The Grandparents, John and Marie, neighbors, and friends from the nearby church were all there to celebrate the birth of the long expected Grant child. Trudie was named after Corinne's Grandmother, Trudie, who had shared her love of plants and medicine with Corinne from a young age. It was her grandmother's legacy to have a namesake. It made Corinne's heart burst with love, knowing that she had a daughter to share her passions with.

Lucas was an overjoyed father, who doted on his little darling every moment that he could. He wrote his parents back East to brag about his firstborn, knowing they would be thrilled to know they had another grandchild. Lucas was often at home that winter. Corinne laughed when he would take extra breaks throughout his day, making little excuses for coming home for a quick visit. There was something so very charming to see her strong husband, so capable and hardy, holding his daughter. He made many special trips home. It was the winter after all; a farmer's work was not as busy during that season.

The winter had been a snowy one, but the cold was not felt much in their warm cabin, the fireplace crackled and the place was alive with new life. Violet, the young housekeeper at the Grant's house was a godsend. Violet was a great housekeeper, and a superb cook, but her nurturing and care went beyond just an employee and Corinne felt so blessed to have her, especially those first few weeks after giving birth. It took a while to adjust to the schedule of the baby but adjust they all did. Baby Trudie was not the only one to catch naps during the day.

Trudie's dark hair stood out in tufts as Corinne scooped her up for her morning kiss and cuddle. Trudie was generally a happy baby, but hungry often, and Corinne knew she only had a minute or two to get that girl ready for feeding. Corinne brushed back the baby girl's fluffy brown hair and gave her a gentle kiss or two before she was settled into the rocker for feeding time. She had been shiny bald when she was born but her hair was coming in finally.

The girl was growing fast and was sitting up and grabbing for anything she could get her hands on. Corinne wondered how soon it would be before the crawling started, it would be quite interesting to keep her out of the fireplace and away from the dangers in the kitchen.

Corinne was still able to do her work, but her rhythm had definitely slowed at first. Now it was easy to wrap up Trudie in a sling that Lucas had made and take her into the greenhouse. The laboratory was more difficult, with glass bottles and jars and hot steaming copper pots, was not a place for a child, but Corinne had lots of help, between her housekeeper Violet, her Step mother Marie, her sister-in-law Chelsea, Angela, and her newest neighbor, Edith Sparks. Everyone around was a huge support and Corinne thanked God for them every day.

Corinne never knew that kind of feeling before, very different yet the same kind of all-encompassing love that overwhelmed her at times. How could you love something that much?

London, England
April 1852

Sean Fahey stood above deck on the ship, The Atlantic, a thoroughly modern steamer-ship. He would travel in luxury with his packet ticket, allowing him a pleasant journey home. His cabin was small but it had a comfortable bunk, fresh linens, and a small chest of drawers with a washbasin on top. It was a far sight better than his accommodations had been when he was a child, and his family traveled to Boston. That room had gotten smaller every day with four people staying in it. Their parents had been wealthier than most but it had still been cramped quarters back then. His sister Angela had been four or five years old at the time. Sean tried to bring up the good memories but was at a loss to find them, his parents both dying a few years later.

Sean buttoned up his wool coat higher against his chin, the wind was brisk and he pulled his green scarf out from the inside of his jacket and tied it tighter around his neck to warm his chin. He breathed a few puffs of his own breath into his cupped hands to warm them. There were a few braziers on deck but Sean did not want to push through the crowd to get to them. He saw the other families on deck, all waiting for the departure from Liverpool, England and saw the excitement on their faces. Many of these people looked to be traveling to America for the first time, as his own family had done almost fifteen years before.

He prayed that their journey would be any easy one, he knew many would be in steerage, a harder way to travel, all the bodies sharing a space below decks, with no privacy or amenities. It would be a completely separate experience than he would have. His prayers were for the safety and health of every soul on board. In the past, he had never thought much about the needs of others. He was hoping that his heart was growing softer and more loving as he learned to lean on God. His faith was new; it had been on a rocky path for several years.

More like a decade. He thought with a grimace.

His companion and mentor Willie Shipley had had a rock-solid faith and had always challenged Sean to think of 'the good Lord'. It had taken his death the year before and a long journey to Ireland for him to find his faith again. He was not certain why he had left California territory at first, being a knee-jerk reaction to Ol' Willie's death. Sean recognized recently his propensity for running away from grief.

He had been sitting in a grand manor house, just north of Kilkenny, Ireland; the enormous fireplace had crackled heartily. His Great Aunt Felicity, whom he barely remembered from his childhood, had been chatting with him over tea and biscuits when he realized his folly in so much running.

Aunt Felicity had been the one to find him, through a lawyer in Boston, thanks to a caring friend of his sister Angela. It was a complicated web for him to fully understand. However, receiving word from Ireland that he had family still living was just the distraction he needed.

Aunt Felicity's home was grand with sprawling woods and pastures that were worked by sturdy farm hands. Her son was well beloved and paid his tenant farmers well in a time when other landowners in Ireland were fighting their tenants over every penny. Sean had spent long enough in the land of the free to understand more about these things than when he had been a child. Seeing the health and happiness of those people here made him proud to know that his family had some integrity. The more he got to know his Aunt the more he understood the reason why their situation was so rare.

Felicity Eileen Fahey was a strong-minded woman, with a heart that was full of compassion. Her father had worked for the Fahey's to manage the estate when she was a child. She and the eldest Fahey son had been married when she was only a day past her sixteenth birthday. She had spent her life on this land and knew every person in the area.

She had shared stories of his father and mother, even memories from when he was young that he had long forgotten. She brought out the letters from Sean's mother, from when they first reached Boston and had written of the hard journey and then the letter announcing her nephew's death. Sean had a child's memories of those days; many of the details had been lost in the fog of pain and loss. He copied every word into a journal, knowing that somehow he would pass along these words to his sister if it were ever possible.

It had been a grand time reconnecting with Aunt Felicity for the first few weeks in Ireland. Aunt Felicity was a sweet lady with a fine sense of humor and a generous heart.

Aunt Felicity fully explained how she had finally found him. She had posted an ad in the Boston Gazette every year, searching for (Mother Fahey) and never hearing from anyone, until last year, when she received word from a lawyer in Boston, who had been involved in the case against Sean and Angela's stepfather, who had sent them to a work orphanage.

"I had been so saddened to hear of that wretched man's actions." Aunt Felicity had held his hand as she looked into his eyes, her expression so sincere. "I wept bitter tears over the loss of your parents, but to know the depths of selfishness of that man." His Aunt had paused, being overwhelmed again by her feelings. "I was happy to finally have found you, but I mourn the way in which your lives were affected by your parent's death."

"Your Uncle was soon gone, and he wanted to be certain you were both taken care of, hence the inheritance that would have gone to your father will now go to you both. Your Great Uncle was a firm believer in saving for all of his kin. He would be so pleased to sit with you now. It is a shame that your sister could not be with us now." She had patted his cheek and smiled a faraway kind of smile. "You look so much like your father."

Sean had pleasant days with her and marveled over how life had taken such a turn for him.

Ol' Willie had only been dead a week when he had received that letter. Sean had been devastated and lost in grief; the letter proclaiming his great Uncle had passed and left him an inheritance. It had spurred him into action. He bought a ticket and was sea-bound within a few days, packing up his few articles of clothing, and placing the other items in storage in Sacramento. Sean had no plans to return to Ol' Willie's cabin, somehow he knew that he would have to find his own way, and stop living like a wandering nomad.

The trip was pleasant enough, he had used the time aboard to mourn the loss of his dear friend, but he put all thoughts of any other serious thing away. Choosing to play cards in the ship saloon every night to pass the time.

It was that day, months later, with his Aunt, who would no longer be persuaded to avoid all talk of his sister, that he finally broke his silence.

"I abandoned my sister... twice." He had said when she brought up Angela again. His throat had been tight as the words escaped.

He went back to the days when his father died, then his mother remarrying. The stepfather, who no longer had a face to Sean, had deposited them into a work orphanage soon after their mother had passed away. It had been a blight on his memory, and he tried so very hard to put those days behind him. The squalor and the beatings had been torturous. He had run away the first opportunity that arose. His sister Angela had only been 7 or 8 years old. He had left her there and never turned back.

He spilled the story out to his great Aunt, her large tears spilling over her wrinkled cheeks. There was no anger on her face but Sean felt his own shame over each tear. They were tears he should be spilling, but he could not cry over it, could not summon the emotions that seemed to be locked away.

He told Felicity about the great strides Angela had taken to find him in San Francisco and how he had turned her away. He had told her that he did not want her in his life. She was 'already dead to him,' he had said. He had to be the most unfeeling and callous brother on earth. He knew it, but could not find any way within himself to be any other way.

His Great Aunt had come closer and taken his rough hands within her own. "God help you boy, you have been running away for a long while now." She said with her Irish lilt that held no judgement.

Sean had felt shocked to hear it spoken so plainly. He instantly knew her statement to be true. He had broken down and wept. His Aunt held him and let him pour out every thought he had about how vile a person he was. They had talked until the wee hours of the morning. Felicity had shared her faith and read many passages from her family bible, persuading him to lean on God to overcome these feelings of shame. The last weeks had changed his perspective on everything.

He had indeed inherited a fortune from his Great Uncle, who had passed months before, but he left Kilkenny, Ireland a new man. His Aunt had sent him off with a few family treasures, some things for him and others for his sister. The thing he would most treasure though were her words of comfort. She had never been pushy or bold, but sweet and uplifting with every word and gesture. She had help lift him out of a dark place in his mind. Sean was more than grateful.

Sean had handled his inheritance business in London and he shopped and stayed there a week, enjoying the grand hotel he could now afford, and the sites of London. He even attended a church service at a grand old church on his last day in London. His first step into a church since his mother had passed.

Sean had received a family bible from his Aunt, a cherished and old tome, but felt he needed something to read along his journey. He purchased a handsome new bible at a shop in London on his last day, as well as a leather bound journal. He had a long way to travel and he may need to write out his thoughts.

Sean pulled out that journal aboard the Atlantic Steamer-ship as it began to pull out from the dock. The crowds along the railing waved frantically to those along the shoreline. Sean pulled out a small pencil from his pocket and jotted down a few words.

The ship sails from Liverpool. My mind is renewed. I am leaving the land of my birth, for the second time. I take with me a new faith in God and a renewed sense of self. ~ S.F.

It was twelve days aboard the ship before the shores of New York was in view. He spent those days in his cabin, writing out all the stories that his Great Aunt had shared, still fresh in his mind.

He made a stop to Boston and spent a few days reminiscing over the fleeting memories he had of his parents. He bought a few new suits, clothes, and luxury items that were hard to come by still in the West. He handled his money, having his fortune sent forward to the largest bank in Sacramento. He did not want to carry that kind of wealth on his person. All the paperwork was soon in order and he was back aboard another steamer-ship. He had to pay dearly for the extra cargo he was taking along. He had splurged in New York and Boston, knowing with every purchase that the cost would be more than it was worth to purchase to carry it to the West but he was the newly rich. He laughed over his money spending, having always prided himself on living simply. His new mindset had freed up his stubbornness and he reveled in the new thoughts that sprang to him.

He set forth over the sea again, his mind made up. He would sail to Panama, then to Sacramento. He would settle his affairs and head off on a new quest.

Sean Fahey would find his sister; he would make amends. He was going to Oregon.

Chapter 2

Angela Greaves

Angela splashed the water from the washbasin on her cheeks, and then chided herself for not taking a minute to warm the water. The cold water was a shock to her skin, she could not help but gasp, she grinned to herself over her silliness. Her husband, Ted, was in the kitchen, frying up the last of the bacon from the butcher in town. Angela wiped the cold water from her face and joined her husband. He seemed to love the morning routine as much as she did. He liked cooking alongside her every day, they worked well together, bumping into each other a few times every morning, little kisses and touches as they got their day started. Angela found it romantic and sweet the way he doted on her. Marriage agreed with them both it seemed.

"Good morning, Angel." Ted would say every day. His eyes would watch her as she rolled out the biscuits.

She would separate the cream from the fresh milk that Warren would deliver to the back door. They had just purchased a second milk cow that was pregnant. They would have a birth any day now. Angela felt an inner thrill. She loved the animals.

"Heading to town for supplies after breakfast." Ted announced as he pulled the sizzling bacon strips from the pan and placed them on the plate he was holding. Angela ran a hand distractedly through his blond curly hair on the back of his head. He gave her a look that made her blush.

"Ah good, we should make a list." Angela suggested, trying to recover her wits. "The pantry is in desperate need of some help. I was looking through last night and was sad at the state of it. We went through all of our goods over the winter months. I'm guessing our root cellar isn't much better."

Ted chuckled and nodded. "All we have left in the root cellar are some moldy potatoes and a pathetic bag of rutabagas. Never been a big fan of those." He stuck his tongue out and pulled a disgusted face.

"I'll work on a list while the biscuits are baking." Angela smiled. She was learning her husband's likes and dislikes; it was an entertaining past time.

"Henry Sparks will be coming with me." Ted said and plopped the plate on the counter next to the hot bowl of oatmeal. He stirred in some brown sugar and butter into the oatmeal. He tasted and declared it good. He took a free hand and slid it around Angela's waist trying to distract her from her work. The biscuits had to wait a minute to be placed in the oven while Ted pulled her close. Angela made no protest.

She was so happy that Ted had agreed to let the Sparks come and live near them. It gave Angela such a feeling of family and togetherness, just knowing they were close by. Henry and Ted were quick friends, perhaps even closer than that already.

She finally pushed her affectionate husband away and set him to task to set the table.

"Go on, git yerself away so we can eat soon." Angela laughed and kissed him one last time before she grabbed up the biscuit cutter. Her hands worked quickly as she pressed the cutter into the dough and then carefully scooped up each roll and placed it on the cooking tin. She pulled open the stove; put her hand inside to check the temperature. It was ready. The biscuits were baking and Angela grabbed up the fresh butter from the day before and the last of the blackberry preserves from the pantry.

She twisted on the jar of preserves and could not get it open, Ted jumped in behind her, trapping her with his arms, he grabbed the jar and with a grunt and a lot of effort he wrenched it free.

"Someone must have gotten the jam on the edge." Angela said with mirth.

"Mmhmm." Ted said slowly, he put the jar down and then wrapped his arms around the front of her, fully surrounding her; she was defenseless against his charms. He just held her for a long minute then kissed her on the right shoulder then pushed her away, kissing her above her old scars. It was becoming a habit of his.

Those scars on her right shoulder had been an insecurity for her, a reminder of her frailty and imperfections. Ted, the ever patient, had taught her to accept her scars, reminding her of all that she survived, how strong she was. He made a habit of kissing or touching her on those scars on her shoulder, where she had been pierced with rocks and branches as she fell down into that ravine years ago. How he could take something so painful and frightening and turn it into a blessing she would never know. But she marveled at his patience and love. He was teaching her to accept herself, and he took his job very seriously.

Angela leaned against him and let herself relax.

Soon they sat at the table and worked on the list for town.

"You going to the butcher and the grocer?" She asked as she pulled out her small notepad.

Ted nodded then added. "A few other places too, we have some business to do at the lumber yard and the carpenter. May get an order in for our own wagon, we need to have our own, instead of borrowing from the Harpoles."

Angela agreed it had been in the back of her mind as well. "We'll need another horse then."

"I'll probably get two. We are needing to break ground for more trees, hoping for some good horseflesh to pull stumps and break sod." Ted's eyes held a faraway look. She enjoyed seeing him envision their future. He was a good, hard-working man. She had no worries that he would always be that way.

Angela wrote down a few ideas and jumped up to check on her biscuits. They were golden brown and she fetched them out of the oven. Ted grabbed the bacon and oatmeal he had made and took them to the table. They chatted and got ideas as they ate their meal.

Angela said goodbye to Ted as he headed over to the barn to talk to Warren before his trip to town. Warren was a godsend, a solid and capable young man. Angela wondered how long they would be able to keep their work hand. He would be a man soon enough and want to branch out on his own in a few years certainly. With Oregon still having land available to any man of 18 she knew their time was limited. She and Ted would miss his help when the time came.

Angela put on her dark green coat and grabbed her list; she went through the back door and headed down the hill toward the Spark's cabin. Ted and Angela had built the cabin for the Spark's family, and they had arrived in the previous fall. Angela held a deep affection for Henry and Edith, since they had nursed her back to health a few years before. Mama and Papa Sparks were as close as family again. Angela felt so blessed.

Angela watched the sky as she walked, the clouds were coming in, dark and brooding; a few flurries of snow were floating past. The wind was picking up and the chill in the air was colder than she had hoped for. The snow was still clinging to the ground and it crunched under her feet as she walked.

She saw the blond head of Peter Sparks dashing around the yard; he was alone but seemed to be having a grand time at whatever game he was playing. He gave her an enthusiastic wave before he ran off to continue his adventures. The cabin looked homey with curtains on the windows and smoke curling up from the fireplace. Spring Creek's icy waters was beyond the cabin and Angela saw a family of deer bending their heads down to drink. Then there were two females that were heavy around the middle. She held high hopes of glimpsing a few fawns with their white spots and sweet faces when the weather finally warmed.

She took quiet steps forward and reached the door and her hand was nearly on the door to knock when it opened to Mama Sparks, giving Angela a smirk.

"Ya know, Angie dear, you needn't knock." Edith laughed and bundled her inside. It was warm and smelled of apples and cinnamon. Edith had pink ruddy cheeks; her ample waist and bosom were covered with a generous apron.

"Smells good." Angela shrugged out of her coat and pulled the list out of her coat pocket.

"Ah... just some dried up apples I am baking up into tarts. They were some sad shriveled things." Edith patted on the front of her apron and then untied it. Her cheeks were rosy and hair pulled up into a high loose bun to keep it from her eyes.

"I should check on mine. Haven't been in my cellar for weeks." Angela said as she leaned into hug Edith. They shared a warm hug. "Though Ted said we only had some moldy potatoes and rutabagas." She made a face and Edith laughed.

"I heard birds this mornin'." Edith declared.

"Yes, me too." Angela grimaced. "Then I saw snow flying on my walk over. I declare, snow in April is a bit of an insult."

Edith laughed again, agreeing. Angela told her about the deer.

Edith laughed. "Yes, Peter likes to watch them."

She looked about the place, Edith's kitchen was tidy with all her baking tins hanging up on nails and pegs along one wall, and a china cupboard along another.

"Come sit yerself down. Don't mind the laundry." Edith said cheerfully.

"I miss hanging the line outside." Angela lamented, it always was soft and fresh when laundry was dried by the sunshine and breeze.

Heidi, the eldest child sat in the parlor in a cushioned seat with a bit of sewing in her lap.

"Hello Heidi," Angela greeted, trying again to create a cheery mood between them.

Heidi looked up to Angela and smiled cordially. "Making a shirt." She said.

Angela was a bit perplexed by the young lady, it was hard to get to know her. She was sullen and quiet a lot. Her features could be quite pretty, but her moods left her looking melancholy most of the time. She was still young, and may take some time to get used to living in a new place.

"Let me see." Angela walked over to the young lady. Normally she would have reached over and laid a hand on her head, with affection. But Angela held back, knowing Heidi was not wanting that from her.

Heidi lifted the shirt and showed it, her face showing no emotion.

"That is fine; your stitch work is very good." Angela praised, hoping to get a smile.

"Thank you." Was all the girl said.

Angela tried not to sigh or show any signs of frustration. She would just have to work all that much harder to get to know the girl.

"I brought my list for town, Edith. Our husbands are heading out soon. I wondered what you needed. We can bombard them with our big list." Angela sat in the rocker by the fireplace.

"Oh good. Needing a bit to get through the next month or so. Cannot wait to start on my gardenin'. I stare out the window of my kitchen and dream about that garden plot." Edith said and plopped down onto the loveseat.

Edith opened the drawer of the side table near her and retrieved a pencil and small journal.

"The wait gets harder when the hints of spring come and then it hides again." Angela laughed.

They began plodding through the lists. Ideas came and they got off course a few times, as they started and stopped discussions on anything and everything. Within the hour, Henry Sparks peeked into the cabin to give his warning.

"Heading out, my love." His voice was low and cheerful. His mustache was even bigger than it had been a few years before. It always made him look like he was smiling, curled up in the corners. His medium blond hair and mustache was starting to show a little lighter than years past.

"We have lists for you, dear." Edith announced and got up to stop him before he escaped out again.

Henry came all the way in and retrieved the papers from the ladies. He gave Angela a big bear hug in welcome.

"You are looking fine Angela. Good to see that Ted is taking care of ya." He let out a barrel-chested laugh.

Angela blushed and nodded.

"Iffen he ever treats you different you let me know. I may be past my prime but I could whoop him into contrition if I had to." He laughed again. They all laughed, even Heidi joined in.

"Past yer prime..." Edith harrumphed and muttered. "Only 45 years old." She harrumphed again.

"I'm heading out." He announced and gave his wife a kiss on the cheek.

"Me too." Angela announced. "Going to see Corinne in the green house, to say hello to my new almond tree saplings. Silly, I know." Angela smirked.

"You should tag along, Heidi. You haven't been there yet." Henry suggested. "You need to get out of the house more."

They all looked to the young girl and saw that she wanted to protest but she nodded and gave a half smile to Henry.

"That's my girl." Henry spread his arms and on cue, she got up and walked into them. Allowing him to hug her warmly.

"I need a moment to tidy up." Heidi said after the hug ended.

Angela nodded cheerily, hoping in some way that the girl knew she wanted to spend time with her.

With Heidi gone, Angela looked to Edith. "Any improvements?" She asked with concern.

"Not much with me... she is lost to her grief still." Edith frowned, a line creased between her brows.

Angela placed a comforting hand on Edith's shoulder.

"She has bonded with Henry more than anything. I am praying that she can find some peace. The adjustment has been so difficult." Edith said, her kind eyes were misty and held the pain of trying to love someone that pushed her away. When the three children had lost their parents in a river crossing the Sparks had adopted them all.

Heidi was the oldest and still dealing with the many changes that had taken place.

"I am praying too." Angela said sincerely.

Henry patted his wife's shoulder and then pulled Angela in next to him for a sideways hug.

"She will find her way through it. Some souls need a bit more time than others." Henry said wisely.

The women nodded.

"Here's the lists, if you want to give this new one to Ted." Angela handed over the two slips of paper that had been torn from the notebooks. She felt a little silly adding so much more to the list, but she had some good ideas while brainstorming with Edith.

They spent the next minute talking of plans for spring and hope for the warm weather to come.

Heidi had finished prepping to leave and Henry coaxed a smile from the young girl before he left.

Angela bundled back into her coat and scarf and Heidi pulled on her own wool coat. The blue of the coat made her blue eyes stand out and Angela wanted to tell her how pretty she looked but refrained. The whole relationship still felt forced so they wordlessly left.

"You have fun ladies!" Edith waved at the door. Young Fiona had come out of her room and waved next to Edith, hugging against the side of Edith's hip. Angela was glad to see it, knowing that Edith cherished those children with every breath. Edith had lost a young child long ago, and never was able to have another. She had prayed for many years to be able to mother a child. Edith felt blessed to be able to have these children now and love them, she would never want a child to go unloved. It was a tragic way to be a mother, but Edith had shared many times with Angela how she knew that God was watching over these young people. She and Henry just got to be His helpers.

Angela led Heidi over the small hill and across the road. The weeping willow that sat next to Spring Creek was sad and gray, its branches dangling over land and water dejectedly. Angela looked forward to the Spring when she could sit beneath its branches again.

Angela walked on, after crossing the road, they passed the Laboratory where Dolly worked, and then they saw the greenhouse.

"It's pretty." Heidi said, breaking the silence.

Angela looked back and saw the hint of a smile on the girl's lips. Angela nodded and smiled, sharing the moment.

"It is warm in there; we will be shedding our coats soon." Angela said. She turned back and kept walking but was so very pleased to see the girl was happy. She knew what it felt like to lose her parents at a young age. She prayed so much for the girl but hadn't yet found the way to bond over their shared pain.

The green house was upon them and Angela opened the door and felt the rush of warm and moist air that rushed out at them.

"Hello!" Angela called out. The place was green and alive, the smell was earthy and made Angela long for summer.

"Hello!" A call came from somewhere.

Corinne peeked from behind a row of tall plants, and then walked briskly towards the door.

"Oh Angela!" Corinne said. She embraced her friend. "And Heidi, so glad you have come!" Corinne's cheeks were bright and pink from the warmth. Trudie was snuggled against her chest, the sling holding her snugly. Trudie's dark eyes were open and looking at Angela sweetly.

"Thank you." Heidi said before she was swept into an embrace by Corinne. Trudie reached a hand up to touch the blond braid of Heidi's.

"No, no Trudie." Corinne said gently and pried the fingers of Trudie's from Heidi's hair.

"I don't mind." Heidi said sweetly. Heidi gave Trudie a grin and patted at the tufts of brown hair. "She is growing so fast!"

"Yes she is. Oh, this sling is making me so warm in here." Corinne swiped a hand to fan her face.

"Oh, let me take her." Angela declared quickly. "Auntie Angie is ready to take over."

Angela reached out with eager arms. Corinne gave an experienced tug and released the child from the sling. Then she sighed with relief.

Angela proceeded to lavish kisses on Trudie's face and fingers.

"I would love to show you around Heidi, if you would like." Corinne offered, knowing Angela was lost in cuddling Trudie for a few minutes at least.

"Oh yes, this place is so lovely." Heidi said enthusiastically.

Angela looked up to see that Heidi's face lit up and felt such relief. Angela looked back to Trudie and said a thankful prayer to God for the unexpected gift of that smile. Trudie's eyes widened at Angela, making her day even brighter.

Dolly Bouchard

Dolly escaped the laboratory with her work done early. The bottles for a shipment of lavender oil were all labeled and boxed up in the special crates that Lucas Grant had built. So far, the glass bottles had survived the shipping with minimal breakage, which made everyone happy. Lucas and the local woodworker Amos Dreys in town had cut a woodblock stamp to make the labels easy to make after they had designed the pretty labels. It looked very professional and soon hundreds of bottles would travel to different ports along the pacific coast, with a few crates making the long journey east, to Boston Harbor.

Dolly enjoyed her labors, creating oils from the powerful lavender blooms was still exciting to her. She planned to spend a little time in the greenhouse with Corinne before she went back to her current home. She was staying again with Chelsea Grant and her growing family. She had a nice room to herself where she would lock herself in most evenings and work on her drawings. She was trying to get the leaves just right on the peppermint plant she was drawing. She and Corinne had plans to publish a book on healing herbs and plants. It was a labor of love.

Dolly washed her hands several times to get the scent of the glue from her person. The sticky sap worked well to keep the labels on the glass bottles but if Dolly didn't get it all removed she would be sticky all evening.

The night before the children at home had laughed when Dolly's fork stayed in her hands without her holding it. The memory of it still made Dolly smile.

She rinsed and dried her hands, realizing that there was still a stubborn spot that was just not coming clean. She would have to be careful to not touch her hair or she could lose a few strands.

Dolly closed up the laboratory and walked across the flagstone path toward the green house. She could see through the frosted glass that there were visitors.

She heard Angela's voice before she even opened the door. Angela looked happy and beautiful with a baby in her arms.

"It is funny Angela, in my village, the elder women spoke in the same tone to the young babies." Dolly said with a knowing smile.

Angela looked up, away from the trance she was in with the baby, and smiled warmly.

"That is interesting. I guess all cultures speak baby talk." She murmured sweetly.

"At least the Shoshone do, and everyone I know here." Dolly said with a laugh.

"Well, cause babies are just so irresistible." Angela said and made a face for Trudie, who rewarded Angela and Dolly with a chuckle.

"There is no better sound on earth than a baby's laugh." Dolly said simply.

Angela met her gaze and nodded.

"Have you said hello to your sproutlings yet?" Dolly asked and sat next to Angela on the little bench.

"No, you want to take Trudie?" Angela offered.

"I had better not. I still have glue from the labels on my fingers, cannot seem to wash it off." Dolly laughed and made a gesture of surrender. "If I wash them anymore my skin may just fall right off."

Angela laughed and hiked Trudie up on her hip, in the way most women learned since the dawn of time.

"Lead the way, Dolly dear." Angela let Dolly take the spot in front and they walked through. Angela being careful to not let Trudie's grabbing hands get ahold of anything.

A row of twenty potted saplings lined the back wall of the green house. There was twenty more on the other side that were smaller.

"Here is the batch we will plant outside this year. We wanted to give them a good start but they seem strong and should be able to handle the weather." Dolly instructed. She was a lot like Corinne and took every chance to tell everyone about every plant they knew.

"More baby trees." Angela said in a high voice for the benefit of Trudie who was getting a bit squirmy. Angela gave a few rhythmic jumps to keep the baby happy. "I think this gal wants her mama back."

Trudie confirmed the sentiment and let out a pathetic cry that was sad and heart felt. Angela made a pouty face and jostled Trudie with a few more shakes to try and cheer her.

"I'm coming!" Corinne hollered from the back of the greenhouse. Corinne came around a corner with Heidi at her heel.

Angela handed over the crying child and then within a moment of contact Trudie settled right down.

"There she goes. Mama's girl." Heidi said shocking everyone. Heidi looked to Trudie and brushed the brown fluffy hair on the sweet head with obvious care.

Dolly knew from talks with Angela that they were all praying for Heidi, who had been sullen and grieving. Dolly had met the young lady a few times but had never seen her with a smile. It was refreshing to see her now with a little color to her young cheeks.

"I should head in soon." Corinne explained. "It is near to her feeding and nap time." Corinne let Trudie lay her head on her shoulder and gave her a soothing rock. Heidi patted the girl's back affectionately one more time before Corinne made her way to leave.

"Thanks Mrs. Grant for showing me around. It was so lovely." Heidi said with a big smile.

Dolly and Angela gave each other a surprised look that said volumes without even speaking.

The door closed behind Corinne and Heidi began to talk excitedly.

"Isn't this just the neatest place. I never expected to find a greenhouse out in the West." Heidi said with animation.

"I do love it in here." Angela said with a smile.

Dolly was trying not to laugh at the shocked look on Angela's face as Heidi kept talking.

"I saw a greenhouse once; I think it was in Ohio. It was bigger than this but I think I like Corinne's better." Heidi said and took a glance around the place.

"We have big plans of adding on to it every few years." Dolly said to encourage the conversation on. It was fun to watch the girl come alive.

"I do hope I can come again. Maybe Corinne would let me come sometimes." Heidi said wishfully.

"I am certain she would love that. We love enthusiastic visitors. We will talk your ear off and force you to listen to us jabber on about plants until we run out of breath." Dolly said and couldn't help but laugh when Angela agreed.

"True story." Angela said with a chuckle.

Heidi pressed her hands together in front of her, almost like a prayer and smiled brightly.

Dolly and Angela shared a look of happiness between them. Finding a way to make a sad girl happy was a precious thing to behold.

"Ok, well then, let me start by introducing you to Angela's almond trees. Here is the batch to be planted when the time is right." Dolly went on to explain in great detail how Angela's orchard was going to grow into the best almond trees in the region.

Angela Greaves

Angela watched Heidi as they walked together from the greenhouse. *Has Heidi ever had that pink glow to her cheeks?* Angela wondered.

She walked Heidi to the front door of her cabin and paused to say goodbye but changed her mind and decided to peek in a to get word to Mama Sparks, thinking her friend needed to know a secret to make the young woman smile again.

The aroma of the apple tarts was still lingering and it made Angela realize that she was hungry. She stuck her head in the door as Heidi went through.

"You in here Edith?" Angela asked softly.

Fiona peeked her head around the back of the kitchen table and gave a mischievous grin to Angela, she held her finger over her lips in the gesture to 'shhhh'.

They must be playing a game. Angela smiled and nodded conspiratorially.

Angela crept in and sat on a chair by the kitchen counter and pretended to see nothing.

She heard Peter's voice shout out. "Ready or not, here I come!"

He zoomed from the back hallway and was looking around the room with wide eyes, a grin from ear to ear. Angela looked and saw that there were two feet behind the loveseat that were sticking out a few inches further than they should have been. Angela tried not to stare for too long so she didn't give Peter a clue.

Peter looked at Angela. He was surprised that she was there. He was listening intently.

Fiona let out a tiny giggle and Peter shrieked and found her, both of them going into a round of giggles. "You are next!" Peter pointed and laughed. Fiona's cheeks were flushed and her identical smile was infectious. They looked so much alike, her and Peter.

Peter slunk around the back of the kitchen counter to look for his mom, ignoring Heidi who was standing over the teakettle that she had put on the stove. Heidi reached out and rumpled her younger brother's hair as he went past her. Angela was glad to see that her good mood was lasting.

Peter swept back around to the fireplace and finally checked behind the loveseat. Edith yelled out a 'Boo', and Peter jumped out of his skin and gave out a whoop.

Violet Griffen

Violet Griffen had lived through much in her short life. In her 21 years, she had known abuse, and the joys of first love, and then loss. Her last year had truly been the hardest of her young life. So much pain and suffering in such a short amount of time. She was not a woman that wanted to live in fear. Violet knew who she was. She was quiet and strong, and had a heart that could be full of joy, who could learn to see past the pain of her past and just let God heal her, slowly.

She still felt that fear building up inside herself, she imagined it every day, it always came as a shock to her. The picture of the rope, going over her father's head. She had walked away from his execution; she had walked away... But still the image came every day.

She could be making bread, pounding out the dough, the soft give of the ball as she tugged and kneaded, then suddenly all she could see was his body dangling from the gallows.

She might be cleaning up the dishes, letting the water swish around her hands as she went about her work, just doing what she needed to do... Her job... she loved the Peace that surrounded her job. Caring for others – it was her gift. But yet... the thought could come at any time. The sway of his body, dangling from the noose, his face darkening as the last breath he had taken was stolen from his lungs.

She could always feel her own heart start to pound when these thoughts came. *I didn't watch it!* She would sometimes say to herself. Trying to convince herself that it wasn't really a memory. Just her imagination trying to steal her sanity, but yet it still came. At least once a day she had to tell herself. *I did not kill my father.*

The looking glass showed a young woman, not overtly pretty, but winsome enough features to be pleased when she gussied herself up

24

for Sunday service. She tried to see all of her attributes, her long blonde hair, and her cornflower blue eyes; but mostly she saw that she was damaged goods. She could not push that thought away entirely. She knew that she was loved by God, that was a hard won battle. But she wasn't certain that she loved herself as much as God loved her. That seemed impossible to her mind sometimes, but it felt true. She felt good and right when she helped others, that was the only way she felt complete. She prayed every day for her insecurities to fly away. But they held on. They burned a hole through her on the hard days, when the memories came back.

The daily passage of time is said to heal all wounds. Violet firmly believed in this. Hadn't she overcome so much already? Her beautiful and charming husband Eddie was a brief happiness that had given a glimpse of the future. A bright and glorious reminder that she could be cherished and loved for simply being. He had known her secrets and had loved her. It hadn't been an eternal love... she knew that. She had faced it... the reality of that young impulsive love that they shared. They had been poor and he had seen the announcement of gold found at Sutter's Mill as the salvation from poverty. She had watched the excitement fill his eyes, as he got more and more excited about leaving. He was pulling away from their perfect love and going away. It had been so very hard to watch. He promised over and over that he would return and they would get a plot of land. The promises were beautiful visions of a life full of love. When he had left she held onto that love, only a few months' worth, for a lot longer than that love had actually lasted.

She had struggled those first few weeks after he passed, knowing so few details about his passing. The fever he had died from. She had seen him, squatting in some miner's camp, or a small homemade hovel, dying alone and without a soul to nurse him. But the images had passed and when she had suffered her own fever, she had said goodbye to mourning him. She wore black for a time. But she felt in her heart that she was still alive.

She could watch a sunrise, see the smile on baby Trudie's face, or even the rise of her own bread baking and find herself thankful for the simple pleasures of life. She was glad for these moments and could see God in these simple things.

The image of her father dying had plagued her for months now and she had no way to see through it. She hated the way it took her breath and made her heart pound in her chest. She prayed and the feeling would pass, but again the next day it was like a new wound that she had to overcome.

Violet was learning to live with it. She stared out the frosty window, watching the snow flutter down as she recovered from another memory. She reminded herself again that she was alive, and that she hadn't sentenced her father to death. The town of Oregon City had done that. He had chosen to abuse her... She had given him the choice to back down. He had ignored her warning but she didn't know what there was left to do. She had done the right thing. She prayed again and again. A thousand times to push away the guilt. Perhaps it would never have happened if she had just spoken beforehand. If she had just been, brave enough. Perhaps he would have been run out of town, or gone away himself. He would still be alive but far away. A part of her wished for that.

He could just be gone – Living his miserable life somewhere else. Her mother would have been devastated, and her brothers would have been younger and confused. But they would not have the stigma attached to them all. Violet took a deep breath. Not enjoying the line of thoughts that tumbled through her consciousness.

A part of her wished that she didn't have to see her family again. The remnants that were left over after the carnage that Timotheus Smithers had left behind.

Her brother Tim was still in shock. His smile was a ghost that only hinted at happiness. Her youngest brother Harold was even worse for a time, barely smiling at all. They were the worst casualties, with no choices in the matter, just dragged through the emotional trauma of a childhood with a monster. Violet was still lost when it came to speaking to her mother. It was a stunted and strained relationship that teetered on the edge of insanity in Violet's heart. Forgiveness was there, in its fractured way. But it was so very hard. Violet had to force herself to look in her Mother's eyes when she made her visits. She forced herself to go back to the Watermill at least once a month, for her brothers. They had never given up on her, and she wouldn't give up on them. Especially after they had sided with her, against their own father.

Her Mother's eyes... within the depths there was always shame. Violet didn't want to see it. It made her heart ache in that way that daughters feel when they have been raised to feel it. She knew she had to forgive and forget. It was a daily battle. Perhaps someday the urge will be easier. The urge to let her mother's betrayal go when she really wanted to hang on to it.

When she had been young, she and her brothers had been out playing along the edge of the creek. Just an afternoon in the sunshine when they didn't have chores or obligations for a brief and glorious window of time. Violet had a rag doll that her mother had made for her. It was her constant companion and Violet had dropped the doll, tragically, when a skunk had invaded the secret grove they were playing in. Her baby brother Harold was scared, he couldn't have been older than three years old, she had scooped him up and they escaped the spraying from the skunk with only moments to spare.

Violet was rewarded with kisses from her mother but Violet was worried about her baby doll. Before the sun set she went back to the little grove and her dolly waited there for her. The scent of skunk was overwhelming and the dolly had not escaped the spray. There was no solution to clean the noxious scent from the doll. Her mother had tried everything in her power to save it, but the stench was persistent. Violet remembered the tears and cries when she had to admit that the doll could not be saved. Her father had wanted to burn the doll but Violet had run off with it and hidden it behind the barn in an old flour sack. She would visit the doll when she had playtime and would come back smelling like the dreaded skunk day after day.

It had taken a lot of talks with her mother but finally Violet had to realize that the doll was no longer a joy to her. But something that had to be replaced. She had watched through buckets of tears the doll burning in the fireplace. She had thrown in it there herself. The pain had been so real and raw, but the healing had come when her mother had pulled out her fabric scraps and they made a new rag doll together.

The feeling in her heart when she looked in her mother's eyes was like the memory of that favorite doll. A stinking reminder of something loved but lost to her. It would never be the same to hug and cuddle her. It was a wasted and soiled love.

Violet watched Corinne walk through the snow through the small window of the kitchen and welcomed the distraction. She needed to overcome this feeling of loss and hardship. She loved her new family, in some ways more than the flesh and blood one that was south of town. It was easy to love them. Corinne and Lucas were her employers but they were also her dearest friends. She cared for them like family, because she loved doing it. She cooked and cleaned for a salary, but she would have walked through fire for them. She embraced the feeling and let it wash over her as she felt the grin spread across her cheeks.

Corinne was trying to shiver out of her coat with Trudie in her arms. Trudie was flushed with moist eyes.

"Look who is sleepy..." Violet spoke with a pout and reached for the baby. The girl reached out for Violet and it gave a tug at her heart. She was needed and loved. It was enough for today. The healing was here, in this place and she gave the girl a little hug and cuddle against her chest. Violet ran a hand over the brown tufts on the soft head and felt the warmth there.

"Thank you Vie." Corinne said. Corinne began to unbutton the front of her dress to feed her daughter but she gave an appreciative smile to Violet that also tugged at her heart.

This was so simple. This house was the place she was loved, accepted, and needed. It had never felt forced or coerced, but just real and powerful. Violet was thankful.

Chapter 3

Galina Varushkin

Galina huffed out a frustrated breath as she scrubbed at the pans over the tub of warm water. She was using every ounce of anger she felt at her father on the stuck on porridge. Their relationship had never been a good one. She had spent years working on controlling her anger when it came to his actions. First, leaving her family behind a few years ago to run to the gold rush in California territory. Then he did little to help her as her mother and brother were dying of yellow fever just a few months back. The grave of her mother and brother were just down the road near the small church. Galina walked to visit the grave every few days. Renewing promises to her mother, to take care of her brothers, and to keep the peace with her father. Her heart was still broken, and a few months of grieving had created a false peace in her household. But that seemed to be over. Her father's announcement had brought her temper back to a boiling point.

Now she could not believe her father had the nerve to announce his new engagement over breakfast. Her mother and baby brother had not been dead for even a year. The thoughts broiled in her head, the anger and disgust she had for the man made her stomach ache painfully. She felt a pain in her chest at the disloyalty.

Galina felt foolish, not realizing that his many visits to town were to find a new wife. It seemed all so simple in his mind certainly. Slava Varushkin felt he needed a wife, so he just trotted into town and found one. A nice young widow, he had told Galina and her two brothers while they stared at him over their untouched bowls of porridge.

Her father's smile had faded when Galina began yelling. She was not listening to her inner voice to remember to hold back her opinions. They just burst forth.

"Your wife, Magdalena, is barely in her grave." Galina had said with obvious anger. "You couldn't even mourn her for a few more months or pretend too."

Her father had stood, his fists clenched when she had said that. The boys responded by shrieking and ducking under the table. Galina held her breath, knowing that look on his face. He had been a hot-tempered man, but he never got as angry at anyone else like he did with her. He had grabbed her brothers before, by the arm, and given them a roaring scolding. But he never would get as enraged as he always did with her. She couldn't really understand it. It was a mystery in her mind. She watched his face turn colors and his eyebrows go down in his enraged face that he saved only for her.

"I better never hear another word like that from you again... Or I will not hold back." He said. His face was red and his chin bunched up angrily. Galina was actually surprised he hadn't let his fists fly. He had struck her with less instigation. She had never seen him strike her mother. He saved it for her. Galina felt a small sense of relief that he had held back but she was resigned to this happening again. That window of calm since her mother's death was at an end.

Galina wiped the pan and set it on the nearby towel, trying to pull up any kind of control she could find over her emotional state. She wanted to punch his face, and make him hurt for once. She knew it could never happen, she was a small female. He was a large framed man, with endless strength. He had never refrained from punishing her when she lashed out before. She knew she was lucky that he had not struck her recently, but she didn't feel lucky. She just was enraged. She sat down near the fireplace and cried out her anger. Her brothers were off to school and the house was now so very lonely every day. She still missed her mother so desperately. How could her father be so heartless?

The small cabin she shared with her father had been a gift, only a few years ago, when his family had been hovering in a linen tent outside of Oregon City. Her father had left them penniless to search for gold in California territory. They ran out of food and were living in filth and squalor when the Spring Creek Fellowship Church had refurbished this cabin for her family. Galina wondered now about how things had happened. Her father had returned, but things never did get any better for their family, yes, they had a roof over their head, but his moods made life so tense and unbearable. She had tried repeatedly to make her father happy but it was never enough for Slava Varushkin. He would always look on her with disdain, and today was another example that she could do nothing right in his eyes.

Galina felt that stab again of loss. The pain of losing her mother was bitter and stabbing through her gut at least a few times a day. Her baby brother, Radimir, was a hard loss to deal with, but Galina's mother was felt the deepest.

Galina just wanted her mother back for so many reasons and she had to remind herself daily that there was nothing she could have done. Yellow fever had taken many lives in the Valley, and her home was not the only one to feel the pain of death.

All she could do is to keep ahold of that tiny shred of faith she had that God had a plan for her life.

Galina took a deep breath and wiped down the rest of the clean dishes to put them away. She was going to the Grant house to do some laundry. She knew that spending a day with Violet Griffen would help her through the mood she was in. Violet was only a few years older than Galina, but her joyful outlook always rubbed off on Galina. Violet was someone that Galina wanted to be like. Despite the tragedies that Violet had faced, she still held onto her faith in a way that Galina could respect.

Galina wiped away her tears and hung her mother's apron on the hook by the bedroom doorframe. She would leave the quiet house gratefully. Soon her father would bring in some other woman to take over, and things would never be the same.

Clive Quackenbush

Clive Quackenbush took a heavy stick and punched it through the ice. The water splashed out and gurgled up through the hole and Clive stuck his hand into the hole, he gasped at the frigid shock of his hands in the icy cold water. He pulled up the iron trap, a large beaver was caught and Clive grunted to pull up the wet beast.

The crunch of snow under his boots was loud in the silent morning. The mist of his breath floated around his face as he tugged the beaver out of the water.

The beaver made a slapping noise on the crispy layer of icy snow. Its thick wet coat looked almost black against the brightness of the snow. His buckteeth a bright yellow orange protruding from its mouth.

Clive grunted a little and breathed a few extra puffs of air from the exertion. He was glad to have one less beaver on the land. Too many of the pesky critters always create havoc every spring when they build up the dams and force the small creek to overflow on one side and reduce it to just a trickle on the other. He loved trapping, it allowed him a chance to be outdoors and be one with the land. He looked at every creature with respect, but over population of any creature had its dangers. Too many deer can lead to starvation amongst the herds. Too many black bears can cause them to go further down the mountain bluffs and then they threatened the farmers and their families.

Understanding the balance of nature was a mountain man's trade. He had high hopes that he would always keep that balance within himself and teach it to the younger generations.

His neighbors always came to him with reports on the animal activities of the area, and he was pleased to do his part.

He would use every part of this animal to its full potential. He would draw the musk gland out and save it for further trapping, scrape the hide to preserve it, then used the brains as a tanning method to make the hide soft and supple. It was a tedious task but he enjoyed every step of it in his own way. The meat would make a pretty decent stew to use up his winter stock of vegetables in the root cellar.

Clive put his leather gloves back on after he dried his hands, the joints of his fingers were cold and the bite of the wind was unforgiving.

He looked up at the gray sky, wondering when the hint of Spring would show through with at least a little bit of sunshine.

"Not today..." Clive muttered to himself.

He grabbed the trap from the beaver and unhooked its jaws from the beaver's head. He put the trap in a basket he would sling over his shoulder. He lugged the wet beaver onto the wooden dolly to drag through the snow. His old cabin was only a mile or so away.

Soon he would have to make a decision about his land. He didn't want to part with it, but his life was taking on some changes. Perhaps he could find the right person to rent the land to, or someone who would stay and work the land. He wasn't sure what he could do legally. He would have to talk to a member of the land committee and see what his options were.

He had fixed up the house that was closer to town. His beautiful bride-to-be was pleased with the large front porch and the interior. He so wanted to make Olivia smile. It was a fresh start, he was over sixty years old but he had another chance to be in love. God never ceased to make Clive wonder. She was getting her own second chance and Clive was somehow glad that he was able to do that for her too. Olivia was witty and talented in her own way. Clive would have to keep on his toes to be able to keep up with her.

Clive tramped through the woods and watched as his cabin grew closer and closer through the break in the trees. The dolly slid easily through the icy snow.

Clive was glad though when he finally reached his trapping shed and got the beaver hung up on a hook.

He made quick work of skinning it, setting aside the innards in a pail, then settling the meat on the worktable. He took care to do a thorough job of getting all the red meat from the hide.

The scented musk sack called the castor gland from the front had been cut out and Clive put it into the beaver bait jar. It stunk to high heaven, but worked really well for setting new traps.

All in all, a successful trapping morning. He had several hides that he needed to work on, but his hours have been fuller than usual over the winter months, he would have to stay on task to get all these hides tanned once the weather got warmer.

He needed to make sure his smoker was working properly to get that golden color on the hides when they were finished.

Clive washed the grime and blood from his hands and rubbed some of the ointment that his neighbor Corinne had made for him. His hands would always get so cracked and dry before. He was more than a little tickled when she had given him the ointment for a Christmas present. Pretty certain that Corinne Grant, and her husband Lucas would be his lifelong friends. It was good for the soul to be amongst such good folks.

Clive took the meat to his cabin and settled it on the counter to cook later.

He started up a good fire in the fireplace. He needed to get warmth to his bones before he started up his next activity.

He had a few things on his list for the day. Including a wedding gift for his betrothed. He wanted her to have something special of her own in their house together. Carving a wooden chest seemed like a sweet and thoughtful gift. He could see the design in his mind and was eager to get to work on it. He had the lumber already cut to size, he needed to get it assembled before he got out his chisel. His heart felt that pleasant thump whenever he thought of her. Such a pleasing thing after sixty years of living... To still feel that lovely thudding in his chest over the love of a good woman.

The reminder that his wedding was coming soon was bringing back old memories. The dust of the trail when he made that first trip west. He came out with a few other trappers. He spent a season on the Snake River back in the 1820s. He made a good fortune that first season and built a small rough cabin before he went back to get his wife and children. It was a rugged life but it was so very exciting. Clive had been a young man when he read about the exploits of Lewis and Clark. He was on his own at a young age, doing his own exploring, first the Midwest, then the West. He has had quite a life so far. Knowing this new chapter was starting soon made him think about his early days here in Oregon Territory. The struggle to get by, the few people that were here had to work together to survive the winters. He remembered helping to put the roof on the Hudson Bay store for the original owner, before he pulled up stakes and sold it to Clive, who was ready for a change.

Clive wondered if he had lived nine lives like a cat.

Corinne Grant

The weather finally broke in the afternoon and the snow clouds cleared away to allow a little blue sky to peek through. Corinne was glad of it. Her daughter went to sleep after her feeding and Lucas came in from burning stumps with his brother Russell. He had some serious mud caked on his boots and was seated on a stool near the front door, trying to wash off the mess without tracking up the clean wood floors.

"Greetings husband." Corinne placed a kiss on the top of her husband's head, surprising him. She was pleased when he jumped a little bit.

Lucas let out a breath and chuckled softly. They were all learning to be quiet with a baby in the house.

"How is the eastern field coming along?" Corinne asked him when he had recovered from the shock.

"Ach, it will go better when the ground thaws out more. I think we are wasting a lot of energy trying to get the stumps out now. Tomorrow Slava and his crew are going to go back to fellin' more timber until the snow is gone." Lucas shrugged, he hated to admit he had calculated anything wrong. "I guess I'm not always going to get this farming thing perfect."

"No one expects perfection, my dear." Corinne smiled as she pulled up a chair next to him.

"I do." Lucas gave her a wide-eyed look that was adorable.

"We are all getting impatient for Spring." Corinne patted his shoulder.

Lucas gave her a serious look for a second and leaned over to give her and unexpected kiss. She was surprised by it.

Corinne looked down at his boots and saw how shabby they were looking. "You need a new pair?" She asked.

"Probably, this set has been pretty beat up." He said giving his boots a sad glance.

They sat at talked for a little while, making a plan for the next day.

"I think a trip to town would be good, if the kinder weather holds out." Corinne smiled at the thought.

Chapter 4

San Francisco
Sean Fahey

The port town of San Francisco was bustling and chilly when Sean arrived. His many trunks were unloaded by the hulking dockworkers. It had been almost a year since he had left this stinking and lawless city but he had felt a stirring in his heart when he saw the fog over the harbor. There was beauty to be found everywhere, he was learning, but sometimes you had to look for it.

His leather bound journal was tucked into the inside breast pocket of his coat and he had jotted down a few thoughts as the boat had come to shore. The long dock that was new was a nice addition and Sean was impressed with the city's growth. He could look past some of the dirty dwellings and ramshackle buildings to see more solid brick structures. The town was a boomtown, so many hordes of men seeking their fortunes. But he could see that there was a large effort to make this a real town. Under the filth was the start of a foundation.

A dockworker got his attention and Sean pulled out a few silver coins to pay to rent a few wagons to load his haul. He felt a little ridiculous, having so much, and he felt the stares from folks around that he must be a wealthy man to be able to afford to have that much shipped from the East. He wanted to make a fresh start here and bringing gifts and luxuries to the West seemed like a grand idea when he was in New York. He was now reminded again why his ideas were not well thought out. Everything was heavy and cumbersome. Getting all his boxes and trunks to Oregon was going to take a miracle. But Sean thought that he was going to need a few miracles to make things right with his sister Angela. So what's a few wagonloads of treasure to deal with. As long as he had money to pay the laborers, he should stop feeling guilty. He would help put food in their mouths and a little jingle in their pockets. He had once been like them, working hard for every penny.

He had arranged with a steward from his hotel in San Francisco to have his items stored safely for the week he would spend there before he would take a ferry to Oregon City. He felt eager to be on his way but knew that the time here would help him to say his final goodbye to Ol' Willie.

Sean got settled in at Harbor Hotel and was pleased by the grand room he could afford. The city may have been growing too fast but a few establishments were doing a good job of staying classy. He was so relieved he wasn't holed up in some saloon or inn, with harlots and rowdy music playing at all hours.

The street he stayed on was lined with a few saloons but he found a nice family restaurant that served Italian food that was very tasty. He tipped his waiter generously and took a stroll along the water to watch the fog fade over the water.

He took out his journal from his pocket with the small stubby pencil that was tied to the ribbon bookmark.

The bay in San Francisco is peaceful. The many empty ships that haunted the harbor last year have been sunk or used for building materials. The many men that have traveled these waters searching for that elusive happiness have met with poverty or despair. I hope my journey back brings me the thing I long for more than anything. Redemption...- S.F

Sean stared at the grey-green water and let the calm absorb all his doubts. His prayers over the last weeks had been endless but he knew that worrying would not bring about anything. He would do the hard thing and face the thing he feared the most. Every part of his heart was expecting the worst from his sister. But he had to give her the apology that she deserved. Would she be able to forgive him? Only time would tell.

❖◆❖ ❖◆❖

Megan Capron - The Hampton House

Megan enjoyed the applause as it rolled through the dining room of the Hampton House, an upscale restaurant near the center of town in San Francisco. She had taken the stage name Rosie Green over the summer, her middle name was Rose, and her mother's maiden name was Greensborough. That was an easy thing to decide. Another easy choice was her decision to put herself under the influence of the wealthy Mr. Hampton. What had started as a simple flirtation during an evening meal had created a series of events that left Megan few choices.

When the young man she ran away with had abandoned her and stolen all of her money she could have called her parents, but Megan didn't want to see their looks of disappointment. She had made her choices and now she was well set. Her benefactor, the owner of the restaurant had set her up well. Her darling Pruitt Hampton was very generous with her, showering her with fine dresses and a few lovely pieces of jewelry. Her favorite thing above all was her own little apartment on the top floor of the Hampton building. She had been allowed every luxury she asked for, even a fine cushion settee that she had seen at a local shop when he had taken her out for a stroll in the early days of their relationship. Pruitt was twice her age, and some days she wondered how long she could pretend to be attracted to him. But over time she grew better and better at her deception. She still considered herself an actress in her heart, and this was just a role she was playing at. The doting mistress of a married business owner.

To the staff of the Hampton House she was the entertainment, Rosie Green was the singer that graced the stage every Wednesday through Saturday night. Pruitt had had good success with the orchestra, but the greatest success came when Rosie had taken the stage. Her voice was gifted and her charm won over the customers. Most nights the restaurant would be full of dancing and singing and made the Hampton House a rousing success. Every Thursday the local newspapers would run an advertisement mentioning the Hampton House and Megan thrilled over seeing a beautiful drawing of herself.

The Hampton House - Featuring **Rosie Green** *and orchestra for fine dining and superb entertainment.*

Megan was pleased with her situation and enjoyed the role she was playing still. Some of the staff had caught on to the relationship she had had with the owner, but so far, everyone kept their tongues from wagging too much. The Hampton House was a fine job for them all and no one wanted to deny the owner from having his fun.

Everyone, including Pruitt called her Rosie, he knew her real name, but after the first week of working there it was never mentioned again. A part of her could truly put her past behind her. She could easily forget about her parents and family members who were possibly worried about her and her disappearance. Rosie was a girl with no past or encumbrances. She could live the way she wanted with no feelings of guilt or shame. It was the way she wanted it.

Megan took her bows after her last song of the night, reveling in the applause. She gave her brightest smile to the audience before she slipped backstage. Her corset was extremely tight tonight to show off her small waist in the pale white silk dress she wore. She caught her reflection in the large mirror that was backstage and was pleased with her appearance. She looked so very elegant, her new ladies maid was a marvel at pinning up Megan's blond curls into the latest styles. Her 'Darling Pruitt' had seen to getting her every Paris fashion booklet, magazine and pamphlet he could get his hands on.

The orchestra was taking a break and she made certain to thank the conductor for his fine work for the evening. She knew that he appreciated her gushing over him. She never flirted outright, especially in front of Pruitt, but she made certain that the conductor was always pleased to work with her. She was figuring out her place in show business, it was all about stroking the many egos involved.

"As always, Miss Green, you were a pleasure to work with." The conductor kissed her hand with a flourish and gave her a wink that was bold.

Megan blushed, as she was supposed to, and made her way up the back stairs towards her apartment. She rang for her maid the moment she was inside. The small brunette was there within a minute, which pleased Megan.

"Help me out of this." Megan declared a bit more firmly than she intended. She was feeling trapped in the tight corset, and didn't want to be in it one second longer than she had to be.

"Mr. Hampton was right behind me." The young girl spoke up.

Megan huffed out a breath, he would want to see her in the new dress. She would have to endure the pain in her ribs a little longer.

Megan looked to the girl absently, forgetting her name. "Could you order me a plate of food?" Megan asked a little more politely. "I'm sorry, what was your name again... Julie?" Megan guessed.

"Emily, Miss Green." She said swiftly. "You want a steak or something else?"

Megan thought for a long moment, wondering if her belly could handle a heavy meal. She thought it wise to eat something light.

"Roast chicken and potatoes please. Thank you Emily." Megan repeated the girl's name over again a few times to cement it in her memory. She was horrible at remembering details like that.

Pruitt came into her apartment without knocking, it was a habit that she found irksome, but she didn't know how to broach the topic. He paid for this place, he was no boy she could toss around with pouting and a temper tantrum. Megan looked to Pruitt with her stage smile and gave him a warm kiss on the cheek when he approached her.

"You were an angel on stage tonight." Pruitt purred at her and grabbed her hands and gave her a once over, his eyes drinking her in. "That dress is a delight!" He praised her often, she tried hard to enjoy it.

"Thank you, darling!" Megan said enthusiastically. She had met her match and had to keep up appearances with him, even when she was tired.

"You will be pleased with me, my Rosie." He said and gave her a kiss that was warm and tasted of scotch.

"Oh, you do spoil me." Megan said automatically. She knew what he wanted to hear.

He took her hand and led her to the settee and pulled out a large box from behind the small table.

Megan smiled at him warmly and waited for him to present her with the gift. His presents were always grand but they always had strings attached. She wasn't sure she was up for his expectations but she remained firmly in her role as doting mistress and kept her mask on firmly.

He handed her the box and she opened it up. Megan unwrapped the paper that surrounded the gift and pulled out a snow-white wrap, made from the softest fur she had ever felt.

"Pure Ermine!" Pruitt said with a wide smile and rosy cheeks.

It was indeed the loveliest fur wrap she had ever beheld. Her own mother had a grey fox wrap that was a fine specimen, but it was not as fine as this.

"Oh, Pruitt!" Megan said with a real thrill. This was adding something substantial to her collection of fine things. Everyone who saw her in this would be green with envy.

"Put it on, my dear." Pruitt urged her. His left hand stroked her shoulder affectionately.

She gladly put on the wrap, feeling its weight around her shoulders, the satin lining felt fine on her arms and the warmth was lovely. "This is the most stunning gift, darling Pruitt." Megan smiled, indeed glad for the gift but wishing that she could just rest for the evening. She said the right words, though, and saw that he had appreciated them.

He pulled her into an embrace, she tried to ignore the deep sense of shame, the reminder that she was not raised to be any man's mistress. She had made her choices, though. She had to live with them now.

Chapter 5

Violet Griffen

Violet got a ride to town from Lucas, and she walked through the main street, with her coat pulled tight against her. She looked up to the light gray clouds above and hoped they would not rain on her today. She did not need any more reasons to dread the trip further.

She wanted to see her brothers Tim and Harold desperately, having time with them was important to her, but every visit gave her fresh doubts about her own mother. There was nothing said or done that could give Violet any true reasons to avoid it, but the constant looks of apology and sadness from her mother made her completely uncomfortable.

How was she supposed to do this? She asked the Lord many times in her moments of prayer. She spent the last years trying so hard to forgive her parents. Now that her father had been punished for his sins what was left for her to do? The town council had made him pay the ultimate price for abusing Violet, but what now to do with those deep scars left behind.

Her mother had never believed her when she was young, and even stood by her husband in the courtroom after Harold was a witness to the horrific abuse. She saw her brothers every Sunday at the small church outside of town, and that was always a bright moment in her week, but she had found lately that her eldest brother, Tim Jr., was noticeably quiet and withdrawn. The pressure of running the mill was now in his hands. He didn't seem to want to talk with her after church with a crowd around, and with their mother at home, perhaps the weight of everything that had happened was just too much for him. Violet was praying constantly for wisdom on how to help her siblings.

She got to the edge of town and prayed with every step that the visit would go well. There was no way to know how it would go ahead of time so she just strengthened her resolve to hold on to the peace that she had within her heart. She had done nothing wrong in the sight of God, and that meant a lot to her. But in the sight of her own mother, that was a different feeling altogether and she felt that internal pressure whenever she was around her.

Violet saw her brother Harold as she reached the opening in the trees along the road. Harold swung his axe with precision and split the chunk of wood evenly. He reached down, grabbed the pieces, and chucked them into the large stack behind him. He finally noticed her and his face split into a happy grin that warmed her heart. He had seemed to bounce back from the tragedy better than everyone else in the family and his cheeriness was such joy that was infectious. Harold swung the axe into the stump.

"You are getting taller." Violet said and he ran up to her and gave her a warm hug, he proved his strength by lifting her off her feet.

His grin deepened as he let her down when she squealed. She smiled at him but she felt that bittersweet recollection that she had missed him growing up. She would give almost anything to have been able to be the big sister to him. He seemed to sense her thoughts and he placed a hand on her shoulder. It was a wordless way to tell her things were just fine between them.

They walked into the house together. Tim was settled at the table going over papers while her mother was washing dishes. Violet could tell that bread was proofing in the kitchen from the scent of yeast and dough that was heavy in the air. Tim looked up and smiled a half smile to see her. Her mother's look as she turned away from her wash water was less than pleased. The feeling between Tim and her mother was tense and Violet knew she had missed something.

"I'm sorry I've missed coming the last few weeks. The weather has not been very cooperative." Violet said and sat in the chair next to Tim.

"Don't fuss over that. It has been a harsh Spring." Her mother said from her spot in the kitchen. She was wiping her hands with a towel and she came over to join them.

Tim was staring blankly at the papers in front of him, unseeingly. "Mother has a grand plan. She may as well tell it."

"I think it is for the best, son." She said flatly.

Her mother sat down on the far edge of the table and she brushed at a wavy strand of her blond hair that had come loose from its hold. Violet felt that tension soak in as the tension in the room was deepened by the silence.

Her mother sighed, a deep and ragged breath that she let out slowly.

"I am leaving in a few weeks." She spoke softly, she faced the table and fidgeted with her hands.

Violet felt that internal gasp at the announcement. Where would her mother go? She wondered. There was no part within Violet that would encourage her mother to stay. In many ways, it would probably make life easier.

"My sister lives in Michigan with her family. They have a farm there and I have received word back from her that I am welcome to come." Her mother spoke and her eyes were sad.

Tim huffed out a breath. "You are doing what you always do." He slapped a hand down on the table. "You run away when things get hard." His blue eyes looked coldly at his mother.

"You are right in many ways, Tim. But I believe that things will get better for you when I am gone." She wrung her hands and then patted at her dirty apron.

"You have never told me about family ever." Violet spoke up, feeling confusion start to well up within her.

"They never approved of your father. They had probably been right about his temper. No one could have known about the other things but it was in the past." She said shakily. She gave them all a look, one by one. "You are all stronger than I am. I cannot stay here any longer when it feels like my presence causes so much continual pain."

Violet saw the resolve and nodded in agreement. Her mother's presence was difficult and she wondered if that would ever change. Her mother was never one to be extremely sincere in the way she spoke or acted, it was hard to trust that she wasn't living there because it was convenient, not because she truly wanted to make amends.

"I cannot do my work, for no one in town will buy my bread. I made a crucial mistake when I stood by Timotheus. I was wrong. I know that." A few hot tears ran down her pale cheeks. Violet felt like a cold and heartless daughter when those tears didn't affect her. She was running out of pity. Forgiveness was easier somehow.

"I hope this is a new start for you, mother." Harold stood behind his brother, his hands on his brother's shoulders. He didn't seem sad and it made Violet wonder at how much pain they had all suffered this past year.

"I know God can forgive me for what I have done to my children, the blind eye that I turned to keep the peace. But I am not certain I can forgive myself. All of you are trying so hard to let the past go, and I do see the effort you all have done but I just am not certain I can find true happiness here any longer. Too many know my sins. It is a dreadful thing to live with. I long to go to church but I'm always nervous that people will stare. Or even worse they would be kind and I would always wonder if it was false kindness and then the gossip would begin again." Their mother spoke again and Timmy looked up to watch her speak.

Tim let out a breath, noticeably calmer than before. "Those are good reasons." He nodded in defeat. "I still think you could have tried to stay, and make this work. But I can understand wanting a fresh start." Tim suddenly looked tired and worn from his internal battle.

"I will write to all of you from time to time, I want to hear about your lives." She looked hopeful.

"I will write back." Violet volunteered, feeling more reasonably about her daughter duty. It was a lot easier to see a future of writing a few letters a year, instead of these awkward visits that always made her feel worse afterwards.

Both Harold and Timmy agreed that they would write as well. The tension eased as she laid out her plans to leave in a few weeks. She would go by boat back to the East coast and then take a train back to where she was born.

Violet only stayed for a few hours, and then walked back to meet up with Lucas and his wagon full of beef, pork and food stores. She felt wrung out and tired but as the minutes passed by she was more and more hopeful that she would be able to grow closer to her brothers. The years of abuse were done, the damage was coming around full circle. Her mother was paying her debt in her own way. The journey would be a long one and Violet prayed even now for her safety. It would be a day-by-day journey for Violet as well, to forgive completely and to find a way to love her again. For now, she would keep leaning on God for the rest of her own healing.

❦

Violet Griffen took a deep breath and let the earthy taste of the air into her lungs. She had dumped out the wash water from her round of dishes and she settled the wooden tub on the ground. The mountaintops were glistening white on their rugged peaks in the distance. Two bright beams of sunlight broke through the clouds and dazzled her with their intensity as they streaked across the open valley.

The hint of warmth was there and breaking through the winter chill. She needed that moment and drank it in. Her heart had been in winter. Stuck under the frozen block of ice of grieving the loss of her husband Eddie, and the pain of her childhood memories that had haunted her for too long. It had been a few days since her mother's announcement and she had accepted it. She wouldn't fight it or think too much about it beyond knowing that her mother was getting a fresh start.

Violet was due for her own new season, she mused as she delighted in the snowmelt. She watched the sky for a long minute, waiting for the clouds to break the spell and hide the sun again, but the moment didn't go away.

Violet let the moment soak in before she scooped up the tub to go back inside but she paused as she saw the ranch hands in the far off fields breaking a new horse. She knew the strength and determination it took for a man to force his will over a horse and appreciated the beauty behind it. Some horses were broken too hard and were forced into meanness, but others took the creature and coaxed it into obedience without breaking the horse's spirit.

She walked closer to the edge of the Harpole fence and settled her arms on the edge. She watched for longer than she thought when she felt a little body nudge up next to hers.

Violet looked down to the little girl that climbed up next to her and gave her a warm smile.

"Hello Lila." Violet said softly.

"That's gonna be my pony, there." Lila gave Violet a delighted look that showed off her happy face and the few freckles that were sprinkled across her cheeks.

Lila, only six years old, was a ray of sunshine all by herself with her love of horseflesh radiating out of her whole body.

Violet watched Lila's hand gesture toward the tan and white pony that was making its way around the circular pen that was the closest corral to them. Violet watched appreciatively as he put the pony through his paces.

"He is going to be mine iffen my pa says he is gentle enough." Lila said, but never took her eyes away from the horse again.

"Reynaldo is doing a good job I see." Violet said, smiling to herself. Lila had a special place in her heart that she could never explain fully to the little girl. It was a bittersweet love already that bloomed within Violet.

"Rey has taught me a lot already." Lila said as she watched.

Violet couldn't help but settle a hand on the girl's shoulder. Feeling the warmth connect with her like a spark. She had almost become an adopted sister to Violet last summer. It had started a wild fire of pain and rumor through this valley that had nearly broken Violet, but this winter had been a good quiet time to let that all go. She could see this girl, every freckle and hair on her head was precious to Violet. And the whisper of the Spirit of God within Violet told her that he felt that same way about her. All of that confession and heartbreak was Violet's chance to break out of her shame.

"He is so beautiful." Lila said wistfully.

Violet had been thinking about God and how he was indeed a beautiful Father to her, but she knew the girl was speaking about the horse that galloped with abandon around that corral.

Violet was so thankful that the Harpole family next door had taken the girl in. She had wondered at first if the close proximity would be hard, but it never was, miraculously. Violet got to drink in the site of the happy child. Replacing her own childhood memories somehow with the ones that this girl was now experiencing. She couldn't explain it, but it was doing good healing work in her heart.

"Do you have a name?" Violet asked.

"Dolly taught me and Cooper some Shoshone words. I like Bungu." Lila peeled her eyes away and gave Violet a perfect grin.

It sounded like 'boon-goo' to Violet's ears.

"Bungu..." Violet said to get it right.

"Yea." Lila sighed. "It means horse in Shoshone."

Violet thought that was perfect. She knew that Dolly would love hearing these children use her native words spoken in her new home. It would always be something special to her.

"That is lovely, Lila." Violet said sincerely.

The next few minutes they watched Reynaldo put Bungu through his paces, making sure he obeyed every command that Reynaldo spoke. Bungu was a quick study and within a short while, he had a training blanket over his back and a harness on his yellowish tan head. He took a few hesitant steps away from Reynaldo when the cowboy urged the bit over his head but the soft tone that Reynaldo used could be heard and it soothed the pony and soon the horse was obeying his words again. He gave his head a hearty shake a few times, not enjoying the feel right away but that was normal.

"Tomorrow I will get to go into the coral and do it all again. I have been making visits to his stall every day this week. Talking to him softly and letting him get used to my scent." Lila said proudly.

"That is a good thing." Violet said to encourage her young friend.

"Papa and Reynaldo are the best horse handlers ever." Lila praised, certainly in awe. "I want to be just like them."

Violet was certain that she would. There was something that Lila was just born with, that love and passion would probably be with her... her whole life. Violet mused.

Violet stroked the girl's shoulders one more time with affection and took a step away from the fence, tearing herself away from the long break she had taken to get back to her work. Reynaldo had looked over just before Violet turned away and gave her a wave. Violet waved back and smiled. His smile was broad as his eyes caught hers. She could tell he was enjoying his work. Just as much as she enjoyed her own.

"Gotta get back to my kitchen, Lila, got bread ready to go into the ovens. Come by later for a few loaves for your mama." Violet said.

"Oh yes!" Lila promised.

Violet walked back with her wooden tub, seeing every little spot where the snow was melting away and the rich black earth beneath was peeking through. Her heart was full.

<hr />

Reynaldo Legales

Reynaldo watched Violet walked with her long strides back toward her home. He saw her nearly every day like that, he was aware of her quiet presence on the property next to where he worked every day. He had gotten to know her in small ways over the last few years but lately his thoughts were always drawn to her.

He drew his gaze away reluctantly and put his eyes solidly back on his work. The horse he was working with had some spirit and he had to be fully aware of what he was doing. He gripped the rope with his calloused hand and pulled the horse Bungu close to give the horse some praise. He rubbed his hand down the muzzle of the creature and was rewarded with a passing understanding between man and beast. Bungu tugged at the bit and shook his head a little. Reynaldo kept his calm demeanor to encourage the horse to remain just as calm. He spent several more minutes like this, just silently

48

communicating to the animal that he was in charge but he enjoyed it. Lila watched from the fence line still and he knew she was eager to ride her pony soon. He knew in his heart that Bungu and Lila would be a good pair. He could already see in his mind them running the fields together. Lila had a heart for the horses and needed a horse with a little spirit.

He thought again about Lila and it made him think of Violet, everything seemed to tie together with her. How Violet's bravery had really saved this young girl. He, like Violet, hoped that the girl would never know the truth about how her adoption came about. How she was first intended to go to an undeserving household that has first abused and misused Violet. He couldn't truly express the respect he had for Violet, even knowing what had been done was secondary. Her bravery at facing her past made such an impression on him that he hasn't been able to stop thinking of her. He had never in his life had these feelings, he wondered how he ever could move past them... did he even want to?

He took Bungu to his stall and invited Lila to join him with a wave. Bungu went into his stall without complaint and Reynaldo took a brush to his mud covered boots, then to his pants. The snow and muck from the corral clung to him in the chill and he looked forward to a warm meal and a cozy fire in his cabin in the woods beyond the bunkhouse. Many of the other ranch hands eyed his small cabin enviously, the privacy and coziness. He had earned his place as Ranch manager but some still held a few grudges, him being a Mexican being at the forefront. John Harpole was an amazing Ranch owner and Reynaldo was surprised that he had promoted him years ago, looking beyond the ethnicity, but to the man and his skill. Reynaldo enjoyed the work and aspired to continue to help grow John Harpole's ranch. Many of the ranch hands had the desire to save up and make their own ranch. Somehow, Reynaldo felt he had landed where he wanted to be. He was making a very good income and knew within a few years he was promised a prime spot of land on John's land to build a bigger place. It was a grand scheme in his mind, somehow the vision of putting down roots was growing in his heart. He didn't want his own ranch, he wanted to continue to partner with John Harpole if that was what God's will was. He had talked with John and that seemed to be the agreement between them. It was good to be needed.

Lila came along and he walked her through getting the horse's feed and she was excited to be able to be a part of the process. Lila and Bungu had started to bond already over the corral door but he knew the day would come soon when she would be put to work brushing and caring for the animal daily.

"Papa said we are building a new stable over by Aunt Corinne's property." Lila said as she patted her hands together to shake off the oats on her hands. She looked up at him with those hazel eyes of hers.

"Yes little lady, we are. I drew the plans myself." Reynaldo said. He tousled her hair in play and loved the small shriek she made.

Reynaldo watched Bungu to see if the noise spooked him. It didn't and he was pleased. A pony that spooks easy will not be a good fit for her. Bungu had all the makings of a great match for this young lady.

"My papa says that it will be for the family horses and this stable will be for the bred horses to sell." Lila said, looking proud to be able to talk about grownup things.

"That's the plan." He smiled at her infectious energy.

"When do you think I can ride Bungu?" She asked nearly every day. But he didn't mind. He had been young once himself with the thoughts of his first horse.

"I hope to be riding him tomorrow. I will make sure he is safe and ready for you soon. You will be the first to know. Your Papa has to approve." Reynaldo said and smiled broadly when he saw her excited grin.

She ran off to go back home and Reynaldo walked out to meet up with John Harpole to discuss the plans for the rest of his day. He took a moment to glance back over his shoulder, just to look toward the Grant cabin, knowing that Violet was there.

Chapter 6

Sean Fahey

The ferry had whistled shrilly a few minutes before and Sean had eagerly gotten off the bustling deck. He had a satchel with a few belongings but the rest would have to be unloaded. It would take some time.

A wagon for hire was waiting outside the staging area of the ferry docking. Sean arranged for all the trunks and luggage to be loaded. He wondered if he should hire a porter to come with him. He realized that he would need more than one trip.

Sean looked around desperately for a moment wondering who he could trust.

Sean was told to wait a few minutes, because drivers always come after the ferry whistle blew. Townsfolk were always interested when the ferry arrived. He saw a few vendors setting up their wares along the bank and realized that some men used the ferries to sell their goods. That would indeed bring people around.

Sean put his wool jacket on and straightened himself. He felt travel weary and rumpled but he wanted to be certain he didn't look it. If for any reason he saw his sister, he wanted to make a good impression.

Sean stood next to the loaded wagon and waited. He watched the people scurrying around, the air was crisp but the sun was making an effort to poke through the clouds. It had been a little warmer in San Francisco and Sean could tell that Spring was slow to come here this year. There were still a few signs of snow scattered around. The shadowy patches under trees and along the edges of the road the remainder of icy snow clung to the ground.

Sean had a good coat packed away that had belonged to Ol' Willie and Sean would probably need it. He would suffer through the chill now.

The wait finally produced more wagons and Sean was able to hire another wagon. The second wagon had an extra hand and he was thrilled for the money for loading his trunks. Sean was generous and they proved to have plenty of information. He knew who to talk to in town to find storage for his goods and had been promised a good night's rest at the boarding house in town.

He was pleased to have a good place to settle in before he would try to find his sister.

The ride to town was not very long, the port was a mile north of the town. The town was small, but very neat and tidy compared to San Francisco, he saw a livery, a general store and even a grocer while he was chatting away with the driver.

He was happy to see this western town doing so well. His sister had picked a pleasant little community it seemed to him.

The mountains were grand and he felt that tug to get a horse and see the wilderness that surrounded. There would be time for that.

The place felt different from California, the ocean wasn't far away in miles. But it didn't feel like a port town. It felt like a rural community.

Sean jumped down when the wagon stopped in front of the fancy goods store.

The driver spoke up. "I'm Casey Mackenzie but please call me Mack. I just moved here a few months ago. I'm staying at the boarding house too. I got my land claim but will be building my cabin north of town. You want to go speak to Clive or JQ inside. They have some storage space for ya, reasonable pricing and good men to know. I'll wait here." Mack was a big brawny guy. His son, Daniel, was in his late teens. He was quiet but nodded next to him.

Sean spoke to the other man, who also agreed to wait.

Sean went in and heard the tinkle of the bell on the door. It was a nice little store that he was certain to explore another time. He saw a woman at the front counter. She smiled and gave him her full attention.

"Hello, I'm Sean, I was told to look for Clive or JQ." Sean said and smiled to put her at ease.

"Oh yes, sir. Just one moment." She said.

He looked around while she took a step back into a hallway. There was the aroma of bacon and fried eggs lingering in the air and Sean was reminded that it had been hours since he pushed the meal around his plate in the early morning hours. He had been thinking too much and not eating. It had been that way for most of the trip. The nearer he got to his goal the more distracted he was.

"They will be right out." The woman came back. She was pleasantly rounded and was dressed fashionably, with a lace collar and her hair done up, just so. San Francisco was lacking in women, and according to every newspaper, he read that the west was lacking in quality women. "A land of uncouth and lawless men." A newspaper had declared when he was in New York. He somehow guessed that this small town was not what everyone thought of when they imagined the Wild West.

Sean gave her a smile.

"Is there a local church in these parts? I just arrived." Sean asked to be polite.

"We have two grand churches, one in town and one that serves the rural community." The woman smiled. "I am Millie Quackenbush, glad to make your acquaintance." She shook his hand and gave him a once over.

Two men came out from the back hallway, looking very similar. One had dark hair, one with bits of salt and pepper. Sean assumed they were father and son. It was easy to see.

"I heard you were lookin' for the pair of us." The older man spoke up.

"Yes, I heard from a pleasant fellow named Mack that you were the ones to see about storing some trunks and luggage I have." Sean said and gave them both a handshake.

"Yessir!" The younger man said.

"I'm Clive Quackenbush..." The older man said and raised an eyebrow. Sean could tell Clive was more curious than his son was. There was a wit behind those eyes.

The other said "JQ," with a nod as his greeting.

"A pleasure. I just arrived." Sean smiled and patted his pockets for his billfold. "I'm Sean Fahey."

He watched the play of glances that happened when he spoke his own name. A spread of dread traveled through his chest as he watched the three of them exchange glances. His name was not unknown.

JQ and the older man laughed together identically. The woman pursed her lips to hide her amusement.

"Well, Lord be praised." The eldest spoke and chuckled. "The prodigal brother..."

Sean waved to Mack and his son Daniel when they left the storage area, promising to look them up in the next few days. They were good folks and Sean was happy to continue a friendship.

He walked back into the fancy goods store to face the Quackenbush family again. Those first few minutes had been more than awkward. Clive claimed to be very good friends with his sister. That was enough to make Sean's blood run cold.

Clive was extremely amiable and Sean could not find a single fault in his customer service though. If he was honest with himself, he liked Clive and after a few minutes gained more information about his sister than he had expected in such a short time.

"She is doing very well. You needn't worry. She is a newlywed." Clive had said on the walk over to the storage building behind the store. "She lives outside of town."

Sean hadn't said much. Making the reply that was needed. "Oh..." And "Thank you..." When appropriate. He had expected to get more time to prepare himself to answer questions or meet her first without having to explain himself.

Sean heard the bell ring as he walked back into the store and wondered if this was how it felt to stand in front of a firing squad. His legs felt rubbery. He was shaking in his boots.

Clive was waiting for him and both JQ and Millie were watching him like a hawk. They all had a hundred questions certainly. But they weren't asking yet. He knew it was coming though.

"I heard you mention you were headed to the boarding house." Clive offered and smiled wide when Sean nearly lost his nerve and was contemplating running from the scene.

"I just need to square up with you for the storage space." Sean pulled out his billfold and pulled out a few dollars.

"No chance of that... I don't charge family." Clive said with a wink. Sean was certain he had misheard.

Sean faltered, his hand still holding out the dollars for a long moment.

"Well, yer sister is going to be my niece in a few more weeks." Clive couldn't hide the smirk on his face.

"Niece..." Sean nearly choked on the words. His world was shrinking and he wondered what had happened in the small space of a few years.

"Yep, my wedding is coming up quick." Clive patted Sean on the back. Sean's arm was still hanging in the air. "Put away your cash, lad. It is no good today."

Sean came out of his stupor, still not understanding but letting the mystery continue. He didn't have the energy to ask any questions. He was suddenly very tired. It was still mid-day. All the signs pointed to it being a very long day indeed.

Sean followed the man out the door. Sean felt rude by not saying his farewells to the other two but he was feeling a bit lost.

They were out the door when Clive slowed and took up his stride to match Sean's.

"I'm supposing you are wanting to surprise your sister then?" Clive asked. Sean was pleased at the question. It wasn't rude or accusing. Quite friendly actually.

"Yes sir." Sean said. He was going to be respectful.

"I suggest you use Smith or something until you see her then." Clive said and gave him a nod to infer that he knew something.

"Oh?" Sean saw that the man was amused but he seemed kind.

"Yes, she is well known, and the only Fahey in these parts. Won't take but a minute to spread the word. Small towns have an amazing sense of communication. Better and faster than any telegraph wire ever made." Clive pointed up the street to guide Sean as to where they were heading.

"Thanks for the heads up." Sean finally said when Clive looked away.

He is giving me space to do what I need to do. Sean mused. *His son and daughter-in-law at the store are actually on my side.*

It was instantly heartwarming. He was shocked. It was the first sign in all these days that he was doing the right thing.

"I have a house up the way. If I come by 'round six could I interest ya in some supper? I could loan you a horse for a few days and help ya get yer bearings." Clive kept his gaze forward as he spoke. Giving Sean a chance to think on the proposal.

"I think that would be grand." Sean finally said. It was just what Ol' Willie would have done. Suddenly, Sean's heart was lighter.

The Orchard House was a pretty place, with a fresh coat of paint and was nicer than a lot of boarding houses he had seen in his lifetime. Clive went with him and chatted amicably with the proprietor. A kind lady named Gemma Caplan was very good at her job, who set his mind at ease immediately. Sean dropped his leather luggage and gave her a hearty handshake. She gave him a tour of the place and showed him to a nice room with a good-sized bed, fresh sheets, and a homey quilt. There was a small wood stove and crate of firewood. It was more than he expected.

Sean said his goodbye to Clive and promised to be out front to meet up with him later. Sean shook his head and unpacked his bag. Hanging up his other suit and hanging them up in the small wardrobe in the corner. He pulled his journal and the small stubby pencil from his breast pocket and put it on the bed stand. He sat on the bed and took a few deep breaths. He felt accomplished that he was here. But he couldn't push away the anxiety of waiting to see her. Wondering if this was how she felt to travel so far to come to him. The lingering guilt was lodged in his heart but he knew he was doing the right thing.

To make amends is not without a certain amount of bravery.

Sean went down to the main room to see if he could find a newspaper or a book to read. Gemma had a plate warmed for him.

"We just served our lunch a little ways ago, but I know that you probably came in on the ferry. I pieced together a few odds and ends for ya, lad." Gemma's eyes were crinkled kindly with a smile and a sparkle in them. She certainly loved caring for her tenants. He thanked her several times and took his plate to the front porch to get some fresh air. He needed some quiet time, to relax and distract himself. He needed to clear out his mind.

◆━◆◦◆━◆ ━ ◆━◆◦◆━◆

Megan Capron

Every lesson my mother had ever taught me was proving to be true. Megan Capron thought bitterly. She swatted at her bonnet that was stubbornly tied in a knot at her chin. She had visited the small doctor's office across town and had felt the doctor's judgmental stare as he gave her his opinion. She waited for weeks longer than she should have and the results were exactly what she expected.

"I see no ring on your finger Miss." He had said and she wanted to scream at him. Her cheeks had flamed with her indignation.

She had to control her temper and resist her urge to pummel him with her fists until he bit his puritanical tongue.

Megan finally pulled the ribbon's knot apart and sat on the cushioned settee in the fine apartment her benefactor had given her. She was surrounded by luxury but extraordinarily miserable. She was near to bursting the seams on all of her clothing. Certainly, people were bound to notice soon. She had been a fool to ignore her fears.

Until this very moment, she knew she could easily escape her situation. One telegram to her parents and they would take her back, there would be lectures and long talks but she had refused to budge, thinking somehow she would make her own way for herself. Now she was doomed.

She would remain Rosie Green, the singer at the Hampton House until she could no longer. She would have to convince Mr. Hampton to continue her funding somehow, even if she was carrying his child. She knew somehow that he would not be pleased.

She took off the outer jacket she wore and looked over the sheet music the band had sent up for her to look through. She was distracted and somewhat panicked. How would she survive if Pruitt sent her away? She had a small wad of bills she had saved from her earnings but she knew now, better than she had before, how quickly those funds would spend.

She settled the music sheets in her lap and stared out the window, her brow furrowed in worry. This new problem was weighing on her and she didn't feel like singing. Megan stood and paced the room for a few minutes, thinking but no solution came to her mind. She sat at her vanity and fussed with her hair nervously, her blond hair was behaving in her padded wings, puffed out on both sides of her head, the latest fashion. She knew it a simpler style and disliked the harsh look of it. She grabbed at the pins, pulled her hair down around her face, took her brittle brush, and took her frustration out on her hair. She applied the pink lip stain that her maid had found at a fancy goods store across town, it was not garish or flashy but it brightened the pale look that she had for the last several days.

She had been ill every afternoon and was nervous about eating anything before her evening performances. Megan rang the bell for the maid and had her order up a plate of bread and chicken soup from the kitchen. That seemed mild enough to keep her stomach settled. Her doctor, after his judgmental stare-down had told her that she should be beyond morning sickness, but that wasn't always the case. Megan was still annoyed with the man but there was nothing else for her to do. She would eat a peppermint candy after she ate her meal. That sometimes helped.

She ate sparingly, just enough to make sure she wouldn't swoon during her performance and got ready.

The practice with the orchestra had gone well but she was realizing that she was tired and still hungry but also a bit nauseous. She sat back stage, sipped on several cups of tea, and nibbled on a piece of dry toast while she waited for her time to sing. It was a busy Friday-night crowd at the restaurant, she put on her fake smile, and the show went on. She knew she was not her most vivacious and personable, but there were no obvious complaints from the patrons. By the end of the evening her feet were hurting from her tight shoes and the corset around her waist was cutting into her sides painfully.

She made quick time up to her apartment to get more comfortable. She had to stop denying the fact that her waist had grown. She was beginning to show in her pregnancy. There was not much time and she had wasted her chance to get away from Pruitt. Now she certainly would have to rely on him. She could never send a telegram to her parents now. There was no escape.

Megan put on a nightdress and a soft plush robe and settled onto a settee, she had seen the look in Pruitt's eye during the performance and she knew that he would come to see her that night. She would have to tell him her news.

If she was the praying kind she would have prayed just now, for Pruitt to find her news to be fortuitous and that he would support her through this. Her heart did flip-flops as much as her queasy stomach at the thought of what his decision would mean.

The door opened a while later, her maid had left her alone for the evening and she was certain the heavy steps across the floor were his. Megan let out a breath and prepared herself for her speech.

"Oh, Megan, I have some dreadful news!" Pruitt said in his bombastic voice. His brows were lowered and his pallor wasn't his usual rosy cheeks.

Megan stood, wondering if he was unwell. She wanted to say, 'I have some news as well...' but her courage faltered as her mouth opened. Instead, she stood slack-jawed as Pruitt approached her.

"My wife sent word and it just reached me. She is arriving any day by ship." Pruitt took her hands in his.

All thoughts of revealing her secret disappeared when Pruitt squeezed her hands. She felt at this moment something momentous was about to happen.

"Megan darling, you have to leave town." Pruitt kissed her to perhaps soften the blow but her mind went into a spin.

How could she leave? She had nowhere to go now.

"I do not want you to panic my girl... I am working on a way to take care of your needs. I have set aside a stipend for you and even found a great job for you." Pruitt rubbed his hands over her shoulders.

Megan felt wide-eyed and panicked. Certainly, he couldn't force her to leave without making a fuss. He had declared his love for her over and over. Now his wife, whom he hadn't seen in two or more years, shows up and she is tossed aside like a discarded toy. Anger started to bubble up within her but she felt that inner voice telling her to wait, and see his plan before she exploded her wrath.

"A grand hotel is in final phases of construction in Portland, Oregon. A business associate of mine is planning live entertainment, an orchestra. I sent a telegram to him this morning. Seeing if he would be interested in a high-class vocalist." Pruitt said. His hands on her were annoying her. He didn't have the right to touch her any longer. She felt like a piece of garbage being thrown out.

Megan tried to pull away, she didn't want to listen anymore.

"I know you must be upset darling. I do know how close we have become. I have no choice but to appease my wife. Her family money is invested into this place. I am certain that she will not stay for long, perhaps only a season or two." Pruitt reached for her, trying so hard to keep her calm.

"So you expect me to pack up and move to Oregon, with the cows and farmers to wait until your wife returns back to wherever she came from. Also you contacted this friend of yours. Will I be known there as your mistress, cast aside? I could never show my face." Megan said emphatically.

"Of course not, my dove." Pruitt declared and tried to kiss her again. She pulled away. "I know this is not what either of us want. I just said you were a talented singer and available. You can create whatever story you wish once you arrive." Pruitt knew she didn't wish to go back to her conservative family. Now she was almost certain that they would not take her.

"That is awfully close to Oregon City... I am no fool. I could be discovered." Megan argued.

She already wondered if her cousin Corinne would ever travel to a fancy hotel in Portland. It was highly unlikely. *She was probably a mother now.* Megan mused.

"It should only be for a short time. I will also give you plenty to live on. There is no reason that it should last more than a short few months. If you want, you wouldn't have to work at all."

Megan wondered about that and scoffed. She enjoyed the accolades a little too much to give it up now. If he gave her a stipend, and she could set aside a little more money than she could save enough to go back East.

Pruitt gushed and made promises for several minutes. Even pulling out a small pamphlet with a drawing of the hotel she was supposed to go to. It was a nice prospect, she had to admit. The risk was small for anyone to recognize her. If Pruitt provided her with money she certainly could get by, any money she would make singing should be saved to get back East.

She pretended to care for him for a few minutes and he lavished praise on her. She knew there was no way out of this situation if he didn't support her financially. She would do what she needed to do.

After a while, she shooed Pruitt out, declaring that all the distress was causing her head to ache, which wasn't far from the truth.

She laid in bed that night, staring at the walls while she schemed and planned. She had been in worse predicaments before. She pondered a story to tell her potential employer in Oregon, she would go by her stage name full time and perhaps no one would be the wiser. She knew exactly how much money she had set aside to get her fresh start, feeling foolish for all the money she had spent on silly things since she began working at Hampton House. She would have to be more strategic about her goals now.

Megan thought briefly of the child she was carrying. Her story would have to be a good one. She thought of Violet, from Oregon City, the housekeeper at her cousin's house. Megan knew she had been a sweet young woman, though Megan had treated her with a little snobbery, just because she had been a housekeeper. But she had remembered the woman's story, it had been talked all over town about her husband dying in California territory. Suddenly Megan knew she could pretend to be her, a young wife, whose husband went to the Gold fields and she hadn't heard from him again. She plotted, planned, and finally went to sleep. She woke in the morning and wrote down the story she would tell. It would work. No one would question the story because husbands left so many women these days. No one would give her those sideways stares about being pregnant. She would have to handle that eventually, but perhaps by then Pruitt's wife would be back on a ship and gone. Once she got word from Pruitt that his wife was out of the picture she would send him a letter, telling him about the child.

She imagined that there would be some challenges along the way, but she felt certain that she was fast on her feet. There was nothing that could stop her.

That morning she walked a few blocks down the boardwalk and stepped into a jeweler's shop. She bought an inexpensive silver wedding band. She placed it on her left hand and knew that the deception was just beginning.

Chapter 7

Galina Varushkin

Every week for a more than a year Galina Varushkin has spent her weeks doing work for several neighbors throughout Willamette Valley. She washed laundry at Grant's Grove, Angela's, and the Harpole's, and she even got extra work at the Boarding house in town. She also did odd jobs, babysitting, and being an extra hand during harvest for cooking and baking, whenever she was needed Galina was willing. Every single time she was paid, she had to dutifully give her expected pay to her father, with the excuse that it was always for family expenses. She was a hard-working contributing member of the family. Galina had swallowed down her resentment and replaced it long ago with a sense of accomplishment. She tried too, anyhow.

Her father gruffly reminded her of this obligation every few months, even though she hadn't murmured one complaint. The only time she ever kept any money was when she was paid above the normal rate. She snuck a few half pennies away, in the special hiding place she had with the few books that she had managed to hide from everyone in her household.

Since her father didn't believe that she should bother with being educated, Galina was good at hiding her reading. The small purse of coins was slow at growing, her mother had encouraged her to set aside whatever she could. Being a young woman was a dangerous business and if anything ever happened, she should have a little money for herself.

She had lately gotten a raise from the Grant's and Angela and Ted, she mused that they had been in it together when they found out that she couldn't keep any of her earnings. Both Corinne and Angela had confessed to her that it chaffed them to know that she wasn't benefitting from her own hard work. The extra coins were starting to add up and Galina was relieved to know that eventually she would have enough money to get new fabric for a dress or something just for herself with the money that she was able to set aside.

With the snowmelt coming and the chilling air starting to make way to warmer days, Galina had a concern that her small stash could not afford. She dreaded the issue for weeks but the time had come.

Her boots had been new two years before, but a recent growth spurt and last summer's rain and mud had completely ruined them. The sides were tearing where the laces pulled, the sole was splitting, and holes had worn through the bottom of both shoes. Galina had been putting bits of cloth inside her shoes over the winter months but the problem was getting worse by the day.

She settled it within herself that politely asking her father for shoes was within her rights so she went about waiting for the right moment to ask him. It had been a few days since their last altercation and she had been pretending politeness as well as she could lately. She was avoiding one of his tyrannical outbursts. She no longer had her mother's protection and the boys ran and hid when their father was in one of his moods so Galina took it upon herself to handle pleasing him with every chore she did, and every word that came out of her mouth.

She kept the cabin tidy, her brothers were always clean and presentable for their classes every day for school. She did up the laundry just as her mother had done. She was not as good in the kitchen as her mother was yet, but she made a pretty good stew, and thanks to Violet Griffen, she was learning to bake bread and rolls better than before. It had been a good solid month of soft rolls and chewy bread in their little cabin. Galina was bone tired most days, taking on all of her jobs, and also trying to take her mother's place as a housekeeper. But she had no choice. She felt her mother's smile on her when she was doing her jobs and she didn't want to let her down. Every moment her heart spent missing her mother made her work all the harder toward taking care of the family that she had left behind.

When Galina came back from walking to town, delivering the clean tablecloths and towels to the boarding house, she felt her right boot rip through the bottom when she was walking along the muddy road toward home. The wet ground did its work and her foot was thoroughly soaked and muddy when she walked into the cabin. Her brothers, Pavel and Milo happened to be at the table when she pulled the boots off.

"Your boots!" Pavel, the youngest boy, pointed and announced the sad state of her shoes.

Galina could have kissed his little cheeks for bringing it up instead of her. Now she would look like the dutiful daughter that hadn't complained.

"Yes, they have seen too many days." Galina tried to keep her voice light, she added in a little chuckle and winked at Pavel.

Her father, Slava, stood up from his spot at the table, his large frame was always intimidating and Galina watched his face as he perused the damage to her boots.

"How long have they been like that?" He said gruffly. His face didn't look angry but his tone was tense. Galina tried to make her face calm and serene.

What did that verse say, *a soothing tongue castes away wrath?* Her mother had said it a thousand times. She couldn't remember now.

"I was managing, the way mama taught me." Galina gulped and kept a half smile on. "But today this shoe opened up even more on the rough and wet roads." Galina said softly. She couldn't hold his gaze for long, and dropped her eyes, hoping he would take that as a sign of humility.

"Well, you should have taken better care of them." He sat down in the chair, the table jostled and the flatware jangled. Milo and Pavel looked first at their father, then to Galina.

"They are several years old Papa. I am certain that the money I have given to the family fund would more than cover a simple pair of boots." Galina said, she hadn't said it as softly but her tone was still polite, mostly.

"That money has been spent." Slava said simply then took a bite of the stew she had left for them on the stove. He chewed on the food she had cooked and that bitterness tried to creep back in. She had worked so hard on her keeping her tongue under control and she was not going to lose her battle over a simple pair of shoes.

"So, I should go barefoot?" She asked, even smiling a bit, remembering something he had always said when they were growing up.

"You can make do with what you have." He said and scooped up a bite of food. He looked away from her, which made her angrier than his words. He was trying to dismiss her problem.

"I thought your family would always have shoes on their feet and clothes on their backs. You said that to mama all the time." Galina pushed a little. Her father said nothing but looked up at her coldly.

"How has all that money been spent?" Galina looked around, there was nothing new in the house. They still had food in the larder and the root cellar. She would know if there had been food purchased.

"You need not be asking what I do with my money, child." Slava was settling his fork down. He was trying to be calm.

"Actually, since my money was spent too, I think I can ask." Galina blurted, and then waited for the sky to fall.

"I bought a new suit." Slava announced, he put his hands down flat on each side of his bowl. "And a few things for Guadeloupe and her little baby."

Galina nodded, unbelieving. "A new suit..." She said it as quiet as a whisper. Then she said "Guadeloupe?"

"For the wedding next month." Slava lifted an eyebrow, it seemed he was daring her to say something.

Galina took a deep breath, trying to remember the face of her mother, the many times she had sat on her mother's side, asking for advice on how to talk to her father. The advice was hard to hear now, her anger was like crashing waves that was building along a rocky shore. Her mother's voice was too quiet to be heard.

"All I ever heard from you when I was a child was that you worked hard to supply us with everything we need. I have worked hard also. And was obedient and gave you the money I earned, with cracked and bleeding hands. I clean your clothes and take care of all of you. What consideration do I ever ask?" Galina said so very little of what she actually felt, this was just the tiniest fraction of her frustration and she yet knew she had said far too much.

She watched him stand again. His thick arms and muscled torso always filled the room.

"You had better shut your trap, child." Slava reached for his belt.

"By all means, whip me into submission." Galina backed away from the table as she yelled at him. "Whenever the girl gets outta line, gotta put her back in her place! You are no man, you are a monster!"

Galina shrieked and ran to the door when he lunged at her, his large frame was clumsy in the tight cabin and he knocked over the chair and sent a bowl flying to the floor when he past the table.

Galina knew that his boots were off and he may take a minute to get them on before chasing after her. Galina knew that she was foolish with every ounce of her being for speaking to him in that way, but in that moment she was tired of taking care of this ungrateful man, giving him all her earnings, and seeing his coldness.

The ground was cold and wet, her boots and stockings were in the spot where she had left them, as well as her wool coat. She thought she was faster than her father but the rocks and cold earth were taking their toll, her feet burning as they crushed over the crystallized snow patches. She was in a panic, her lungs burned as she breathed heavy from the running and the fear that raced through her faster than her feet could carry her.

The dusk was falling and Galina took a moment to slow her mind to figure out where she was going. She paused to turn and head toward Grant's Grove when her father got a fistful of her hair. She screamed as she went down backwards. Unimaginable pain gripped her as she felt her body fall back with the violent tug he gave. She could hear herself screaming.

Her father's voice was hoarse as he cursed and yelled at her. She kicked and flailed as he drug her the long way back to the house. He had grabbed her arm when she had tried to beat on his legs as he dragged her. He snatched her wrist and used that to pull instead of her hair. She had blood already dripping down into her eyes by the time they were by the cabin. She could hear Milo and Pavel crying.

"Get out here boys!" Slava yelled. "You watch and see what happens when you let the devil rule your tongue."

Galina knew she was whimpering but she couldn't really hear it anymore. She was only aware of her brother's faces, so young and sweet. They had never shown any signs of the anger that their father held so close to the surface.

Dear Father God, please protect them. Galina prayed.

Slava never took off his belt, he used his fists instead.

<hr>

Corinne Grant

The tea kettle sang out and Corinne grabbed the quilted hot pad to grab the handle. The steam poured through the spout and Corinne deftly poured the water over her tea strainer. One cup for her and a cup for Violet who was knitting near the fireplace.

The weather was starting to warm up during the days but the nights were still chilly, and the fire was crackling and cozy.

Lucas was visiting with his brother's family as they were planning an addition on their cabin. Corinne was amazed at how much those two brothers could accomplish when they put their minds together.

Corinne stirred in a bit of honey into each cup, Violet liked it extra sweet. She settled the cup on the small table next to Violet, who murmured a 'thank you' but was deeply absorbed in her counting.

The sweater she was creating looked complicated and Corinne was amazed to see it grow.

Corinne settled into her favorite chair and listened in the quiet for any peep out of Trudie, who seemed to be down for the night. Corinne was relieved. Trudie was having an irritable day. Her Stepmother Marie thought it was probably teething. Corinne was glad to have Marie's guidance through this new phase of her life.

Marie had suggested that she let Trudie gnaw on a cold carrot from the root cellar. Once Corinne peeled it and gave the little stumpy carrot to her baby, she gnawed happily on it with her gums. Her big brown eyes got droopy and she stopped her fussing. Marie was a godsend.

A small knock at the door brought Corinne quickly to her feet, trying to answer before a louder knock woke up the baby.

Milo, the oldest Varushkin boy, stood in his bare feet, shivering in the doorway.

Corinne gave him a startled look. Before she could ask anything, he reached his cold hand through the doorway, grasping her own.

"Galina, she is hurt." He said, his voice was scratchy and raw with emotion. He began to whimper and cry.

Corinne nodded and pulled him in, not caring about dirty feet and clean floors at such a time.

"What happened?" Corinne said as she reached for her boots and her mind scrambled for a way to cover this boy in something, so his feet wouldn't freeze.

Milo was wide eyed, Corinne wondered if he was stunned. She had seen that happen in many tragic situations.

"It was Papa..." Milo finally said. He was still breathing heavily. Corinne was assuming he ran the whole long way... More than a mile certainly.

Corinne's heart was pounding a bit faster.

"Violet?" She turned to her friend. Violet nodded.

"I will stay put, you go. Get yer Pa." Violet suggested.

She looked Milo over, the thought came that Cooper may have a pair of shoes to borrow for Milo's feet... and a coat... she added to her mental list.

"Come with me." She pulled on her wool coat and hat. Shoving it on her head as she pulled the boy out the door.

"My Pa is going to do the same to me..." Milo muttered as they ran across the yard.

"No one will hurt you Milo." Corinne promised. Fear gripped her when she heard his confession. What had happened? She knew from hints that Galina shared that Slava Varushkin would sometimes punish her a bit too harshly. But if Milo is this scared, how far had a punishment gone?

Oh God, please be with Galina... Help me to get to her... She was going to add 'in time' to her prayer but she didn't want to think that way. Certainly her Pa hadn't beaten her to death.

She prayed the whole way up the path. Her mind racing with the 'what ifs'

Corinne reached the door to her father's large cabin. She knocked softly and waited, she watched Milo lifting his cold feet in a little dance. The ground must be so cold on his feet. She wished that she would have grabbed him a pair of stockings or something. She was feeling irresponsible. Why had she let this little boy suffer? Hadn't their family been through enough?

The door opened. Her father, John, was there, looking distressed at a late visit.

"Galina has been hurt, I don't know how. Can Milo stay here? Lucas is gone. Would you come with me?" Corinne rushed over her words, hoping that she made sense.

John pulled them both inside. He rubbed a hand over Milo's head. "You did good son." He said to encourage the boy who had tears streaming down his cheeks still.

Marie was on the davenport and was reading a book to Cooper and Lila. Abigail was sitting next to her mama looking sleepy.

Cooper and Lila waved at Corinne and Milo. Corinne gave them a half smile, but worry over Galina made her feel absent from any real emotional connection just then.

John asked Marie to help warm up Milo and made sure she had the situation understood with very few words. He certainly didn't want the children to worry.

"I'll hitch up my wagon, Corinne, you know where Rey is staying?" He asked Corinne quickly.

Corinne nodded.

"Tell him to send for Doc Williams. You want Galina at your place?"

She nodded again. She wanted to protect her, if she could.

She ran off toward the small cabin next to the big barn. Rey had his own place, as Ranch Manager.

Reynaldo answered his door quickly. He smiled a welcome smile, seemingly unperturbed by the late night disturbance.

Corinne explained quickly. He whole-heartedly agreed and took no time grabbing his boots and coat. Corinne thanked him and ran back toward her father. Hoping he had hitched up the wagon in record time.

The horses were jittery from John's hurrying but John was almost finished. He got the harnesses in place once Corinne was seated in the front. John pulled himself up and clicked for the horses to go just a minute later.

It was only a mile, but it felt an eternity as they moved down the road in the darkness. John had thought ahead and grabbed a lantern and Corinne held it as he led the team. Corinne could only imagine the worst-case possibilities as they neared the turn off toward the Varushkin Cabin.

Oh, please let her be okay.

Galina was such a good-hearted girl, with spirit and spunk. Corinne didn't want to see her hurt in any way. She considered her a friend, was looking forward to watching her grow into a strong woman. Corinne wanted to wring her hands and cry but she took deep breaths and reminded herself that she needed to remain calm, she could not help the girl if she lost her wits.

The cabin neared and the front door was swung wide open, the lights from the lamps inside shining through the doorway.

They stopped the wagon on the edge of the path, just twenty yards away from the doorway light. Corinne could see that there was a shape on the ground just in front of the door. Corinne's heart dropped, the lump was probably the girl. Corinne could not see any movement. The moment stretched out long and Corinne felt a scream or a wail lodged in her throat. The quiet was deafening as Slava's large frame filled the doorway.

John got down from the wagon first. Corinne seemed bolted to her seat, not knowing what to do.

"You seen my boy?" Slava said roughly.

"Yep." Said John, very matter of factly. "He is warming up now, having a sleepover with Cooper."

Slava huffed. "You send him back in the morning after breakfast for chores."

John nodded. "We came for the girl. We heard she got hurt. Corinne does the healing around here."

Corinne knew that Slava knew that and wondered where her father was going with the conversation but stayed silent and still.

"You take her. I'm done with her." Slava huffed again.

John nodded. "We will take good care with her sir." John said with a softer tone. There was no implication of anything in the words that he had said. Corinne finally realized what her father had done, casting no blame, but just offering help.

Slava turned and shut the door behind him. Leaving them to take Galina away.

Corinne jumped down, not even waiting for her father to help her down from the tall wagon box. The lantern jostled in her hands but she hit the ground running.

She was at Galina's side in a swift moment. The lantern settled next to the girl's face. Corinne could see swollen lips and eyes, bruised cheekbones, she was nearly unrecognizable. There was sticky blood on her scalp and bruises and blood on the girl's hands. Corinne's eyes saw blood on Galina's work dress and even some on the snow surrounding her. The red blood shown bright against the white and icy ground.

"She is breathing…" Corinne whispered to her father in relief when she saw the rise and fall of her chest. Corinne ran her hands along the limbs of the girl, checking for any obvious signs of anything broken. They laid Galina out flat and Corinne ran a hand along her right cheek, barely brushing the skin, as to not cause her any more pain.

"I am here Galya." Corinne said, using the girl's pet name. The name her mother would have used.

A moan escaped the girl's lips.

"We are taking you somewhere safe." Corinne promised.

"Do you think I can pick her up?" John offered. His brows were creased and his frown showed his distress.

"Can you move your head?" Corinne asked. Galina nodded, and then groaned.

"What hurts the most?" Corinne looked her over, wondering at the injuries she couldn't see.

"He kicked…" Galina croaked and then flinched. She moved a hand and pointed to her ribs.

A stray hair blew over Corinne's forehead and she tried in vain to brush it away, she felt the sticky blood on her hands and felt her heart drop. Slava had left his daughter out in the snow to bleed. Galina's blood was soaking into the ground and now Corinne would soon be covered in it. The thoughts were dark and full of anger as Corinne made her plans to help the girl.

"John is going to carry you to the wagon. It will hurt but we will get you to a nice soft bed." Corinne took the girl's hand and held them softly to give her any kind of comfort before the pain would come again.

Any kind of lifting with bruised or broken ribs was going to hurt, no way to avoid it. Corinne gave her father a nod. He took no pause and carefully scooped her up, as gently as he could. Galina cried out and began to sob but John didn't pause a moment, he carried the girl to the wagon and got her settled in. Corinne climbed up beside her and did her best to be a friend and a calm voice amidst her pain.

The ride back seemed so much faster and Corinne held Galina's hand as the cries softened. Every jostle of the wagon would cause Galina to gasp and stiffen and it reminded Corinne so much of that horrible time on the Oregon Trail when Angela had fallen down the ravine. Corrine was reliving every fear she had for her closest friend, as she prayed for this girl.

Ted Greaves was waiting at the front of the cabin. He was pacing and looking grim as Corinne watched the light from her own windows grow closer as the wagon creeped along. The wagon pulled to a stop. Ted reached inside and grabbed a heavy blanket.

"Would this make it easier to carry her?" He asked. Corinne saw his genuine concern and felt that surge of warmth for Angela's new husband. Ted was such a good man. She was thankful in this stressful moment to have another friend nearby.

John Harpole nodded and jumped from his seat.

"Rey came by on his way to get the Doc. He thought an extra set of hands was a good plan. I sent my work-hand Warren to get Lucas." Ted gave Corinne a look that was full of understanding.

Corinne patted Galina, who was quiet and holding still. Corinne slid out of the wagon box when her father lowered the back gate. She didn't want to shake the wagon any more, knowing that Galina would suffer enough in the next few minutes.

71

Corinne gave instructions to the men on how to carry Galina. She tucked the blanket next to Galina's side and after taking a deep breath, she got into the wagon.

"This will hurt but make it easier to carry you." Corinne offered, wishing there was a better way.

"I understand." Galina said weakly.

The process was indeed painful to get her loaded. John hoisted up her feet and Ted grabbed her shoulders and with a swift move then got her on the folded blanket. Galina sobbed again with that simple movement. Corinne was worried about Galina and rubbed her bloody hands on her forehead to think. An idea came and she made the men wait and ran to her greenhouse that was nearby. She grabbed a recently made shelf that Lucas had built for her, it was leaning against the back wall and was going to be added to a new unit that he was going to put together in the next week. It would work now to get Galina safely inside. She found it and carried the bulky wooden shelf. It was long and heavy but Corinne ran with it, hoping she wouldn't be her normal clumsy self and trip.

She made it down the dark path and John knew just what to do. He slid the board under her feet and Ted lifted her shoulders and John expertly shoved at just the right moment.

That made the rest of the process easy to get her inside and through the hallway to the spare bedroom. Corinne saw that Angela was sitting inside, her and Violet both distressed and sitting next each other on the davenport.

<hr />

Galina Varushkin

Galina was so relieved that she was settled on the bed. Her face was throbbing and hot from being cleaned and handled. Her eyelids were swollen nearly shut. She could see a lamp through the slit of her eye but it was blurry and it hurt to have her eye open. Everything hurt so badly. A part of her had been relieved to be rescued. She was no longer on the cold ground, suffering and shivering.

She was not sure she was relieved anymore now that she had a moment to think through the haze of pain. Everyone would know that she was a shameful daughter and her face would show the proof for a long while.

She let the pain wash over her, every part of her face hurt and the sharp pain in her ribs with every breath was a good punishment for what she had done. When would she learn to control her own tongue? She had her mother's example. Forbearance is a gift, and to have patience and a humble attitude was the true mark of a good woman.

Her father's words as he was beating her had been the truth.

"You are a worthless complainer." He had said when he had slapped her against her cheek.

She had not fought back but covered her head as he stopped slapping and moved on with a closed fist.

She heard his words as he talked to the boys.

"She is no daughter of mine. There is no room in my house for children that talk back to their father." Slava had said.

Once she had had enough, she laid on the ground and sobbed.

Her father had stood over her. "Children are to obey your parents, as commanded by God."

She had heard her brothers crying. She had brought this shame upon herself. She had known better.

"In the old country they would have called you the devil's daughter." Slava had put a boot into her side.

Galina remembered screaming but the moment went dark soon after.

Surely, God would forsake her.

Galina lay in the soft warm bed and felt her heart turn to despair. She wasn't certain she had ever hurt this bad in her life.

<hr />

Corinne Grant

Corinne spoke soothing words to the girl but she seemed unaware that Corinne was with her. Corinne had a loving father, who had spanked her behind when she was a child, but had never crossed into beating her. She felt loved and disciplined. Certainly not an easy task, especially since after her mother's death Corinne knew that she had been a bit of a handful. Corinne brought the lamp close to Galina's face to get a better look at the swelling and was even more horrified than she had been earlier. Galina would be lucky to be able to see at all for a few days, the purplish swollen eyelids made Corinne wince.

Corinne had asked her father to cut off a piece of ice that they had in the root cellar, they could use it to make cold compresses to take down the swelling. Corinne hoped that the doctor had something to help her with the pain. He was always studying up on the latest medicines.

Corinne heard someone walk in and looked up. Angela and Violet wanted to check on the patient.

"We just want to pray over her." Violet said. Angela nodded, there were tears in her eyes.

Corinne gestured them to come in.

"Dear heavenly Father, we lift up this sweet girl. It says in your word that we are your children and I pray you comfort your daughter right now Lord. Heal her body quickly and help us to show her that she is loved. Please guide us to know how to help this girl." Violet prayed but lost her voice when a whispered sob escaped. Corinne knew Violet had to understand firsthand what a betrayal it was to be mistreated by a father.

Angela whispered her prayer. "Please guide the doctor's hand, help Galina to recover and to find joy even while her body recovers."

Corinne put her hands on the girl, wishing she had the faith to be a healer like those in the bible, who could lay their hands on the sick and they would be healed. The only words she prayed. "Give us Wisdom, Lord."

Hot tears flowed down each woman's face as they waited for the doctor. They didn't leave her side until the horse's hooves could be heard outside.

They quietly left and joined with everyone who was by the front door.

Doc Williams knocked but Ted got the door open in a brief moment.

"Come in Doc." Corinne said and gestured for him to settle his things on the table. She helped him shrug out of his coat.

"Thanks for going Reynaldo." Corinne said as she saw him peek his head inside. He probably only knew Galina as an acquaintance but it was kind of him to be so willing to ride out on this chilly night.

"No bother at all. I am praying for the gal." Rey said with a weary smile. "Is she well?" He asked.

"She was badly wounded." Was all Corinne could say. The part of her that was so angry that a man could beat his own child wanted to shout it to everyone in town. But she opted for discretion at this point. She needed to find some inner peace before she could figure out what to do next.

She heard Trudie whimpering in her room. Violet stood, placed a hand on Corinne's shoulder.

"No worries, I will care for her now. You go be with Galina." Violet said. Her eyes were misty with tears.

The doctor was ready to be filled in so she gave Reynaldo a wave. Everyone else went into the parlor and found a seat while Corinne and the Doctor talked. They would do whatever was asked of them, but they all knew enough to let the doctor and Corinne alone to do what they needed to do. Violet sat down with Trudie who was bleary eyed and snuggling against Violet's chest, looking content. It warmed Corinne's heart in a moment, realizing that she had so much love and support in this room. Her daughter was in good hands.

"So you know exactly what happened to Galina?" Doc Williams asked.

"She has been beaten badly, I believe he used his fists on her..." Corinne said, disgusted. "Her ribs are hurting her, she mumbled something about being kicked."

The Doc made a face, and grabbed up his bag. "Is there a lantern in there with her?" He asked.

"Just one..." Corinne said.

"Grab another if you have a spare. I want to be able to see what we are dealing with." He said and started to walk back to the bedroom, Ted showed him the way as Corinne went for another source of light.

Corinne lit a spare lantern from the kitchen and went to Galina's bedside.

The doctor was talking to the girl in a soothing voice and he looked her over.

"Let's get her more comfortable." The doctor took out his scissors and snipped off the girl's top that was buttoned down the back. Corinne knew it was wise but was already planning to ask Marie to make another. Knowing this girl didn't need any more disappointments.

Corinne gently helped the doctor remove her cumbersome skirts and petticoats.

Doc Williams had helped deliver almost every child in Oregon City and always was kind and considerate to every woman, but Corinne wondered how Galina was fairing in this trying moment, was she aware of what was happening to her? It was always a challenge to be prodded and poked, and this could very well be the first exam she had ever had by a doctor.

Galina was breathing but she hadn't said a word since they had moved her from the wagon.

"The doctor is here, Galina, we are going to take good care of you." Corinne reminded her, hoping for a movement or a word from the girl to know that she was aware of them.

"Her eyes are dilated. Her breath is shallow. I am worried that she is slipping away from us." The doctor whispered to Corinne.

Under the girl's chemise, her ribs were already bruised and mottled, red and swollen. The doctor felt along the rib cage carefully.

"At least one broken rib." The Doc grimaced as he moved the chemise to cover her. "Let's cover her well, but I wonder if perhaps the men could scrounge around for some snow. We could use that to take down some of the swelling."

The doctor was thorough. Corinne was handed a notebook and she wrote down everything the doctor said.

She looked at the list that grew as he continued.

Two broken fingers, several rib fractures, at least one broken, bruises on her face abdomen and back, facial lacerations, and torn skin on her scalp. Corinne was trying to stay detached as she wrote but she felt her stomach churn with every word she wrote. She wanted to vomit with her anger churning in her gut but forced herself to hold it down. Now was not the time to let her anger out.

Corinne left the room, discouraged. The Doctor was seeing everything that she saw but she had hope that the girl would wake while they examined her.

The men agreed to go find some snow, knowing that by the creek the woods still had some that hadn't melted yet.

Corinne saw the ice that was sitting on a bowl in the counter and took a knife to the small block, shaving off a few chips. She sprinkled the chips into a small bowl and put a few drops of lavender oil in the water with the ice chips. She grabbed a few clean dishrags and took the bowl and rags with her. The icy water would help until the boys had some snow.

The doctor was digging through his satchel and pulling a small brown vial when Corinne came back into the room.

"I got a shipment from China last month with some laudanum pills. I won't use them but sparingly, since many say they can be dangerous in high doses, but does wonders for traumatic injuries. I'm concerned that the pain is more than she can bear." The doctor said.

She set down the bowl of ice water.

"That will do for the swelling until you can use a snow wrap." The Doctor seemed pleased.

Corinne pulled the stool close to the side of the bed nearest to Galina's face and dipped the rag into the frigid water, getting it very damp. She settled it over Galina's eyes.

"I put lavender it the water, hoping it would sooth her." Corinne said and felt foolish. She felt like making excuses. Just wishing there was more she could do.

"That is good, every little thing we do to help can bring her out of her stupor." The doctor took a close look at the back of Galina's head.

"It looked like a chunk of her scalp has been yanked. A chunk is pulled out and dangling there." Doc Williams point to the bloody clump on the back of the girl's head.

Corinne had a vivid imagination and could see that Slava had probably dragged his daughter by the hair. Corinne's heart was already broken, this just added a fresh lump to her throat.

"I want to give her this laudanum, if we can get it under her tongue the pain will be dramatically decreased."

Corinne was handed a small round pellet and the doctor pulled the girl's chin down as Corinne worked to slide the pellet under Galina's tongue.

"It should only take a few minutes to take effect. I will be listening to see if her heart rate gets stronger." Doc pulled out a long tubed device and put one end on Galina's chest, and the other to his ear.

Corinne doused another rag and dabbed at Galina's swollen lips, clearing away the crusted up blood and dirt that was caked on her. She needed a soothing bath but knew right now they needed to get her to wake up, if she had injuries inside her body they couldn't know until she woke.

Corinne spoke soothingly, saying everything they had done, even repeating things.

"We are cleaning you up, sweetheart. The doctor gave you something for the pain. You should be feeling better soon." Corinne said again and again.

It was a few minutes in the quiet room and then the girl moved a hand toward Corinne's finally.

"Oh good Galina. We are right here." Corinne said just above a whisper, so relieved to see a sign of any kind of spark.

"Thank you." Was all the Galina said but it was enough to raise Corinne's hopes.

"Squeeze my hand if you don't want to speak, okay?" Corinne said. "Once for yes, two for no."

Galina squeezed her hand once in response.

"Are you still cold?" Doc Williams asked.

She gave Corinne two squeezes. Corinne shook her head for 'no.'

"I gave you some laudanum for the pain. Is it helping yet?" He asked.

One squeeze. Corinne nodded, relieved.

After he talked with Galina about staying still he said they would start on a few stitches when the medication was in full affect. Galina had squeezed Corinne's hand once, she understood.

"The boys will be bringing in some snow, to help with the swelling on your face. You are safe and should recover. Just know that you are safe." Doc Williams put a hand on Galina's shoulder and felt her shaking. "We will get you cleaned and stitched up. You will be in pain for a while, but this is the worst you will feel. It should get better." His voice worked to soothe even Corinne.

A muffled sob escaped the girl. Corinne was at a loss on how to help the girl through the pain that no one could take away.

The only thing that she could think was to talk to her through her crying.

"We are all here for you... Angela and Ted are here, Violet, and Reynaldo came by, and Marie is praying for you next door. Right now Ted and John are tramping through the woods to get snow for you." Corinne tried to keep her voice soothing and calm. "We are with you every step of the way." Corinne dipped the cloth back into the cool water to refresh the coldness. Her eyes looked a little better, the swelling was atrocious but some of the blood and dirt was gone.

The girl began to relax and her sobs slowed. Her stiff body was relaxing.

"You getting sleepy from the medicine?" Corinne asked. A soft squeeze told Corinne that it was a yes. That laudanum was truly a miracle.

Corinne placed the cool rag over Galina's eyes again and the doctor gestured for them to walk away for a moment.

"We need to keep her still and calm. I don't see any signs of swelling in her abdomen. The bruising is mostly to her chest and back. She should not be moved, use a bedpan and check her urine for blood in the next few days. If she starts coughing, or shows any signs of spitting up blood you come fetch me immediately." The Doctor said with a low voice only for Corinne's ears. "I'm going to get some warm water to clean her head, I'll do the stitching soon."

Corinne sat down with Galina and worked with the rag to clear away any blood or dirt from all of her scratches and scrapes.

Corinne wanted to joke with the girl, to make her feel better but the words stayed lodged in her throat.

'Looks like you tangled with a bear.' Corinne could have said but she just couldn't say it. She dabbed at Galina's lip, swollen and still oozing blood slowly in two places. Corinne pulled the lips back to check on Galina's teeth, hoping none of them had been damaged. She couldn't see any cracks in the ones that showed so Corinne left it be to ask tomorrow if Galina could talk more.

Doc Williams got settled in next to the other side of the bed.

"Is your pain almost gone?" The Doctor spoke. Corinne grabbed Galina's hand again.

Galina squeezed once and even muttered a whispery 'yes.'

The Doc heard and prepared the hooked needle with the thin silky thread.

"I am going to start stitching your scalp, this may still hurt, but I need you to keep as still as you can. I promise to make this as swift as possible." He said sincerely.

He gave a look to Corinne to keep Galina calm and still without saying a word.

He began to wash out the wound, bloody water ran down the side of Galina's head and Corinne caught it in a towel. He wiped at her scalp with a clean rag and made certain that no debris or dried blood remained. Galina was breathing deeply, her tongue jutting out to lick her swollen lips. Corinne squeezed her hand in support when the cleaning was done.

The doctor put Galina's scalp back in place, his hands gentle and sure as he did his best not to hurt her any further. "You will feel a pinch. Just squeeze Corinne's hand when you need to."

Galina muttered and took a deep breath and let it out shakily.

The doctor started the stitching with smooth even motions, it took more than ten minutes to get the two pieces that had been hanging haphazardly from her skull re-attached. Corinne wondered at the ability for the body to heal and hoped for the best. She desperately prayed that this girl would have no long-lasting marks or scars from today's beating but time would tell.

Galina had stayed still throughout the whole thing. She squeezed Corinne's hands a few times at the beginning, but Corinne had talked to her calmly as she watched the doctor do his work. She was impressed with his even and small stitches.

"All done, good job Galina." He said softly. "No washing your hair for a few days. I want to see if the stitches take before we go jostlin' your head around. I've seen worse scalp wounds than that that healed up so good that no one could even notice." He smiled but Galina's eyes were too swollen.

Corinne patted Galina's hands.

"Doesn't hurt so bad." Galina slurred and turned her head just an inch toward the doctor's voice.

"No moving around. We'll help you get settled in more comfortable once we get you all cleaned up." He said and put a hand on an uninjured shoulder.

"You feeling drowsy from the medicine?" He asked.

"Ya..." Was all that Galina could slur out.

Corinne couldn't help but smile. She had heard that Laudanum could make people feel dizzy or silly.

The doctor listened to Galina's heart again. "Your heartbeat is stronger. I am glad to hear it."

"Hank you..." Galina said breathily. She smacked her lips together and licked them again.

"No more talking. You just rest and we'll take care of you." Doc Williams insisted.

"I'll go make some broth and send Angela or Violet in to sit with her. She is probably a little thirsty." Corinne offered and saw the doctor nod.

"You were an excellent hand in here tonight." He placed his capable hand on her shoulder. "Someday soon, there will be many capable women doctors, just like you."

Corinne gave him a look. He had told her that many times, his wife even piped in sometimes. She was no doctor, but the thought of women as doctors and scientists made her glad inside. If the world could just change a little...

Corinne escaped his smirk and headed down the dark hallway. She had to fill everyone in on Galina, glad she had some better news than the unknown. Galina had a lot of recovering to do, but she was safe.

* * *

Galina Varushkin

Her face was ice cold but her head felt so thick. She could hear people talking but she felt like she was underwater, like the river was frozen over and she was stuck under it. She could not open her eyes no matter how hard she tried.

For the longest time she felt pain but it was covered by the ice now. She was floating through a haze of darkness but the pain lingered there under the ice, trapped with her but not clinging to her so much now. She held onto the memory of her brothers, who had been crying by the cabin door, watching her. She had been running, but she couldn't remember just now what she had been running from. But she could see their faces, red-rimmed and so very sad. She saw her mother there too now, just standing and watching her dark eyes brimming with tears but she couldn't say anything.

Galina felt something on her head, like a sort of tugging pain but it was far away, it didn't feel real. She just wanted to sink back into the darkness that wanted her to sleep but the tugging was keeping her awake. The doctor had finished the stitches, she remembered, but she still could feel the pain on her head. So much pain, but it was easing some, she admitted to herself, trying to find a morsel of thankfulness within her.

She tried to focus, she felt an urgency for something, the reminder of some desperate need. She thought hard and tried to move her arms. They felt heavy and wooden. She pressed her cold lips together, trying to urge some kind of sound out.

She heard a voice, maybe her friend, Corinne.

"Don't move... the doctor is done stitching you up. He found another spot on your scalp that was bleeding. There was a bad cut on your forehead too. It is over now." Corinne's voice sounded far away.

She pressed her lips together again... "I need..." She tried to say.

Her thoughts were so distant but her body finally cooperated and she tried to move.

81

Her tongue was dry but she finally spoke into the darkness. "Outhouse..." She said. Her lips felt frozen and the pain crept past the fog.

"No, don't move. I'll help you take care of that here." Corinne's voice was there again. She could barely feel fingers along her scalp.

"I'm done. I think the stitching will hold nicely, there are no gaps. Let me help you get her seated." Doc Williams said. His voice was soothing and kind.

She was so very tired, but the urgency was there again, reminding her that her body had needs.

She heard herself groan as hands lifted her and got her settled. She lifted a hand to touch her face, she could not see. A distant worry surfaced. *Am I blind?* She wondered.

"No... no... Galina. Your face is swollen. We will help you." Corinne's voice soothed.

Galina tried with enormous effort to open one eye and felt the thick pain just as a slice of light made her aware of the room. The room came into a hazy focus, but she could make out Doc Williams carrying a bedpan over to Corinne. Corinne's dark hair hung down in waves over her shoulders.

Galina saw the look of concern and care on her friend's face but the pain in her side made her groan again. Every part of her was coming awake to the memory. The beating, she remembered it now as exquisite sharp pain shot through her side. The throbbing began to pound through her face. She felt hot tears squeeze through her eyelids and she fought off the urge to sob, knowing how even that would hurt.

She got through the next few minutes, the mortification and degradation was nothing compared to the pain. Corinne and Doc Williams got her settled back into a more comfortable position on the bed after they took care of her needs. She didn't want to cry but she felt overwhelmed again. The memory of the day taking over, and she felt the shame again.

She slept for a while, dancing through the fog, she was warm now. She dreamt of those moments in the cabin, being so very angry with her father. Her running through the snow. She got much farther in her dream than she did this night.

She heard voices again. She whimpered as hands pressed against her belly.

"I believe her shoulder is dislocated." The man said.

"Should we put it back now or wait?" Corinne's voice said softly. Galina was waking up more fully. The pain was returning and the fog was lifting.

Galina muttered something but her lips were too swollen, it sounded like gibberish. She wanted to tell them to fix her arm.

She reached for Corinne's hand, she squeezed it to tell her it was okay.

There was some talking and Galina could tell what they were going to do. She didn't know how she did it but she thought about her mother and steeled herself to the pain that was coming.

It hurt while they shifted her body flat. Corinne leaned over her and held her body down, to keep her still. Galina took a few deep breaths, burning pain ripped through her side were her ribs hurt so desperately. She wanted to cry out, but bit it back. She could cry another day.

The doctor had her hold something, her eyesight was still just like looking through foggy glass, she didn't know what the doctor was doing exactly but she trusted him.

"This will hurt but be over quickly." Doc Williams said. He twisted the object in her hand. Galina wanted to jump from the bed. The white hot pain was exploding through her. Corinne pushed down on her shoulders to keep her down. The loud snap followed a fraction of a moment later. Corinne let her go and tried to soothe her. But Galina had lost her steely resolve. She sobbed again.

She heard the doctor saying something about her pain. She was urged to open her mouth. She complied. "Swallow this tablet." The small pill was placed on her tongue. Then a cup with cool water was placed against her swollen lips. She drank in tiny sips, letting the water soothe her dry tongue.

She swallowed and sipped a few more times before she laid her head back down.

"You are going to be very sore, Galina, but we are right here for you." Corinne's voice was soothing and Galina stopped fighting the pain, her tears would dry, her sobbing had been short lived. Then she let her body relax as the thick wave of darkness took over again.

The voices were still there but they got further and further away. She was back in the icy river but she was becoming used to it. She let herself be drawn away, she didn't want to feel anything.

Sean Fahey

Sean stretched and prepared for bed with a settled resolve. The dinner had gone well with his new acquaintance. Clive let Sean talk and talk, he had that way of listening and absorbing. Clive talked about his upcoming wedding and a little bit about Angela, but Sean felt that Clive was letting him find his own way to get to know his sister in a broader way. Sean knew that Angela was happy and married and that she had built a fine home outside of town. But any more than that would be for Sean to discover. Sean had a plan to go back to the place where his trunks were stored and find that one crate that he had marked with the first gifts he wanted to take to Angela the next day.

His stomach fluttered at the thought but he was more than determined to move forward with his plan, he had come this far. He would complete his journey and make the first steps toward reconciliation.

He brought out his journal, sat in his nightshirt, and wrote for a while before he brought out his bible.

I spent a pleasant evening with a new acquaintance - Clive Quackenbush. He has a lovely home just outside of town. In a few ways he reminds me of my dearly departed friend, Ol' Willie. They both have that wisdom that comes from experience.

I feel a bit foolish, after spending most of the evening prattling on and on, I may have told the man my life story. There is something about his open countenance that made me feel at home there. He is a good listener and I come away from my evening feeling humbled and somewhat relieved.

I feel better prepared to face Angela on the morrow.

I am pleased to know that Angela had this man as a mentor- he seems very protective of her and that warms my heart. He shared a few things about her that I should know- she is recently married. Which is hard to imagine, but also that she owns the boarding house I reside in.

I'm still wondering if I am making a huge mistake, if I should just turn tail and run away again, thinking it would be better for her if I just stay out of her life. But I want to make things right, I owe that to her and to my parents. I want to be a better man. - SF

Chapter 8

Angela Greaves

A dull thudding headache filled Angela's head as she tried to ignore the pounding rain outside. The storm had started hours before and the rumble of thunder had woken her throughout the night. The heavy drops of rain rapped against the window glass whenever the wind gusted. The stormy gloom was felt inside of her, after she saw the damage Galina's father had done to the girl. Angela had cried against Ted's shoulder when they went to bed the night before. Holding on to the image of Galina's battered face. It had taken her a long while to fall asleep.

Amelia Greaves was coming by today, her mother-in-law. Angela had been preparing herself for the visit but after the night she had had, she was in no mood to deal with the potential of the day with someone with such determined opinions. Amelia had a special way of putting Angela on the defensive.

Amelia had made her some lace curtains and she was bringing them over to get them hung in several rooms. Angela checked her appearance in the mirror and smoothed her hands over her hair as she waited. The roast chicken in the oven was making her home smell good but it didn't break through Angela's mood. She was so worried about Galina, and she just wanted to be over at the Grant's home to be helpful.

Why does everything get in the way of what I want to do? Angela wondered selfishly. She tried to keep her impatience to a minimum but she was grumpy and irritated. *I am probably just tired.* She said to herself.

The water on the stove was boiling and she put her apron over her pretty green housedress, a simpler frock than one with all the hoops and petticoats that was the latest fashion. She refused to wear corsets and frilly things when she was home. She wanted to dare Amelia to make a comment about it. The way she looked at her sometimes, judging her with a raised eyebrow. It just made Angela want to scream.

Ted walked through the back door and she heard him stomp his boots a few times.

"Is your mother here yet?" Angela asked with an irritated tone.

"Not yet." Ted said from the backroom.

She heard two thumps before he walked into the kitchen without his heavy boots on. He gave Angela a look and raised his eyebrows.

"That is a serious frown there darlin'." Ted said with a smile and leaned in to kiss her on the cheek.

Angela took a deep breath and let it out. She felt tense and out of sorts. "I'm sorry." She said and sighed again. The lack of sleep and headache was taking its toll on her.

"I am just in a foul mood. I want to be helping with Galina today, and I feel a bit anxious about your mother coming. I would just rather do something else today." Angela sighed.

"We can make it a quick visit. We will have lunch and you can do the curtains another day." Ted said with practicality. "If you explain about Galina then I'm sure she will understand."

Angela nodded but she wasn't sure that Amelia would understand. "I just feel uncertain..."

"About what?" Ted asked as Angela headed to her kitchen counter.

"Just everything feels a little topsy turvy today. My dear friend is so very hurt. And your mother doesn't really approve of me..." Angela felt a hot tear escape and she wiped her cheek with a shirtsleeve.

"She doesn't disapprove of you, you know that. She is sometimes a little hard to handle, but I plan on being here the whole time." Ted said and walked up next to her at the counter.

Angela drained the water out of the chunks of peeled potatoes into the waste bucket and then scooped the potatoes into the boiling water. She checked the fire in the cook stove and shoved another piece of firewood inside, the coals were red hot and the heat was warm and dry as it rushed out of the opening. She closed the door of the stove and hung the handle up on the little hook on the wall.

"I do know that, I'm just feeling a bit fragile today." Angela admitted when she turned back to her husband. His face showed a little concern for her and that made her feel a bit better with her sincerity.

A knock came to the front door and Ted ran to get it. Expecting it to be his mother.

"It's Dolly." He announced as he saw through the window.

The door opened and Ted let her in. Dolly carried a basket and touched Ted's shoulder in greeting before she ran to Angela. Dolly put her basket down and ran to Angela for an embrace.

"I cannot say the words." Dolly finally said as she pulled away.

"About Galina...?" Angela asked. She was surprised by Dolly's affection; it was unusual for the quiet girl to show her emotions.

"I am headed over to see her, I stayed behind with Chelsea Grant last night. But when Russell came home with all the details I just cannot say how much my heart..." Dolly pressed a hand to her chest. She seemed to be searching for her words.

"My heart is broken too." Angela offered and Dolly nodded. Her dark eyes were misty with tears.

"I came by to deliver something from Chelsea Grant, she stayed up almost all night baking. She was so upset. I stayed up until my eyes burned from tired... no exhaustion." Dolly corrected. Her English was good but she lost herself sometimes when she was upset. Dolly reached into the basket, brought out a parcel, and placed it in Angela's hand. "Just blackberry tarts. She made some for Corinne and Lucas too." Dolly looked like she was ready to cry. Her dark cheeks flushed red and she took an unsteady breath. "I wanted to ask if I could stay in my old room for a few days, so I can be close and helpful to Corinne and taking care of Gal..." Dolly's voice broke.

Angela was so surprised to see so much emotion from her half-Hopi friend, who was also so guarded.

"Of course you can stay anytime. We would love to have you, and I'm certain that Corinne would be grateful for the help." Ted spoke up.

Dolly looked at Ted with tear-filled eyes and then back to Angela, whose eyes had sprung a few leaks themselves. Dolly leaned into Angela's embrace and she began to sob.

The two women shared their grief together for just a minute or so. Letting the shared emotion flow between them. Another knock came to the door and Ted left to get it.

Angela and Dolly tried to scramble to wipe away the evidence of their tears.

Amelia Greaves strolled in with a greeting and a kiss on the cheek for her son. She looked surprised to see two red-cheeked women but she didn't say a word for a full minute.

"Hello, Mrs. Greaves." Dolly broke the silence. She gave a sniff but took a few steps forward to shake the older woman's hand. "I was just leaving, but I am pleased to see you again." Dolly said.

"It is lovely to see you, I do hope that you are well, my dear." Amelia spoke, she gave Dolly a kind smile that pleased Angela.

"A friend of ours was hurt, it was a shock but I'm going to help Corinne with her care now." Dolly said and walked back to get the basket she had left on the counter.

Angela took Dolly's hand quickly. "It is settled, you come back with your things later. I will have your room all cozy and warm for you." Angela looked into Dolly's eyes briefly, trying to express that the woman was truly welcome to stay. Dolly smiled and gave the slightest hint of a nod.

Dolly left a moment later and Angela turned her full attention to her new Mother-In-Law.

"I'm sorry for the emotional scene. It has been a trying time." Angela said and was pleased when Amelia came forward and gave her a kind embrace.

"I want to hear all about it, my sweet girl." Amelia patted Angela on the cheek affectionately and Angela felt her tense nerves relax.

"Let me check my potatoes. Ted, could you get your mother's coat and umbrella?" Angela saw Ted nod, and he kept his mother busy as Angela got back to work on her lunch preparations.

Ted and Amelia talked for a few minutes, he shared a simple version of the previous evening's events as Angela got everything ready for the meal. Angela pulled the two chickens from the oven and settled them neatly on a platter, then poured the drippings into a smaller saucepan. She made a gravy as she listened to the conversation between the other two.

"Oh, that poor child!" Amelia had gasped. "Her mother and infant brother just passing away." Amelia seemed genuinely upset to hear the news. "My prayers will certainly be with her."

Angela felt a bit of her heart lighten as she realized that perhaps she hadn't given Amelia enough credit. The rocky road between them had made for a rough start, but Amelia was not without compassion.

The gravy was coming together and Angela blew on the spoon, gave it a taste before she declared it good, and pulled it from the hot stovetop. She ground some fresh pepper over the gravy and the chicken and then went to her china cabinet to gather up the plates to set the table.

"You sit wife, and let me." Ted jumped up from his chair and pulled out a chair to let Angela sit. She gave him a grateful smile and sat next to Amelia.

Ted set a fine table.

"You have grown close to Galina, Ted is always telling me about you and her when he comes into town to check on us and make sure we have plenty of firewood and essentials. He says you have been helping her with her reading and writing over the last year." Amelia said and took Angela's hand. "Oh my..." Amelia held a hand to her cheek and looked distressed. "Sophia is going to be so very sad for her friend." Amelia took a deep breath and frowned.

"Yes, Sophia and Galina were fast friends." Angela agreed. She wondered if they had been able to spend much time together, they were both busy with their own jobs, Galina with her laundry, and Sophia with her lace. "I can tidy up another room for Sophia, if she would like to come and stay. Once Galina is up for visitors. I would love some time with my sister-in-law too." Angela found a small smile within herself. Trying to make something brighter out of this horrible day.

"Oh yes, dear. That would be grand for them both I believe."

They talked through a few details and Amelia even seemed enthusiastic about it. Wanting them both to be happy.

"It is such a shame..." Amelia frowned again, her eyes shifting away from Angela's gaze uncomfortably. "I married a bit of a foolish man. But he was never one to abuse a child so terribly. I cannot imagine what is going on in that man's mind."

Angela shook her head, but felt connected to Amelia's thoughts profoundly. She could not understand the need to brutalize anyone, especially a bright and caring girl like Galina.

There was a pause between them for a moment. Only Ted shuffling about in the kitchen could be heard as these two women sat in silence thinking of the tragedy that happened to an undeserving young girl.

"Galina has been learning to read from you and Violet, yes?" Amelia asked. She cleared her throat.

"Yes, she is doing so very well. She is honestly such a bright girl. She has such an amazing gift to tell stories and since her father..." Angela felt emotional just mentioning him and she paused to keep herself from growing angry again... "Her father forced her to go to work and didn't let her finish her schooling... Well..." Angela was flustered and didn't know what else to say.

"I believe some men just cannot look past the feminine physic to realize that women can be educated and have gifts." Amelia said with feeling. "My daughter Sophia just loves Galina and has sung her praises at home. She will be so distressed to hear this news." Amelia's eyebrows were pinched with distress. "Sophia will come bearing gifts. I have a few books I will donate to Galina's reading selection." Amelia sighed. "It is not everything she needs certainly, but it is something." A few tears escaped her blue eyes, and traveled down her cheeks. Amelia wiped at them. "Lord please show mercy on the girl." She whispered.

"We will see that Sophia's room is ready to go within a few days." Angela offered, agreeing with the prayer for the Lord's mercy.

"Oh, Angela dear, that would probably be such a good plan. Sophie will be beside herself. Knowing she could be closer to her friend would make it a little easier." Amelia took both of Angela's hands and gave them a hearty squeeze.

Angela smiled sincerely, feeling that inkling of love she wanted to have for her mother-in-law starting to bloom into something bigger. "After lunch we can take a look at the bedroom and see what else we need to prepare." Angela offered, knowing that Amelia would appreciate being included in the planning.

"Well, with Olivia leaving in a few weeks that will give my sister and I some time alone to chat about her future. She is beside herself in love with Mr. Quackenbush." Amelia grinned. Certainly glad to be on a happier subject.

Ted was finally done and carrying the platter of chicken to the table. The shiny platter looked so becoming on her lace tablecloth that Amelia and Sophia had made.

"I will serve, you ladies need anything?"

"Some cold milk would be grand; your dairy cow has the best milk I've tasted. I buy our milk and butter from the grocer, but yours is better." Amelia declared and scooted herself closer to the table.

"Well, I am pleased to share." Ted said with a chuckle and got busy bringing all of Angela's fine cooking to the table.

Angela felt her sour mood lift as she ate lunch with Ted and his mother. She always got so nervous, but she could really see that Amelia was improving since her widowhood. It was sad to realize how much energy Angela had spent dreading her mother-in-law's visit. She was determined to make a better effort to accept that God had answered the many prayers she had about helping Amelia find her joy again.

An hour passed pleasantly as Angela, Ted and Amelia wrote out a detailed list of the items the spare bedroom needed. Amelia gushed over some of the new cabinets and side tables that the woodworker in town had.

"That Amos Drey is such a talent. I am bartering a fine set of lace curtains and tablecloth for his mother back East for a new display case he is building for our little storefront." Amelia said as she was preparing to leave. "Ted, I will leave those curtains behind and you hang those up for your dear wife." She patted Ted's cheek. "I will head home now so you can visit with Galina and the Grant household. I will be praying." Amelia gave Angela a kiss on the cheek. "I think I will keep this story just between me and my own household. That girl has been through so much, I will be looking to hear how she is fairing." Amelia watched them both nod and accepted her coat, hat and umbrella from Ted's hands.

"We will send word; I may just come myself tonight if I can get away." Ted offered.

"Tomorrow is soon enough, my dear. I love you both dearly. Take good care of yourselves."

Ted helped her into her coat and she was settled into her hat.

The hired driver from town was waiting with the covered buggy just a few steps out from the door. Angela and Ted waved goodbye as she pulled away.

Angela prepared herself to go to visit at the Grant's house for a while, and Ted was going to get a stepladder and a few tools to hang up the curtains.

Angela gave Ted a sweet kiss before she left. She said a thankful prayer for the good visit with Amelia. She had such a sweeter hope for the future of that relationship.

Angela walked across the road and headed past the two buildings before she got to the front door of the Grant cabin. She steadied her heart by saying a quick prayer. She didn't want to be so fragile about seeing Galina in her battered condition, remembering her own time in recovery, she wanted to be strong for her friend.

Violet greeted the door after Angela's knock.

"Why do you knock, Angie?" Violet said with a hint of a smile. "You come in, you are family here."

Angela came in and gave Violet a hug. "The doctor is here again, checking on them. I have some fresh coffee just made."

Angela hung her coat on a nearby peg and accepted a fresh cup of coffee with cream. She and Violet visited for a few minutes before Doc Williams came out with Corinne.

"You can give her one of these tablets every 4-5 hours as her pain continues. I think the snow is helping some with the seeping but it will be a few days before she can open her eyes fully. Encourage her to get lots of rest and some good broth with a little soft bread will be the best." He said to Corinne as they entered the parlor.

Corinne thanked the Doctor for coming and he was gone with a wave to Angela and Violet.

Corinne sighed and sat next to Angela and gave her a sideways hug.

"What a night." Corinne said with a weary look.

"Where is Trudie?" Angela asked, suddenly realizing that she hadn't seen Violet with her. It was too early for a nap yet.

"Marie came by a little bit ago, she will take Trudie until she gets hungry. Dolly just left her a few minutes ago to fetch some things to take to your house. It has been a whirlwind of activity around here." Corinne leaned her head to rest it on Angela's shoulder.

Angela wondered if she had come at the wrong time. "How is Galina doing?"

"She is in a lot of pain, but she wakes up every few hours when the laudanum wears off." Corinne said without moving off Angela's shoulder. "She will be asleep most of the day. I am so very tired myself."

Angela let the moment grow quiet and saw Violet watching Corinne from her chair with her yarn and half-completed sweater sitting in her lap.

"You should get some rest. I can go back home and get Dolly's room ready." Angela offered and heard Corinne sigh.

"I don't want you to go, I would feel bad to make you leave." Corinne said and then yawned.

Angela felt a sting, she wasn't needed here and was actually denying her friend some rest.

"Can I do anything for Galina while you take a nap?" Angela offered. She reached over, took Corinne's hand, and patted it.

"No, she is asleep again, she ate and I cleaned her up a bit more. She ate some broth and seems to be out now that the laudanum is doing its job." Corinne said sleepily.

"I want you to send for me if you need any help. But I will leave you alone to a quiet house." Angela said firmly. She didn't need to be a burden. She may have wanted a visit but she would not add an encumbrance on Corinne's already overburdened shoulders.

"I love you sweet friend." Corinne said and squeezed Angela's hand. "I think in a day or two Galina will be up for more visiting and comforting."

Angela knew that from her own experience. A visit while resting wasn't actually helpful.

Angela gave Corinne a hug and got up to go.

"You are such a good friend, please keep praying." Corinne said. Her cheeks were flushed and her eyes red-rimmed.

"I will not stop praying." Angela said with a small smile that was meant to comfort her friend.

Angela said goodbyes and was out the door. She walked back to her house trying to fight off her disappointment. She had wanted to be a helper and get a chance to do some good, but she really hadn't been needed. Galina wasn't sick, she was horribly injured and her heart knew the difference. Corinne seriously needed some rest or she herself would get sick at a very inopportune moment when she was much needed.

Angela said a prayer for everyone in the Grant household and also prayed that God would show her what she should do to be a help and not a hindrance in this whole situation. She faced her disappointment and knew that it was natural to feel helpless in this situation. Not everything had an easy fix.

She walked up the porch steps to her home and was pleased to see her new lace curtains hanging prettily. Ted had made fast work. She heard some shuffling upstairs and wondered if Ted was working on some other project.

She walked up the staircase and saw that Ted was putting firewood in the small woodstove in Dolly's room. He had opened the green curtains and the cloudy sky was seen out the window.

"You read my mind." Angela said.

"You are back sooner than expected." Ted turned to face her from his kneeling position.

Angela explained how the short visit had gone.

"I suppose I can spend some time getting things done around here. Feeling a little disappointed but knowing that Dolly, and perhaps Sophia, are coming to stay is starting to cheer me up." Angela smiled wearily to Ted. He turned back to the wood stove and closed the door.

They walked to the bedroom across the hall and talked over a few plans. Ted promised to go into town to get a few things to make the room ready for a new guest in a few days.

They soon went downstairs and Angela carved up the chicken that was left over for lunch and was getting it ready to take over to Earl and Warren in the cabin they shared on the other side of the property when Dolly gave a quick knock and came right in.

"I saw you through the window with your hands busy." Dolly looked chagrined at coming in without being greeted.

"Oh, please don't knock. You just always come right in." Angela said and smiled. Since Violet had said the same thing to her just a short while ago.

Dolly brought in two satchels and shrugged out of her coat.

"That chicken looks good." Dolly said as she hung up her coat.

"I baked it with some onions and rosemary. Edith Sparks shared the recipe with me." Angela smiled and grabbed a small plate and made a little snack for Dolly.

"I can smell the rosemary even more now than earlier." Dolly raised her eyebrows and smiled when she saw the plate that Angela was making. "Let me take these up and then I will come back down."

Angela called to Ted who was in the parlor. "Ted, could you take this food over to Earl's cabin?"

"Sure thing." Ted gave her a kiss and then kissed her shoulder in his endearing way and was gone soon after.

Dolly trotted down the stairs and thanked Angela while she went to retrieve a fork from the cutlery drawer.

"I am hungry, I am relieved to know Galina is resting, but I wanted a chance to visit with her today." Dolly said and sat at the table. Angela joined her with a cup of tea.

"I was too." Angela shared how tired Corinne was and that she left to let her rest. "I had my day all planned out. Now I am a little out of sorts. My emotions are all over the place."

"Mine too. I'm sorry for earlier." Dolly said and looked embarrassed.

"You never have to apologize for your feelings." Angela said.

Dolly ate her snack and then complimented Angela's cooking.

"I wanted to talk with you about a package I got in the mail this week." Dolly said after she finished eating.

"Oh...?" Angela asked.

"From Reggie," Dolly offered and then blushed.

Angela's eyes widened.

"He sent me a book about China, a tin of tea leaves that he got in Sacramento from China, and a few letters." Dolly said and then she frowned.

"Why do you look upset, that was kind of him...? Or were the letters bad news?" Angela asked. Dolly didn't talk much about Reggie, but Angela could tell that it had upset her when he had left. They had been nearly ready to start courting, or so everyone thought, when Reggie just left to go back to California territory.

"His letters were kind and full of interesting news. He is leaving on a trip to China and he sent those gifts I suppose as a sign of his excitement." Dolly shared, but she looked perplexed still. "I just wonder why he wrote at all. He said such amazing things to me last year, then I left, and by the time I came back, it had all changed for him. I had started to care for him." Dolly admitted for the first time to Angela. Angela wasn't surprised, but she didn't have any good advice.

"Did he make any proclamations of coming back for you?" Angela asked.

"No... more the opposite. Really confirming that he feels called to live his life on the sea." Dolly sighed. "I do wonder why he would bother to say all this again."

"Understanding men sometimes is a futile act." Was all that Angela could offer.

"I am almost hoping he doesn't write again." Dolly placed her hands on the table with resolve. "I need to forget about all the sweet words."

Angela thought for a minute in silence, watching the show of emotions crossing Dolly's face.

"You have been more open lately." Angela said. Hoping she wouldn't offend Dolly.

Dolly smiled at Angela and nodded. "I have decided something..." Dolly paused. "Before I was always between... the two parts of me" Dolly explained her face serious and thoughtful. "I did not know where my future would lead me and it made me feel small and not myself." Dolly put her hand to her cheek. "I was a girl, without a say or a voice."

Angela knew that feeling, having used to be a servant in a world of wealth but no opinion of her own.

"God has given me this chance to live here and now, with freedom to speak and live the way He has given me. I am no longer in between."

Dolly looked to Angela's face, seeing if her words made sense.

"I think I understand." Angela said with her own smile.

"I don't want to hide within myself anymore." Dolly said.

"It is a good feeling to be free, yes?" Angela asked.

Dolly laughed and nodded, it was a good sound that filled the room. Angela had never heard Dolly laugh like that.

Angela heard a knock at the door and wondered what else could interrupt her day. She saw the dark shape in the doorway. She pushed herself up from the table and took an angled glance to see who was there waiting beyond the doorway.

What Angela saw stopped her cold in her tracks.

◆━━◆━◆━━◆━━◆━◆━━◆

Sean Fahey

Sean's heart was in his throat, thudding a frantic rhythm that threatened his sanity. There was no feeling like this in his previous experience. He took an unsteady breath as he saw a pale hand draw back the curtain of the nearby window.

The time has come. He said within himself.

The door opened slowly, perhaps tentatively, he thought. Angela was there, looking older than a few years ago. Her green eyes wide with questions lurking in them.

"Hello sister." Sean said, he was holding a package in his hands and felt foolish. He should have thought ahead. He could attempt to give his sister at minimum a handshake. If things went well he could have embraced her.

They stood for a moment looking each other over.

"What are you doing in Oregon?" Angela asked finally, breaking the silence.

"I came to apologize to you." Sean tried to look her in the eye, but he dropped his gaze. The look of hurt and confusion on her face was immediately felt.

Angela took a deep breath. He looked her over seeing a ring on her finger and hoping her new marriage was a happy one. She was dressed nicely, her home was charming and elegant. He could see that she was doing well.

"Pardon me, please come in from the cold." Angela said simply, her tone was absent any emotion but the look of confusion was in her eyes.

"Thank you, kindly." Sean said politely, feeling like a fool and a terrible person. How many days had this visit been overdue? He deserved every bit of coldness that she could throw at him. The fact that she was allowing him in was at least a small chance that he could talk with her.

Sean walked in and wiped his feet on the rug. He handed the package he was holding to Angela, she quickly placed it on the table. She was going through all the motions of politeness. He removed his coat and placed it into Angela's arms. She hung it on a nearby hook.

"Sean this is my dear friend Dolly Bouchard." Angela gestured to a young lady who stood up from the dining table. She was elegantly dressed but Sean could tell she was an Indian. "Dolly, this is my brother, Sean Fahey."

"A pleasure..." Sean said and reached out for a handshake. Dolly came forward and gave him a firm shake. She barely smiled but he could see the challenge in her dark eyes.

"Likewise..." Dolly said.

Sean saw Dolly purse her lips in judgement of him and he wanted to smirk, but he held back showing any emotion yet.

Sean looked back to his sister, her stance was rigid and she wasn't looking confused anymore. She looked on the verge of anger. He had better start talking soon or this crowd may yet kick him out on his heels.

"I want to begin by begging your forgiveness for my atrocious behavior before." Sean saw Angela lower her gaze, and felt a rush of frustration. He wasn't sure he deserved attention, but he wanted it. Angela said nothing. He spat out what he needed to say. "You came all the way from the East to see me and I was rude and dismissive and afraid. I am sincerely sorry." Sean said and was pleased that Angela looked up at him.

Angela took a deep breath and let it out, her face serious and pale. "I appreciate that." She said coolly.

"I mean it. I want to make things right with you." Sean reached out to take his sister's hand, hoping to show her that he sincerely wanted to mend the breach. Angela didn't really pull away, but she didn't reach towards him either.

A door opened and Sean heard sounds from the back of the house.

Angela and Dolly turned around to watch a tall blond man come in through a door into the kitchen behind the women.

"Who is this?" The man stopped and gave Sean a once over.

"This is my brother." Angela spoke softly. Angela turned back.

"Sean, this is my husband, Ted Greaves." Angela's eyes were glassy with tears. Seeing her upset was not what he wanted but he was relieved that she was looking him in the eye again.

"I am very pleased to meet you. I do apologize to arrive without any word sent ahead. I wasn't sure of your location until just yesterday." Sean said, feeling his heartbeat jump again. Ted stood still for a moment before crossing the room. He shook Ted's hand when it was offered. Ted shook it wordlessly, looking him in the eye, his piercing gaze was sizing him up and Sean felt the challenge in those eyes.

You had better not be here to upset my wife. Ted seemed to say.

"I promise I come with good intentions. I just arrived but I will say it again. When Angela came to California a few years ago I acted horribly and sincerely apologize for my dismissive behavior." Sean watched Ted accept his words thoughtfully and gave the smallest of nods before he took his wife's arm.

"Let me get you settled in the parlor before I see to your horse, I assume you rode in?" Ted offered and led them off without even looking at his wife. She had a red flush to her cheeks.

Their parlor was cozy and a small fire was burning low. Dolly excused herself. "I'm going to get settled in upstairs." She said and ran up the staircase, her footfalls on the wooden stairs echoing through the silent room.

Angela gestured to a leather chair by the hearth, Sean took it wordlessly.

Ted kissed Angela's cheek and she sat on a love seat on the opposite side of the fireplace.

"I will be back in a few moments." He said to Angela, she gazed into his eyes for a long moment before she turned to face Sean.

Ted gave Sean a nod and left the room at a brisk pace.

"I appreciate you letting me come in." Sean said and felt foolish. He should have written a letter or something to her, preparing the way. This was more than awkward. He felt that urge to run again, to make his way to the front door and just escape, but he knew that nothing would ever be the same. He wanted to be better than a man that runs away from hardship or confrontation. He saw his sister, her fair skin marred by red-rimmed eyes and reddened cheeks. He knew he had to keep talking to get her to open up.

"You have a lovely home." He said lamely, he tried a half smile.

"Thank you." Angela looked down, she was staring at the floor or her shoes. Maybe she was waiting to talk until her husband came back for support.

How sad, Sean thought. I botched things so badly in San Francisco that she cannot look to her own brother for support. *I will endeavor to change that*! Sean decided within himself.

"Angela, I failed you when I saw you last. I failed myself too." Sean admitted. "I've spent years of my life running away from every hurtful thing and my addled mind put you in the mix of pain from my past. I know you cannot possibly trust me now. But I hope to earn your trust again." Sean watched her lift her head, her eyes were full of tears and one escaped down her cheek. He took a deep breath and sighed. He could hear Ted coming through the back door again and wondered if things would go better.

Ted came in beside Angela and sat next to her, the silence in the room was eerie and Sean could hear someone upstairs, probably the friend Dolly, her footsteps echoed throughout the house.

"I was just apologizing again." Sean said as Ted gave him a look. The fact that Angela had barely spoken was making him more and more nervous. He wished she would just yell and rail at him rather than remain silent.

"I recently got back from a trip to Ireland. I saw our Great Aunt Felicity Fahey near Kilkenney." Sean said, hoping that would bring Angela around. He saw Angela raise her gaze, the tears in her eyes were gone. That was encouraging.

"Oh?" She finally said. She tilted her head to the side, a tendril of her red hair escaped the braid and he saw how much she still looked young and vulnerable.

"Yes, we had a good visit, but I will say that the best thing that came out of that trip was the many talks I had with our Great Aunt. She talked about memories of our parents. I brought you some letters from her. She hopes to correspond with you now that she knows where she can reach you." Sean saw her face lift from her sadness for a brief moment.

"I appreciate you bringing them all this way. Though you easily could have sent them through the post." Angela said then pressed her lips together. Ted took Angela's hand and she gave him a look that Sean didn't understand.

"In all the conversation I had with Aunt Felicity the most profound one was when I spoke of my behavior with you. I..." Sean did not want to delve into emotional issues, actually, he would rather take on an angered brown bear than face Angela at this moment but he knew if he would ever break through this wall that Angela was constructing he would have to go to the dark places within him. Aunt Felicity had reminded him in her goodbyes, that confession was good for the soul.

"I abandoned you at the orphanage." Sean said, his voice grew thick.

Angela gasped and her eyes grew wide. Ted put his arm around her and tears flowed down her cheeks instantaneously.

"When I saw you in San Francisco I felt so much guilt. I wanted to run away. What kind of brother does that?" Sean stopped because he was on the verge of breaking down. He was ashamed that it mattered to him but crying right now seemed a horrible way to express himself. He swallowed and his throat was tight. "I was ashamed of leaving you at that horrible place, so I left you again in California. It was despicable." Sean said finally through a hoarse and dry throat.

Sean couldn't look at her any longer and put his head in his hands and faced the floor. Trying to fight off the urge to leave this house again.

"I never blamed you for leaving that place, Sean. It was not safe for you." Angela said and he could hear the emotion in her voice.

"I blamed myself." Sean said, not looking up. He took a few deep breaths, willing the tears that pricked at his eyelids to go away. He vividly remembered the squalor of the work orphanage. The cold dirty windows that let the weather in, and the bugs. The older boys that used their fists on him and the younger boys daily for scraps of bread that was never enough. He would if he could knock down every brick of that place to erase those memories.

"Let me get you both some water." Ted stood and Sean saw his feet pass him by as he went through the doorway to the kitchen.

Angela left her seat and sat before Sean in a moment of surrender. She placed an arm on Sean's in a gesture that tore through him. She had reached out to him. He took his hands away and saw her green eyes looking to him again as her brother.

"I forgive you!" She said finally and her breath caught.

He felt his own tears break free and he took her hand. "I am so very sorry for everything." He said thickly, meaning every word. She nodded and stood up halfway to hug him. He stood up the rest of the way and gave his sister the hug he should have given her in San Francisco and so many more since then. He felt her crying on his shoulder and he knew that he had succeeded in doing the first part of his goal. She would allow him back in, even just in this little way. To forgive the unforgivable behavior was truly a miracle.

❖

Angela Greaves

Angela felt a swell of embarrassment as she pulled away from the hug with her brother. She wanted to hide in the fireplace after she had gotten so emotional. She promised herself the moment he came in that she wouldn't be a gibbering, crying female. As soon as he brought up the orphanage, she had crumbled. She truly didn't want him to wallow in guilt over that. It was their stepfather's fault that they were there.

On the other hand, she didn't want to let him by with his actions. In San Francisco, he had been terrible to her, practically calling her a corpse. She did not want him to feel like everything was forgiven. She knew that sounded cold, and she knew that wasn't what God would want from her but she just wasn't there yet. He cannot just show up and say a few sentences and everything just be swept under the rug. She didn't know what to say but she stood back and wiped away her tears, determined that she would be stronger.

"You never hurt me in your childhood Sean, but in San Francisco you..." She searched for words, trying hard to find the right way to say it. "You crushed me." She said, knowing that didn't explain anything.

"I know I did. That is why I am here." Sean said.

Ted walked into the parlor with two mugs of water.

Angela saw her brother take a sip, his eyes were blood shot and he was still shaking, like he had been when he walked through the

102

door. Knowing he was nervous should have made her feel better but it didn't.

Ted sat down and Angela followed his example.

Sean took the cue and sat back down, he took a few sips of water. Angela watched him carefully, his hands were growing a little steadier and the emotional tension was easing out of the room.

"My companion and mentor, William Shipley passed away quite a few months ago." Sean said quietly, his voice and face showed how much that had hurt him. "Within a short time I got a packet of letters from a lawyer in Boston. Our great Uncle had passed away in Ireland and I was asked to appear in Ireland, to talk to the lawyer there. I was grieving and desperate to get away, I didn't take a moment to pause, I put everything I owned in storage and went to Ireland. Running away from my pain and the memories." Sean looked up from his mug and the corners of his mouth lifted into a hint of smile. "I am good at running away from things."

Ted grabbed Angela's hand and she felt a little twinge that Sean was winning her husband over. Then she felt guilty because Sean was actually trying. *What is wrong with me?* She wondered.

"My trip was such a blessing, because Aunt Felicity helped me see some things I have been avoiding in my life. I blamed God so much for our parents dying, and for the orphanage. I had put up so many walls."

Sean continued telling his story and Angela tried to listen, but her thoughts were wandering. She wondered how she could still be so mad, when he was pouring out his heart. Declaring his new found faith in God. She should be thrilled, but she wasn't.

After he spoke for a while, he went to get the package he had brought.

"I got so much more, but this was a start." He opened the parcel and handed her a packet of letters.

She read the flowing letters,

To Angela Fahey,

You were a small girl when I saw you last. I can see a green dress in my mind, and tiny little white shoes on your feet as you played in the yard with a cat that was fond of you. I believe the cat was named Grady, he lived to an old age for cats. The thoughts of you and your

103

brother have never been far from me. Always wondering and wishing the best for you. Your Uncle and I were very concerned when we lost track of your parents so long ago. He went to Boston a year or two after receiving the last letter from your father, we were never able to track you down. For that, I am so very sorry. You were never forgotten. It took a few years but we finally got news from a lawyer in Boston.

My heart grieves more than I can say for the way you were all treated after you were orphaned. One day, such places will be burned to the ground, never to harm another soul.

I have a letter from your mother, from when you had just arrived to America. She was so very happy. I wanted to share them with you to remember her and her love.

"Sean has grown tall and thin from the journey, spending every moment he can pestering the crew. He claims he wants to be a pirate or a sailor now. He was most impressed by the big ships in the harbor when he landed. Angela was not a fan of the boat as much; she was seasick for a few days when the journey started but she rallied well. She was such a help to me. She is learning her letters and anxious to practice her reading every night. The hotel we are staying at near the dock is so much bigger than the small room we had aboard the ship. I may be spoiled after just a day of being here. My dear husband is seeking out a friend who will help us find a home here. Your nephew has already secured a job, he has been such a patient and amazing husband. Angela is my sweet girl who still loves to sit in my lap and give me hugs."

Your mother loved you so very much. I pray you remember her sweet and loving smile. Your father was also so very proud of you both.

I will search through all of my old letters, and share when I find them. I wish above anything that nothing bad had ever happened to you. I long to hear from you, praying that you have found happiness and freedom in your life.

Please never doubt that somewhere far away, someone loves you dearly.

Sincerely,

Great Aunt Felicity Fahey

Angela felt her heart swell at the thought of someone so far away still caring about her. She could be thankful for this gift. She could try to extend some courtesy to Sean.

"I have something for you, if you give me a moment." Angela set the beloved stack of letters on a nearby table and went to her room. She opened the family trunk and instantly knew where to look for something she had set aside years ago for her brother. She also took down the picture that had hung on her wall.

She returned to the parlor where Ted and Sean were chatting about his voyage. She felt that twinge again, seeing them get along was making her feel pressure. She didn't know if Sean deserved his friendship yet. She wanted Ted to remain neutral. She felt that inner pang of conscience, knowing that Ted would never be rude, and the Christian duty to forgive was required but she was desperately struggling to hold on to her manners.

"I saved this for you, I have a trunk of belongings. I thought you would appreciate this. I seem to recall that this was our father's and his father's before him." Angela sat and handed over a carved wooden pipe.

Sean took it and held it with nearly a caress. "I remember this. Oh sister..." Sean said softly. His words full of such gratitude that Angela felt a momentary break in her resolve to be angry.

He called me sister. She thought to herself.

"I have had this hanging up on my wall. But I wanted you to see it." Angela showed him the framed drawing.

She saw the tears fill his eyes again as he let the faces of his family soak in. He took long minutes tracing every line and every face.

"You look like Papa." Angela said finally, her heart touched by his reaction. She may be angry, but she wasn't heartless.

"You look like Mama." Sean said and looked deep into Angela's gaze, unwavering and so very thankful for this moment shared.

Her eyes burned with emotion but she fought off the tears. He was breaking down her feeble attempts to remain untouched. Angela had spent the last two years wishing for a relationship and declaring to herself that she longed for her brother. Now he was here, trying to mend the breach and she fought it within herself. Part of her wished she had slammed the door in his face, but the other part of her enjoyed sharing these precious mementos of the family they had both lost.

Sean handed the frame back to Angela and took the pipe back into his hands. His fingers running along the smooth edges. His voice was husky as he spoke. "I know that it may be hard to forget those words I spoke when we last met. They are burned into my heart, and I regret every single thing I uttered that day. But I am determined to earn your trust and to make amends." He said and looked at both Angela and Ted with resolve. "I plan on settling nearby and I do pray that over time we can be family again."

"Oh, you plan on staying?" Ted said with a little more interest than Angela would have liked.

"Yes," Sean said and smiled fully. "God has led me here, and I don't plan on running again."

Angela looked down, she swallowed the uncomfortable lump that was lingering in her throat. She hadn't thought of him staying, or disrupting her life here. She had dreamt of it before. Now she dreaded it. She tried to pull out a fake smile, to say the right words and they felt stuck as she looked up.

"I'm sure time will tell." She said, and realized it sounded like she doubted him. That hadn't come out right but it was out.

"I have a lot to prove. Oh... before I forget." Sean opened the second parcel. "This is also from Ireland, Aunt Felicity said that it was left to you. It was from the Fahey side. It has been in the family for many generations."

He handed her the brooch that fit into the palm of her hand. It was indeed old, the circle of silver was dark in places, a few green, blue and red stones that were deep set. It was precious and to know she was holding a piece of her family history was a heavy feeling in her heart.

"Thank you Sean..." Angela said softly, not knowing if she could say anything else.

Angela saw Dolly's head peek around the edge of the archway into the parlor. Angela smirked a little, knowing her friend was checking in on her. She saw Dolly slip out the front door a moment later.

"Where are you staying?" Ted asked and pulled Angela's attention away from the antique brooch that captivated her attention.

"Well..." Sean smiled and wiped a hand over his chin. "I am staying at the boarding house, which I recently found out from a new acquaintance that my own sister owns it." He laughed, and Ted joined in. Angela's eyes grew wide and she wanted to glare at her husband but resisted the urge.

"You needn't stay in town. I'm sure we could get another spare room ready for you until you figure out your next course of action." Ted offered congenially. Angela wanted to scream, but held her voice in check. She took a few deep breaths and concentrated on not throwing her new brooch at her husband.

He cannot stay in *my* house! She wanted to yell. But that was not anything she could ever say out loud. Her husband and her brother would both be insulted with one small phrase.

"Oh please accept my apologies, but I don't think that would be wise. I have come with no notice, and stirred up enough trouble for now. I am comfortable in her fine establishment and can come to visit when I am invited again. I do hope to see you both again soon but I do not want to force the issue. I am here, as a brother to make things better." Sean said and stood. "I should get going. But I cannot thank you both enough for letting me in and giving me a chance to apologize."

Angela let out a sigh of relief and thanked him again for the letters and gift.

"I have many more things from Ireland and more than a few crates of things I brought from New York. I hope to bring some by on our next visit." Sean said with a smile. Angela was feeling more tired as the moments dragged on. She just wanted him to go so she could lay on her bed and cry for a long while.

"Goodbye Sean. Thank you for coming." Angela said stiffly. She knew that her tone was a bit cold but she didn't know what to do about it at this point. She was just exhausted.

Sean waved as he headed through the door. She watched his dark shape through the window as he stepped down the porch steps. A part of her wished he would never return.

Chapter 9

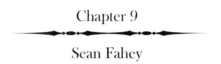

Sean Fahey

Sean could tell that Angela was growing tired of the visit and he was glad he left. He saw the clouds rolling in and he knew he would have to get back to town quick or he would get soaked. He walked around the back of the house and figured his horse was in the barn. The property was stunning and atop the hill behind her grand house Sean could see the lay of the land, the barn down the hill, a small cabin and what looked to be some fruit trees to the East, another cabin that had smoke billowing out the chimney to the West. He could see a chicken coop and a few goats searching through the brown winter grass to look for anything to nibble on. They had the start of something good here. Sean was glad for her and her new husband Ted. He just hoped that he would be able to be a part of their lives in the future.

Sean walked down the path to the barn. The bright red color was vivid in the grey brown of the late winter landscape. He saw the white caps on the mountains in the distance, the winter was trying to hold its last grasping breath here. But in just a few weeks, he could imagine that the world would dramatically change. So far, he was very pleased with the area his sister picked to settle. He could see himself enjoying this rugged landscape. The wilderness beckoned him.

Sean found the barn door and found a young man and the woman he met inside, Dolly, he remembered.

"Hello..." Sean said tentatively and saw Dolly and the young man turn away from their discussion.

Dolly lowered an eyebrow then spoke. "This is Warren, Warren is going to leave now." Dolly stated. She gave a signal for Warren to go, the young man with broad shoulders had an uneasy look. "Warren, he can saddle his own horse! I wish to have some..." She paused, she seemed to be searching for the right thing to say, "I wish to talking, to talk with him." She said finally and pressed her lips together impatiently.

Sean watched the young man mutter some apologies before he left. Sean put his hand up in a little wave and couldn't hide a smile.

Poor Warren... he was not ready for dealing with a strong-headed female quite yet.

Sean could see that his saddle was nearby, he gave Dolly a nod. She was standing against the door where he could see his borrowed horse was sitting.

"This is Clive Quackenbush's horse." Dolly stated. Somehow, Sean knew there was a question in there.

"Yes, I ran into him in town. He gave me directions to find my sister's home." Sean watched her face. Her thick dark hair was almost black and she had it pulled away from her face, but it was long down her back. Her dress was very fashionable. Not a common sight for a young Indian woman. *I think she is angry with me.* Sean pondered and hid a smile.

Dolly seemed to accept his explanation and she was staring at him with half closed eyes. "Why did you come here? You will only make her more upset when you leave again."

"I don't plan on leaving, I hope to settle here." Sean said, trying to convince another person that he meant only good, not harm.

"You say that now, but men say many things. What do you plan on doing here, Mr. Fahey?" Dolly pointed to him.

Sean was beginning to feel defensive. He knew somewhere in the recesses of his brain that Dolly was trying to protect her friend. "I hope to get a piece of land, grow some vegetables, hunt and fish. Nothing nefarious, I promise."

Dolly looked at him for a moment, the angry look was gone. "Nef-air-ee... I do not know this word." She said simply.

"Nefarious, means wicked, like a criminal action." Sean said.

Dolly said the word twice. "Thank you for teaching me a new word." She looked toward the saddle and went to it. "I will let you go, I smell a storm coming. Just promise me you will not hurt my friend again. She has cried for years over you. If you make her cry again I will be ashamed of you." Dolly looked Sean in the eye, her dark eyes sought his and he wondered at this mysterious creature.

"I promise..." Sean said and he never looked away from her dark gaze.

Dolly lifted the saddle and Sean opened the stall and let the horse out. He grabbed the reins and let the horse to the open section of the barn. Dolly effortlessly got the horse saddled and ready to ride. Sean was very impressed.

"Just up the road is the church, you should come on Sunday. That would be good for you to be seen to all her neighbors. They will all want a chance to threaten you as well." Dolly smiled for the first time as she stepped away from him. He saw her grin.

"Well, I will certainly be there." Sean promised again.

"If you stay around, as you say, then I will show you some good hunting spots." Dolly said.

Sean wondered at this girl, she was a mystery for certain.

"That would be grand. Good day, now." He said and grabbed the reins to lead the horse outside.

All together a very strange day... He would have plenty to ponder as he rode home. A few fat drops of cold rain hit his shoulders and back so Sean kicked his heels and let the horse pick up the pace. It felt good to get in a good ride after traveling by ferry and boat so much.

❦

Violet Griffen

Violet made a fresh pot of coffee on the stove and perked up the fire. She could hear that Lucas was outside chopping firewood and she knew he would be coming inside for dinner soon. Today had been a strange day, the doctor was here for a while, and then a few visitors, Corinne sent out requests to any visitors to gather a few things for her. Pastor Whitman had spoken to Corinne a few minutes ago and was heading out to the Varushkin cabin to speak to Slava. Violet had a few knots in her stomach trying to imagine that meeting.

Her own fresh experience at confronting an abusive parent was not the best example of how these things could escalate. The story with her father had ended when she walked away from the town square with her own father's head in a noose. Now there was no punishment for spanking or even taking a belt to a child. Here in the West it will probably be the case that most people will look the other way. Certainly most people would just tell you to mind your own business. Violet knew Lucas was not the kind of man to take it lightly that a man he employs had used his fists against his 15-year-old daughter. Corinne had even said that Galina had said something about being kicked. Violet felt a shudder go through her. She had her own past to forget, she did not need to imagine how Galina felt, she knew.

110

Violet prayed as she went about her preparations. She needed to get some more fresh butter but she hadn't been able to get away. Perhaps she could now.

Violet peeked in to check on Galina, Corinne is awake and sitting with the girl.

"Is she awake?" Violet asked softly. She couldn't see any movement.

"She was a few minutes ago. But she fell back to sleep again. The laudanum will wear off soon. I will warm up some broth for her. She may want some real food later." Corinne looked up to Violet and smiled wearily. "Would you be willing to go get Trudie. I'm sure she is going to get hungry soon too. Corinne held a hand to her chest. "I'm getting a bit uncomfortable myself. I think I will have to change my dress." Corinne blushed.

"I needed to go to your father's to get some fresh butter anyhow." Violet said just above a whisper.

Corinne nodded and turned her attention back to Galina. Violet stood for a moment and watched over the scene. Corinne's dark hair hung long down her back. Her friend was such a comfort to everyone who needed help. Violet sincerely hoped that Corinne knew how much she was appreciated.

Violet felt the chill a few minutes later. Dusk was falling and the temperature was dropping quickly. The sky had the brilliant dark blue and the sun shone orange over the tops of the trees to the West. She stopped and told Lucas where she was heading.

Violet walked on the worn path toward the Harpole house.

She made it to the door just as Reynaldo was coming toward her from the opposite direction.

"Hello, Mrs. Griffen." Rey said politely. His arms were full with a burlap sack.

"Oh, hello." Violet said, she felt a blush creeping up her neck. His smile was charming and he made her feel flustered.

"I was able to find some clean snow; I've heard that Corinne still needed some for the young woman in her care." Reynaldo said, he nodded his head toward the sack.

"Oh, I'm just here to gather up Trudie, and to get some fresh butter." Violet said. She was fidgeting with her hands. "I suppose I should knock." Violet felt the urge to giggle nervously and wanted to escape the discomfort of Reynaldo's gaze. His eyes were warm and his smile suggested that he found her amusing.

"By all means." His smile grew broader.

Violet turned away, certain that her cheeks were scarlet. She knocked.

Cooper Harpole answered the door with young Lila a step behind him.

"I will stay out here. I don't want this snow to melt any more than it already has." Reynaldo claimed. "I will wait and walk you back, iffen you don't mind." Reynaldo said before Violet walked into the cabin.

Violet whipped her head back around. "Why certainly." She said without thinking. She turned back quickly and wondered why her tone bordered on flirtatious. She really must be tired to allow herself to flirt with this nice man. He certainly hadn't meant anything by his offer. She would have spoken like that to her Eddie, but she was not in any state of mind for that kind of thing.

Violet went inside before she embarrassed herself further.

Marie Harpole had Trudie on her hip, bouncing an obviously upset child.

"I've come to check and see if Trudie was ready to be fed." Violet said then added. "I also need some butter if you have any to spare. I have not had the time to churn any." Violet offered to take Trudie with arms outstretched.

"Oh, yes, Trudie just started to fuss a few minutes ago. I think we tuckered her out fully. Lila and Cooper were good little helpers today keeping her busy." Marie looked to her son and adopted daughter with love in her eyes. She handed Trudie to Violet.

Trudie was more than willing to be transferred to Violet. She cuddled against Violet's chest and let out a withering sigh that bordered on a hiccup. Her lip was distended in a pitiful pout.

Marie walked away and Violet placed a few kisses on the top of Trudie's head. Marie was back a moment later with a full bowl of butter.

"It's fresh, just churned today." Marie grinned, her lovely dimples showing.

"You amaze me, fresh churned butter and managing four children in the house today." Violet praised.

"Oh, don't be too impressed. My new housekeeper Mrs. Franklin has been working full time now. My husband has declared that it was time that I gave up the fight. I still do most of the cooking, but now I can focus more on other things instead of the housework. He spoils me so." Marie said with a grin.

Violet smiled, she had seen Mrs. Franklin walking up the path just that morning. She knew that she would make an effort to get to know her one of these days.

"I should get going. But I want to thank you so much on behalf of Lucas and Corinne." Violet offered.

"You get going. You can save the thanks. It was certainly my pleasure." Marie covered the bowl of butter with a tea towel she was holding and Violet took it awkwardly with a spare hand.

Violet was out the door just a minute later. Reynaldo was waiting, as he had promised. Looking handsome with his dark hat and kind eyes.

"The young lady is ready for her mother." Violet said and began walking.

"Wait, let me get that for you." Reynaldo took her shoulder and she turned, looking up to his face while he took the bowl from her. "I've got it." Reynaldo held the sack in one arm and the bowl with his free hand now. Violet was speechless.

She began walking at a fast pace to let the brisk air cool her cheeks.

She was so thankful when she reached the doorstep to the Grant's home.

"Thank you Mr. Legales." Violet found her manners as she opened the cabin door.

"I thought we had settled on you calling me Reynaldo at least." He stepped in next to her and nudged the door open with his shoulder.

Lucas stood inside and was giving Violet an interesting smile.

"Of course, I'm sorry... Thank you Reynaldo." Violet's eyes were wide as she realized how close he stood to her. Lucas was watching them, she could tell he was quite amused. They both came inside.

"Hello Rey." Lucas came over.

"I brought some snow for the Doctor Lady in the house." Reynaldo said and handed the icy bag over to Lucas and placed the bowl on the nearby table.

"Don't let Corinne hear that. She gets her stockings in a twist if someone calls her the doctor." Lucas laughed. "She will appreciate the snow, though. We don't have many snow drifts around here to pilfer anymore." Lucas gave Reynaldo a slug in the shoulder. "Thank you so much. It will do some good for certain."

"Is Corinne still in with Galina?" Violet asked. Glad that Reynaldo's attention was on Lucas now.

"No, she should be out in just a moment." Lucas said.

"You want to stay to supper?" Lucas offered. "I'm sorry Violet, I should have asked if we have enough for a guest.

Violet's eyes grew wide. "Why yes... of course." She stammered then placed a hand on Trudie who was beginning to fuss.

"Oh dear, sweet girl, Mama is here." Corinne walked into the room and reached out her arms for her baby girl.

Trudie nearly jumped out of Violet's arms to get to her mother. Violet had to grasp ahold the wiggling child to keep her from falling. Reynaldo slipped an arm around the child and around Violet's back to steady her.

Corinne grabbed ahold of the girl and everyone laughed as the tragedy was averted. Corinne comforted the girl and excused herself to a back room to take care of feeding.

"Let me get cleaned up and we can talk before dinner. We'll let Trudie get settled in before we eat." Lucas offered with a friendly smile.

Violet attempted to keep her hands busy as Lucas and Reynaldo cleaned up at the basin. She hadn't been amused by the gleam in Lucas's eye as he invited Reynaldo to supper. She was a widow; she was above such nonsense.

Violet got the butter separated, a smaller portion on a plate for the table, and the larger portion in a crock. She started a pot of water to boil on the hot stove to warm up for washing dishes after the meal.

She checked the bread in the dutch oven and it was ready to come out, all golden brown and smelling good. She had made a simple stew, but she had added a few dried herbs from her dwindling stock, it added some nice flavor. Violet pulled out the bread and let it cool on the trivet on the counter.

"You need some help?" Lucas asked as Violet was reaching to grab the pot of stew off the stove.

"Yes, thank you." Violet said demurely. Both Lucas and Reynaldo invaded the space behind the counter near the stove and Violet felt heat creep into her cheeks again. Violet had to press herself against the counter to get out of their way.

The men made quick work of the heavy stew pot. "It is ready whenever Corinne is done." Violet said. She was out of tasks to do and felt the men watching her, which unnerved her greatly.

She scrambled for any ideas of what to do to keep her hands busy when a knock came to the door.

A booming voice came from the other side of the door.

"Lucas, I need to talk to you!"

Violet was certain that it was Mr. Varushkin but it gave her a chilly reminder of her own father's tone when he had been here last year. Violet felt herself shrinking within herself. She just wasn't certain she wanted to be involved in any kind of scene.

Lucas answered the door. Reynaldo stood behind him but he kept turning to give Violet a few concerned looks.

"I'm here Slava, no need to holler." Lucas kept his voice even.

"I had my son gather up Galina's things as you asked me to this morning." Slava shoved a linen sack through the doorway. Lucas grabbed it and settled it next to him.

"I appreciate that." Lucas said.

"I need to be getting back to work Lucas." Slava said, he was such a large man that Violet wondered if he was trying to intimidate Lucas.

"I understand that. I am struggling, I will be honest with you. I am so disappointed in your behavior concerning your young daughter." Lucas spoke softly, but Slava reacted strongly.

"It is none of your business what I do concerning my own children!" Slava said with force. Violet watched his hands form into fists and felt fear trickle through her.

"It becomes my business when your daughter was bleeding in my back bedroom, when the doctor had to sew her scalp back together." Lucas's voice rose with his own anger.

The tension in the room was palpable and Violet wondered if she would see more violence.

Slava was seething, she watched his cheeks redden.

"Seems to me, that you are treading on dangerous ground Slava." Lucas spoke up again. "The last time a man so severely mistreated his daughter he found himself on the wrong side of a rope. I don't think you have much of a leg to stand on."

"I am allowed to discipline my child as I see fit." Slava said, his lips were rigid and he was spitting as he spoke each word.

"I am allowed to hire who I wish, and fire them." Lucas put a hand to his chin.

Violet couldn't tear her eyes away as Slava worked out the dilemma that he had created.

"What do you suggest Mr. Grant?" Slava said, noticeably quieter. He was on thin ice and about to lose a good paying job.

"I suggest you give us guardianship over Galina, I will deduct Galina's earning over the last six months from your wages to repay her for everything she had rightly earned from her work. I also want you to talk with Pastor Whittlan every few weeks to make certain that you have some advice on how to manage that temper of yours." Lucas said all this calmly and with no anger. Violet wondered how any man could actually accomplish that with a man like Slava, who radiated anger, and just standing a few feet in front of him.

Slava's hands formed into fists again. He took a deep breath and looked down, obviously in defeat. "I agree." He muttered.

"You will behave and I don't want to hear one word about you smearing her name to anyone. If I ever hear of you taking a hand or fist to anyone in your household ever again all deals are done. I will ruin you for any job in this town." Lucas said low but forcefully, his eyebrows low and serious.

Slava nodded. "Do I start back up tomorrow?" Slava said with less bluster. He knew he'd been beat.

"That is fine. But I never want you coming to my door shouting again. You come talk to me with civility..." Lucas put a hand to his forehead, he wasn't happy with any of this. Violet could tell by his demeanor.

"I will, sir." Slava nodded and pulled his hat down as a goodbye. Violet watched from the kitchen as the large man turned and walked away. Her stomach was tied up in knots and she let out the breath she was holding.

Lucas finally closed the door and let out a breath himself. Reynaldo clapped a hand on his shoulder.

"You handled that pretty well." Reynaldo said and he chuckled nervously. "I wondered for a moment or two if we were going to have a brawl before supper."

"I talked with John Harpole and Pastor Whittlan today and got some good advice. I knew this confrontation was coming. I am not pleased that he came to my door shouting, but I am glad we got things settled. I wanted to terminate his employment. I am disgusted with his actions. But John Harpole and the Pastor advised against it. Saying it would only fuel his anger more." Lucas ran a hand through his hair and sighed deeply again.

"It's certainly going to be awkward working with him for a bit of time." Reynaldo clapped Lucas's shoulder again.

Lucas laughed and nodded. "I'm going to check on my wife. Make certain she wasn't affected by his bluster."

Reynaldo smiled and let Lucas go.

Violet watched Lucas leave the front room, her heartbeat slowing after the confrontation but somehow not understanding why she suddenly felt so emotional. It was so much like her father, the yelling and violent temper that always made her feel so small and insignificant. It took her straight back to those horrible days that she wished so badly were banished from her memory.

Violet knew that she was losing her resolve when a few hot tears streamed down her cheeks. She looked at the floor and willed herself to let those memories go but they were there, confronting her again.

She took some deep breaths and closed her eyes.

In may have only been a minute, her swirling emotions and memories colliding in her mind, making her feel like she was 8 years old again. But she felt a presence at her side and looked up.

Her eyes were full of tears but she could see through the blur. Reynaldo was next to her, watching her with concern.

"Angry men bring back some memories?" He asked softly.

Violet nodded and felt a rush go through her. She never understood why a little bit of sympathy would always make her cry harder, but seeing that look in Reynaldo's dark eyes. Knowing that he had his own memories of the past to overcome. It tipped her over the edge. Reynaldo stepped in close and Violet leaned into his chest and let the sobs roll out.

His brown flannel shirt had the scent of the woods, fresh air, and the hint of pine. Violet's tears ran out quickly as she realized with a deepening sense of mortification that she had lost her composure.

"Do pardon me..." Violet said through a scratchy and tight throat.

She escaped the room, made it to her own rooms, and never looked back.

Violet washed her face and made certain in the looking glass that her face showed no ill effects of her weeping. She changed her blouse as an excuse to Lucas and Corinne for her leaving, not that they would ask, but she was prepared anyway for the question.

Violet went back to the main room and was pleased to see that Corinne had joined them. Corinne helped Violet serve up the supper

117

and Violet never looked away from Corinne. She was so embarrassed by crying on Reynaldo's shoulder she avoided eye contact at all cost.

Dinner was delicious and the conversation held a serious tone to start but ended with the talk of plans for the spring. Violet stayed mostly silent. Everyone tried to coax her into the conversation but she claimed that she was tired a few times. They finally let her be.

❖◆❖ ❖◆❖

Megan Capron

Megan watched the gray-brown water fly by her as the porters walked around the top deck of the steamship. She had her bags and trunks around her, she already had money to pay a porter to get her luggage off the ship. She had high hopes that the day would go smoothly. She was tired and travel weary from the journey. She had her severance funds tucked away on her person, not trusting even to put her money in her bags. She would quickly deposit those funds in a bank as soon as she was settled in. She was assured an audition at The Portland Grand Hotel. She was confident that she would assure her position, she knew she was a good entertainer.

The steamship finally docked and by midday Megan, now to be known to everyone as Rosie Green, got her bags and trunk on board a wagon and she road into town. Her mint green traveling suit was rumpled and she longed for a hot bath. She wondered as she made her way through town, seeing the small buildings along the street, that a boardwalk was along the buildings, which impressed her. She did remember when she was in Oregon City that they had been talking about building a boardwalk. They hadn't at the time she had made her exit. It had seemed like it had been years but it hadn't been that many months since that day. She wondered how that had played out, certainly Corinne and her Father would have sent telegrams to her parents. Megan was getting agitated as the bumpy road nearly knocked her off the seat. She sent a glare to the grizzly looking man who drove in the seat in front of her.

"Are we almost to the boarding house?" Megan tried to keep her tone pleasant, but she heard the edge in her voice. She would have to work on that. "I am just anxious to get settled." She smiled sweetly as the man turned around to look at her. His expression didn't change.

"Almost there Ma'am." He said gruffly.

118

She huffed softly and settled back into her seat. The wagon squealed and squeaked over the bumps. She was glad to be off the steamship, but looking around this small town made her wonder again about being back in Oregon.

How in the world could a town like this support a Grand Hotel? She wondered and shook her head.

She saw men on horseback and even a few women walking through the streets. There were a few shops and a tavern. No one was dressed in the latest fashions. This felt like the same kind of town as Oregon City. She rolled her eyes as she passed the tavern. She wished again somehow that she had enough funds to just leave and head back East, but she needed to have more money, in case her Grandmother Rose Capron would not take her in. She certainly didn't want to live below decent means. She had a certain dignity, and she would not live like a pauper.

They finally got to a large white building with a large front porch with bright blue shutters on the windows.

"Here we are Ma'am." The bearded man said as he pulled the wagon to a stop.

Megan stepped off the wagon with the help from the driver. She noticed his rough hands and worried for a moment about her gloves being soiled. She smiled her fake smile at him then checked her gloves for any evidence of being tainted.

He went to work to unload her baggage and Megan took a chance to go inside and secure her room.

The man who ran the place was found within a few minutes. His wife seemed pleasant enough, but Megan thought that she was typical for the region, slightly underdressed and rather frumpy. The man walked in, he was wiping his hands in a towel before he reached out to her to shake her hand.

"I'm Kevin Landers, my wife here is Sadie."

"I'm Mrs. Rosie Green, originally from Kentucky, but most recently from San Francisco." Megan shook both of their hands, trying to make a good impression.

"We have been expecting you, we have a two room suite set aside for you. Everyone is so excited about the new hotel. We are so pleased to have talented musicians coming in." The wife Sadie said.

Megan removed her gloves and talked with the owners for a few minutes, making polite conversation, but inwardly wanting to just rest and get settled in. After they went over the schedule for the provided meals, they finally let her go.

Sadie led Megan up to her room.

"Do you expect your husband to join you?" Sadie asked as they were walking up the staircase to the second floor.

Megan was prepared. "My husband Edward is still in California territory. I just felt that San Francisco was not a safe environment to stay in for a lady. He owns a gold mine west of San Francisco. His letters say that he plans to sell it for a big profit in a few months." Megan said. She had almost said Pruitt, but caught herself in time. She had practice the lie so many times in her head. But habits were hard to relearn. She would stick with fiction. She had heard so many stories from miners in San Francisco that she pieced her story together from their experiences. She knew she had taking a large portion of her story from her cousin's housekeeper, it was the easiest to remember.

"Well, I am glad to know you are here. I couldn't help but notice. You have a bit of a glow to your cheeks. Is it presumptuous of me to congratulate you on a blessed event?" Sadie smiled sweetly as she asked.

Megan was annoyed but glued her smile on and even lowered her head as a lady would at the mention of being in a delicate way. "Well, I guess I cannot hide it any longer." Megan said. She knew that being new in town people would be curious about her. "I am just a private person."

Sadie nodded and led her down a hallway.

Megan was pleased with the room Sadie had led her too. If she was honest with herself, she hadn't expected such a nice room. It had pretty windows that faced the back of the property, there was a pretty garden area, with a bench and what looked to be some small trees. Once the weather warmed that would be quite charming, she mused. Megan huffed and settled herself on the loveseat in the sitting room. She would have to make arrangements to have some help with her wardrobe and need a maid at least a few times a day. She would have to go back downstairs to talk with the owners. She dreaded it. The nosy Sadie Landers seemed like a woman who was going to always be prying into things that were not her business.

Megan removed her bonnet and checked her hair in the mirror on the wall. She fixed a pin and smoothed over the sides of her hair.

It only took about thirty minutes to set up the times for a maid to come and take care of helping Megan dress when she had to perform, she also paid extra to have someone take care of other cleaning needs. Megan may be living in Oregon, but she was not going to clean her own chamber pot. That was not acceptable in her mind.

Her meeting with the owner of The Portland Grand Hotel went extraordinarily well. He was a lot like Pruitt, a round, jovial businessman, who responded to her with the expected bowing and scraping. He was married, and to him, Rosie Green was married, but she flirted and flattered just enough to make him feel comfortable. She was offered the job of singing with the Orchestra on Thursday through Sunday, a lunch performance, and then a full evening performance. She did explain that she, Rosie, was expecting to be upfront. Her new boss congratulated her and her fictitious husband on the good news. Her lie was going to work.

Megan walked a few blocks through town with a smug smile, she was truly a magnificent actress in her own mind. There wasn't anyone she couldn't fool.

Chapter 10

Angela Greaves

Angela was certainly in a foul mood. She had cried herself to sleep for two nights in a row. Her head in a muddle between Galina's beating and her brother showing up. She was numb and confused. She had tried to pray in the midst of her tears the night before, she felt like her prayer was stilted and she couldn't find the words. She didn't know what she was asking of God and her heart felt like a stone in her chest. She had lain in bed for the longest time, sniffling and crying, her husband sleeping easily in the bed next to her. It really chaffed her that Ted had no trouble with anything, he was calm and cool-tempered about just about any crisis that came along.

When Angela woke in the morning, she saw the sunshine break through the doorway as it streamed through the eastern window of the kitchen. She smelled coffee and saw that Ted was at the counter. Angela shifted and turned on her side, the bed made a tiny squeak from the movement.

"Good morning wife." Ted turned his blond head and smiled his best smile for her. He was so handsome and charming she wanted to let her foul mood run away like a skittish creature. She smiled the best she could manage.

"Hello, my husband." Angela sighed. She needed to put away all her negative thoughts and be thankful for a new day.

Angela stretched and closed the door to get dressed, since they now had a houseguest. She dressed in a simple blouse and skirt and threw on an apron so she could immediately get to work on cooking. She planned to throw herself into a task so she would get out of her own head. Angela had learned a lot from Violet over the last few years, doing good for others can lift you out of the darkest of mood or memory. Just that reminder made Angela take a pause as she tied her apron around her waist. Angela had certainly not had the easiest of childhoods, but Violet had overcome so much and had the sweetest spirit. Angela felt that inner pang that she was being childish and petulant. She finally found a few words and said a quick prayer.

"Oh, God, please show me how to find Joy even when I just don't understand the world around me." Angela said softly.

Angela felt a sense of relief. It was always hard to explain, but knowing that she was getting out of her own way was a start. She was not Galina, broken and bleeding, or even Violet, a widow who had watched her father hang just a few months ago. She had a lovely home, a husband who loved her, and her brother had come across oceans to see her and make amends. Certainly, her life had been blessed, Angela needed to remember all the good things.

Angela joined her husband in the kitchen and gave him a kiss on the cheek, feeling the stubble of his reddish blond beard on his cheek.

"Your cheek is rough!" Angela said with a tone lighter than she had felt in a few days.

"Sorry dear, I haven't shaved yet." Ted bent and kissed her neck and then grabbed her tight and rubbed his stubble on the sensitive skin of her throat.

Angela shrieked and tried to escape his clutches. The mood shifted in the house and Angela laughed as the morning routine took on the normal play between them. Angela was so thankful.

❖

Sean Fahey

Sean Fahey had gone to bed early the night before. The bed in the boarding house was comfortable and the fire in the wood stove was cozy. Sean was asleep within a minute of his head hitting the pillow.

Sean was pleased when his room was bright the next morning. There was the unmistakable sounds of robin-song that trilled outside nearby... The sound of spring.

Sean ate breakfast with some of the other tenants. Gemma Caplan, the manager of the Orchard House was sweet and had a funny sense of humor as she served up extra helpings and talked with the guests as they came in and out of the large dining room. He decided to spill the beans about his identity and let Gemma in on his real name. Gemma was in raptures about having Angela's brother in the house. He kept things simple, not going into the troubles from the past, not knowing how much Angela had said around town.

Gemma had no negative sign of any thought but that this was a 'Miracle from Above!'

Gemma raved on about his sister's generosity, and how her farm manager, Earl was a constant visitor and the handy man around the place.

"Angela has done everything to make this place a showpiece for this town. My husband and I owned it before. Once my husband passed on I just wasn't able to keep it up." Gemma held a hand over her heart and smiled sweetly. Sean wondered if a fond memory was captured within that peaceful grin. "Angela let me stay on here to do what I love, which is take care of people. It just blesses my heart to do it." Gemma had a few wrinkles around her eyes and some deep smile lines around her cheeks but her genuine warmth made Sean glad to know her. She was just the kind of lady that you wanted as a friend.

123

Sean ate heartily, Gemma's company lifted his heart but also having seen his sister and taken that first step, he had freed a heavy burden. He had a lot to do, he wanted to do some exploring and get a better feel for the land. There was that tiny tug in his heart, going out without his old companion, William Shipley. He could imagine how excited Ol' Willie would have gotten about going to find the deepest, densest of woods to settle in. Sean felt that page had turned in his life, wondering if he ever would find another friend as close as Ol' Willie had been to him. A part of his heart was missing.

Sean dressed casually and headed out to see more of what this small town offered, he already liked it more than the bustling and busy cities.

The streets were a bit muddy, that was normal for early spring, he imagined that as the snow melted off the mountain tops the Willamette River would grow and expand. He saw several businesses that he made a mental note to visit sometime as he walked along. The morning was early and a morning mist clung to the air. The bright sunshine made the mist nearly glow yellow and hazy through the trees.

He found the livery across the street from the fancy goods store, where his new acquaintance Clive was probably already busily working. Sean would stop in to say hello when he was done with his first task of the day.

The livery was a big lofty space with an open corral behind it, with several horses munching at their meal. Sean saw a young man hanging tackle on the pegs on a wall inside, Sean walked over to seek his attention.

"I'm in the need of some horseflesh." Sean said with a smile.

The young man gave him a nod and they went to the corral together.

Within the hour, Sean had a new saddle and a spirited mount, a fine dapple-grey, promised to be sure-footed, a good mountain rider and workhorse. Sean wasn't looking for speed but a solid mount that could handle himself in the rough landscape. Sean paid for a few weeks boarding, plenty of feed, and was pleased. Having his own mount again was a good step. He had sold his and Ol' Willie's horses before he left for Ireland.

Sean planned to come back later in the day to take his new horse out for a ride to see the landscape. First, he wanted to have a good chat with Clive and see what needed to be done to apply for land. It

124

was the next step, one that gave him a bit of trepidation, he had never built his own cabin and knew that he would likely have to. It would definitely be a challenge.

He walked into the fancy goods store and gave a hearty hello to Mrs. Quackenbush, who was sipping tea at the front counter.

"Oh, please, you get to call me Millie, dear." Millie gave him a generous smile.

Sean nodded and looked around, he found a few flannel shirts that would fit nicely, and some handkerchiefs, he plunked the coins on the counter to pay for them. Millie offered him some tea.

"Oh, no thanks, I'm wondering if Clive is around." Sean asked.

"He's out back in the warehouse, you go right ahead and head back." Millie gestured him to follow her. "It's a slow morning. I expect it will pick up soon with the sun out, people flock to town when the spring sun peeks out of the clouds." Millie led Sean through the back rooms and let him through the back door.

Clive was indeed just outside the back door and gave Sean a hearty wave.

"Thank You, Millie." Sean placed a hand on her warm shoulder.

"Oh, you are most welcome dearie." Millie patted his arm and went back to her post at the front of the store.

Clive was wearing a blue shirt with black suspenders and dark pants. He lifted his eyebrows and gave Sean a grin.

"You are out bright and early." Clive walked over and gave Sean a backslap.

"Yessir, just got myself a horse, working through my list of things to get accomplished." Sean said.

"Oh you'll have to ride by my new place sometime and let me get a look-see." Clive chuckled.

"That I can do." Sean promised. "I was going to ask for a bit of advice. I'm looking for some property."

"Well, I've been living in these parts a long while. What kind of land you looking for?" Clive scratched his chin.

"I'm wanting enough room to get in a garden at least, but I hope to get back to some hunting and trapping. I've never built a cabin before, but I will if I must." Sean said and wondered if anything he built himself would last a winter. He knew his strengths.

"Well, I do know of a place that would fit those needs. As well as a few others." Clive offered. "Before I go into that..." Clive gave Sean a querying look. "You talk with your sister yet?" Clive raised an eyebrow.

"Yesterday, I went by, she was certainly shocked." Sean sighed at the memory of her face, the hurt behind those green eyes would leave a lasting mark on his heart.

"Well, I can imagine that." Clive chuckled softly. "She has a sensitive heart."

"Let me make you an offer, I have a cabin and piece of land that I don't need anymore. I have moved closer to town, now that I am getting hitched again it makes more sense for me. I will take you by the place and see what you think of it. I can also show you a few pieces of land further from town that you could get by going through the land office." Clive said and bumped Sean with an elbow. "No pressure on your decision, but you look a bit nervous about building your own cabin."

"Never attempted it before." Sean shrugged. "Might be an eyesore iffen I tried."

"I'm guessing you are a smart lad, you'd figure it out. But I can show you around and see if my place would do for ya. I would love to know that someone would be on the land, trapping and hunting like I used too. I keep the beavers off the creeks and nearby rivers too. They will take over the place if you let 'em." Clive laughed and gave a holler. "J.Q.! I'm heading out for a bit."

Sean didn't see JQ, but he heard him from the back of the warehouse.

"See ya later!" Came the voice from the back.

"Well, I get to see your new ride sooner than I thought. Let me grab a jacket and we can get going." Clive left for a minute and was back with a thin brown coat.

They walked across the street and Sean saddled up his dapple-grey. Clive was waiting out front already mounted on a tall dark brown beauty.

"Oh that is a handsome sight." Clive clucked and nodded with his approval.

"Thanks, John Harpole has a fine selection. I got a good one!"

The men rode out of town, Clive leading the way. The morning sun was bright and the blue sky was promising a delightful day. The road opened up as they got out of town and Sean enjoyed seeing the mountain splendor. It was a stunning sight, even with the trees still brown and drab from their winter slumber.

"My place is to the North; I hope you don't mind going off the main path. There is a rough road that goes near my property but today I will show you the way as the crow flies." Clive said over his shoulder.

Sean smiled and gladly went with him, seeing Clive in the outdoors was like seeing a man freed. He could tell that Clive was an outdoorsman just by the way his whole being seemed to light up once he ventured out.

Clive shared some tidbits along the way, names of creeks, and pointing out different properties and who owned the land that they passed by.

"Beavers are drawn to this creek especially; I have been asked several times to trap them for the farmers along this route. Beavers are such a mighty nuisance." Clive said with a grimace.

"I would be glad to help out on that score." Sean said and laughed with Clive. "I do love trapping and understand the damage a wayward critter can do to the waterways if you let them have their way."

Clive gave Sean an appreciative nod before he continued. They climbed to the top of a hill and got a good look over a good portion of acreage. Seeing a few farms spread out, with cabins, barns, but also plenty of woods and forestland made Sean excited, this land was tamable, but held that kind of rugged beauty that drew him in.

"Since you have the heart of a hunter and trapper I will tell you that the reason I chose my plot was the rich variety of wild game. I have a few creeks that run through the dense woods on my property. It would make a good place for you to keep that up." Clive gave him a wink as they sat on the top of the hill.

Sean's mount was stepping around, seemingly eager to keep moving forward so they both took the cue and clucked their horses back into motion. Clive pointed off toward the north.

"We're headin' that way. Let's give these fellows a little run in the open stretch ahead. I think we are all glad for the snow to be gone, gotta let the winter blow off of us." Clive gave his mount a little kick and his mount eagerly let loose. Sean's horse didn't need any encouragement but joined in the chase to catch up with the other horse.

Sean reveled in the wind that brushed his cheeks and the cool spring air. It was refreshing and exhilarating to be free in the open air, with the mountain view surrounding him and the sound of the pounding hooves beneath him. He had missed this kind of freedom.

They slowed the horses after letting them have a good run, Clive led them across a small creek. Sean was pleased that his mount gave him no difficulties, but instead was willing to accept any change in terrain without baulking.

The woods were darker and the scent of wet earth and moss gave him that familiar tug. The memories of hunts with Ol' Willie in many a woods like this. Sean was seeing the possibilities and looked forward to exploring again. He would have to make new memories in this new life, but knowing the familiarity with the sights and smells made him realize how much he missed this part of his life. He really felt that he was finished with traveling the world. He had been gone for far too long.

"We are getting close. This is part of my land here. This spot is good for fishing and trapping." Clive said and pointed to a large rock on the side of a trickling creek that widened out. "I have caught some good suppers sitting at that rock." Clive grinned and kept moving forward. Sean paused and took everything in, the sound of the creek and the way the sunlight played on the water. It would be a very good place to find some peace and quiet, a good place for prayer, as well as some fishing.

"My place is just a few more paces." Clive said as he weaved around a berry patch. "Watch out, the thorns will snag ya if you don't give em' a wide berth."

"Sure thing." Sean said lightheartedly. Sean was betting that Clive had a story about that bush catching him unaware by the grin on his face.

The woods did open up after just a few more minutes and Sean could see a nice little cabin up ahead. They rode up to a fence post that Clive pointed to and tied their mounts up.

Sean liked the look of the cabin, it wasn't a huge one, but it looked big enough to have a few rooms, which is a fair-bit larger than the cabin he lived in outside of San Francisco. That had been a two-room cabin, and was pretty shy on luxuries. There had only been one glass window in his previous cabin. This one was bigger, and looked to be tall enough for a loft up above. Sean eyed the roof practically, it looked solid with no signs of sagging or damage.

"Let me get to work. I put up my bear-protection just a few days ago. I didn't want any unwelcome guests." Clive laughed and set to work getting the front door open. Clive picked up a few rough boards with long spikes sticking up.

Sean was surprised to see the gruesome steel nails.

Clive chuckled. "You seem concerned." Clive held up the wood. "These spikes aren't sharp enough to puncture the tough feet of a bears paw... but they will be uncomfortable to stand on them long enough to get the boards off the front door. It's a trick I learned from a fellow a few years ago. If you take this place, I'll leave them behind for ya. The black bears on the bluffs will be making their way down as they get hungry."

They got through the boards and got the front door open. Sean was pleased to see a nice big room with a fireplace, and a decent kitchen with a wide cook stove. There were even some pretty windows and some curtains.

"I hadn't thought of needing any of these furnishings so it can all stay if you like it. I just have a few little personal things in here I'm supposin'." Clive said.

"It is way better than my last place already. My friend Ol' Willie was not much for luxuries, like rugs and soft chairs." Sean chuckled and Clive gave him a slap on the back. "I have a shed out back, but you may want to build yourself a small barn to hold your horse or a wagon. My barn was pretty rickety, I took it down for kindling after my wife, and kids were gone. I always kept my horse at a neighbors place up the ways." Clive walked Sean through the place. He pointed up to the rope ladder that led up to a loft. "I haven't been up there for years; the dust may swallow you up if you dare go up there." Clive opened his eyes in mock fear.

"I'll be careful." Sean smiled. Everything about this place felt homey and peaceful. It wouldn't take much at all to make this place his own. "I think I'll take it." He decided and felt a calm warmth fill his chest.

"You want to see the bedrooms first?" Clive asked.

"I'll see 'em, but I'm happy. This place is grand. It will do nicely." Sean reached a hand out to shake Clive's.

Clive's grip was strong and his smile was approving.

"May God bless your days and nights spent here, Sean." Clive spoke low and Sean felt the blessing down to his toes. It felt like something a father would say to a son, and he hadn't known that he needed that.

He was getting the fresh start that he needed. He had faced something that he had been running from for so long. It was good to finally start to let those guilty feelings go. He had followed that path that God had led him towards, and the blessings were following.

Chapter 11

Galina Varushkin

Galina was able to see... it was such a relief to see the light of day through both eyes after several days of pain and drowsiness. The warm brown logs and the bright colors of the quilt were strange to her. She remembered where she was but still had to take account of how she had gotten to Corinne's house. The light from the window was bright and she looked away from the intensity of it. Memory had come back to her slowly as the minutes passed by. There was still a lot of pain, especially in her ribs and her face when she tried to lick her dry lips.

Her eyes adjusted and the window had pale blue curtains that were pulled closed but the sunlight was seen through the small opening and a beam of sunshine shown from the window to her bed. It was a sweet sight after the dark days.

There was a little bell next to Galina on her bed, she took ahold and let the bell ring out softly to let someone know she was awake. Galina was certainly eager for some company and some help to get up.

"Oh, you are awake." Corinne said sweetly as she opened the door, her smile was radiant.

Galina wanted to smile back at her friend but the attempt made her cheeks hurt.

"I have some water right here." Corinne poured some water into a small mug and sat next to Galina. Corinne held the cup and helped Galina get a few sips of water. It was delightful on her tongue.

Corinne grabbed a jar from the side table and dabbed a finger in it. "Just some oil for your lips. I'll be gentle." She promised.

Galina was glad for Corinne's tenderness while spreading the oil, as her lips were still a bit swollen, but she could tell that they were improving from some of her cognizant moments of wakefulness over the last two days. She wished the memory of pain would go away.

"Thank you so much." Galina heard her scratchy voice and wondered at it. She still felt a bit dull-witted and her tongue still was a bit parched.

"Not a bit of that, I am here to take care of you. God calls us to take care and love one another." Corinne said and placed a soothing hand on her arm. It was a kindness that made Galina so very thankful. She didn't want to tear up but she felt the salty tears leaking from her eyes without her bidding.

"You probably need to take care of some needs." Corinne patted her arm and gave her a smile. Galina nodded slightly. "Then we will worry about getting some more fluids and even some food in you. You are going to waste away if we cannot get you to eat something. Violet will be happy to know you are going to be eating, she has been thinking up all sorts of things to cook for you."

Galina let Corinne help her up to sitting and they took care of her most pressing needs. Corinne helped her wash her face and hands and promised her a bath later if she was up for it.

"I would like that." Galina said softly as she settled back into the soft pillows on the bed. Her backside was tired of being in the bed, but sitting up and moving had made the throbbing start back up. Too many parts of her were still so very painful.

Corinne left and within a minute Violet was in the room. Her blue eyes dancing and her smile so loving.

"I have been waiting to see you awake, rather impatiently." Violet admitted.

Galina felt the corners raise up in a slight grin, it didn't hurt too badly, she would have to remember that grin motion for the future while she healed.

"You are through the worst of it." Violet met Galina's eyes and somehow looked right into her heart. The words meaning so much more than a simple phrase. Galina nodded.

"I just want you to focus on getting better. You are safe, and your brothers are safe. No need for you to concern yourself about any of that." Violet offered, then told a brief version of what Lucas did to ensure that no beatings will go on from Slava Varushkin again without dire consequences.

Galina felt brave enough to speak a little. "Thank Lucas for me." Galina pointed to the glass and Violet helped her drink a bit more. Then she spoke again. "I'm glad he didn't lose his job, but I'm more glad that he will talk to the pastor." Her voice was hoarse but she needed to talk out a few things. "I don't know how I will go back home. I am so afraid." Galina felt Violet's hand squeeze her arm.

"Oh dear Galina, you aren't going back."

Galina's heart thumped painfully in her chest. He had said something that night. She had heard it but she couldn't remember.

"He has kicked me out then?" Galina asked softly, her eyes staring down at the bedspread. The bright reds and blues were blurry as her eyes filled with more tears. *He had not ever wanted me. I was a burden.* Galina said within herself.

Violet stood and stepped away for just a few moments and sat next to her. Her shoulder up close enough for Galina to feel the warmth of her. Galina sniffed and was handed a handkerchief.

Galina wiped carefully at her face, not wanting to cause pain but to clear away the signs of her distress.

Violet shuffled a few pages and placed a hand on Galina's back, comforting her.

"Isaiah 40, verse ten says. 'Fear thou not; for I am with thee: be not dismayed; for I am thy God: I will strengthen thee; yea, I will help thee; yea, I will uphold thee with the right hand of my righteousness.'"

How could God possibly wish to ease her fears? All she had done her whole life is dishonor her father. Galina thought. Certainly, her punishment on earth is only a portion of what she deserves. Galina thought and felt the tidal flow of emotions burst within her.

Violet rubbed her hand gently down Galina's back as she wept.

"No one deserves to be beaten that way Galina." Violet said soothing her. Galina knew her thoughts had been silent, but somehow Violet had known what she was thinking.

Galina nodded but her tears would not stop.

Violet flipped the pages of her bible and read again. "Ephesians 6, verse four, 'Fathers, provoke not your children to wrath: but bring them up in the nurture and admonition of the Lord.'"

Galina met Violet's eyes, wondering how her friend could have survived her own ordeal with an angry and demented father.

"What about 'Spare the rod, spoil the child?'" Galina asked through a throat that was tight and raw.

"He did not spank or scold you Galina, he beat and kicked you. He broke your bones. Your brother told me when he came into the house crying, that it was over shoes?" Violet's light blue eyes were full of her own tears.

"I called him a monster." Galina admitted and hung her head low.

"He is a monster." Violet laughed and swiped at her angry tears.

Galina felt that strange emotion and felt a tiny laugh escape as tears still filled her eyes.

"Have you attacked him or your brothers?" Violet asked.

Galina shook her head. "No."

"Refused to care for your brothers?"

Again, she replied. "No."

Violet went over so many scenarios, from burning down their house, refusing to obey, making up lies about her father... all of them Galina could honestly say no to. It slowly sank in that she had not truly been such a horrible daughter, but she held on to those words of her father's for a bit longer. That look in his eyes, the hatred and loathing was hard to forget.

Galina sat with Violet for a time, trying to calm herself as they spoke together about her healing and what would happen. Galina was thankful that Corinne and Lucas would take care of her. She felt a sense of awe, they were young and wealthy with their own problems and responsibilities. She wondered absently all afternoon what they would do with her long term. They were kind people, but she was not family. What was in it for them?

Violet went to get Galina some soup, and Corinne came in and sat with her a while too. She was friendly and chatty, but Galina was distracted and hurting, emotionally and physically. She ate as much as she could and felt tired again. Corinne gave her a small portion of the laudanum again, hoping she would sleep some more. Galina was thankful for the drowsy oblivion. She didn't want to think or feel anything for a while.

Angela Greaves

Angela was wearing a simple brown skirt and soft cotton flannel that she borrowed from Ted's work clothes. She tested the weather on the front porch and decided on a sweater to wear instead of a coat. Her red wavy hair was in a simple braid down her back. The sun was shining brightly and she was ready to take her mind off her brothers' visit. She was still a little irritable and temperamental and was scolding herself every few minutes about her own attitude. She had been pleased when Heidi Sparks had knocked on the back door after Ted had left the house after breakfast. The house was quiet and Angela was feeling more distracted by the silence of the house. She had cleaned up the breakfast mess quickly so now the walls of the house were closing in on her. The knock was perfectly timed to cease her silent insanity.

Edith Sparks had invited Angela to prepare the garden area for spring planting. Angela was overjoyed to get outside and be useful.

Angela dug out her grubbiest pair of boots from the box under her bed. They would be perfect for a day outdoors. She felt that inner fullness when she thought of getting outside and getting dirty, it was a remedy for certain.

She left a note for Ted and Dolly on the counter, in case she was still gone in the afternoon. She escaped through the back door and walked down the hill and past the barn. She waved a hello to her chickens, making a mental note to clean out the coop in the coming week. She said a little thankful prayer for the coming of spring. So many promises in a simple season change.

Edith was outside the cabin, sweeping off her front porch with Peter and Fiona underfoot, Edith looked up toward Angela and gave a bright smile.

"I know it's too early darling girl, but I just had to get my hands in the dirt." Edith spoke loudly to carry the distance.

"It shall be lovely, Mama Sparks." Angela smiled back, feeling so happy all of the sudden.

Angela took a few faster skipping steps toward the porch and let Mama Sparks give her a welcome embrace. It was warm and inviting.

"I'm ready to get dirty!" Angela announced when she pulled away from the long hug. She took some deep breaths of the fresh air and was rejuvenated.

"I have plenty of gloves for all, we shall wrangle the children to help. I think Heidi is willing. The younger ones may be distractible. We may have to promise them something extravagant to keep them on task." Edith said with a chuckle. She reached into a satchel she had sitting in the rocking chair that was sitting on the porch. She handed Angela a pair of tan leather gloves.

"Oh, these are too pretty to get dirty." Angela saw the fine workmanship and put her hand inside, they were soft and supple.

"Clive sold these to me a few days ago, I thought the same thing. But he says they should be sturdy enough to handle the work." Edith shrugged. Heidi was over near the garden gate and Edith grinned and tossed a pair to her, Heidi caught them and grinned herself. Heidi laughed and gave a silly curtsy. Angela smiled as she watched, it seemed everyone was feeling better out in the fresh air.

The group made their way into the cleared plot for the garden.

"We should expand it further over time." Angela mused as she looked around. The simple fence would be easy to move.

"Henry and I spoke of it often over the winter months, all the things I want to grow. Corinne has some seedlings growing in her greenhouse from seeds I gave her that I brought with me. I went over yesterday and Dolly showed me their progress."

Angela nodded, knowing that with a nearby greenhouse that the season for vegetables and fruits will be longer than usual.

Edith pointed out where they were going to get started and tools were handed out. Angela was glad for the brown skirt when she got down in the dirt and started pulling weeds, sticks and rocks from the garden bed. The ground was cold and wet but there was a joy in the simple activity. They all chatted, talked the morning away, made plans, and discussed nothing serious or important. It was like a balm to Angela's heart.

The noon hour came and Edith brought out simple sandwiches of roast chicken, they sat on the ledge of the front porch and looked over their progress.

Heidi and the children were done eating and Heidi volunteered to take them down to the bridge so they could play and run off some energy. Edith let them go with a smile. "No one gets wet or muddy, or everyone has to take a bath."

Angela laughed when Peter made a face of horror and despair. They ran off with Heidi playing the part of big sister, already bossy and taking charge.

"No bath?" Angela asked with a laugh.

"I've no doubt that Peter will end up wet somehow. I was planning a bath night anyway. We have that big washtub; it will get some use tonight. Those two lil' ones cannot resist getting filthy every chance they get." Edith chuckled and patted the crumbs off her dress front. "I'm going to need to find every scrap of dark material I can to keep their clothes from stains."

Angela smiled. She looked away from Edith and looked over the property, the trees were still gray and leafless but the snow was gone. The sun had done its job and cleared away the remnants of ice and snow except for the secret dark places in the woods where the sun had to work to sneak into.

"Have you heard that my brother found me yesterday?" Angela asked, not looking back but speaking loud enough for Edith to hear.

"Yes, my dear, I did." Edith said and she scooted a few inches closer to Angela on the ledge.

Angela looked into Edith's eyes for a long moment. The loving compassion was there and it was just what Angela needed. She spilled the whole story, every fear, and angry moment, as well as all the scolding she had given herself. Her heart was raw and exposed by the time Edith spoke to her.

"There is no right or wrong way to feel right now." Edith said, as she rubbed Angela's back while she shared her story, the feel of her hand sliding up and down was comforting to Angela. She needed it more than words or platitudes.

"Thank you..." Angela muttered, wiping away another few tears that were cold with the breeze blowing in her face.

"I know that you weren't ready... just as he wasn't ready when he saw you in San Francisco. Your bond was broken a long while ago, when harm was done to ya as children. I don't think it has to stay broken forever, though." Edith said wisely. It gave Angela a few things to think about, and she did in the silence.

Edith was a rare treasure. Angela thought, she could sum up this impossible situation so simply. Angela felt that moment of calm come over her. If she could allow for a grain of forgiveness for her brother's actions a few years ago, then she may be able to let their bond be healed in God's timing. She took a few deep breaths and let the breeze dry the rest of the tears from her cheeks. She closed her eyes and faced toward the bright sun, enjoying the quiet, and the peace.

◆◇◆◇◆

It was a half an hour or more before the children came back with Heidi dragging Peter by his shirt, shivering and angry. His boots and pants were wet up to his hips. Angela had to smother her laughter as Peter was placed in front of the porch.

He would look no different if he faced a firing squad. Angela mused.

The case was put forth to the jury, Mama Sparks, who was a mild judge that declared the sentence for going into the creek was set forth immediately. The accused was sent inside to change out of his pants, with extra chores, and the dreaded sentence of the evening bath that weighed heavily on his young shoulders. Peter walked into the cabin like a young man condemned to a life in prison. Edith and Angela

137

shared a good bit of laughter over the whole proceedings. Heidi surprised them all by sitting right next to Angela and she joined in.

Angela gave her a pat on the shoulder. Heidi didn't seem bothered by it. Angela felt that was a step in the right direction.

"I do declare..." Heidi smiled. "That boy moves faster than is natural." She laughed again. She wiped at the mud on her own skirt. "I guess this skirt is doomed. She looked at the faded blue fabric and wiped away at it, hopelessly convinced that it was ruined.

"Ach... no worries girl. Boys will be boys." Edith said. "That skirt was getting a bit short for you anyhow. Keep it for outdoor chores for now. I want all of you to have new clothes anyway. I was also thinking of asking our new friend Marie Harpole to make you a nice set of Sunday clothes too. She does fine and fancy work I've heard."

Heidi smiled and nodded. "I was wondering, Mama Sparks." She looked down at her hands. "I was thinking of asking Mrs. Grant iffen I could work an afternoon or two at the greenhouse, since it's bigger now and with her havin' a baby...." She paused and looked up. "I was hoping that you could spare me after school and before my chores. I do love it there." Her face was full of vulnerability and that hint of sadness she always had hidden in her eyes.

"Oh, sweet dear. I think that is a grand idea. We can broach the subject with her when her hands aren't so full with Galina's mending." Edith offered.

Angela enjoyed the fact that for Edith the Sparks children had adopted her nickname, Mama Sparks. Angela watched the small smile that played at Heidi's mouth. The girl nodded and stood up and slid on the work gloves.

"Thank you." Heidi said and her lip quivered pitifully.

Edith stood and pulled on her own gloves. Heidi took two quick steps and gave her new mother a hug. Angela knew that this embrace was a rare gift and she soaked it in. The story of orphans and adoptions is not always an easy tale, but love can find a way into all the loss and heartache.

Fiona grumbled when it was time to get back to pulling weeds, but she was shushed when Heidi gave her a glare.

"Don't be complaining too hard sister, think of all the yummy food that will grow here. I know that you do love strawberry pie more than just about anything else in the world. If we don't grow 'em how would you be able to eat it?" Heidi scooped her sister up and fussed with her light blond hair.

"I do love strawberry pie..." Fiona said softly. She gave an untrusting look to Angela, still being a bit shy sometimes.

"I do too, it has been a long while since I had one." Angela confessed. "But I am looking forward to having my root cellar full again. All I have now is some shriveled rutabagas." She was rewarded with a grimace from Fiona.

Peter came out with a fresh new outfit and they all got back to their dirty work. When the sun shone, there was that hint of warmth that soaked into their bones. It was a lovely time.

Chapter 12

Clive Quackenbush

Clive climbed out of the saddle, tied his horse to a fence post, and pulled out several parcels from his saddlebags. The sun was setting to the West but it was still early enough to make a house call. He knocked on the Grant's door and a few warbling birds were settling in for the evening. He smiled as Lucas Grant answered.

"Ah, Lucas. I heard a rumor that Galina is awake today." Clive said quietly. He extended a hand and Lucas shook his hand and pulled him through the doorway.

"Yes, word of mouth in these parts is fast as a racing horse." Lucas smiled.

"I was just visiting in town with my bride-to-be." Clive smiled and took off his leather coat. Lucas hung it up for him on a peg. Clive settled the armload of wrapped goods on the table.

"How is Olivia and her family?" Lucas asked.

"Oh, they are all well and good. In a tizzy over the discussion of our up-and-coming nuptials." Clive gave Violet a nod when she looked up from her dish washing at the counter.

"You are looking fine Mrs. Griffen." Clive winked at her.

"You old fool. Stop your flirting with me, Galina is awake, use your wiles on her. Cheer her up a bit." Violet gave him a wry smile and stuck her tongue out at her friend.

"That I will, milady." Clive gave her a slight bow.

"I brought gifts all around. For you dear girl a book and a wire whisk. All the way from London." Clive winked at her again.

"Oh, well, Clive you flirt all you like!" Violet dried her hands on a hand towel, came to him, and gave him a kiss on the cheek.

He pulled a whisk out of his jacket pocket, and handed it over. "I've ordered several of these. Got a big box of them."

He handed over the leather-bound book.

The Young Cook's Assistant and Housekeeper's Guide

Violet grinned and held the book close to her. "You are a gem." She kissed him on the cheek again.

"Two kisses from you. My dear Olive will be quite jealous. There are hundreds of recipes in there dear, I certainly hope to sample some..." Clive smiled warmly.

Violet looked over the whisk in wonder. "This will make cakes a lot easier I'm supposing. No more using twig bundles." Violet couldn't hide her grin.

"My daughter-in-law Millie read some advertisement about them last year and begged me to find a supplier. Took a while but I finally got a source. The kind British gentleman sent me a pamphlet about other fine kitchen miracles. I'm certain Millie will get around to showing every soul in the valley." Clive saw Lucas chuckle. "It's supposed to add air to eggs and many other wonders. Just be sure to keep it as dry as you can. Who knows how quickly the thing will rust."

Violet nodded soberly. She settled the wire contraption on the counter, and the book on the table. She went back to doing the last of the dishes.

"Thank you Clive, sincerely." Violet said as she walked away. She made eye contact with him and he saw how he had made her happy. That was his goal.

"Alright, Lucas, take me to Galina. I shall do my utmost to cheer the girl. I heard that you had a talkin' to with her father."

Lucas nodded and shared the interlude that he had with Slava Varushkin. Clive nodded and was pleased that it went as well as it did.

"I'm glad he kept his head. We don't need any more violent outbursts." Clive said. He patted Lucas's shoulder like a son.

Lucas took him back to Galina's room and Corinne let him in.

"She just ate, she probably will get tired again soon. She has had a few visitors already today." Corinne said softly through the doorway.

"You've done a good thing here, Corinne. God bless you for it." Clive said and planted a kiss on the top of her head. Corinne looked up wearily at him.

With that, a cry was heard from the next room.

"Oh, Trudie is fighting off sleep again. I do believe she is in a foul mood tonight." Corinne said.

"You go sit in the parlor, Cori. I'll sooth her." Lucas offered.

Clive was pleased to see that Lucas was being a helpmate. Watching the young people learn to be supportive in marriage was satisfying, it reminded him too that soon he was to be a husband again, with all the challenge and sacrifices that came with all the benefits.

Galina was laying on the small bed, the quilt pulled up to her chin. Her face awash with colors of blue, red and purple, swollen still beyond what Clive had imagined, to prove that the rumors were indeed true that she had been beaten with fists and worse. His heart broke and he fought the weary sigh that built up heavily in his chest.

"Oh, Clive." Galina opened her eyes a little wider. Probably causing pain... He mused.

"I'm here girl. No moving. I'll come to sit next to you." Clive said softly instantly feeling that protective anger that made him want to pummel her father the way he had hurt this girl. She was so young. His heart ached.

He pulled up a chair next to her with a prayer on his heart.

Lord, give me the words to cheer this girl... Your sweet daughter Galina.

They sat and visited. He gave her the books he had brought for her, for when she was able to sit up and read. She seemed happy to receive them and promised to treasure them. She was quiet and he could tell she was tired but he was pleased that he made her laugh softly at least three times. He had done his duty. Thanks to the good Lord.

Sean decided to visit with his sister before he moved into Clive's cabin so on moving day he sent a note with a young fella he hired outside the livery.

I am hoping to visit today around lunchtime if that would suit you. Please send back word.
Sean Fahey

He paid the lad enough to rent a horse and gave him instructions to wait for a reply then bring it to the Orchard House.

Sean went back to his rooms and packed up his belongings. He was eager to get everything ready and he didn't have to wait more than an hour to get the reply that he was hoping for.

Ted and I would be pleased for a visit. I hope you like fried fish. Ted got some fresh catch in town.

Angela

Sean smiled as he grabbed up his bag. He settled it near the door, he pondered taking his bags with him as well as getting a few food goods at the store. He took a moment and made a list on a small pad of paper.

Bread, matches, butter, bacon, canned goods, and coffee.

It would do for a day or so. He had a lot to accomplish but he had lived on simpler fair.

He stopped in at the fancy goods store, bought an ax and a hatchet, and chatted for a few minutes with Millie Quackenbush. She was kind and offered a few glass jars of her stew to keep in his cupboards. He thanked her profusely.

He paid for the rental of a cart at the livery and went shopping for more goods at the grocer. He put all of his goods in the back of the cart and tipped the man at the livery to make sure it was untouched until he was finished with his visit.

He rode out on his horse, which he named Shipley, in honor of his friend. He and Shipley were bonding well and he was pleased with his new saddle. His new life was shaping into something pleasant and Sean was thankful for the easy transition to this life in Oregon.

He rode out a few minutes before the noon hour and enjoyed every minute of the ride. The valley was so lovely.

Angela's house was bright in the noonday sun, the front porch cheerful and white against the pale blue of the sides. She had built a fine house. With so many cabins in this valley, a fine house like this certainly did stand out. He looked forward to someday sitting on that front porch with his sister and new brother-in-law, having a pleasant conversation without any hard feeling or apologies needed. It was a good goal to work towards.

He saw the work hand Warren working next to the barn and Sean got his attention. Warren took his mount and Sean gave him a nice tip. Warren tried to pass on the money but Sean insisted. He had heard a rumor in town that Warren was dreaming of owning his own farm someday. Sean wanted to help him in little ways to achieve that goal. He was a mild-mannered young lad, and according to everyone he talked to, he was a godsend. Sean had asked around about Earl too, mostly brotherly concern and curiosity about who was working for Angela and how it all was going. Everyone had glowing praise. His sister had good mentors and workers, even before she was married.

He was proud of her, her courage and her smarts. It was something he wanted to tell her, but he wasn't sure there was a way to say it yet, without sounding condescending.

He wiped his dirty boots on the grass and walked up the steps. He saw through the window that Ted was standing next to Angela in the kitchen, a kiss was shared and Sean felt himself blush at catching their intimate moment. He was glad for her, that she looked so happy, and that Ted seemed happy too. It took him back to a long forgotten memory of his own parents who were never shy about showing their simple affection. His Papa saying something about love, the words were gone, Sean couldn't remember them, but the meaning was still hidden in Sean's heart. That children should always know the love that their parents have for each other. It was a good memory buried inside of him, where so many bad ones tried to darken. Sean hoped that more memories like this one would work their way to the surface. It made him smile.

Sean knocked and Ted answered a moment later.

"Brother Sean!" Ted said and beamed a welcome smile. Sean couldn't help but smile back.

"Blessings on the house!" Sean said and took off his hat.

Ted took his hat and hung it on the hat rack beside the door. Sean kicked off his cowboy boots on the rug.

"Fish is almost ready, brother." Angela said lightly. She looked to the side, away from the sizzling pan, and her grin was genuine. Hearing her say 'brother' meant more than anything else.

"It smells good." Sean offered.

Ted presented Sean a place at the table. Ted spoke of local news and pleasantries while Angela scooped the last of the fried fish onto the platter.

"I'm serving today, Ted, don't get up." Angela said with a little harmless attitude. Ted was halfway out of his seat when he plopped back down.

She settled the platter on the table, and then went back for the butter and the red potatoes.

"This is the last of the good potatoes from town. Everything else is too far-gone and will get planted. All the potatoes in our cellar are trying to grow new plants." Angela laughed as she placed the serving forks in the bowl.

Ted said a quick prayer over the meal. Sean was so very pleased at the beginning of the visit that he hoped that his announcement wouldn't change the mood. He felt the moment needed to be soon though, before he lost his nerve.

"I wanted to say something, before we go too far into the conversation." Sean settled his utensils down and gave a look to his sister. Trying to see if she would be upset before the words even came out of his mouth.

Angela's face was open, and she didn't seem unwilling to hear anything from him.

He continued. "I got a piece of land outside of town and I wanted your blessing."

Angela took a pause and considered it a moment. There was no frown, but he could tell that she was thinking hard.

"I don't think you need my blessing, Sean." She said finally.

"Well, I feel I do. If my quest to come here and rebuild this relationship is causing you pain, I sincerely don't want to cause anymore." Sean said, wishing he could say more.

"If I said that you were causing me pain... would you leave?" She faced him, looking into his eyes, searching hard for something.

Sean was taken back by the question, a part of his heart breaking and another wondering if this was a test of some kind.

"I would certainly not leave unless you asked me too, even then I may be close enough to..." He thought of saying to keep an eye on her... but that was not right, he was not her father. "I don't know, Angela. I'm sorry. I don't know what to say." Sean sighed.

Angela smiled at him, just a lift of the corners of her mouth. It was enough to calm his nerves a little. She was asking questions; it was better than not speaking at all.

"Am I causing you pain?" Sean found the courage to ask.

"No... well yes... but not really about you. Some of it is memory, and some of it is just confusion." Angela said. "Eat, Sean, the fish will get cold." Angela pointed at his plate with her fork, and her eyes flashed at him playfully.

Sean obediently took another bite of his fish while his sister thought through things. Sean gave a look to Ted, but Ted seemed to be enjoying himself silently.

I guess he is letting us work through this mess. Sean mused.

"I am glad you are here." Angela said and nodded, as if she was agreeing with herself.

"Me too." Sean muttered then took another bite. The fish was good.

"I think my initial reservations were normal, and also a little irrational. I tend to get emotional before I come down to assess what I feel and deal with it." Angela confessed.

"I am a bit that way too." Sean offered and they both laughed, finding a humor in the sharing.

Ted couldn't help but chuckle. "You both laugh the same." He was chewing on his food and trying not to choke.

Angela gave Ted a glare and then smiled at Sean. "Where are you going to stay?"

"Clive sold me his old property a few days ago." Sean said.

Angela nodded and took a pause. "You and Clive are probably thick as thieves already. I should feel betrayed, but somehow I just don't. You both have a lot in common." Angela swirled a piece of potato around in the melted butter on her plate before she took a bite.

"That was another thing I was worried about. I am not trying to usurp any relationships you have. I promise you." Sean said.

"Well, Clive has a pretty big heart. He knows your story probably better than you would guess. We had a lot of time to talk about my past in the years since I've known him. He helped me find you in San Francisco."

Sean wasn't surprised. It was the kind of man that Clive was.

"When you moving in?" Ted asked when his plate was clean.

"Today actually, I have half of my worldly possessions in a wagon I rented at the livery, I wanted to talk with you both first." Sean said. He was suddenly filled with the full measure of excitement. Having his sister open up to him and give her blessing was the push that allowed his heart to stop feeling so much guilt.

Thank you Lord God. Sean prayed within himself. He was just so grateful he had followed God's lead.

"You have enough food and firewood to last ya?" Ted asked, he was forever practical.

"Food I am covered with a few staples. I think Clive left some firewood in the box behind the cabin. I'll be busy this week getting things settled. But I got enough to get through a few nights if they get cold." Sean smiled. This was an adventure and he felt that lightness in his chest.

"I wouldn't mind stopping by later... if ya don't mind it." Ted asked. His gaze was direct.

"I would welcome you both, anytime, day or night." Sean said sincerely.

Angela asked him a few more questions, just what his plans for the land were. He found her to be knowledgeable and bright on the subject.

"I'm thinking that the garden will need some serious attention. Clive was not very patient about that. I think Dolly did most of his weeding out there. Oh, Dolly, she will probably need to ask you about something." Angela held her chin.

Sean tried not to let his face show too much interest, but Dolly was indeed an interesting woman.

"Oh, did she want to buy the land instead?" Sean hoped he hadn't stepped on anyone's toes unknowingly.

"Oh, nothing like that. She just has a few plants that she harvests on his property in the summer months I think." Angela waved it off as nothing serious. "Once things settle down next door I want you to meet some friends of mine." Angela had a secret smile that she shared with Ted.

Ted laughed and stood to the clear the table. He picked up Sean's empty plate. "You want anymore?" He asked.

Sean shook his head; he had eaten his fill.

"I think you may have a spitfire to deal with when you meet Corinne Grant." Ted gave a warning. "I would bring a gift, and be prepared to defend yourself."

Angela laughed.

Sean's eyebrows raised playfully.

"Corinne is the closest I have to a sister. She will be ready to cook you over an open flame. I talked to her yesterday. But she will want to look you in the eyes and get to know you. She is a fierce and protective person." Angela said, then added. "She was the friend that hired a lawyer years ago, and got our inheritance back to us."

Sean remembered, it was coming back to him, how much that friendship had probably meant to Angela. She was a servant and this friend, Corinne, was the reason that Angela was able to get her own freedom. It was something to be thankful for and it led to him being able to reconnect with the family back in Ireland. His own inheritance was due in large part to this young woman. He was humbled by the impact that Angela's friend had made. He would have to pray about a way to thank her properly. He promised to write in his journal himself tonight about this. He didn't want to take any of this for granted.

"I look forward to meeting her." Sean said quietly, feeling overwhelmed over his feelings.

Ted settled the dishes on the counter with a rattle.

"I'm certain she won't murder ya." Ted laughed.

"No, I'm certain there is some censure that I most certainly deserve. I guess I just realized how much I owe her." Sean looked in Angela's eyes, hoping she could see how much this visit had meant to him. "Thank you for today. It is far better than I deserve." He sighed.

"Oh, if we all got what we deserve..." Angela sighed too. "But for the grace of God we all would be in the gutter." She took the few steps between them and held her arms out in an invitation. He gladly took it and gave his sister a hug that healed more of the breach. He was forgiven.

Chapter 13

Sean Fahey

The cart creaked along the rough wagon path that Clive had pointed out, and Sean watched the scenery go by slowly, trying to soak in the landmarks as he went. The cabin came into view before too long and he felt a pride to own his own place. The bluffs to the north were the edge of his property, promising a few wild animals as his neighbors. Clive had given him plenty of warning to be careful with his hunting, with full knowledge that wildcats and bears could be close enough to give him trouble.

The afternoon weather was kind but to the west, there were a few clouds that could prove to bring rain overnight.

Sean pulled the cart up to the front porch, as close as he could. He unhooked Shipley from the cart and tied him to the fence. Sean grabbed a bucket of oats from the cart and settled it next to the horse to allow him to nibble on it while Sean unloaded.

Sean had to free the front door from the bear proofing and the door opened with a squeak.

His home welcomed him and he made quick work to get his few things put in their proper place. He then went outside and checked the box, it had a decent stack of firewood that would last a few nights. He started his mental list to get busy over the next few days to fill the box and then add more to the shed.

"I'm gonna need a barn." He spoke aloud to himself. He was pleased that the garden spot was not so bad. It needed some care but he could see that a good fence would keep the critters out of it. He saw quite a few deer tracks, and the telltale signs of rabbit infestation. "Yep... a good fence."

Sean opened the simple door to the shed and peaked inside to see a few tools, buckets, and some rope, most of the space was empty. Beside the shed was a lumpy tarp that revealed a small plow for breaking sod underneath. Sean nodded to himself and was about to take a closer look when he heard a voice yell out his name.

He expected Ted to come but it seemed a bit soon, since he had only left their house just a little while ago.

The man he had met his first day in town, Mack, was waving near the wagon path. Sean smiled and gave a holler. He had been meaning to go see Mack's property, but hadn't gotten around to asking him. He heard through the grapevine at the boarding house that he got his cabin finished with a few hired hands a few days before.

Sean jogged over to his friend with a smile.

"Hey there neighbor." Mack said with a grin. He had trimmed his bushy beard closer around his face.

"Hey there Mack, you caught me just getting a full glimpse of the land I took over." Sean said cheerfully.

"Well, I heard word that you took over this property. I just bought the land south of here. We are neighbors." Mack gave Sean a slap on the back.

"That is grand news. I didn't know you would be so close. That is fortuitous indeed." Sean was pleased to already know a close neighbor.

"I heard that this land belonged to Clive." Mack said. He gave a look around. "He must have liked the solitude out here. It is a pretty property." Mack nodded with a face that seemed to be pleased with what he saw.

"Indeed, he said he has been living here on and off for 20 years." Sean added.

"Well, my other neighbor, Mr. Hynes who runs the paper said that Clive trapped all the land around here. Kept the beavers from cutting off the water supply." Mack said. "Mr. Hynes, Gomer, is that way, to the east. I can take you by in a few days once you are settled." Mack offered.

"Clive told me about the trapping, I do enjoy that myself and will gladly take over. I have some traps back in storage in town, I'll bring them out and get to work soon. I've got a lot to do." Sean sighed and took another look around. The air was fresh and the sight of tall trees and fertile land was inspiring.

"Glad to hear it. I got the new cabin built. It still needs some work on the inside but my son and I are getting settled in. Got the fireplace done yesterday." Mack said. "Oh, the small barn on my property has plenty of room for your horse. Until you get your own barn I would be glad to help ya out."

Sean reached out to shake his neighbor's hand. "I would be most obliged. Don't want a wildcat taking out my horse."

Mack laughed loudly. "Did Clive scare ya with stories of bears and wild things?"

Sean allowed the teasing. He had heard in town that wildcats sightings were rare, but not unheard of.

"I'll keep my eyes and ears open, but I would hate for any animal of mine to get hurt for lack of shelter." Sean said, smiling..

Mack nodded. "I'm only teasing ya lad, I'm glad to help you out. A few neighbors have helped me out tremendously this week. The cabin that was on the land I got was not livable, barely more than a shack. I will have my son fix it up enough to use it as a shed. No wonder it was left behind..." Mack chuckled. "There were holes in the walls big enough for a squirrel to go in and out at their leisure." Mack nodded, his eyes wide. "Glad the barn was in better shape."

Sean gave Mack a simple tour, talking about his plans. It was nice to get some advice and the offer to help with building a fence and some other structures as time would allow.

"You taking the cart back today?" Mack asked as he was turning to leave.

"I've rented it out for the week, I plan on buying a wagon but until I have a place to keep it out of the weather I will keep renting from the livery." Sean said, shrugging.

Mack nodded. "If you like I can take yer horse with me now, and get him brushed and fed for the night."

"That would be grand!" Sean thanked him again.

"I'm just down the path, the first cabin on the left side, just past that tall group of pines." He walked over to Shipley and spoke a few kind words to the animal.

Shipley seemed happy to go with him.

Sean waved and watched his neighbor go and smiled to himself at the providence of having a helpful neighbor. The Lord was truly good to him.

Sean saw the water barrel against the side of the cabin and walked over to it, he lifted the wooden lid and checked it. Seeing that it was empty and it didn't have a moldy or rotten smell and rejoiced. He got a few buckets out of the shed and took a walk to the creek that was nearby that Clive showed him. The water was higher than it had been just a few days ago with the snowmelt. He was glad the creek was close enough to be convenient, but far enough away to keep it from overflowing into his cabin. Clive was a smart man and built his home on a nice little rise.

Sean filled the buckets and made a few trips to fill the water barrel. Sean tasted the water and enjoyed the fresh flavor that only a mountain spring could create. Sean was so pleased.

He grabbed an armload of firewood and took it inside to get a fire going in the fireplace. The temperature was beginning to fall outside and he wanted a cozy fire for the evening. He would use the fireplace to warm up his dinner. He was going to put some of his things away and tidy up before he had any more visitors. He got his clothes and belongings put to order pretty quickly, and he settled into the soft leather chair that Clive had left behind. It was comfortable and Sean was thankful for the luxury of it.

It wasn't long before he heard the sounds of a wagon coming up the lane. Sean made his way to the door to greet the visitors.

Ted, Angela and Dolly were there, all smiles and waves as Ted pulled the wagon to a stop.

Sean stepped onto the porch, so proud and pleased to see them. Wondering at how, in such a short time he could be so very blessed.

Sean got a firm handshake from Ted and Dolly, and another heartfelt hug from his sister.

"I suppose you have been here before." Sean said with a laugh.

Angela and Dolly nodded.

"Once or twice..." Ted offered.

"Well, you are welcome in either way." Sean smiled.

"We brought supplies." Angela said and without pause her and Dolly went to the back of the wagon. They each came back with several baskets.

Ted was fussing with his own haul.

"You have outdone yourselves." Sean was surprised.

"We nearly arrived with at least fifteen people and a full on housewarming party, but we opted to bring food and gifts to get you started." Angela grinned. "A dear friend and excellent cook made some fresh bread, another neighbor Marie sent some canned goods, Edith Sparks had some leftover apple tarts, and I scraped together a dinner of ham and beans for you."

"You needn't have done all that for me." Sean took a basket from each of the women to take the weight off their hands.

"Oh hush." Angela said and her smile was sincere.

"I just brought some extra firewood for ya."

Sean was humbled again by the generosity. He helped everyone into the cabin with the gifts they brought. Angela was thrilled to look

152

around and offer a few suggestions to get the place freshened up. She offered to make him some new curtains and he happily agreed to let her.

Ted talked over helping him build a fence around the garden with some long vines, with a technique he used by soaking long vines then wrapping posts that were placed sturdily in the ground. Ted said he would bring a diagram by after he drew it up.

Dolly was the one surprise to Sean. She remained remarkably quiet throughout the visit. The first day he met her she had spoken with him easily enough. Now she stood back from the conversation, her dark eyes taking everything in but not saying much.

Sean tried to draw her out finally with a question aimed at her. "Miss Bouchard," he nearly forgot her surname but he breathed a sigh of relief that it came to him as he opened his mouth. "I heard you have used this property to find certain plants in the past." Sean looked over her face, she was good at keeping her expressions neutral.

"Yes, Mr. Fahey." Dolly said, she gave him a once over that made him nervous. "I have in the past, along the creek bed and deep in the woods I have found many medicinal plants."

"I would be happy if you kept on that tradition." Sean said and smiled warmly, trying to seem sincere, but now even more curious about this woman with the warm eyes but stoic attitude.

Dolly nodded. "I had done a little hunting on this property too. I could show you some good locations for traps that Clive taught me over the last few years."

Sean was glad that her shoulders relaxed and she even attempted a smile. "I would certainly be pleased to learn about the land. What kind of hunting have you done?" He was hoping to draw her out even more.

"She is quite skilled with a sling, but over the winter she has impressed us all with her archery skills." Ted said proudly. "Mostly just with targets over the winter months, but she uses a bow she made herself." Ted's praise made her blush.

Dolly looked flustered for a moment and seemed to loosen her rigid stance.

"That is an amazing skill set to have. I haven't used a bow to hunt in many years. I would love to see you in action." Sean said and smiled. He saw that Angela was watching him closely and realized that his interest in the mysterious girl named Dolly was not going unnoticed.

"I could show you." Dolly said, she lowered her head for a moment. "You may call me Dolly, I thank you for letting me continue to come out here. Clive's land is special. The deep woods are so near the mountain." Dolly's eyes lit up for a moment and Sean was drawn in.

"I feel the same way." Sean said low and sincerely. There was something special here. He looked forward suddenly to having a quiet morning, perhaps being shown the secret quiet corners of this land by a woman that was so knowledgeable.

"We should get going, let you get settled in. Will you be coming to church on the morrow?" Ted asked as he reached out to shake his hand.

"I would not miss it." Sean promised. After shaking Ted's hand Angela gave Sean another embrace, making up for lost time between them. Dolly took his hand and shook it firmly and for just a moment Sean held it longer. Her dark eyes looked up to him, inquisitive and deep. She was searching him, for his character. He hoped that she found what she was looking for.

<hr />

The next day the church service was pleasant for all. Sean enjoyed the preaching, a good message on understanding how Faith in God can apply to so many aspects of life. Sean took notes in his journal and was hoping to talk over his thoughts in the next weeks with his new friends and neighbors. He had spent a good portion of his life ignoring God, he wanted a fresh start to be one that revolved around his rediscovered faith. He sat by Ted and Angela during the service near the back. He could see a few people he knew.

Clive sat next to his bride-to-be. A pretty woman who seemed a few years younger than Clive, but the way she smiled up to Clive while singing the songs he could tell they were very much in love.

Sean met Corinne and Lucas Grant, her Father and Stepmother Marie. They had all been pleasant to him. Dolly introduced Russell Grant and Chelsea as well as their children, Brody and Sarah.

Edith and Henry Sparks seemed like very kind people, but he did promise to come by for a proper visit over the next week. The oldest

154

girl Heidi had barely said a hello before she was scolding her younger brother for climbing on the chairs. Edith and Henry took over with the discipline. Sean chuckled at the boy's energy, remembering suddenly some moments like that with his own parents. He had been so very young.

Mack and his son, Daniel were in attendance, and Sean introduced them around. He was a new face too, and Sean was pleased to see how kind everyone was.

Corinne and Lucas invited Sean, and Ted and Angela to lunch at their house. Angela seemed excited to see a girl that was staying at their house. He did notice her close friend Corinne giving him plenty of perusal during the visiting time after church. Sean was pleased that the community of believers here were very vocal and it seemed everyone stayed.

"You will get to meet Violet, at our home, maybe Galina if she is ready to get out of bed." Corinne told Sean. "Violet is our housekeeper, but most of all she is family." Corinne smiled warmly. Her daughter, Trudie, reached a hand out towards Sean, her dark eyes wide and curious.

Sean reached a hand out to let the chubby fingers grab his thumb. He smiled at the child and was rewarded with a smile. A baby tooth was peeking through the gums in front. It was charming to see. It had been a while since he had been around children. His thoughts went back to the work orphanage from long ago, the squalor, the fights, and the forced labor. No children in these parts would suffer that fate. His heart was warmed by that realization.

Sean brought his thoughts back from the darkness of the past and made a few faces to the child, puffing out his cheeks comically. The chuckle that burst from the baby was charming. There was no sound like it to lift your spirits.

Corinne smiled up at Sean, giving him a warm look that made him see her acceptance, in part, already. He knew that she would have concerns. Why had he shown up out of the blue? Along with others, he wasn't afraid to answer. He was done running away. He had faced his fears and Angela, and he was on the right track to rebuilding something that could have easily been lost to him forever.

The group slowly dispersed and Sean mounted up on Shipley to follow Ted and Angela over to the Grant house.

The morning had been quiet and peaceful for Violet. She had sat with Galina and read through a few chapters of the bible. Violet stuck with Psalms, and she skipped around and found encouraging verses that could lift Galina from her sadness. Galina had spent the day before in tears off and on, trying to accept that her father had not only hurt her terribly, but also would not allow her home.

She is on the verge of despair. Violet thought and was discouraged.

Galina ate some chicken broth that Violet had made and added some rice to see if she could handle more than just broth. Violet was worried to see the girl going so many days without eating anything substantial.

Galina finally declared herself full and she wished to rest some more. Violet cleared the bowl and teacup from Galina's room and left to let the girl sleep. She still looked a fright, with bruises and cuts and scrapes over her face. Violet was growing used to it, but every morning she wished that the swelling would be gone. Time was not so kind on healing. It would be a longer road than anyone would want.

Violet busied herself in the kitchen, singing a song from church while she mixed up a batch of oatcakes to bake. She enjoyed the breeze through the open window, the weather proving to be milder than she expected. The lace curtains fluttered happily, as she added cinnamon to the bowl and stirred it in with the sugar. The scent was delightful and Violet let her voice ring out at she worked. She knew from experience that Galina wouldn't hear a thing from her room on the far side of the house.

Violet was scooping the oatcake batter onto a flat baking pan when she heard a chuckle just outside the window.

Violet's eyes went wide as she saw Reynaldo standing outside. He was in his Sunday clothes, a dark blue shirt and black pants, even dark shoes that looked polished. Violet stood at the window, her hands covered with sticky oatcake batter.

She wanted to ask him why he was there but she said nothing. She snapped her mouth closed when she realized it was hanging open.

"I'm sorry to frighten you. I was on my way home from Sunday service. I heard your singing as I passed on the path. It was lovely singing, Violet." He said softly. He dropped his chin and gave her a look through the window that made her neck and cheeks warm.

Violet gathered her wits. "Well... I suppose that is what I get for singing with the windows open." She said and was proud to have gathered herself. "I stayed home to care for Galina." She said, realizing that it would look bad that she had stayed home from services. Not that anyone was forced to go, she mused. But she usually only missed if she was unwell.

"I stopped after service and Corinne said how kind you were to stay home today." Reynaldo said.

Violet thought it was silly that they were talking through the open window. Should she invite him in?

She looked to her hands and was flustered for a moment, wondering what to do. Would it be appropriate to invite him in?

"I'll be moving on. Just was pleased to hear your angelic voice on this Lord's Day. It was a pleasure, Violet." Reynaldo put his dark hat on and gave her a nod, with that ever present smirk of his.

Violet shook her head as she went back to her work. Certainly, every woman in these parts were bound to blush at his smiles. She only allowed herself to feel a little foolish. He was more than a little bit handsome and he probably smiled like that at every one.

Violet tried to make herself forget about the interruption as she put the sheet of oatcakes in the oven. She tried again a few minutes later when she checked on the roast beef that was warming up on the stove. She never did start singing again, but instead she hummed softly as she used her new wire whisk to stir up the beef gravy in the pan. She smiled playfully as she thought of his handsome dark eyes. There was no harm in it, certainly.

Sean was stuffed to the gills as he pushed away from the dinner table at the Grant's house. The talented cook, Violet, was a sweet-tempered woman and they were lucky to have her there. He hadn't eaten that well in quite some time.

The conversation around the table had been exceedingly pleasant. Corinne and Lucas asked him a lot of questions, mostly about his recent travels. Corinne had asked him a little about why he had decided to find Angela again, but it had gone so well that he felt even better about his decision.

Angela had warmed up a lot since that first visit, and she was peppering him with questions about their Great Aunt in Ireland, and how the place looked. Ted kept looking happily at his wife, probably happy to see her smiling more now. That first visit had probably brought some unneeded stress to his wife. So it was a pleasure to see that she had recovered.

After the supper Angela and Ted offered to show Sean around the property with Lucas, Corinne wanted to check on Galina, who had slept through the meal. Violet was happy to stay in and care for Trudie.

Sean was impressed with Lucas, he had a sharp mind and a grand sense of humor. He seemed to be an easy sort of man that could fare well in almost any company. He knew an extraordinary amount about farming and caring for the land. After learning about his education at Yale University Sean was even more impressed. He now knew whom to ask about any gardening concerns. He could see that Corinne's father's ranch was a well-run property also.

After a tour of the land and some more lighthearted chatter, he left, feeling better about his place in this new life.

Over time, he would cultivate the relationships he had started today. He spent the evening tidying up the place, clearing out the weeds and debris that were gathering around the edges and corners of the cabin and small shed. He walked the flattened land, in his mind seeing the perfect spot for a small barn. Nothing grand in scale, but enough room to get his plans moving forward.

He might just talk with his new acquaintance Lucas Grant, and see what he would suggest.

He slept well that night; well fed, and well beloved by God.

Chapter 14

Galina Varushkin

The next week passed slowly as Galina healed. After a few days of maximum efforts she was able to get up and around a little more. Though any jostling or leaning put pressure on her broken ribs, and

158

she was forced to go back to bed pretty quickly. She found her mental state was ever on the precipice of emotional outbursts and she was frustrated.

Galina wondered how long she would be tolerated at the Grant household, for she didn't really see any reason for them to keep her on. She was of no use to them now. She worked harder than she ever had in her life to not complain but on a few occasions, she spoke before she could think and snapped at Violet, and even Corinne. She apologized again and again, but each time her heart was grieved. Corinne soothed her with kind words.

"Sweetheart, no one is ever at their best when they have been hurt." Corinne had stated practically. "You never heard me yell at my father when I disagreed with him."

Galina doubted that Corinne had ever been argumentative. Corinne would just laugh at that. She told Galina about a fight she had with Lucas just a few years ago. When she had kicked him out of the bedroom and huffed all night like a child.

"No one is perfect all the time, dearie." Corinne said. She shook her head. "You will heal, but the road is a bumpy one... I was helping the doctor a few months ago, a lumberjack cursed us up and down for setting a broken leg. He was not very pleasant. You grumbling about some pain is reasonable. I just hope you know it doesn't scare me."

Corinne had to help Galina through so many unpleasant and embarrassing tasks and Galina grew grumpier still. She was growing impatient and bored from the lack of anything to do. She hurt too much to do anything but her mind was aching for something to think on besides the state of her life.

<hr>

Violet Griffen

Violet watched her mother board the ferry with mixed emotions. Tim and Harold were stoic and quiet all afternoon as Violet visited. She was helping her mother with all the last minute details and packing. She wasn't taking much with her, mostly just her personal clothing and a few belongings. But Violet tried to encourage her to take some of the money Violet had set aside for her.

"No, Violet, I could never accept any help from you..." Her mother had said. It was unsaid but implied that she felt she didn't deserve anything from her children.

Violet took some time and fussed with her mother's hair. Braiding her hair up the way her mother had taught her as a young girl. It was a bittersweet moment, to be so close to her mother after so many years. It was an intimate thing to do and Violet felt hot tears on her cheeks as she put in the finishing pins.

Her mother waved from the deck of the ship. Violet waved back. The motion of her brother's hand waving beside her was blurry as she watched through the welling moisture in her eyes.

This chapter of her life was truly over now. Nothing will ever be the same within this family. The only thing she could do was heal that gap between herself and her brothers. She felt that pain in her middle, knowing it would be easier now with their mother gone. It was a horrible thought, but it lingered in her mind.

Violet sighed and watched as the steamship filled up and pulled out. She really had no words for how she felt. It was a tangle of regret, pain and relief. She needed something pleasant to think but the pain was too fresh. Her heart was heavy as they all walked back to town together. She gave her brother's each a long hug before she left to head toward her own home, and they to theirs.

The walk was refreshing as the sunshine warmed her face and shoulders. She started praying some as she walked along the road, trying to spot the signs of spring. She thanked God for everything she saw, and moved on to thanking God for the time she had with her mother, even if it had been difficult, there had been some moments of closure and healing. She prayed for the strength to move forward with her own life, and her brothers that they would draw strength from Him as well.

By the time, she crossed the Spring Creek Bridge she was feeling lighter. Her tears were dry and she was ready to tackle any job she could. She was always so relieved to keep her hands busy after a trying situation. She would see if Galina needed anything, perhaps a craving for something decadent. Violet would show Galina her new cookbook and have her friend challenge her to make something new from it.

Violet smiled as she got to the cabin door.

Clive peeked his head out the door just as she meant to walk in.

"Greetings fair lady!" Clive said and gave a tip to his broad hat. His smile was broad and mischievous.

"Oh, Clive, you are in proper good spirits." Violet grinned.

"Well, yes ma'am I am." Clive placed a hand on her shoulder. "I'm getting married again in less than a week. I may just be the luckiest feller alive." He gave Violet a wink. It lifted her mood even higher.

"I'm looking forward to making the groom's cake for your party." Violet said.

"Oh, I am certain it will be delicious!" Clive smacked his lips together.

Violet gave him a kiss on the cheek.

"What was that for?" Clive gave her an amused look.

"Oh, I just needed a little cheerin'." Violet said, not afraid to be real in front of Clive.

"Well, I am always happy to do that for my friends." Clive touched a hand to her cheek. The warmth of his palm was soothing. Something a father would do. It touched her heart deep down.

She felt on the verge of tears again but held them back. The comfort of the gesture was meaningful and she accepted it.

"You are such a good man Clive. Olivia is one lucky lady." Violet said, her voice thick.

"Well, I think you should jump on this train too. Wedded bliss would look good on ya." Clive gave her a wink.

Violet huffed out a small laugh. "You silly man."

Clive gave her a knowing look, like he knew something that she didn't. That usually meant that he was up to no good.

Violet talked over wedding plans for a few moments and let him go on with his day.

Violet went inside, did what she had planned, and went through the cookbook with Galina. The girl was moving around better and the swelling on her face was improving dramatically every day.

Violet spent some time gently brushing Galina's hair as the girl went through the pages. The doctor had declared that her scalp was healing very nicely. She said it was tender still but she was very relieved that her hair wasn't falling out.

Galina's hair lay soft and wavy around her shoulders when Galina decided on a recipe for Violet to try.

"Baked Apple Dumplings!" Galina said with a full smile. Her eyes lit up a little and Violet was glad to see some of her old spark coming back.

They read over the ingredients and Violet was happy to have some apples in the pantry that she had recently bought from the grocers in town.

Violet was about to tell her so when a knock came to the bedroom door. Corinne peeked in.

"I have two boys here to see you Galya!" Corinne's face was excited and she opened the door wider. Galina's brothers, Milo and Pavel, ran past Corinne and bolted to the side of the bed where they stood, silly smiles on their faces.

Galina didn't hesitate a moment but gave them both a savage embrace. Sweet tears were shared all around. Galina gave them kisses on their cheeks and patted their heads with affection.

Violet took the book and took a step back to watch the family reunion. Misty tears in her own eyes.

"Papa wanted to go into town, so he allowed us to come and visit." Milo said as he laughed over the kisses that his sister was giving him. He wiped at his cheek when he stepped away.

Galina patted the bed next to her and Pavel climbed up next to her. He was careful not to bump her too much.

Corinne must have given them instructions to be careful with their sister. Violet mused.

Milo sat at the end of the bed and Violet made her excuses to leave and let them have a proper visit.

Violet heard laughter and talking as she stood outside the closed door a minute later. She was so very thankful that the boys had a chance to be with their sister. She knew from personal experience what it was like to be separated from family. She sighed and let it out slowly, it had been an emotional day but she had some baking to do. She hoped that the boys would stay for supper. Giving the siblings a long chance to visit and talk. It was priceless in Violet's thoughts.

Galina Varushkin

Galina finished reading a fairy tale from a book she had received from Clive, and settled into her bed. She knew she should go to sleep but felt restless. She didn't want to stir but she knew she was long off from sleeping. She sat in the quiet, knowing the household around her was sleeping peacefully. She prayed for a little while, but her mind wandered. The stories always stirred her up lately, wishing for something that she didn't even know she wanted.

She sat and listened to the sound of the wind outside, wondering. She thought of the stories and tales she had learned from her mother over the years. She daydreamed about those stories all the time but she mused if she could write down her mother's stories. Perhaps make a story for her mother with a happier ending...

Would anyone want to read anything she would write? Galina wondered. Her education had been a strange one. But she knew she would find pleasure in saving these stories, even just for herself. The thought bubbled inside her happily. She lay back contentedly, daydreamed, and planned.

She had a pencil, and her journal nearby. If she sat up with a pillow at her back, she could write down her thoughts.

There was so much swimming inside her head and she was tired of being still.

She stretched her arms above her head until the strain was felt along her ribs. The healing there was slower than everywhere else on her body.

Her scalp had itched for several days but now her head was doing better. She was more than a little pleased that her hair hadn't fallen out. She had written a thank you note to the doctor the day before, but she wanted to rewrite it. She had a lot to say to him and Corinne both for all they had done for her.

There was a misconception in her mind that had been formed from her childhood. Mostly because of her father. She had been born in a lumber camp, north of where they lived now. Her mother, Magdalena, had told her many stories about how the poor were treated where she lived growing up. Her father and mother had decided soon after marrying to leave Russia and cross the ocean with a lumber company, advertising good wages on the shores here. Trappers, lumber companies and others came here to get a fresh start.

Slava had always complained that the lumber company mistreated all the loyal men that came and worked torturous hours, in deadly conditions for such little pay, after being promised so much. Slava was the one who planted within Galina the idea that people were selfish and would never be kind to anyone that was different or poor. Galina remembered from when she was young that most of the neighbors they had in those lumber camps were so poor and unhealthy. No one helped each other, but instead everyone was so suspicious of one another. The children would go to school but often Slava would discourage friendships with other children, saying that the only people you could trust were those in your own home. Galina had learned a hard lesson with her father, he was so untrustworthy with everyone else, but she could not trust him.

In her heart there was a warmth growing, seeing the generosity at first from the small church when they helped her family get a roof over their heads when Slava left them destitute to search for gold. Then now again, after her own father had punished her so severely. They were embracing her like a daughter, lavishing love and concern on her in a way she had never felt before. It was hard to reason her old thoughts with the people she was surrounded with now.

Corinne and Lucas promised to care for her with no motives. She truly wondered if she could have that much love in her own heart to do that for someone else.

Galina saw the sun break through the clouds and light came through the window. She stood from her bed carefully, walking slowly to the window. Her bare feet on the smooth boards, It felt good to be up. There was a mirror along the sidewall and she saw her reflection in it. The swelling and bruises had gone down. Her face was not as distorted any longer, she was beginning to feel like herself again. She was glad that the pain was less too and she no longer had to take the laudanum to sleep any more. There was a strange part of her that yearned for the blurry escape of the medicine, but the freedom from the dull floating feeling was more pleasant. She had been told by Corinne that laudanum was known by some as addictive and she wanted Galina to know that it would be harder to do without it the longer she took it. Galina did not want to become addicted in any way. That strange yearning for it was enough of a reminder to make her want to cease its use. She would deal with the pain from now on, it was certainly less now. Corinne had been making her a white willow bark tea at night for a few days, that had been enough to keep her pain under control for the most part. Though some nights her ribs ached badly. She would fight through it.

Galina put on a loose dressing gown over her nightgown. She had to move slowly and she winced a few times loudly but she was tired of being in this room. She had to see more today than this small room.

She turned the knob of the door and walked slowly down the hallway. Violet sat at the table, Trudie in her lap with a grin. Violet looked up to her, her eyes bright to see Galina up on her own.

"You are looking better today." Violet offered.

The sun shone through the front windows and her blond hair had a halo of sunlight around her.

Galina took slow steps and Violet pushed a chair out for her with her free hand. Galina sat slowly, as to not disturb her ribs.

"I saw in the looking glass that the swelling is going down." Galina smiled and placed her hands to her cheeks. She touched her lips and was pleased that there was little to no pain.

Violet nodded with a warm smile.

Galina gave a big grin to Trudie, happy within herself that she could smile again, for not only the pain was gone, but also that she actually felt a bit of actual joy at holding the baby girl. There was a pang in her heart, missing her baby brother Radimir, and of course, her mother, but she could find a peace in knowing that life did move forward.

"I needed to see something besides my small room. I see that the morning rain is gone and the sun is out." Galina said and looked toward the sun coming through the window.

"I can set up a chair for you just outside, you can sit for a few minutes in the sunshine." Violet said with a lifting of her eyebrows.

Galina wondered if it would be indecent in her dressing gown. Galina looked herself over.

"Oh, do not worry about that. The men are all out in the far pasture plowing up a new field. You are covered and decent, and recovering. I will give you a blanket to throw over yourself if anyone comes nearby." Violet offered. She stood and balanced Trudie on one hip. "Corinne should be back in a little while; she was helping Dolly in the lab this morning. Trudie gets a little too grabby to be in there. But she would definitely agree that the breeze and sunshine is good for healing." Violet said wisely. Galina knew that she spoke the truth so she nodded. Violet was such a warm soul, it was hard to disagree with anything she said.

After a minute, Galina was settled into a chair in the front of the cabin. Her eyes closed and was happily soaking in the sunrays. There were no words that could fully describe how wonderful that felt on her skin. The warmth and joy that was in the sun, it soaked in to skin and went to the bones it seemed. There was truly nothing like it on earth. She took some time to thank God there, absorbing the light within her.

Oh, Lord, I thank you for the good friends you have led me to. I thank you for showing me that I am still your daughter, and that you love me. I thank you for forgiving me of my faults, but also showing me that I am not a wretched creature but worthy of being loved.

Galina felt a rise of emotions a little from confessing these things to God but also felt strengthened by even thinking them. She knew somehow, that God was watching over her.

She stayed quiet, taking several moments to open her eyes and see the world around her. In early spring there are signs everywhere of the world coming back to life. She spotted a squirrel darting over by the fence line, in a flurry another squirrel came by and a grand chase was on. Galina watched the play between the two, even laughing once as the leaping and chasing became very animated.

She paused to close her eyes again, soak in more sun, and listen to the quiet. After a few minutes like this she heard footsteps nearby. Her eyes opened in alarm and she looked up, her eyes blinded a bit from the bright sun. It was Warren, the farm hand from Angela's house next door, walking down the lane. She reached down slowly, her ribs protested and she winced loudly enough that he heard.

"Don't worry, you are fine." Warren ran forward, a basket in his hands. He was at her side within a minute. He plopped the basket next to her and he scooped up the blanket and discreetly turned to let her cover herself.

A moment later, he gave her a smile. "It is good to be outside on such a fine day." Warren said. He was tall and broad shouldered, but his cheeks were red from blushing. He was a few years older than her, but was well known for being quiet and shy.

Galina felt like crawling into a hole. Embarrassed for being outside in a dressing gown, of all things. But there was no undoing it now. She felt like making an excuse. "Violet said I should get some sun." Galina said lamely.

"Oh my Ma would say the same. Nothing heals quite like the sunshine. It just does somethin' to lift the spirits too." He smiled again.

It was the first time she had ever spoken to him, but she was glad in that moment, even with the embarrassment that he had come by.

Galina smiled and held the blanket right below her chin.

"I just came to drop off some extra eggs for Angela, but she will be so pleased to know you were up and around a bit. We all have been praying for ya, nonstop." Warren gave her a wink that made her blush. He was a nice young man, her mother would have said.

Warren gave her a little wave and then knocked on the cabin door.

He was there and gone within a few minutes but Galina felt profoundly better for quite a while after the visit. The sunshine and the exchange with the handsome young farm hand had done wonders to cheer her up. She knew that she was still bruised and a bit of a fright to look at, but somehow she forgot all about that for just a little while.

Galina went inside a while later. With a secret smile on her face.

She was excited to know that Sophia was coming to stay with Angela for a week or more. She could talk and visit with her friend almost every day. She had a few things to share with her that weren't all bad news.

She would cling to the happy thoughts for a little while.

❖◦❖——❖◦❖

Sophia Greaves

Sophia looked like a vision in pale pink in her day dress as she came into the cabin. She had a bundle in her arms but quickly placed it on the table. She didn't even greet anyone else in her excitement but went to Galina's side in the loveseat by the fireplace.

Galina was getting around better, but she still got tired so easily. A short walk from her bedroom, and simple movements would tucker her out.

Galina felt Sophia's hand in hers, and received the kiss on her cheek with a warm heart.

Sophia had come a few times to make short visits in the first weeks after the incident but now Sophia was staying nearby, at Angela's with a promise to come every day.

The night before Galina had spent an hour with her journal and began to write out a story from her childhood, a simple tale her mother had told her, but over the years as she had told her brothers that story it had grown and changed as Galina's imagination had taken flight. It was just a child's story. A squirrel who learned a lesson about storing up food for the winter. It was now a more in-depth story, and Galina had made up a few extra woodland friends to add to the story.

She was excited to show her friend, the only one she trusted yet to share this story with. Somehow, to tell a story was different than writing it down. She wanted some private time to let Sophia look through it, to make sure that Galina had her words right, and there was nothing misspelled or embarrassing about them. Her heart thudded nervously just thinking about showing her friend, but she knew she would have to show someone, it was nearly bursting within her chest to share it.

Sophia sat next to her. "I'm not hurting you?" Sophia asked. Her dark blue eyes like sapphires. Her eyebrows lowered in concern.

Galina shook her head and smiled.

"You are looking so much better." Sophia took her hand and stared into her eyes, probing her the way only a friend could.

"I am doing a bit better, though I get tired easily." Galina shared.

"Well, you had better kick me out whenever you need to rest." Sophia gave her a bossy look and shook her head at her, her blond curls swishing around her pretty face becomingly.

Galina sat and chatted with Sophia for a few minutes before she invited her back to her room.

Violet brought in tea and ginger snap cookies for them to enjoy and Galina finally got up her nerve to show Sophia her story.

"I want you to see something I wrote." Galina said nervously, staring into her teacup without looking up to her friend. Her stomach was tied up in knots.

She felt a hand on her arm and finally looked up.

"You wrote a story?" Sophia looked at her with awe and genuine happiness.

"It is just a short children's story, a little like one my mother told me when I was young. I just expanded on it." Galina said quickly. She didn't want Sophia to think it was very important. Just something that she had always wanted to do.

Sophia clapped her hands. "That is so exciting!"

Galina felt heat in her face. Suddenly her stomach flipped as she thought about the consequences of telling someone. She would look like a fool, certainly. She was just a poorly educated girl after all.

Galina sighed.

"Are you going to let me see it or read it to me?" Sophia asked. She took a hand and tipped up Galina's chin to look her in the eye.

Galina saw the smile on her friend's face. She would hopefully be kind if the story was terrible.

"You can read it." Galina said softly. She couldn't imagine reading it aloud.

Galina slipped the journal out from under her pillow and flipped the pages over to where the story was. It had taken a few drafts to get it done but the final version was there, in her simple handwriting. Her letters were better now but still not as fancy as others she had seen. She sighed again. This was much harder than she expected.

She handed the journal over to Sophia with as much bravery as she could muster.

"My hand writing is not…" Galina started and was shushed by the look Sophia gave her. She needn't have said a word. Sophia knew how hard she had worked to learned to read and write, while hiding it from her father. She needn't make excuses. Galina smiled a little at the friendship she had. Sophia accepted her and that was enough.

Sophia smiled and put her head down to read the story. Her grin never left her face as she read. She took a sip of tea and then giggled.

"I like Sawyer, he is a funny little fellow." She smiled and laughed again.

She kept reading and slowly Galina felt better. Even if the story wasn't complete, she felt a bit more relieved. She had made Sophia laugh. It was a good feeling.

Sophia giggled twice more before she finished and handed the journal back to Galina.

"It is so charming! I wouldn't change a thing." Sophia settled her teacup down and grabbed Galina's hand. "You are a writer."

She would never understand why her eyes welled up with tears. She had said something kind, but she felt suddenly so very overwhelmed.

"You really do like it?" She finally asked over the lump forming in her throat.

"Sweet Galya, I loved it. You should go to the schoolhouse when you are feeling better and read it to the schoolchildren. They will love it!" She suggested.

Galina's eyes widened at the thought. It made her nerves flutter again in the pit of her stomach but she wondered at hearing the children laugh at her little story. That would be grand.

Galina nodded at her idea. The stubborn lump in her throat made speaking seem a bit daunting. If she squeaked out an answer just then she would feel like a dunce.

"Well, you should. Do you have any more ideas?" Sophia asked her with bright eyes.

Galina swallowed. "Yes, I have a few floating around in my head. You know me and my stories. I am used to telling them more than writing them down, though." She felt suddenly a rush of happiness. Sophia was taking her seriously. It was an odd sensation.

Galina told a few of her ideas to Sophia and they went through most of the plate of ginger snaps before Galina felt tired again.

Sophia helped Galina get settled in her bed and they chatted for a few more minutes.

"I am so glad you showed that to me Galina. I know it must have been hard. I have some of my lace creations that I have kept hidden myself. Too nervous to show my mother. She doesn't always like my ideas." Sophia shared. She patted Galina's hand.

"You have been through quite a lot lately. Having this to help you through your healing may just be a blessing."

Galina felt emotional again and that pesky lump was forming. She nodded.

"God is good to us." Galina said hoarsely, not even caring if she sounded foolish.

"Indeed He is." Sophia leaned down and kissed Galina's hand. Her broken fingers had healed but Sophia was gentle.

"Rest, sweet friend." Sophia smiled down at her. Making her feel so very lucky to have a good friend. "I'll come back tomorrow."

Galina snuggled under her coverlet and went to sleep as soon as Sophia was gone. Her worries had flitted away.

***

Galina Varushkin

The next few days were good for Galina as Sophia took her mind off her worries and the aches and pains that still lingered. They giggled over the story Galina told her about Warren, scaring her out of her wits in her nightgown. Galina was worried that perhaps Sophia would get jealous that she had talked to Warren first, but she wasn't. They both thought him sweet and handsome but nothing more than girlish interest. They had time to grow into those kinds of things.

170

Sophia had gone back to town one afternoon and Galina had a quiet day at home, she enjoyed sitting with Trudie when Corinne and Violet had their hands full with a job or a project. Galina could handle a little movement, and Trudie's smile had its own healing factor.

Sophia dropped by just before supper, Violet was covering the freshly baked rolls on the kitchen table and welcomed her in.

"I hope this is a good time?" Sophia looked nervously at Violet.

"Galina may be napping in the lump of blankets over there. But I was going to wake her. Corinne and Lucas are getting cleaned up for supper. I can easily set an extra plate." Violet smiled sweetly.

"Your cooking smells divine." Sophia praised.

"Steak and potatoes with gravy... I am pleased with Lucas and his dealings with the butcher today." Violet went back to her work, grabbing plates and utensils while Sophia walked toward the davenport. She finally saw the sleeping form of Galina. Her face peaceful, still showing the hints of green and blue around her cheeks. Her heart just could not handle it very well without anger sneaking back in.

Sophia spoke softly, pulled over a cushioned footstool, and sat next to her friend as she woke up from her nap.

Galina immediately smiled. She stretched a little and let out the tiniest wince.

"Your ribs again?" Sophia grimaced.

"It is so much better than it was." Galina tried to soothe her.

Sophia thought it should be the other way around.

Sophia dropped the subject. "Dinner is soon, but I thought I'd like to give you a gift while we wait."

Galina smiled at her with a suspicious glint in her eye, her brow lowered.

"You don't need to get me any gifts."

Sophia hushed her.

Galina pulled at the brown parchment paper. Inside was a black leather book. She opened the pages, expecting it to be a New Testament bible, which she already had, but instead the pages were blank.

Galina sighed happily. Knowing this was Sophia's way to encourage her to keep writing.

"Here is the other one." Sophia handed her and oddly shaped gift that was easy to recognize.

Galina opened it quickly and saw a fancy pen, with a bottle of black ink.

Sophia reached into her satchel and brought out a stack of light brown parchment.

"For you to practice with the pen." Sophia said with a grin. "I think you will pick it up in no time."

Galina was pleased and gave Sophia a warm hug.

"For my continued education. I am thankful that my right hand doesn't hurt at all, not sure I could have written anything lately if my other fingers had been damaged." Galina said with a shrug.

Sophia had to take a breath and calm her anger again. Her father wasn't a very wise man, but he would never have harmed them. He just didn't do much to provide for them.

<hr>

Reynaldo Legales

Reynaldo stepped up to the doorway of the Grant's home, feeling a bit anxious about seeing Violet. Hoping she wasn't angry because Lucas had invited him for supper. Lucas was excited about the plans for the barn raising and he wanted to discuss a few things with him after supper. He hoped to be able to talk to Violet a little too.

He pushed his nerves aside and rapped on the solid wood door. Lucas was there momentarily and welcomed him in with a smile and a hearty back slap.

"I hope you brought your appetite." Lucas said.

Reynaldo let his gaze float around the room. He saw Violet at the table, placing a gravy boat down in the center.

"I always do when I come here." He said. He looked back to Lucas. His friend had caught him staring. He just gave the smallest shrug, to announce to Lucas that it could not be helped.

He saw the young girl Galina walking in with a young woman.

"This is Ted Greaves sister. Sophia Greaves..." Lucas introduced.

Reynaldo gave the young lady a nod and the 'how do ya do's' were exchanged.

Galina had a little more pink in her cheeks since the last time he saw her. She was still moving slower than normal but she was moving. He was glad for it. He had said a few prayers for her that first night and every time the thought came to him. He had felt a few fists from his father, he knew the scars that stayed behind.

Corinne came out of the back hallway and gave Reynaldo a kiss on the cheek before they all were seated around the table. Lucas had added a leaf to make room for the full house.

"Well, there is plenty for everyone." Violet beamed at her eager guests, her cheeks flushed from working in the warm kitchen.

"Let me serve." Lucas jumped up. "You have certainly earned the seat of honor tonight for this feast. I don't want you to lift another finger tonight."

Reynaldo jumped up to help.

"You might reconsider that when you see the stack of dirty skillets, I had to borrow a few from Marie. I think I dirtied everything in the kitchen but the plates. Which we will finish up here in a few minutes." Violet laughed.

Lucas scoffed. "My momma done raised me right. I ain't afraid of no dirty dish." He was mimicking Clive and he did a good job of it. Everyone laughed as Lucas and Reynaldo grabbed up the plates and started serving up the steaks. Mashed potatoes and gravy were loaded on the plates; rolls were handed around.

Reynaldo finally sat before his plate not certain if he was ever anticipating a meal more than now. Of course, with the first bite he was not disappointed. Her food was just one-inch shy of heaven.

The table was surrounded by happy people as the conversation flowed. Galina was more talkative than he had ever seen her and he was so very pleased.

He was certain that he was caught by Violet several times, as those blue eyes would catch his gaze. She was good at pretending not to notice. He was rather hoping she would blush just a few times. He quite enjoyed it when she did.

Corinne shared a story about her day at the greenhouse, training up the neighbor girl Heidi to help in the afternoons.

"That girl is just blooming like my summer flowers. I think she has some great potential." She shared. They all talked about the Sparks family, and were looking forward to all the promise of vegetables from her garden soon.

After dinner, Reynaldo and Lucas discussed the upcoming barn raising over pans and dishes. While the women enjoyed themselves in the parlor. Corinne was more than pleased and praised them a lot. Reynaldo finally got to see Violet blush when he snuck in a wink when she tried to thank them in her sweet and gentle way.

Reynaldo was pleased with himself.

He left later that night, on his walk back to his cabin, as a nightingale called out.

Chapter 15

Mid-May

Clive watched his new bride take his weathered hand as he said his vows. The third time in his life, to promise to love and cherish a woman. Olivia's hand was warm, the skin so soft and pink. His own hand rough from his life of working, trapping, and hunting. How in the world had he gotten so lucky again?

Olivia was bright, and charming, with talent and wit. God certainly had blessed him. It was the only explanation. Her eyes were bright when she looked up to him.

"Until death, do us part." He said and he looked into Olivia's eyes. He saw so much love there. She was still forty-one years old. Only for another month. Clive was sixty-two now.

He listened to the words of Pastor Whittlan. "You may now kiss your bride."

He kissed Olivia, feeling all those same feelings he had had as a young man. He heard Lucas Grant play the violin as he pulled away from the kiss. His heart pounded in the knowledge, he was a husband again. The most joyous part that struck him instantly, he did not have a lonely home to go to anymore. Olive would be there now. He had a companion to live with for the rest of his days, Lord willing.

Olivia looked up to him, her beautiful hair, and the red gold that made her blue eyes sparkle.

"I am one lucky gal." She whispered to him, a smirk on her pretty lips.

He shook his head in awe. He then winked at Olivia and then turned to face the congregation. The faces of all of his friends and family, the dear ones that came to celebrate his third chance at happiness. The smiles of everyone was truly a sight to see.

Galina Varushkin

Galina sat in a pew at the church, she was wearing a new dress, sewn by Marie that fit so perfectly. It had been a week since she started wearing regular clothes but it was still a chore to get into them

175

with her ribcage still protesting over every twist and turn. She was the most pleased that her bruised face had healed so well this last week. The cuts and scrapes were totally healed, and there was only the slightest discoloration on one of her cheeks that was lingering. She felt almost pretty again. She wore her hair loosely, hairpins still being a bad idea, with only a ribbon pulling back some hair at the front. Her long dark hair had been expertly curled by Violet this morning with curling irons and Galina felt good to be out in public again. The morning wedding had been lovely.

Clive and Olivia looked handsome at the front of the church, Olivia was smiling radiantly up at Clive as they walked down the aisle as husband and wife. Galina was seated next to Corinne with Trudie in her lap. Galina caught a glimpse of her father on the opposite side of the church as she watched the bride and groom pass by. Her heart skipped a beat at seeing him, but she forced her eyes to move away from him. She saw that a woman was seated next to him, she had tan skin and dark eyes, and her dress was a dark flowered pattern and looked new. Which made Galina wonder if her own money had bought that fine frock. There was a baby in her arms with dark eyes and long eyelashes. A pretty little baby, she mused. She felt a pang of sadness as her eyes swam over her brother's faces. Her heart missing the mornings she spent with them every day.

She took a shaking breath and let her eyes move to the front of the room. Her eyes blurred and Olivia's gorgeous lacy dress swam as a white shape with no features. Galina felt heat rise to her cheeks and she had an urge to sob. She took a few deep breaths softly, trying so hard to not draw any attention.

Corinne placed a hand down on hers. Galina looked to see Corinne's concerned brown eyes through the tears. It was going to be okay. She was loved, somehow in this pain-filled life she had people who genuinely cared for her.

The urge to sob slowly faded, Lucas inconspicuously handed her a handkerchief. Then one to Corinne. Galina saw Corinne dab at her own, dry eyes, and then give Galina a look. Galina wanted to laugh. Corinne had done it perfectly. Anyone looking would just see two silly females, crying at a wedding. Love filled Galina's heart.

Galina kept her eyes facing front and tried hard to ignore anything else for the rest of the wedding, the signing of the marriage papers, and then the regular Sunday service.

She was a little tired by the end of the morning, feeling like she had run to town and back... But she had survived.

Clive and Olivia were holding a picnic at their new home in a few hours. Violet, Marie and Chelsea Grant would be heading over to get the food prepared as well as Millie Quackenbush. The folks invited would certainly be in for quite a party.

Galina wondered if she should try to fit in a nap before she went. She wasn't certain at the moment if she could last if she didn't.

Corinne and Lucas waited outside, to congratulate Clive and Olivia and to chat for a few minutes with their friends. Galina felt like melting into the back of the wagon to start that nap but she leaned on a small tree to save some embarrassment.

The crowd swarmed happily around the married couple. Galina watched the people, quietly, observing everyone's smiles. She was glad to be out in public again but her exhaustion was proving to her that she still had some resting and healing to do.

Clive and Olivia looked so very happy. It did distract Galina for a few minutes, just seeing them together.

She didn't notice until he spoke that Warren was standing close to her.

"You doing well Miss Varushkin?" Warren's voice was low. His eyes caring and concerned.

"Yes... Yes." Galina gave Warren a soft smile.

"It is good to see you at church again." He said. He was almost a man, but Galina enjoyed seeing his cheeks redden.

She could have sworn that he hadn't even known she existed before there accidental meeting before. He had noticed her at church before?

"It is good to be out." Galina said finally. She tried to stop leaning and stand upright. She swayed a little and grabbed the tree trunk.

Warren was there next to her in a moment, without touching her but able to help if he was needed.

"I'm a bit tired from all the festivities already." Galina sighed and confessed.

Warren said nothing but his eyes said volumes. He was sorry for her struggles.

He was kind. She could see it in his eyes.

"You can call me Galina. No more Miss Varushkin. We are neighbors now." She said simply.

"You staying with the Grant's permanently?" He asked.

Galina nodded.

"Good," Warren said and let the matter drop.

Galina watched the bride and groom make their way to their wagon. The crowd waving and laughing as they left.

Galina felt herself smile. She was so happy for Clive. He was one of the best people in the whole world, in her eyes. He deserved every happiness.

It was only a moment later that Slava crossed her path. Her brothers waved to her but her father's glare covered the twenty yards between them. She felt a cold shiver run through her.

His face wasn't its usual angry one, but the stare chilled her to the bone.

Warren tapped her on her shoulder. Pulling her away from watching her family walk away.

Warren's eyes were just as perceptive as Sophia or Violet. He could see what she was feeling. He didn't say a word. His medium brown eyes just told her that she didn't need to feel alone.

I think I just made a new friend. She thought.

"You going to try and come to the wedding party later?" Warren asked after a minute passed.

"After I take a nap." Galina said weakly. She tried to smile and found that she could somehow.

"Well, iffen you are up for it. I could ask you for a dance." He smiled again. It wasn't flashy like Reynaldo, or flirty like Clive, but it was kind and invited a friendship.

"I could probably manage a slow one, but only if you ask Sophia too. I don't want my friend missing out." Galina felt a little better when he nodded. He knew Sophia because she had stayed at the Greaves house before.

"I wouldn't want that either." Warren said and chuckled.

Galina was rescued a minute later by Lucas who gestured for them to go.

"Goodbye Galina." Warren said. And gave her a half wave.

Galina gave him a nod. "Thanks for the company."

"Anytime at all."

<hr />

Galina had a plate full of roasted lamb, piled high with all the fixins'. She was feeling better after her nap. Corinne and Violet had helped her back into her nice new outfit. The fabric was a celebration of spring with lace and embroidered flowers. Maria had designed it well to make it easy for Galina to get into.

Lucas was playing the violin, some other musicians were joining him and the dancing would get started.

Galina had dawdled as the line for the food had started. She had lots of conversations with all the neighbors who were glad to see her out in public again.

Sophia was next to her, in a blue dress than made her eyes sparkle. She was so happy for her Aunt Olivia, conversation bubbled out of her non-stop. It was good for Galina to have her nearby. She gave Galina that little bit of energy with her very presence.

Galina finally began to eat and Sophia prodded her. Galina had spent so long in recovery that she didn't want to miss seeing anything.

"Welcome, welcome everyone!" Clive announced. His black jacket had been removed but he looked dapper in his black vest and tie. "Today is a blessed day in the sight of the Lord. I feel so honored to have you all here at the home of myself and my beautiful bride, Olive." Clive gave a glance to his bride who stood next to him. She wrinkled her nose at him when he gave her a wink.

"We have planned a long while for this day. So happy to have the sunshine as the Lord smiles down on all of us. Please eat up, and join in to the dancing and festivities." He went on to thank all the women who helped with all the preparations. Making them stand up and blush through the applause from all their neighbors and friends.

Soon the band started playing and the dancing started first with Clive and Olivia taking a turn around the yard. Clive welcomed everyone to join in and the cleared meadow was filled with happy folks, enjoying the afternoon splendor.

Skirts twirled and smiles were shared. Galina watched as she finished her plate. Feeling so lucky to be a part of the day.

Warren made good on his promise and led Galina into a dance when a slow waltz started.

"I'm glad you were able to come." He said as he took her hand.

Galina nodded, feeling tongue-tied and shy.

It was a long moment of silence as he dipped and led her in a dance.

"Thanks for the encouragement today." She said.

He just smiled.

"It is what friends do." He offered.

He danced better than she expected, and caught herself smiling as they moved slow and easy throughout the song. Conversation was light and stayed on subjects that had little to no importance. It was perfect.

Galina thanked him for the dance. He just grinned and gave her a bow. She was thrilled to see him fulfill his promise and the next dance he chose Sophia.

The next number was a group dance, upbeat and the crowd clapped as the dancers took their places. Lucas was fast on the fiddle and the male dancers were in a wide circle, the women in the middle. The swinging and stepping was fun to watch as partners were twirled and swapped in a dance that was well known to all. Galina laughed and clapped along.

A few children outside the group of adult dancers had their own circle going and were practicing the steps their parents had taught them. It was charming and heart-warming and the crowd let out hoots of enjoyment.

Galina enjoyed watching the next few dances, as the dancers switched partners and everyone was having a grand time.

"Well, my oh my. Miss Galina. You are looking pretty as a spring bloom." Clive said leaning down next to her ear.

Galina laughed and grabbed his face closer and surprised him with a spontaneous kiss on his cheek.

He laughed aloud, grinning in his beguiling way.

"I was told the next dance was a slow one, so you better dance with me." He said and gave her a wink.

"But your bride..." Galina looked around.

"She is going to dance with Ted. You are all mine for now." He offered his hand.

Galina accepted gratefully and let Clive whirl her through a waltz.

"It is good to see you and Olive together." Galina said, she couldn't stop herself from smiling.

"It is good to see your cheeks aglow again." He said right back to her. His eyes were deep pools. Friendship and caring were deep within them.

She felt happy today. Letting her new friendships and cares push away all other thoughts.

"Your mama would love to see you in this dress." He said. Smiling down on her.

Galina nodded and felt that presence of her mother watching over her. She would have enjoyed this day.

"You are a good girl." Clive leaned in close and whispered in her ear.

She knew it was Clive speaking, but suddenly it felt like a glimpse of heaven opening up and her mother was telling her. Galina felt that lump in her throat again. It was a happy moment. Somehow knowing that all was going to be well.

She gave Clive a big hug after the dance. No words were needed, just so happy to have such a good man of God watching out for her.

Galina went over to the big table of deserts and settled on a piece of Millie's cherry pie and Violet's groom cake.

She ate every bite of both and felt silly when her tummy protested its overfilled state.

Sophia was busy dancing all the afternoon away, getting to dance with every brother, cousin, or nephew of every neighbor or church member. Galina wasn't surprised. Sophia was blooming into a very pretty young lady and would, in a few years be well sought after, in Galina's mind. She was a good dance partner and her smile was infectious.

Sophia finally sat back down when the band took a well-deserved break.

"You have danced with nearly every single man in town." Galina teased.

Sophia pursed her lips together then shrugged.

"Well, it is not like there are many women to dance with. You will see once you are up and at your full strength. Nearly every man I danced with said there wasn't many pretty young ladies to dance with." Sophia said.

Galina shook her head and chuckled.

"We will have our pick of them." Sophia's eyes went wide. "I read in the newspaper just this week about men sending money to newspapers out east to advertise for brides to come to the west." Sophia nodded when Galina scoffed. "I read that in many towns along the frontier that men outnumbered women as much as twenty to one."

"Well, then, I guess we will have our pick of the litter." Galina grinned and wiggled her eyebrows, the way that Clive would.

Sophia erupted into giggles.

"Though Sophia, I have no intentions of getting married anytime soon." Galina felt she had said it firmly, but the look on Sophia's face was not proof that she was convinced in any way.

"I did enjoy dancing with Reynaldo the best though." Sophia sighed. "But I believe it will only be a matter of time before he makes a move on someone else." Sophia widened her eyes and tilted her chin as a way to encourage Galina to look at something.

Galina saw instantly how Reynaldo's eyes were watching Violet as she talked with her brothers.

They both had the giggles again.

Then Sophia went through all the single girls in town.

"There is Dolly, Violet, you and I, and Georgia Dellingsford, who goes to the church in town. All the other ladies in the valley are older and widowed or married." Sophia said. "I suspect my mother will start getting gentleman callers. She is still attractive, even if she is a handful." Sophia said practically. "There are just so many men that are unmarried here."

"You obviously have been thinking quite a bit on this." Galina laughed again. She was enjoying the silly side of Sophia.

Warren joined them a few minutes later with a small plate with a piece of cake.

"You gals are having far too much fun over here." He said.

Sophia offered him the seat across from them.

"Well, we enjoy watching the festivities." Galina said, feeling much more comfortable talking with Warren after the dance they shared.

"I think another wedding is coming soon." He said and took a bite of cake. He seemed to enjoy keeping them in suspense. Galina thought.

"Well...?" Sophia finally said after they waited after three more bites of cake.

"Well, Gemma Caplan and Earl have been seen out on many an evening stroll." He said.

"Oh, I just love her." Sophia sighed.

"And Earl has got to be one of the best and most generous souls." Galina shared.

The idea of the kindhearted manager at Angela's place and Gemma both finding happiness was just the sweetest thought.

The chatted on and on, solidifying the new friendship forming between the three of them.

Somehow, she felt good about things as the evening drew to a close. When Olivia threw the bridal bouquet, it landed in Violet's arms without her even reaching for it. She took the teasing with deep red cheeks. The crowd had loved it.

Galina rode home as dusk fell feeling very pleased. She was so very tired, but the day had been lovely. Her ribbed ached from all the laughing, dancing and walking as she had visited with her friends.

It was a good day.

Chapter 16

Dolly walked along an old path, noticing a few tracks in the soft earth. Probably a few deer that were looking for shoots of fresh grass that was along the creek. The creek was swollen with snowmelt from the mountaintops. Dolly stopped for a few moments, enjoying the mild breeze that carried the scent of wet earth and moss. She had purchased some tanned leather and made a traditional skirt and what some would consider men's pants to go under them. She had been accused of forgetting her roots last year from a surly Shoshone man named Gray Feather, she hadn't thought of the statement much then, but she considered the thought when she came home. She did not want to lose the skills she had, and having some clothing that matched her upbringing wasn't a crime. It was very comfortable and Dolly knew the moment she put her new leather pieces on that she was somehow honoring the many mothers she had in the Shoshone village growing up.

Her own mother was Hopi, but rescued by the Shoshone tribe, then she married the fur trapper Joseph Bouchard. Her mother had lived in the village with the Shoshone and her father was gone for long stretches to trap in the mountains. He had taught Dolly's mother some English and about God, Dolly's mother had passed along everything she knew to Dolly. Dolly sometimes wondered about her strange life, how many lives she would know.

When Dolly came west with the white people of the wagon train four years ago she had wanted the chance to get to know the ways of different people. Her father was white, and her mother had never taught her to be afraid of them, though many Shoshone were fearful.

Dolly learned English quickly and soon embraced the lessons in the Bible and accepted that she wanted God as her savior. Now she had come full circle, again embracing pieces of her past to celebrate her upbringing without giving up on this new world she was now a part of.

She would probably never return to the Shoshone life fully, but dressing in skins while she searched the forest for plants and game was soothing to her. It felt like a moment to step back and embrace her childhood. So many memories flooded her mind.

The early morning hunts with the boys of the Shoshone village, they first teased her and a few of the other brave girls who would try to go along with the boys in the hunting games. Soon the girls were accepted as part of the group.

Dolly took her chastisements from the elder women for sneaking away from the camp before the sun came up. She was never a girl who was easily tamed. In a way, her lighter skin had given her a small amount of freedom, the women would shake their heads at Dolly, blaming the part of her that was willful on that other blood in her veins. Those kinds of comments never really hurt her, but they always made her aware of the 'other' side to herself. She enjoyed the competition as a girl to be the best hunter she could be, she didn't always win, but any day when she had more squirrels or rabbits to bring home than the other boys was such a sweet victory.

She had been practicing again with a handmade bow and quiver that she had made over the winter months and she was eager to see if she was as accurate as she was as a girl. It had been a long time but she felt that inner thrill of knowing that she would never have to give up that part of herself. She had been praying as she walked through the woods and felt that Peace of God fill her, there was nothing in the world like the quiet of nature to connect her with her maker.

Dolly stepped along the swollen creek and put her hands in the water to scoop out a sip. The water was ice cold and it made Dolly gasp. She smiled to herself at the cold and shock of it.

She had received another letter from Reggie. He had sent kind words, mostly about his plans. He was leaving on a trading vessel, bound for China and Russia. She was disappointed by his words, because there was truly no sign of any kind of affection for her any longer. She had accepted that in small part when he left. But her heart was bruised when his tone of the letter was offering nothing more. He had been truthful when he said goodbye. She had to finally let Reggie Gardner go. She was not certain she wanted to yet. She wouldn't say that she loved him. She could see what love looked like through the example made in others around her. She had never felt that for Reggie, but there had been that pleasant feeling of being cared for. To know his regard had been so very flattering. The day he said

185

goodbye, those moments on the porch had been the strongest feelings she had felt. A wish for something grand to happen and hope of a connection. But he had walked away with a promise to say goodbye before he left for good. Dolly was extremely disappointed that he hadn't fulfilled that promise.

Perhaps his letters are only to assuage his guilt on that fact. Dolly wondered. She took a deep breath and sighed it out slowly. She placed a hand on a tall tree, feeling the rough bark under her hand. She scratched her fingers along the side and listened to the sounds around her. It was solid and still. She let the peace of the moment fill her.

If God could create such a wonderful wilderness, could provide for the smallest of creatures that lived in these woods, then He could provide for her. God knew the desires of her heart. She had dreams and goals and somehow He would lead her toward that place of contentment.

Dolly settled the bruised feelings within herself. She would do her work and be thankful that she had not allowed her heart to go further, and be even more crushed when Reggie realized that his future lay somewhere else.

She felt lighter and began her search through the forest floor again, looking for young plants to transfer to the greenhouse. It was her calling, and the satisfaction of that would have to be enough, for now.

❖ ❖ ❖

Megan Capron

Megan enjoyed her new position and the hotel was grand indeed, as the name advertised. She had seen the advertisement that Pruitt had shown her before she left San Francisco and it lived up to its claims. People did come to enjoy the music. The orchestra was just as good as the one in San Francisco. 'Rosie Green' was regarded as charming and talented in the newspapers and the weekends were especially busy when the dining guests would come from miles around to get some needed culture.

Megan was happy to bank her money and tips every week as the weeks passed. She had a few new dresses made and had to forgo her tight corsets as her waist widened, but everyone that spoke to her believed her story. She told everyone that her beloved 'Edward'

186

would be returning from California territory in a few months. Everyone gave her attention and sympathy, Megan enjoyed every moment of it.

The boarding house was full of interesting people, some of them beneath her in status, but most all of them had funny or interesting stories to tell. She took her meals during the week with the other boarders to keep appearances up of being friendly and courteous. She had learned her lesson from her earlier time in Oregon to get along with people better, even if she had to bite her tongue. She even went to church services a few times, for appearance sake only. People in these parts were quick to gossip if you didn't go to at least a few Sunday services. She learned quickly to have a headache after performing on Saturday night, she made her excuses to sleep in most Sundays. When she did go to church she made no effort to listen, and was able to escape every attempt the pastor and his wife made of her singing for the parishioners. She was not interested.

Once the weather warmed, she took nice strolls in the garden and up to the river. She didn't enjoy the extra weight she was carrying and the walking sometimes made her feel a little better, even if it did make her ankles swell.

She nearly had a fit when she went to the fancy goods store in town and met Gabriel Quackenbush and his wife. She had to cough delicately when Gabriel introduced himself. She hadn't paid much attention when Clive Quackenbush had talked about his family, he had been somewhat amusing when she had seen him at the Grant's house, but she put him in the category of all the other do-gooders that would probably judge her tremendously. Megan had shopped through the fancy-goods store, shaking her head at the coincidence of meeting up with Clive's kin. They wouldn't know her, to be certain, but it did give her a pause to be more aware, she was a little too close to Oregon City than she was comfortable with. She made her purchase but did not make any attempts to talk long with the owner and his pretty wife. Somehow, she thought it unwise.

She walked back to her rooms at the boarding house, feeling nervous. She settled herself and focused instead on her goals. She would work throughout the summer and get enough money to go back East, she would not be deterred.

187

The sky had been dark and thundering all morning but the clouds finally cleared. Galina sat by the fireplace as the small fire that took the chill out of the cool morning was dying and the temperature outside was warming up. Violet's stove in the kitchen was hot enough to keep the place a little warmer than necessary, Galina reasoned. Galina had more strength as the weeks had passed and was eager to do more, just to keep her mind from thinking in its incessant way. She was ready to be busy, but Violet and Corinne, as well as the constantly visiting Doctor, all agreed that she was not cleared for any lifting or bending. Galina would admit that bending or moving fast was still uncomfortable, but she was irritable and tired of sitting still.

Even writing her stories had lost its flair when the call to be outside and have the freedom to roam again was calling to her. She was restless.

She felt the urge to be herself again. Even if her home had been tumultuous and full of strife, it was the only home she had. She missed her brothers daily, more than she could ever express. Galina spent some time watching Violet work, but she was running out of conversation, she wanted to lash out about her forced inactivity, but she knew within herself that no one but her father was at fault. They were caring for her, but she was very tired of it.

Violet was peeling potatoes, and cubing them to fry up for lunch, Galina brushed her hair as she watched Violet's expert hands go about her work. Galina fussed with her hair and tried a few popular styles, before settling on something simple. She had put on a day dress, a blue one that Angela had given her, she hoped if she acted nicely and made a few promises that after lunch they would allow her to walk the property again, as they had done a few days ago. She had walked slowly, and soaked up the breeze and sunshine, and no harm had come to her. She wanted to do it again, but she would keep her real plans to herself. She had a destination in mind.

Violet fried up some thick bacon in the large cast iron frying pan, the snapping and sizzling was loud and Violet jumped as a droplet of frying grease hit her arm She cried out.

"Are you hurt Vie?" Galina asked, lulled from her trance of silent contemplation.

Violet smiled, "No, it just stung a little. I should know better than to stand so close to frying bacon."

Lucas came through the door just then; he was pretty much covered from head to toe with dirt.

"Could you send lunch outside today? Me and the crew are pulling stumps and we are a fine mess, I will wait to wash up until later." Lucas asked. Galina was laughing at his disheveled appearance. Lucas gave her a wink and laughed a little with her.

"No worries, Lucas, I can bring you out some food. How many you working with today?" Violet asked. She took a fork and flipped over the bacon. Then she yelped when another drop of grease got her. Violet glared at the pan, to tell it what she thought of its shenanigans. Galina let out a breathy laugh at Violet's not-so-menacing look.

Lucas thanked Violet and Galina sighed as she watched her friend peel another few pounds of potatoes without being able to help.

Galina finally made her escape, lunch had been simple but delicious. Violet fed the men working and Corinne fed Trudie then ate herself. Galina had eased into the request to be able to walk around the property more. Corinne had agreed with a pleasant smile. Galina had felt that small twinge of guilt over her plans, but she had to push it away. She was feeling smothered and agitated, she needed to make peace within herself and a long walk would hopefully help her.

Galina's new boot heels thunked across the footbridge. The sun was warm, but when any cloud passed over the breeze was surprisingly brisk. Galina was carrying her shawl and put it on when the breeze got cold, then would shrug it off when the warm sun came out.

Galina laughed to herself. Her mother would have said something about 'the joys of spring.'

Galina watched the fields, dark against the sweet soft green of the budding trees in the distance. The lavender would grow and be dazzling in a few months, but now the rich moist earth was almost as black as night. She could see movement beyond a grove of trees, it was probably where Lucas and his crew were working, most likely her father was there, using brute strength alongside horses or oxen to pull out the many stumps they had left behind when they cleared timber. Galina wondered at the scope of work it took to be a farmer. It must be so daunting realizing how much work it would take to make the land break to your will.

Galina shook off the visual of her father working, it was stealing away the hopeful mood as she walked slowly along.

It took her longer than it ever had in her life but she saw her family cabin ahead. A large gray cloud had been covering the sun for a long while, but the bright sun broke through as she drew closer to the front door. It felt like a good omen to Galina, who needed some courage to go inside. A rise of panic threaded through her gut as she stood in front of the door. A flashing memory of just lying there, bleeding, her brother's cries echoing through the twilight hour. Her father's words cutting her more as she bled on the ground. Galina took a shaky breath.

"Oh, please, Lord God, help me to say goodbye." Galina said aloud, her throat was tight and an uncomfortable lump was lodged there.

She walked inside, feeling her heartbeat against the inside of her chest. Her eyes took in the dark space. The boys were at school, her father still working, the inside was more cluttered than normal but it wasn't a scary sight. Galina scolded herself for her fear and willed herself to calm down.

She stared at the wooden counter, a few dirty pans lingered there. She felt that urge to go get some water and start it to boil. She walked over and placed her hand an inch above the cook stove. It was cold as a stone. She really couldn't clean up, she knew it would be a terrible idea if she left any clue that she had been here, but that desire to clean up one last time was inside her. The scent of breakfast, probably eggs and bacon, remained in the air. She would have opened a few windows to let some of the breeze blow through to freshen the house as her mother had done. Her heart ached as her mind visualized her mother doing her chores around the house. She would sing old songs in Polish, she knew a few in Russian too. Her family had lived along the eastern border, her father had been Russian, her mother Polish. Galina wondered absently if her mother would have been an educated woman if her life would have been different. She spoke two languages fluently, and she had a million family stories to share, her memory had always been a good one. Galina sighed and stepped away from the untidy kitchen, it was no use to stay in this room.

She went to the ladder for the loft and climbed up, hearing the familiar squeak of the wood with each step up. The boys had not touched her side of the loft yet. Their side was a mess of blankets and items not put away.

"I had always made them tidy up at least." Galina said above a whisper and tisked at her absent brothers.

There was a wall between the space but the side of the loft that faced the rest of the house was open, Galina usually used the curtain that was on a long rod above to drape around the opening, so she could have privacy every night. It looked like her brothers hadn't felt the need for it.

"That may change with a new woman in the house." Galina huffed. A part of her still angry at her father for remarrying. Another part of her was praying for the change to be good for her brothers. Hoping that the woman would be kind and loving to Milo and Pavel.

Galina crept up to where she had slept, it had been a simple rope bed, with a mattress of hay inside a large linen bag that buttoned closed at the foot. Galina lifted up the corner of the bed by the wall. She grunted at the weight a little.

The second board in was loose and Galina retrieved the items that she had hidden there. A book of poetry, a journal, and a New Testament book. She felt around the dark space, her hands found the small slate but after a minute, she could not find the small piece of chalk she had left. She laid on the ground and reached further back into the tight space, her shoulder pressed uncomfortably against the wooden bed frame, poking her while she searched with her fingertips for the leather pouch. She finally felt it and grabbed at it trying to pinch it between two fingers and drag it toward her. After several attempts, she was able to pull it out.

Galina put the board back where it belonged and made everything look the way it was supposed to. She sat on the floor next to her bedding and looked at her small treasures.

She read through some thoughts she had written with the stub of a lead pencil. It had been hard to come by, and her last pencil had been thrown in the fire when her father had seen her using it a few weeks before her mother's death.

Galina opened the leather pouch and saw that all of her coins were there, safe and untouched. She sighed with relief. Hoping that soon she could go to town and be able to buy a few small things for herself. She had some money that Lucas was paying her from her father's earnings to pay her back.

Galina finally climbed down the loft and crossed over to her parent's room, feeling that twinge of apprehension again. She had a plan and she knew that it was wrong but she needed to make sure that her mother's things were still in the trunk behind the bed.

Her father's clothes were strewn about the floor, the smell that filled the room indicated that they were all dirty.

His new bride won't have much of a honeymoon here. Galina thought with a little malice. *She'll be cleaning for a solid two weeks to get this place clean.*

The floor was dirty and she heard the crunching of dirt beneath her shoes. Galina shook her head and sighed. The floor had probably not been swept once since the incident.

Galina knelt at the edge of the bed and opened the wooden box with a squeak. It was nothing fancy but her mother had kept her things there since Galina could remember. Galina peered through, glad to see nothing had changed since she had looked through it last. She had spent many moments like this after her mother's death, crying tears of loss as she touched her mother's simple things. Her blue flowered apron, the faded green work dress, her red and white handkerchief, a few hair ribbons and more clothes beneath. Galina didn't wipe away the tears as they slipped down her cheeks. She truly just wanted to take the box with her. But she knew the weight of it would cause her pain. She was not so foolish to think her father wouldn't miss it. Galina sighed and picked through the items she wanted. The blue floral apron was the first thing she pulled out. She ran her hand over the fabric and closed her eyes for a long minute. She took the red bandana that her mother had worn to do housework. There was a woolen shawl that Galina wanted and a black vest that her mother had kept from her younger days. Galina took the items and place them on the dining table. She looked in a low cabinet and found an empty flour sack that Galina had laundered herself. She placed all of her treasures inside then went back for one more look through her mother's things. At the bottom of the box was a smaller box, it had a rough carving of a pine tree on the top. She opened it and saw a few very old ribbons, a piece of old yellowed lace and several rocks of different colors. Galina had another flash of a memory, of her mother sitting with these rocks at the table. She had told Galina stories of her homeland, and how her grandfather had been a kind man who would always look for rocks and stones in the stream on their land. Galina knew that she would be taking this box with her. She could not leave it behind.

She closed the lid of the bigger box and with a few more tears said goodbye. It was harder than she had imagined but also somewhat freeing. She didn't have to leave her heart behind for her mother any longer, she was taking her with her to her new life.

She would still feel some pain when it came to her brothers, but there was no helping that. She was no longer welcome here. She had to face that and accept it.

Galina bundled up all of her treasures in the flour sack. She stood by the door and let her eyes float over the space, seeing it the way it was when her mother was there, not as it was now.

Galina felt the warm rush of her mother's presence and her heart was light for a moment.

She remembered something her mother had taught her when she was young.

"Tęsknię za tobą." Galina said softly as she went through the door, meaning *I miss you.*

Galina walked home slower, having to take lots of breaks from carrying the light bag. Her body and mind were very tired, and the two-mile trek there and back was more than she should have taken on yet. But she finally made it back to the Grant cabin. She had decided to find Corinne first, to tell her what she had done. She didn't want to carry the guilt of lying to them on her heart.

Corinne was outside the greenhouse, talking to Dolly when Galina saw her.

Corinne and Dolly waved her over.

"Your cheeks are flushed Galya." Corinne reached out a hand and placed it to Galina's cheek.

"I walked to... I went back home. One last time." Galina said, her voice was tight, and she dropped her gaze.

Dolly took a step closer and placed a hand on Galina's shoulder. The gesture released a sob that Galina had been holding back. Both Dolly and Corinne were embracing her before the moment passed. They had both lost their mother, somehow she knew that they understood the need to say goodbye.

When her emotions calmed she told them about the day, what she had felt, and the things she had spirited away.

They had both understood. Galina had expected a lecture, but it never came.

Dolly placed a hand on her chest, over her heart. "My mother lives here, her words and lessons are with me every day."

Corinne nodded, with misty tears in her own eyes. "I know you will treasure every memory, even when they hurt." She swiped as a tear escaped down her pale cheek.

Dolly soon left, to go back to Angela's house to stay. But Corinne stayed with her. Galina talked for a few more minutes. Spilling out more of her thoughts than she had ever before. She felt that first budding of trust blossoming into something else. Corinne was more understanding than Galina knew in the past. It made her wonder at God's providence, in providing her with the friend she truly needed.

Corinne carried Galina's sack and they went back to the cabin. Galina was happily settled on the davenport within a few minutes with a cup of white willow bark tea for her aches. Her new life had officially started. She had no idea how she would move forward, her heart still hurt more than her body but she had to accept the changes in her life, her inner prayers were constant.

Chapter 17

Clive Quackenbush

Clive and Olivia had spent the first few weeks of their marriage at home, Clive taking a long and much needed break from working anywhere. They spent their days settling into their own little routines, making the home their own. Olivia planted flowers in front of the porch. Clive doted on his new bride with furniture and gifts as they settled into their new life together. He felt young again. His bride was funny and charming, and excellent company. He thanked God every day for her.

They sat many hours in the comfortable rocking chairs on the front porch. They watched the weather come over the mountains to the west, the mist rise in the far off fields. It was a grand time to be alive.

After two heavenly weeks of honeymooning, it had been Olivia who had finally kicked his reluctant self back to work.

"Oh, husband of mine, you will wither on the vine if you stay home so much. You get back to your work, and your visits. I'm certain everyone will be missing ya. I will be here most days doing my work." Olivia winked at him. "I may go into town with you tomorrow though. I can do some work with my sister and my niece a few times a week to visit and help with the business." Olivia was practical and cheerful.

"You are a beautiful and talented woman." Clive said with a chuckle. He was still a little regretful about getting back to his old ways. Wondering if they could honeymoon just a little bit longer.

"You will see me every evening." Olivia patted his arm. Her soft hand was reassuring.

"I may want to take you along on some of my visiting runs." Clive said, hoping that she understood that he really did want her to be with him on his adventures.

"You come and get me whenever you want to." She laughed and smiled.

Clive sat and rocked in the chair next to his beautiful bride, pleased that she was willing to be a part of his life. He sat quietly, making plans to venture back into his life, so many people to visit and catch up with. He felt that old feeling again, that quickening of his heartbeat and the pleasure of having good friends and a good business to work at.

He was pleased to think of showing off his new bride around the county, he spent the last evening with his bride as they discussed the plans of the summer.

<hr />

Corinne Grant

Corinne sat with her daughter settled on her knee. Her one leg was tiring from the bouncing her daughter enjoyed, she switched her to the other leg. She was getting so big, and every week her thick brown hair was getting longer. Corinne was so happy to be her mother.

Lucas, her father John, and Reynaldo were leaning over the dining table with plans and they were in the heavy discussion about the new barn.

All the logs had been gathered and were sitting on a platform next to the build site. But the flat lumber hadn't arrived yet. The newspaper had announced the barn raising for the next week but the plans and details were being decided today. Corinne gave a wink to Marie who was across the room in the kitchen, brewing up coffee and slicing up a crumble cake.

Trudie let out a whimper, Corinne smoothed the dark hair on her head and pulled her against her chest. Trudie's eyes were red and she yawned to show it was nearing her naptime.

Corinne stood and swayed a little, her daughter cuddled her head under mama's chin and was soothed. The scent of the sleeping child was comforting to Corinne as she walked slowly over to the kitchen to chat with Marie as the men did their planning and scheming over pulleys and blueprints.

Galina and Violet had gone home after lunch and Corinne was going to take Trudie home soon but she was glad for the chance to visit with Marie. Baby Abigail, Corinne's half-sister, was growing so fast and had been clinging to her mother's skirt earlier, was now happily playing with her blocks and toys in her wooden playpen next to the kitchen and away from the hot stove.

Marie handed out the coffee to the distracted men, discussing the arrival of the supplies from the blacksmith that would be later in the day, large nails, thick chains, and harness parts. There was so much to keep track of. Corinne marveled at the expansive project.

Corinne knew they would all benefit from the new horse barn, it was going to be a blessing, but she worried over everyone's safety in this undertaking. Corinne had been little when she had been at a barn raising in Kentucky. A rope had broken and a log had crushed a man. Lucas had promised Corinne that every safety measure would be taken, but she still worried. Sometimes it seemed the job of women was to worry... and men's job to shush them for it. Corinne smiled and patted her daughter's back.

◆━◆•◉•◆━◆━◆•◉•◆━◆

Megan Capron

Megan stepped through the doorway of her own rooms at the boarding house. Her feet aching and her side cramping from the walk back from the hotel. The show had gone well but she was not able to sing as loud or hold the notes out so long as she used to. Her belly was heavy and she just did not have the air that she used to. She had given up the corsets almost as soon as she had traveled to Oregon. She was not going to fool anyone, and they were unmercifully uncomfortable. She had hired a local seamstress to make her a few dresses to wear performing, which dipped into some of the money set aside for her trip to the East. The dresses were not as fancy as her normal fare, but she felt a little better once they were on. "A few nice baubles and the crowd will be impressed." She had said to herself in the mirror. She hadn't been wrong.

Now she was stretching the fabric to its limits. She wondered lately if she wasn't going to explode like an overripe watermelon.

This evening had been a chore, she had to take so many breaks that the hotel owner again pressed the issue of her taking time off. She had always shushed him, but tonight she had agreed, a few days off to rest may do her some good. The hotel owner had glanced down at her belly wordlessly. She knew what he was thinking. She was due in a few weeks, perhaps a month. She felt as big as a barge already. She had better talk to a doctor about arrangements for the birth, but honestly, she just didn't want to deal with that yet and pushed it from her mind.

Megan pulled the rope for the maid and settled into her soft settee. She got out of her shoes and waited, her small dainty hands reaching for her shoes to remove them, if possible, when a thought occurred to her. What in the world was she going to do with a child?

She had had months to think on this topic, but now, only weeks away from delivery, it finally dawned on her. *I am going to be a mother.*

Chapter 18

Reynaldo Legales

The building day had come. Reynaldo gathered up the ropes and pulleys he was preparing the week before on the table in his small cabin just as the morning light filled the eastern sky. He heaved the heavy ropes over his shoulder and made his way outside. He had a wheelbarrow out front and loaded everything he would need in it. It would take him a good ten minutes to walk everything over to the building spot across the property.

He always enjoyed a community build. When he was young, the rural community would come together and help build barns and there would always be music and a fiesta. He was pleased to find out that in his new world it was the same kind of gathering. Today was going to be busy, noisy, and probably exhausting, but the chance to connect with others would make it worthwhile in the end.

Reynaldo grabbed a few more of his tools, piled them into the wheelbarrow, gave it a tug upward and pushed to get it moving. He had forgotten to eat in his excitement of the morning but he had high hopes that a few ladies would be setting up early near the build and some fresh coffee would be available. He was hoping to see Violet there as well.

Just the sight of her lately was more energizing than any coffee could be.

Violet with her hidden scars. Blond braids and the smile that was like a small red jewel. Joy radiated from her pale skin, with a pink blush at her cheeks. Despite a sadness that sometimes came over her eyes, she always seemed to have some secret way about her. He would admit the last time he spent any time with her alone she had leaned on his chest and trusted him enough to be close to him. He was intoxicated by her presence and wanted more of it. He certainly knew she would not seek him out. Her ability to trust anyone after her past was something he was concerned about, but he had that blossom of hope that perhaps if he approached her slowly, she could learn that he meant her no harm.

Reynaldo wheeled past the barn and heard the horses stirring, he saw a few ranch hands bustling about the place. He gave a nod, since his hands were full, to several of the new fellows that were working. With business going so well and some new births coming soon, they would be busy all spring.

The grass in the eastern meadow beside the fence was beginning to grow, that lovely spring green that was so pleasant on the eyes after the winter gray. He saw a few tiny buds on the bushes along the fence line that promised new leaves in the coming weeks.

The pile of lumber sat next to the cleared off piece of land, it was bright in the morning sun. He saw his boss, John Harpole, and his wife Marie setting up a few tables. The little ones were probably still inside their home, eating breakfast with the housekeeper.

He saw in the distance that Violet was walking up the stone path from the Grant's cabin. He felt foolish as he noticed the quickening of his heartbeat to see her. He had to make a mental note to watch where he was going or a rock or tree root would upset his wheelbarrow if he didn't pay attention. The weight of his load was pretty heavy and his hands were smarting from the rough wood of the handles, he had forgotten to put on his gloves. He stopped the forward motion and grabbed the gloves that were on the top of his haul. He watched Violet walk closer to Marie Harpole and Reynaldo wished he could help her with the items that she was carrying, her arms were full and he would have enjoyed easing her burden.

Reynaldo reminded himself to stay on the task at hand, lifted the wheelbarrow, and pushed it forward over the uneven ground. He rounded the fence and stopped near the pile of lumber.

That is close enough. He thought.

John Harpole caught his eye, walked to meet Reynaldo, and gave him a slap on the back.

"Weather looks fine for the day so far." John said cheerfully.

Reynaldo looked up to the cloudless sky, the sun was still just peeking through the trees but the pale blue of the sky was a good sign. "Indeed it is." Reynaldo said and smiled distractedly to John. His eyes were drawn to the blonde that was chatting now with Marie at the tables.

"You needing some coffee?" John asked and nudged him with an elbow.

Reynaldo looked back to his boss and saw the smirk that told him that his boss knew what he had been staring at.

Reynaldo smiled sheepishly. "Well, yessir, I am thinkin' so."

John laughed and Reynaldo walked away with a glance back to watch John laugh at his expense. Reynaldo could not hide a grin, John was a smart man and Reynaldo knew he was never good at hiding his intentions.

"Hey Rey!" Marie said and handed Reynaldo a piece of warm bread with butter and jam.

"Oh, you beautiful woman." He gave Marie a winning smile and took a bite to please her.

"Coffee?" Violet asked, she looked down at the mugs and poured him a cup.

He could tell she had done some fancy thing with her hair and the top of her head showed a weave of braids that encircled her face. She looked up to him with pink cheeks. Her cornflower blue eyes were dazzling in the morning light. He forgot everything to say for a moment.

She handed him a hot mug.

"Sugar or cream?" She asked and looked him in the eye.

He paused and felt a heat rise in his neck as he felt mute. "Uh, yes, sugar please." He inwardly praised himself for not being a complete fool.

He took the mug and sipped it to try to save himself somehow. "It's good." He announced and took a few more swigs. He looked over to Marie who also seemed to notice his attentions and she was hiding a smile behind her hand. He gave her a warning look that had no malice and she knew it. Marie stifled a giggle.

Reynaldo thanked the women and sat on a stool nearby to eat his bread and regain his composure.

John Harpole walked forward and gave a wave to a man pulling up on the wagon road along the fence. A tall man with a bushy white beard and weathered hat waved back.

"There's the man I was telling you about Marie." John announced.

"The engineer from Portland." Marie reached to take her husband's arm.

Reynaldo had met the man a few days before in town. His name was Brit Cramer, he was an engineer in London for years before he came to do some design work for buildings in Philadelphia. He was an adventurous man who was settling in Portland to design a hotel but had a break to come and help with John Harpole's project. He was trading his services for a few draft horses that John was breeding.

"His pulley system for the hay storage is a sight to see." Reynaldo stood and gave a wave himself.

Violet caught his eye and he saw the shy look that she gave him before she turned to watch the newcomer walk closer.

"A great man, certainly an asset. He looked over our designs and gave us some good input." John said and took a sip of the steaming coffee he held with his free hand.

Brit pulled his wagon off the road next to the fence and gave a holler. John settled his coffee on the table, gave his wife a smile and a nod, and went to greet the man. Reynaldo decided to join him.

The greeting didn't take long and the older gentleman was ready to get to work, he wanted to look over the materials, ropes and pulleys before the crowd of neighbors were to arrive.

It wasn't long after that the laborers, women and children appeared. Corinne and Lucas had brought a few more tables, and more breakfast food from their cabin, Russel and Chelsea Grant arrived with even more.

Reynaldo took a moment, before the building was to begin to get himself another cup of coffee from the pretty blond that occupied his thoughts.

"Would you mind sharing some more of that delicious coffee?" He asked.

Violet whipped her head around from where she was focused.

"You surprised me, Rey." She said and put a hand against her chest.

"It's good that you call me Rey." He smiled and watched her look down again.

She pursed her lips together. She poured him some coffee and dropped a sugar cube in it. She stirred it with a nearby spoon. She handed him the coffee and smiled becomingly.

"I'll come around later, I've heard you are making fried chicken for lunch." Reynaldo grinned.

"I'll do my best to feed as many as I can today. You fellows will be working so hard." She said.

"Many hands will make the day fly by." Reynaldo chugged the last of his coffee and handed her the mug. She reached for it and he placed a hand over hers on the mug. "I'll be looking forward to that fried chicken." He winked at her and he enjoyed the blush that brightened her cheeks. He let the hand go regretfully and strolled away.

Galina Varushkin

Galina was settled in on a chair, with Heidi Sparks next to her. Peter and Fiona Sparks were excited to see all of the commotion as people were instructed on what jobs were needed. Trudie was holding Galina's fingers tightly as Galina bounced her on her knees. Galina sang an old silly song that she remembered her mom singing to her when she was young. Galina would admit that she still had a lot of healing to do, probably more in her heart than on her body but she knew she could handle the sweet girl she was watching. Heidi Sparks was a few years younger than her, but she promised to take over Trudie's care if Galina needed a break. She was beginning a small friendship with Heidi and was hoping that today would be a good day for them to cement that bond. Galina was also hoping to see Sophia today; she hadn't seen her in a few weeks since her long visit with Angela. Sophia was busy working in town, yet Galina hoped that she would not miss this kind of day. It seemed like the whole town was going to be here.

She saw Clive standing on a stack of wood up ahead, he had a gathering of men around him, presumably getting instructions for their first task. Lucas had told her in detail how today was going to go, she was pleased that he treated her so kindly and never thought her questions were foolish. It was a different kind of life so far at their home. She saw the everyday discussions, had even seen a few disagreements between Corinne and Lucas, that was part of life she knew, but she had never seen him lose his temper or raise his voice, she was pleased to see it. But the thing that made the largest impression was the equality between them. Lucas never treated Corinne, or even Violet, like they had a lesser intellect or that, their opinions didn't matter. It was a new kind of world to her. Seeing it once a week helping with laundry had given her a glimpse, seeing it every day was on a whole other scale.

She saw Sophia finally approached from the path, she was dressed simply, which was an oddity. Sophia was usually dressed head-to-toe in the latest fashions, dripping with lace and embroidery from the fine skills of her family members. Galina smiled, glad that her face no longer hurt to do so.

"Sophie!" Galina said, and was pleased when Trudie gurgled out some gibberish to be heard as well.

Sophia quickened her pace and joined her. Galina pointed to the chairs that Lucas had brought out of the house. Sophia found one that suited and settled it next to Galina and Trudie. Galina made the introductions with Heidi, who had her hands full with Peter mostly, who desperately wanted to get closer to the construction.

"It will be nice to spend the day together. I might just need to hog tie my brother to be able to enjoy myself." Heidi said as she gave Sophia a nod. Peter looked back over his shoulder and his eyes widened, proving that he could hear her when he pretended deafness for most of the time.

"I am pretty good at tying things." Sophia offered with a giggle. She gave Peter a solid glare that meant she was on Heidi's side.

Sophia settled in the chair between Heidi and Galina and held her hands outstretched to take Trudie. "Oh, I need to get some kisses right now." Trudie went willingly and Sophia planted kisses on her cheeks and fingers, as promised.

The three girls chatted as the work around them began. Galina saw some younger boys being loaded with leather bags full of nails and pegs that they were to distribute to the men building. The foundation had been built over the last week so the walls began to take shape over the morning.

Marie Harpole brought Abigail and Lila over to visit with them, Lila and Fiona were becoming fast friends and Heidi mentioned that she was pleased to see it. The older girls watched as the two young girls were lost in their own little world once they were together.

"Fiona needs a good friend to draw her out of her shyness." Heidi said with a smile.

"We all need that." Galina said and reached a hand over to Heidi. Sophia took a free hand too and placed it on Heidi's hand. It was a short-lived moment when Trudie wanted Sophia to bounce her more and let out a grunt of disapproval. They all laughed.

Abigail Harpole was getting so big and Galina offered to take her so Marie could have a break.

"No, thank you, Galina. She is in a mood and I don't want her hurting your ribs. I was giving my housekeeper a little break to eat a late breakfast. Abby has been up since before dawn. I was baking and my poor housekeeper has been taking on Abby's temper tantrum.

Toddlers know just the right moment to bring on the chaos." Marie laughed.

Marie must have noticed that Peter was restless and he kept edging closer and closer to the construction area.

"Peter Sparks!" Marie yelled out, Abby settled in on her hips.

Peter jumped a little and gave a look to Marie who had a no nonsense look on her face.

"You are going to get hurt if you get any closer. If you behave yourself for the next few minutes while I visit with your sister and her friends then I will let you come with me. I may be able to find a way you can help. But only if you behave yourself." Marie offered.

Peter looked excited then sobered to nod his agreement. "I'll behave."

Marie gestured him over with a crook of her finger. He obeyed. She placed her hand on the top of his head and gave it a gentle rustling, his shiny white-blond hair was blowing in the breeze. He smiled up at her in respect.

Galina took Trudie back from Sophia and continued with the knee bouncing, which seemed to be the favorite thing today for the child.

Sophia jumped up and went to help Angela, who was carrying a few heavy-laden baskets. With the farm-hand Warren behind carrying two more.

Galina watched Sophia take a basket and give her a sideways hug as they strode forward.

Angela noticed Galina and beamed at her with a happy smile.

"Oh, Galya!" Angela sometimes used the pet name that her mother called her. It was good to hear it. "It is so good to see you out in the sunshine."

"What did you make?" Galina asked, and then shuffled Trudie, who was wanting to get down.

"Just about a thousand bread rolls. Nothing fancy. Violet gave me the dough and I've been baking all day yesterday and today. We have an army to feed today." Angela settled the basket at Galina's feet and scooped up Trudie, who was wanting Angela's attention. Sophia grabbed up the basket.

"I'll take this over." Sophia gave a look to Galina quickly, with a secret smile, and made the slightest gesture with her chin toward the strapping young man that was next to her.

Sophia and Warren were chatting happily about the big day. Galina was glad that the friendship between them was forming well. In Galina's mind, it was a blessing to have someone close to their age to be friends with.

Galina grinned quickly but turned her attention back to Angela. She wouldn't have minded carrying baked goods next to Warren, but it would look a bit silly to take Sophia's place just now. She knew that everyone would have protested at her carrying anything just yet.

Angela fussed and talked baby talk to Trudie for a minute, and Heidi got up to give her brother a lecture to be careful and obedient as Marie was offering the boy a chance to do some 'safe' helping.

Galina watched Peter nod again and make promises to be good. Heidi smiled as she sat down. Heidi watched Fiona and Lila chat and giggle the way of young girls. It was going to be a full day but it was pleasant to be out with people again. Galina hoped that the whole day would be just like this.

Corinne came by, took charge of the little ones, and offered a chance for Galina, Heidi and Sophia to go watch the commotion. They were eager to watch the framework of the barn go up and they went with swinging skirts to see it all.

———◆•◆•———◆•◆•———

The huge logs were lined up and they each were notched on the edges. There was about fifteen men with axes, hatchets and a few with hammers and chisels that worked together to make the notches perfect. In the center of the foundation an enormously tall beam was towering over the structure. Galina had seen it there for the last week and wondered about how it would be used it this massive undertaking.

Several large teams of oxen and a team of tall workhorses were using ropes and pulleys, with the expert handling by very strong men, to pull the long foundation logs up to the edge of the foundation. So far, there were two rows of beams standing. The notches were cut so well that there were no gaps between the logs, the space was flush. The girls were amazed to see the expert work that had already begun.

Sophia and Galina both pointed at Reynaldo, who was handling a team of horses that was pulling a log up just then. He yelled instructions to the driver and held a whip in his right hand and his other hand was pointing and giving direction. He was a favorite of the

206

two girls, him being a constant sight at church every Sunday, and for being so very handsome. This encouraged Heidi to join in on the giggling, more to be a part of the group than any actual attraction. He was still young, being in his twenties and though no one had more than a passing attraction for him, he was definitely in their conversations when it came to boy gazing.

They watched as the beam was settled in place, a man with a chisel and hammer came forward, while the beam still hung in the air just an inch above the other beam. The horses straining, men yelling for everyone to hold their lines still so the master could chip away at the notch. Within a few moments the beam was lowered perfectly and the work was flawless.

The girls watched in amazement for a time before they headed back to relieve Corinne.

<hr />

Violet Griffen

Violet was glad for the breeze as she stood over the fire, she had four different frying pans on the fire with crispy chicken in each one. Edith Sparks was beside her with more chicken, breaded and ready to go.

There was only a few minutes left before the bell for lunch would be rung. She had two platters full of chicken already fried and ready for the workers.

She had gotten too close to the fire several times and scorched the bottom of her light blue chintz skirt. She was a bit flustered but she kept working. She glanced up from her work a few times and watched the progression of the building as the men toiled even harder than she was.

She used two long forks to flip the chicken over in one pan and checked the doneness of the chicken in another. It would be a few more minutes. She wiped at the sweat on her brow and glanced up to the barn progress again. It was several layers tall now, almost shoulder high for some of the men standing nearby.

Corinne came by and gave her a mug of water to slake her thirst. Violet thanked her and sipped it gratefully. She would be happy to get this job done and join in the feast. She could see several makeshift tables loaded down with food.

There were many chairs and stools being set up nearby for everyone working to be able to rest a bit after a busy morning. Corinne came up behind her and rubbed her shoulders a little to be supportive.

"Oh, you poor thing. It is scorching hot over here." Corinne exclaimed.

"Reminds me of a hot day in August." Violet said with a grin.

Corinne looked her in the eye, assessing if she was getting too tired.

"I will be fine. I only have a few more pieces of chicken to do. I do fear I've ruined this skirt. I wasn't paying attention." Violet laughed. She hadn't noticed someone coming up to her on her other side.

"That chicken is looking mighty fine." Reynaldo's voice surprised her.

Violet snapped her head around. She let out a gasp.

"My part is done for now. I was wondering if I could help at all before the crowds gather." Reynaldo's smile was even more distracting than the heat from the frying pans.

Violet smiled back without thinking. His eyes were focused in on hers and she was more than surprised by the bit of a flutter in her belly.

"You probably just want to steal a piece of chicken before everyone gets a chance to eat." Violet finally said after a long pause. Violet had turned away from those intense brown eyes of his. But she was very aware of his presence behind her. He was so very close.

"I promise I will not steal anything, Sweet Violet." Reynaldo said quietly. There was something behind his words. She looked over just a little and he had moved to her side. Her breath was caught. "Well, I can't promise that I won't steal a kiss."

Violet's eyes went wide and the flutter in her belly returned. She whipped her head back to her work and silently watched the chicken cook in the pan and her cheeks flamed.

"You are quite a charming man, Mr. Legales." Violet poked at a piece of chicken and flipped it over.

"I thought you were going to call me Rey." He said.

"Well, I don't want you to take liberties. You probably are flirting with every young woman here." Violet said, certain she was right. He must enjoy the attention he gets, she mused.

208

"I would never take liberties, Violet. I hope you know that." Reynaldo still spoke softly, only for her ears, but what caught her off guard the most was the sincerity behind them. She turned again, one last time. His hand reached down to hers, still holding the long handled fork. He grabbed her hand and forced her hand to poke and flip a piece of chicken that was done. She pressed her lips together and gave him a questioning glare, wanting him to be kind to her but also not wanting to play a game.

"You are the only woman I see here today, Violet. I was hoping you knew that." Reynaldo said and let go of her hand. He didn't smile then, she could not help but see the serious look in his eyes. Somehow she knew that he was somewhat saddened by her questioning his honor. He walked away and he gave her a grin, but that moment she saw stayed with her.

She got busy, to keep her herself occupied and still her mind from thoughts of handsome men. She filled another platter full of chicken before the lunch bell rang out.

<hr/>

Clive Quackenbush

Clive was enjoying his day thoroughly, but for the burning in his shoulders from a little too much heavy lifting. He was working hand in hand with Brit Cramer, the engineer who had just done a big job in Portland. Brit was excellent at a job site that was certain. He knew just how to keep things moving, always having his thoughts a few steps ahead to keep everyone flowing.

Clive sat with Brit during the lunch break and heard all about Brit's work over the years. Clive peppered him with questions, Olivia joined them and wanted to hear all about the new hotel in Portland, she was especially interested in hearing about the music they played there.

"Oh Clive, dear, wouldn't it be grand to hear an orchestra?" Olivia gushed and sighed. Olivia invited him to come stay at their house since he wasn't able to get a room at the boarding house. She was so excited that she left the barn raising early to get his room prepared. She wanted to hear all about the hotel when he would come to stay that evening. She would be sure to have some coffee and dessert for them when their work was done. Brit Cramer was a jovial man and was glad to have the company and conversation.

It didn't take much for Clive to take a hint from his ladylove. Before the day was gone he got all the particulars from Brit on when a good time to visit would be. Brit promised Clive that he would handle a three-day stay for them at the hotel. Clive was pleased as punch and it made the hard work of the rest of the day seem a bit lighter. He was giving her a fancy honeymoon after all, certain to create a long time memory.

The second story of the barn was starting to take shape, the draft horses were working hard and snorting through the heavy lifting of the timbers. Ropes and chains were checked after each load, John Harpole wanted to be certain that no risks were taken for the health and safety of the men and animals that were working. Reynaldo was in charge of seeing to the health of the animals and had switched out a few workhorses when the animals were showing signs of fatigue.

The day ended with the barn close to completed, the structure anyhow. The trusses would have to go up the next day and then the outside of the structure would be nailed on. This was a large undertaking, but it certainly had been a productive day.

Many of the men promised to return on the morrow to see it completed.

❖━━━━◆━━━━❖

Violet Griffen

Violet put on a large pot of water to boil to wash the empty platters as Corinne was preparing Trudie for bed. Trudie had fallen asleep on the walk over but the jostling had woken her when they came inside.

Lucas had lit a few lanterns and had gotten the stove lit and was now cleaning off his boots.

Corinne got Trudie settled in for the night and Violet put on a kettle for some tea for everyone.

Corinne strode into the room with a smile.

"It was a fine and busy day." She said and walked up next to Violet. "You take a seat for a minute, I'll get the tea. The water for the washing will be a while before it's hot." Corinne patted Violet's shoulder.

Violet was comforted by the friendly gesture and sat at the nearby table.

Corinne reached into the cupboards and got out three sets of teacups and saucers.

Lucas was now opening his tin of polish with a small squeak. Violet watched him work.

"I noticed that you had an admirer today, Mrs. Griffen." Lucas said as he brushed a little of the black polish on his boots. He looked up to her and gave her a wink.

Violet ignored his comment but she couldn't stop herself from smirking just a little bit.

"I indeed saw Reynaldo paying quite a bit of attention to our sweet Violet." Corinne said with a melodious quality to her voice.

"He is entirely too good looking." Violet said and huffed for good measure. She would not be teased, so she thought to put an end to it easily.

"A grievous offense, truly." Lucas said then laughed at his comment.

Corinne laughed too. Then placed her hands on the counter, her eyes intent. "He needs a wife."

"I don't doubt that, he is a good man, with a nice cabin, and a solid career." Violet said with a nod.

"Beside him being good looking, what other flaw would make you spurn his glances." Corinne asked.

Lucas was amused and Violet could hear him chuckling mildly to himself.

"I am not spurning anything. I am certain he has many women vying for his affections. A raven haired beauty would probably be to his taste."

Corinne nodded. "How would you know what his taste is?"

Violet shrugged. "Is the water warm for the tea?" She asked then pointed to her friend accusingly, wishing for them to stop their pestering.

"He seems to stare at you a lot for being interested in some raven-haired beauty, as you claim it should be." Lucas offered.

"Are you meaning to fluster me, Lucas?" Violet sighed.

Corinne was pouring the tea into the teacups and then putting sugar in and stirring. The sound of the spoon swishing in the cups filled the room, everyone was watching Violet.

"I don't know what his tendencies are towards me, but you must be confusing his looks at me. We have a good friendship... as neighbors only! You will see." Violet assured them. She accepted her tea and blew out a breath to cool the hot liquid.

"A friendship?" Lucas asked. He was smirking, and Violet did not appreciate it.

"Yes, our backgrounds have a few similar commonalities." Violet took a sip and enjoyed the warmth and sweetness on her tongue.

"How would you know about commonalities?" Corinne sat next to her. There was no mocking or smirking and Violet was soothed. This was just curiosity.

"We have chatted upon occasion. He had a difficult childhood as well. We both have a tenderness toward those that are mistreated." Violet took another sip, pleased that the conversation was turning away from the teasing.

"I have known him as long as you and I did not know that." Lucas chimed in.

Violet gave him a look that might suggest he go back to polishing his boots. He had only taken her glance as another reason to pester her further.

"Perhaps, I might be overstepping my bounds. That he shared those things with you because he has an interest in you." Lucas offered.

Violet huffed.

"Indeed, Violet, I know we tease, but... I have noticed that he seems to watch out for you, and not just today. He is always sitting near us at the church, and he is always the first one to say hello when the service is over. He does make a habit of checking on us all when the weather turns foul. Certainly he is not that good of a neighbor to everyone in the area." Corinne gave Violet a look that was practical.

"I don't see anything beyond a mild flirtation." Violet settled the tea in the saucer. She was feeling more confused and a bit saddened suddenly.

"I wouldn't suggest anything to be a forgone conclusion. But I have never seen him paying any attention to any other woman, Violet. He is a good man, a good Christian, and a hard worker. Is there any reasons you wouldn't want him to pay more attention to you?" Corinne asked.

Violet had her own fears, mostly silly ones that she would never speak aloud. "I am not certain that you are right." Violet said finally. Her voice sounding as insecure as she felt.

"He might be waiting to know if you are more interested. He may be a cowboy, but he is also a gentleman." Lucas offered.

Violet nodded. She had accused him of being insincere that very day, he had seemed the tiniest bit struck by her thoughts of him.

"Perhaps I should just have a frank chat with him. We are not children. I am capable of just asking what his intentions are. I will not be offended if he was simply flirting. I would say that Reynaldo may be a bit like Clive, who enjoys flattering the female sex, without ever having any kind of malicious intent. Some men are just that way. Reynaldo is certain to clear this whole thing up." Violet said finally, feeling relieved at the very thought of it. He was always easy to converse with. She would just have to take a moment and pull him aside.

"That is wise I think." Lucas said simply, He smiled just a little and went back to his boots, the brush swishing softly over the leather as Corinne and Violet drank their tea.

Sean Fahey

Sean Fahey had enjoyed the day, working alongside the men in the new community he found himself a part of now. He had been standing atop some tall scaffolding helping to guide the large logs to get them into place. He had a few close calls early on, not sure where to stand to stay clear of the logs as they were hoisted. He got the hang of it quickly. He did get his fingers pinched a few times, by not having them in the right place and a corner was caught a time or two. His thumb would smart for a day or two certainly. He had sat with Angela and Ted over lunch and had a lovely conversation with his sister, which he was profoundly grateful for. He had brought over a few more of the gifts and mementoes he had for her from his vast storage a few days before. Every visit got a little easier between them. Though he had to admit there was still a sadness behind her eyes sometimes. Sean was thoughtful of that and only came to visit a few times, not wanting to force his way into their lives. Ted was certainly warming up to him and Sean had a pleasant vision of having a brother. Ted had taken him for a ride around their land just the day before. He was a bright young man and Sean was pleased to know him.

Sean had gotten a chance to see Dolly at the barn raising but she had not been any more than polite. There was something about her

213

that made him wonder. She was such a quiet girl. He wanted to break through her silence and discover more about her, but he wasn't certain how he could accomplish it. He decided to make more of an effort, perhaps after Sunday service.

Sean settled into his cabin by the fire and ate some bread that Angela had sent home with him with some butter he bought from the grocer in town. It would be time soon for him to build his own barn and make the land he now owned obey his whims. Seeing the valley come to life with spring was a reminder that he had a lot of work to do. He said a prayer that God would give him wisdom as he moved forward. He felt a peace fill him, that he was exactly where God wanted him. That was worth more than anything else was on earth.

Chapter 19

Violet Griffen

A week had passed since the barn raising and Violet was pleased see a few laborers from town were on tall scaffolding painting the barn a pleasant dark red. Violet could imagine how bold and beautiful it would be in the fall, with the colors of the fall leaves in all their splendor on the mountains and hills beyond in contrast to the barn. The running horses prancing through their paces.

The summer was growing close and for now, she would enjoy the view of green trees and the wildflowers that abounded. There was no large patch of earth or fence post that wasn't marked by some flower or budding leaf.

Violet made some dried apple tarts from the last of the dried apples in the pantry and was going to surprise the ranch hands with a treat. She had visited with Marie a few days before and heard Marie lament that she had not had the time to bake them any treats as of late. Marie had her hands full with both Cooper and Lila down with a slight cold.

Violet enjoyed walking down the path, the breeze pleasant as she watched a few horses and young foals playing in the corral at her side. She stopped a long minute and watched the foals play. Their skinny legs were knobby kneed and adorable as they practiced all the skills they would need to grow up into strong work or riding horses. Violet couldn't stop her smile at the sight.

"A penny for your thoughts..."

She recognized Reynaldo's voice right away. His Latino accent was rich and charming as always.

"I saw you as I was heading to the ranch house." He came alongside her. His dark eyes were fully focused on her. Perhaps Lucas and Corinne were just a little bit correct. Her stomach flipped, wondering suddenly if she had the nerve to speak frankly with him.

"I was headed to the bunk house myself." She said, her voice was high and nervous. She all but bit her cheek to keep from chattering. She held up the basket finally after a pause. "I made tarts... for the men." She sighed, feeling foolish.

"Lucky fellows." Reynaldo smiled his best smile, it was broad and friendly and Violet felt her stomach flip again.

"I can set aside a few for you to take home... if you wish." Violet offered. Then felt ridiculous for how flirtatious that sounded.

I am almost as bad as Megan Capron. She said to herself.

Reynaldo smiled. "Let me accompany you." He offered his arm.

She didn't even take a moment to think too hard about it but slipped her arm into the crook of his offered elbow and let herself be whisked down the path.

A few ranch hands were lingering outside the bunkhouse and she happily delivered most of the tarts to their eager hands, with a promise to share them with everyone. There were many thanks and smiles from the rugged and hardworking group.

"If you wouldn't mind, I will only be a moment. I would love to walk back with you." Reynaldo spoke near her ear.

Violet smiled and nodded, realizing this would make a good opportunity to have the talk with him.

She was more than certain that Reynaldo would clear up the suspicions of her dearest friends. They were in love, and people in love want to see everyone around in the same state of blissfully wed.

She would admit that she did enjoy his calming company but any more than that was just ridiculous.

Reynaldo joined up with her and they walked at a slow pace. Violet wished that this conversation was over, but she dove in. She had faced worse problems before.

"I wanted to converse with you about something." Violet said. She looked over and saw his charming smile was lit up again. *I wish he would just stop that!* She mused.

"Anytime." He said simply. She looked away and kept moving forward. It would be easier if she didn't look at him.

"A few people have made some comments to me... that I feel are completely unfounded about you." Violet said.

"Well, the rumor mill has news about me. I'm totally flattered." He said. She could hear the mirth in his voice but she didn't look.

"Well, it concerns me. Several people are under the assumption that you are interested in me... romantically." Violet felt a small pressure on her arm.

Reynaldo drew her in like a magnet. His dark eyes serious.

"Well, that is interesting indeed." Reynaldo held her arm.

"Well, since we have a friendship I wanted to settle these rumors by having a talk about it. I see no reason why we cannot discuss this." She stammered on. Why did he look at her this way? He should have said something. Instead of making her keep talking.

"I would be glad to discuss this with you." He said, never looking away.

Why didn't he say anything to deny the accusation?

"Well..." Violet huffed. Wishing for all those words of her practiced speech that had somehow flown away with the warm breeze.

She looked at him, flustered for a long second. Wondering what was going on in that mind of his. She noticed the blue shirt he wore was his Sunday best. He wasn't wearing his normal working clothes. She liked the way his dark brown hair was falling over his brow. He was always wearing a broad hat during the warm days to keep the sun off his face.

"I was actually hoping to run into you today." He said.

"Oh really." Violet lost her nerve when his smirk returned. She looked away.

She took a few steps over to a fence post and leaned on it. Wishing there was something to do, a house to clean, a nappy to change... anything.

"Yes, I wanted to discuss something with you too." His voice was smooth, the way he would talk to the skittish horses.

Violet sighed. She was losing the flow of this conversation into something else. She knew suddenly that she was a fool. An utter fool.

"Ya know, I should listen to my friends more." Violet said.

"Which friends?" Reynaldo asked.

"Corinne and Lucas," Violet said curtly. Feeling suddenly trapped in this conversation that she started.

When was he going to do it? When will he just say want he wants to say?

"They are good friends." Reynaldo said, further driving her into madness.

"Will you just say what you want to say Rey? I am out of words." Violet admitted and looked at him.

"I want to ask you something first." He said softly. Still treating her like a wounded bird.

Violet watched his face.

"If the rumors were true, would you be offended?" His brown eyes looked vulnerable again. Like they did a few days before.

"Well, of course not." She huffed and started walking. She could see the Harpole cabin ahead. She turned around and saw that Reynaldo had stayed by the fence post. She gave a hand gesture, telling him to catch up.

"Violet, you are surely a mystery." He said when he was at her side matching her pace.

Violet was thinking, planning her words. Knowing what he was trying to say without actually saying it. It was her turn to grab his arm.

"It is utterly impossible for you to care for me like that. You are far too attractive to..." Violet stopped before the words tumbled out. Her eyes filled with tears when she thought of the words she was going to say.

"I am far too attractive to be interested in you?" He asked. Why did those eyes of his have to express every emotion he felt?

"No..." Violet said and lowered her gaze.

"Finish the thought, Violet." He lifted her chin.

"You are far too attractive to attach yourself to damaged goods." Violet said what her heart felt finally. It was an ugly thought. In her heart, all the healing she had done, this evil reminder of what her father had done to her still lingered there.

Reynaldo didn't say a word. He pointed to a small curved scar on his neck.

"This is where my father hit me with a board when I was around 9 years old." He said it simply. "Galina is still recovering from what her father has done to her, would you say that she is damaged goods?" He took both of her hands so she couldn't escape.

Violet felt more tears running down her cheeks. "That is not the same." She was losing this argument quickly. She knew his past, but not as well as he knew hers. Everyone knew hers.

He let go of one hand and wiped away the tears on her cheeks.

"If you aren't wanting my attention, I will never, ever, try to..." He paused. "I care enough for you to let you be if you wish. But I don't want you to ever say that about yourself again."

Violet felt that spark, it wasn't expected in her current emotional state. But it was there all the same. Suddenly remembering every time he had looked at her, or spoken to her kindly.

"I am a foolish girl." She said finally. His hand brushed away another tear.

"I am a bit of a fool too." He admitted.

"What do we do now?" She asked.

"Perhaps I could ask you if I could come calling sometime?" Reynaldo asked. He was still holding her hands.

She thought of every argument she could but they all were not founded on anything but her own doubts about herself. "I would like that." She said and felt better. She could be brave again.

"I told Corinne and Lucas that you were too attractive." She smiled, he was watching her so closely. He lifted an eyebrow. "You would certainly be interested in a raven haired beauty."

He nodded and frowned, but in a comical way. He let go of her hands and kneeled down. He got some dirt on his hand and rubbed it on his cheek.

"Is that better?" He asked and laughed.

She reached up to his face trying to wipe it away.

"Don't do that you fool!" She said. He trapped her hand there on his face. His cheek was warm. He grabbed her hand, moved it down to his lips, and kissed the palm, softly, reverently.

She had no words again. She just stared into those dark eyes as he lowered her hand down. He squeezed it once and let it go.

The voice of John Harpole rang out and scared Violet clean out of her skin.

"That gentleman bothering you Violet?" John said without any serious tone. She turned and looked to see John grinning.

"No sir." She said with an equal amount of humor.

"Well, good." He gave her a wink and walked away.

Reynaldo chuckled, a low sound in his chest. He gave her a smile. They had said enough for today about anything serious.

"Want to walk with me tomorrow evening?" He asked when the silence had dragged on between them for a long minute.

"It would be all the better if you came to supper first, around 5:30?" She asked.

"I'll be there."

They parted ways, Violet walked towards her home, strangely calm. It had gone far different than she expected, but she was through being a fool. She would try trusting in something sweeter. She might just be ready for something new.

❖◆❖◆❖

Portland, Oregon
Clive Quackenbush

Olivia Quackenbush sat next to Clive with a contented smile. Her eyes were alight with the glow from the crystal chandeliers that hung from the ceiling, it seemed a thousand candles twinkled above them as the musicians played. Clive was so very impressed by the Portland Grand Hotel and he would never regret bringing his bride here to celebrate their marriage. He had decided on the first night of their stay that this would become a tradition.

Olivia reached over and squeezed his hand affectionately, her eyes full of love and wonder. The swell of the violins filled Clive's chest in the way that only something profoundly beautiful could do. He had never been a man who loved the big city, but he had to admit, he never thought such music would be heard in the untamed land west of the Mississippi River, that it would only stay in the cultured cities of the East. He was so pleased to be wrong in his assumptions.

Olivia had been excited to hear that a singer would be joining the orchestra this evening and Clive was happy that she would get that experience before they left on the morrow.

The orchestra took a break for a few minutes and Clive and Olivia ate their dessert, a vanilla custard that was Clive's favorite. He finished his plate and half of Olivia's who had pushed hers away when she could eat no more.

"I do hope I don't burst my buttons while I sit here, darling." Olivia smiled brightly as she patted her middle.

"Oh my girl Olive, you are such a slip of a thing, you've got some room to spare certainly." Clive gave her a wink. He gave her a once over and wiggled an eyebrow suggestively.

Olivia gave him a warning grin.

The crowd buzzed as the orchestra took their seats again. A lady came on stage wearing a bright yellow gown with some dazzling jewels that sparkled in the candlelight.

The orchestra began and the melody was sweet and lilting.

"I do love this song." Olivia smiled warmly and whispered to Clive. He noticed many were standing to dance. He also joined the crowd and beckoned his wife with an open hand to whisk her to the dance floor.

The poetry of Thomas Moore was sung beautifully by the lovely singer as Clive took his wife around the floor with a slow swirling step.

There is not in the wide world a valley so sweet
As that vale in whose bosom the bright waters meet

Oh the last rays of feeling and life must depart
Ere the bloom of that valley shall fade from my heart
Ere the bloom of that valley shall fade from my heart

It had been Olivia who pulled her eyes away from Clive, her smile was warm and her cheeks pink. She seemed to be enjoying herself so very thoroughly when Clive noticed her face dropped its merriment. Clive slowed his step and turned to look where she was gazing, certain to see something wrong.

He didn't see it at first. He continued his dancing at a slower pace than the music called for. He looked back at his bride and saw that her cheeks had reddened and her eyes were wide.

He wordlessly took her arm, wondering if perhaps the dessert had been too rich for her, and her innards were complaining. He pressed his lips together firmly as he focused on getting his bride back to the table, not an easy task with the majority of the floor covered with dancing couples. The music played on.

Yet it was not that nature had shed o'er the scene
Her purest of crystal and brightest of green
'Twas not her soft magic of streamlet or hill
Oh No 'twas something more exquisite still
Oh No 'twas something more exquisite still

As they reached the table he pulled out Olivia's chair to let her take a rest when she ignored the chair and leaned in close to whisper in his ear.

"The girl singing..." She said in a harsh whisper. She tilted her eyes toward the stage, her eyes flashing.

Clive turned to get a closer look, having paid little attention to the woman before. She was young certainly in face, but she was broad through the belly, obviously large with child. Perhaps Olivia was thinking it was unhealthy for the woman to be performing so close to her time, Clive wondered for a long moment. His head was going to turn back to get a more thorough explanation from Olivia when he had that flicker of recognition. His heart dropped in his chest. Sadly, he knew the young woman.

He grabbed up the pamphlet on the table and held it close to the candle. He read the name of the singer.

Portland Grand Hotel
Tonight starring...
MRS. ROSIE GREEN and Orchestra

Clive ran a hand over his chin and looked to the stage again, where the woman was taking a bow. There was no doubt in my mind.

"She has taken on a stage name. I know her family has been looking for her. I assumed she was in far off parts." Clive leaned close to his wife to speak to her.

"What should we do?" Olivia asked.

"I don't think she has seen us. Otherwise, she would not be taking an encore. I think we should slip out soon. Our ferry leaves early tomorrow. I think we should let Corinne know. She can decide what to do."

Clive and Olivia chatted for a few minutes. They listened to Mrs. Rosie Green sing another song before she gave her last bow.

"I have an idea." He jangled a few coins in his pocket.

A waiter was nearby so Clive gave him a wave and a charming smile.

"My new bride and I so enjoyed the songs tonight. I would love to send the singer and Orchestra leader a small token of our appreciation. They made our honeymoon so very memorable." Clive took his bride's hand and they gave each other a sweet look.

The waiter enjoyed the praise, and congratulated them on their marriage.

"Mrs. Green is staying at the Oak street boarding house. Very nice place. The orchestra leader stays there as well." Clive slipped a few coins in his hand as a thank you.

Olivia chuckled behind a lace handkerchief.

"Life with you Clive, it is sure going to be interesting."

They made their way to their room and packed up their bags for the return trip home. It had been a lovely weekend together.

He was praying that the discovery they had made would do some good. That girl Megan seemed to have trouble follow her around.

***

Corinne Grant

A knock came to the door in the early afternoon. Corinne had a sleepy child in her arms, her dark brown hair still standing up defiantly. Clive stood at the door as Corinne answered it. Olivia peeked her head around to smile.

"Come in." Corinne said softly. The house was quiet, Violet and Galina had taken a walk.

"Trudie gets bigger every time I blink." Clive said and ran a hand softly over her dark hair. She whimpered a bit at the attention.

Corinne led them to the table.

Trudie let out another whimper.

"I should try and put her down. Could you possibly wait a moment?"

They both nodded.

"We'll be here darling girl." Clive smiled warmly.

Corinne felt a bit flustered but she patted and soothed Trudie on the way to her crib in the back bedroom. She sang a soft song and danced slowly around the room until Trudie finally closed her eyes.

Corinne crept out of the room and closed the door softly. Hoping the door latch wouldn't make a sound.

She sighed and returned to her guests.

She smiled a weary smile when she saw them, chatting happily at the table.

Olivia gave her a wink. It was comforting to know they were not impatient.

"How was your honeymoon at the Grand Hotel?" Corinne asked and plopped into the seat dramatically.

"It was indeed grand." Olivia said. "So sorry to interrupt your afternoon."

Corinne shook her head. "I accept the both of you any time, day or night." She answered sincerely.

"I don't hear a peep out of your sweet girl. You did a good job." Clive said. He gave a nervous glance to his wife.

Corinne felt her stomach flip. She was wise enough to Clive's looks to know that he had news.

"We found Megan." Clive said simply, ending her suspense.

Corinne wasn't sure she had heard correctly.

"Megan Capron?" Her eyes were confused.

"Yes, Olivia noticed her first. I am certain it is her." Clive nodded and Olivia did too.

"It was her hair that made me look twice. I was admiring her hairstyle as she was singing. When we got up to dance, I wanted a closer look. My heart nearly jumped from my chest when I realized it was her."

"That is some news." Corinne put a hand to the top of her head. She wondered what to do with this knowledge. Should she telegram her uncle?

"She is pregnant. Due any moment, certainly." Clive said gravely.

Corinne felt her heart drop. That would indeed make things more complicated.

"This morning as we left the hotel I asked if there was a way to reserve a room. In case you wanted to go see her." Clive offered.

"They gladly reserved a room for you and Lucas. They are not busy during the week. If you decide not to go I can easily send a telegram to cancel." He added practically.

Corinne nodded, her mind in a whirl.

He filled her in on the particulars, her stage name on the pamphlet and her location in Portland.

"She is taking a big risk by staying so close to Oregon City." Corinne said finally. Wondering how Megan could possibly think that no one would ever find out.

Who was the father? Corinne wondered.

Clive and Olivia stayed for a while. Corinne made a pot of coffee and Clive headed out the east section of the woods to see if Lucas was free.

Olivia sat and comforted Corinne who was getting distressed about her cousin. She was so very worried for her. The unknowns were great. But knowing she would have a child soon was an added worry. There was no time to waste.

"Olivia, what would you do in my situation?" Corinne added as they sat down with their cups.

"It would be difficult to ignore, but also difficult to chase after her. She tried to steal money from you last year." Olivia must have seen the pained look cross Corinne's face. She reached and patted her hand.

"I am not certain there is a wrong action. If you try to contact her she may be willing, in her state to accept help. If you let her lead her life and ignore this you wouldn't have to feel any guilt." Olivia said, her face grim. "She has made no attempt to reach out to her family."

Corinne nodded again and took a sip. Wondering suddenly if it was Trudie who had run off. Corinne couldn't really imagine that. It was hard to make the comparison to a baby. Megan's parents were still sending her letters every few months, beyond worried about their daughter.

"I have to talk to her. To at least let her know that her family still yearns to talk to her. Perhaps she needs help." Corinne sighed and took a few large gulps of coffee. She needed the boost.

"A lady in town hires out as a wet nurse. I was just visiting at my sister's home a few days ago. The job she had in town was coming to an end. The mother she was working for was unable to nurse. Mrs…" Olivia paused. "Mrs. Travis. She was my neighbor. She still had her milk as of last week."

It was an indelicate subject, but Corinne was grateful for the idea. She wondered how in the world she could manage a baby and a day of travel and the unknown.

"I will definitely have to talk it over with Lucas." Corinne felt overwhelmed again. Lucas had been pretty angry with Megan, and her attempt to take money from their bank account before she left town. He was a very calm-tempered man, but he had limits. He may just say the girl was on her own.

Lucas and Clive arrived just a minute later. Stopping outside the door to stomp the dirt from their boots.

"More excitement from Megan, I hear." Lucas said and grinned conspiratorially.

All said and done, once everything was discussed she was extremely impressed with how well Lucas was handling things.

They had all talked through the details calmly. Lucas agreed with Corinne that it was a hard choice. But knowing her family was so worried it seemed the right thing to do was try.

"We can take Corinne to town to speak to Mrs. Travis, to see if she is available." Clive offered.

Lucas nodded. "I can stay and listen in for Trudie. I can start to make a plan."

"Do you think we could leave in two days? Would that be enough time to get things settled?" Corinne wondered.

"That seems a fair scheme. If we can be certain that Violet would agree to watching over a new houseguest. It is a little unorthodox, but seems like a solid plan."

Corinne left a few minutes later, her thoughts scattered in a myriad of plans. Trying to make her worries settle but failing. She could never know just how this would all work out. She talked to her Lord as they rode to town.

❖❖❖

Mrs. Deborah Travis was a pleasant woman, Corinne thought. Corinne immediately found her pure Kentucky accent to be charming, reminding her of her childhood. She was tall and lean, with medium brown hair pulled back practically. Her clothing was neat and well-tended, but not fancy. She had a broad smile and warm eyes. She wasn't pretty, but she looked friendly and welcoming.

Olivia had come with Corinne and they were welcomed in immediately.

"Please call me Debbie." The woman said enthusiastically.

She was in her mid-thirties and was born and raised in Kentucky.

They sat in the simple parlor of the apartment room above the tailor. Next door to the lace shop.

Corinne got a brief introduction from Olivia but she felt nervous about asking deeper questions.

"I get by on wet nursing and making quilts. I have done housekeeping work before too." Debbie said. She offered them tea but Corinne thanked her and said no. She had consumed two cups of coffee in quick succession. She was going to float away on a nervous cloud.

"You like the work?" Corinne finally asked.

"Oh, yes ma'am." Debbie said.

It felt ridiculous to be called ma'am by her.

"Oh please, Corinne." Corinne felt this same kind of awkward when she had been interviewing Violet.

Olivia sighed and looked over to Corinne, spurring her to ask another question.

"We are in the need of leaving town for a few days. I wonder if you would be available to help feed my child while we are gone? She is almost 6 months old." Corinne smiled a lopsided smile. Hoping she wasn't making a mistake.

"It would be my pleasure. I do love babies." Debbie said with a warm grin.

"Did you lose a child?" Olivia asked.

"Yes, my son Stanley Jr. He was the first one to die in the Valley last year from the yellow fever." Debbie only frowned a moment. "He was a year old, but he had never been well. Doc Williams said that his lungs and heart had been born wrong. He had been sick nearly every day of his poor life. He never did speak." Debbie said, her eyes took on a sad look for a moment.

"In a way it was merciful. He had spent so much of his life suffering. He is my angel now." Debbie took out a pendant on a necklace chain. There was a soft brown curl behind the circle of glass.

"I am so sorry." Corinne said, feeling the woman's loss. Certainly she had read the name in the newspaper. She had mourned every loss with a certain amount of sadness. But to see her face now, knowing her child was beyond this world. It broke her heart.

"You don't mind caring for children?" Corinne asked through a thick voice.

"Not a bit. I was the oldest of ten siblings. I have been taking care of them since I can remember. I had a wicked fall from a barn loft when I was young. I was told I would probably never have children. Stanley, my husband didn't mind. Married me in spite of it. I took on the wet nurse job right after, when I heard through town gossip that a young mother was needing some help. I felt like it was God giving me a chance to mourn and heal while I bless someone else." Debbie shrugged. "My husband didn't handle the loss well. Actually, he never did settle well on being a father. He was gone on one of his trips in the mountains when our boy died."

Olivia sighed. "I cannot imagine."

"My Stanley is an independent sort. He only comes around when he feels like it. I think he is working in a lumber camp now, north of Sacramento. But he may have moved on by now. When I followed him west, I knew his wandering wouldn't stop. He is just that kind of man."

"My first husband was like that." Olivia added.

Corinne liked Debbie's spirit. She was a strong, no-nonsense woman.

"I am sorry for your troubles." Corinne said softly when there had been a long pause. "You have a strength that is somewhat miraculous."

"I trust in the good Lord to get me through. He made me a practical gal." Debbie reached over to shake Corinne's hand. "I would be happy to help you in any way I can."

227

The deal was struck and they talked over details. Debbie Travis would pack a few things and come the next day. She and Trudie would need to make an acquaintance.

"My housekeeper Violet will be there to help in any way. Trudie loves her like a second Mama." Corinne smiled and felt a weight lift as they chatted. Certainly God was working out the details so simply for her. Her daughter would be cared for and fed, and they could easily travel without any undue stress.

Everything had to get finished. Corinne spent that evening in a flurry of activity. She had a talk with her father, to just let him know the news and where she and Lucas were going.

Marie promise to check in on Trudie and everyone here. Making sure everything was running properly.

She gave Cooper a good big sister hug, and Lila and Abigail got kisses on their sweet cheeks.

John Harpole loaned them a cot for Debbie Travis, and also gave Corinne some sound advice, to help her through talking with Megan. He promised to be praying for them on this journey. Corinne was so thankful for the support.

Corinne was amazed at how much she got done as the hours flew by. A short visit with Angela, then her sister-in-law Chelsea. Both women agreed that Corinne was doing the right thing, even though it would be a challenge. Lucas spoke with Pastor Whittlan and his wife to keep them updated on the situation. Corinne felt like she would be leaving with the support of the whole Valley praying for them.

She gave Trudie a few extra hugs and kisses throughout the day. Corinne watched her daughter's face throughout the day. Loving every inch of this darling girl. Wishing that she didn't have to go, but knowing that it was the right thing to do.

"A few days away, and then I will be back darling girl." Corinne said to her sweet daughter.

Debbie Travis arrived that evening. They set up the cot for her in Dolly's room for the night, but knowing that she could just use Lucas and Corinne's room once they left.

All the little details were handled as the evening went by so very quickly.

Debbie and Trudie were getting along. A successful feeding made Corinne feel so much better about the situation and once Trudie went to sleep for the night they all gathered in the parlor to get to know each other better.

Debbie and Violet had such different personalities that it was quite a surprise to Corinne that they got along so well.

Debbie had a spunky sense of humor and everyone was laughing at her stories. Corinne and Debbie furthered their regard for each other with sharing stories about growing up in Kentucky.

Corinne had a fitful night of sleep, thinking through everything she wanted to say to her wayward cousin. Wondering what her responses would be. Had she seen Clive and run away again. The questions were endless in her mind.

Lucas and Corinne were up and dressed early. Violet had a hearty breakfast laid out in quick order.

"Ferry food is never as good as home cooked." Violet said. She gave a long hug to Corinne when she stood up from breakfast.

"You, dear friend, go and save the girl from herself. Do your best, but don't beat yourself up if the girl doesn't respond in the way you wish. We all can do our best, but we cannot force someone to use the good sense that God gave 'em." Violet kissed Corinne's cheek. Her blue eyes just communicating how much love and respect was there.

Going away, even for a short time made Corinne think about how much she truly loved her life. She appreciated every friend and loved one here.

Trudie was awake just as Lucas and Corinne were getting the last of their bags and plans settled. The two-seat buckboard was outside, the horses chomping at the bit to get going.

It was nearly summer and the morning was warm, the dew clinging to everything yet. The sun was barely over the mountains to the east while Corinne kissed her daughter one last time and handed her over to Debbie, who was smiling and cooing to Trudie.

Lucas ran a hand over his daughter's brown hair and gave her a kiss on her fingers that were reaching out to him.

"That's my girl." He smiled so warmly. Corinne felt that amazing stomach flip again, loving her husband even more.

Galina, Violet and Debbie waved from the front of the cabin. Debbie lifted Trudie's hand.

"Say Bye-bye to mama and papa!" Debbie said and kissed the girl's head.

229

Corinne tried not to get emotional. It was only for a few days. But she let a few tears slip down her cheeks on the ride to town. The horses clip-clopped their way to town. The ferry was waiting.

Chapter 20

Angela Greaves

Angela pulled her mind from the darkness of the dream and stared at the morning light that peeked through her window. Her window faced the west, but the soft glow was pleasant. She shook the fog out of her mind and stretched out, squealing a little as her arms reached above her head. Ted was gone from his spot next to her. She vaguely remembered his kiss a while back, and him murmuring something about the barn. She sat up and watched out the window a moment more. Seeing the branch of the tree outside swaying enthusiastically, Angela heard the wind gust. She stood and looked out the window to see the white clouds travel fast across the sky, they didn't look like rain clouds. She smiled and gathered her thoughts for the morning. Her brother was coming over for a lunch.

It had taken a while to fall asleep the night before, her thoughts a bit heavy, thinking about her brother and their reunion. She was proud of herself for giving him a second chance, but sometimes it still plagued her a bit. The memory of his rejection lingered on her mind. She had vowed to herself to forgive him.

She opened her bible to where she had a ribbon placed inside and read again, what she had read the night before. Colossians 3 verse 13.

Forbearing one another and forgiving one another, if any man have a quarrel against any: even as Christ forgave you, so also do ye.

It was so much harder than she could fully express, letting that old pain go. She had thought about Sean's tears, when he had made the long trip to see her, how much he blamed himself for leaving her. It ripped at her heart thinking about his pain. She had never blamed him for leaving the work orphanage. That place was a dark soulless place, full of misery and acute suffering.

Angela had lain in the dark long after she heard her husband's soft breathing of sleep. Thinking about his words, knowing that she had invited Sean over to visit. She had fallen into a fitful sleep. Her dreams of the work orphanage plagued her, the bitter cold in the winters, and the squalor. She remembered the lack of food and the dirty clothes. The boys had been cruel to Sean, she remembered seeing him, the scabs and bruises on his innocent face. She had rejoiced when she heard he was gone. Had been even happier when she had gotten a few letters over the years. She had attempted to escape herself a few times, unsuccessfully. She had gotten the strap across her back for each attempt at escape. Angela could still feel the sting of it. Angela tried to shake off the memories but failed and her eyes scanned over the verse again. Letting the words sink in.

I do not have generous thoughts for those people who ran the orphanage. But I had to forgive them. Why should I not also forgive Sean, who is plagued by guilt? Angela wondered to herself. *Those adults who treated us as slaves have not asked forgiveness, but I did have to invite forgiveness in. Because I knew in my heart to carry around that hatred just ate away at me. Now I need to let my anger go for Sean. He is my brother. In my heart, I love him dearly. I must let his rejection go. I do not even fully understand all that he has been through. I must let it go.*

Angela took a shaky breath. Willing herself to free her heart of its unforgiveness. It was not so hard as it was even a minute before. She felt a Peace fill her. Perhaps the final chapter of those horrible days could close.

Angela stretched fully, her leg aching from the long walk she had done the night before. That long ago bruise from her trip down into the ravine was aching again. She was always reminded when she had overdone things. She and Ted rode horses a few nights ago, which had started the aching again. She knew that she would have to probably not ride horses anymore. Every time she rode, in effort to chase her fear away from being near them, her leg would hurt for days. She sighed and thought of that beautiful saddle she had been given by Clive. It would certainly go to waste.

"Maybe I should give it back to him..." Angela said softly to the empty room. She grinned at herself and decided to get dressed and begin her day. She had slept later then she usually did. She had been so very tired from the late night. She checked the watch pin on her side table near the bed. It was past ten in the morning. She was surprised, she never slept that late.

She thought of Corinne, who had left early for Portland, saying a prayer that Megan would be convinced to contact her parents. Thinking of her own, wondering if the silly, selfish girl had any thought of how lucky she was to still have parents that were there for her.

Angela eased her way slowly into making herself a simple breakfast. She saw that Ted had closed the front windows from the blustery wind. The house was a little stuffy and she cracked a few of them open to let in the fresh air.

She walked around the kitchen letting each step work the stiffness out of her aching leg. She felt lighter after her time of thoughtful reflection on forgiveness. She was ready more now than she had ever been to have a nice visit with her brother. Hoping that her heart was healing from the long journey towards forgiveness. She hummed a song softly as she did a few chores. She nibbled on a piece of buttered toast and sipped some coffee.

She separated the cream from the morning's milking and set aside the cream to churn, she dumped out the cream from the day before and rinsed out the small jar and put some fresh cream in for the day's coffee. She set the rest of the milk and cream aside to take down to the springhouse that Ted and Warren had built the month before over Spring Creek, behind the Sparks cabin. She put the milk in a large jar and screwed the tin lid over the top. Edith volunteered to churn the butter half the time to share the workload. Angela grabbed up an empty box crate with handles and marched the cream and the milk down to the springhouse.

Angela pulled her hair back in a simple braid and carried the crate down the hill. Her leg was still stiff and she slowed her pace down. The wind was indeed gusty as it whipped the braid around the side of her head. A few tendrils were loosened and were waving in the wind and her eyes watered from the onslaught.

Edith was on her front porch with a heap of something in her lap. She waved with some kind of plant in her hands as her hair frantically slapped at her eyes and cheeks.

"I'm heading to the springhouse. I'll be right back." Angela announced and kept her slow pace moving forward. She knew she must look like a fool with her hair flying around her head in the wind.

She opened the creaky door to the dark springhouse, made of stone and a few log beams over the creek. She had to crawl on her hands and knees, and the room was pretty dark, to keep it cool during the summer months. There was an opening for another jar of milk, and the cream had a separate area. Edith had a fresh batch of butter in small jars and Angela took a few to bring back with her.

Her leg was aching fiercely when she crawled backwards through the short doorway. She let out a breath and shook out her skirts to shake off any grass or dirt that was loose.

She stood tall and felt her leg give a protest, a sharp pain shot down her leg. Angela took a few minutes and massaged, painfully, the achy limb. She was growing frustrated again at this injury that continued to plague her.

She finally walked up the creek bank and towards the Sparks cabin to sit for a minute with Edith.

"Ah, my sweet Angie." Edith called out as Angela got near.

Angela smiled and slowly limped her way up the two steps to the porch. She settled the crate with the butter jars down on the porch and sat on the stool next to Edith.

"Well, girl, you look like your leg is fussin' with ya again." Edith's brow furrowed slightly.

Angela waved her hand. "I went out walking last night, had a horseback ride a few days ago too. Just gets stiff when I do that too much." Angela tried to make light of it. She didn't want to complain.

"You need to let Ted take over bringing the jars to the springhouse." Edith said in a mothering tone.

Angela laughed and nodded in agreement. "I will... I will"

Edith grabbed a handful of dirty plants and shook them off over the edge of the porch, clumps of dirt flew down and hit the ground.

"Green onions..." Edith's eyebrows raised and she grinned. "Just smell 'em"

Edith dunked them in the pail of fresh water next to her and then handed her one.

Angela smelled the sweet scent of the small bulbous plant. It was delightful and gave Angela some ideas for a supper or two.

"Oh, that is just heavenly." Angela sighed and handed it back.

"I have some red potatoes that came up just grand, going to use up some of that sweet cream, and these onions, and maybe even some of that cheddar cheese from the grocers. Going to be a delightful baked meal." Edith shook off some more onions and then dunked them in their bath.

"That will be good. I'll want the recipe." Angela smiled, she was so happy to have Edith so nearby. This was the exact reason why they had built this cabin. This was just like family should be.

"I'll bring some up to your house when I bake it up. See iffen you and Ted like it."

Angela nodded and asked about the children.

"Oh, well, Heidi and Fiona are up at the greenhouse, helping Dolly out. Peter went off with Henry to fell some small dead trees to build a fence." Edith pointed with her head toward the northern part of the property. "Ted gave them a few good locations where he had seen some prime trees."

Angela nodded. That was one reason her and Ted had taken that horseback ride a few days before.

They visited a few more minutes and Edith placed a few dozen green onion bulbs in Angela's crate.

"You sure that crate isn't too much for ya?" Edith asked and looked to get up and take over.

"No, no, it is lighter than the cream and milk I carried here, that's for certain." Angela promised. "I'll go slow."

Edith sighed but nodded, knowing that Angela was stubborn.

Angela carried her wooden crate back up the hill to her back door. She was muttering under her breath about the pain and ache that was persistent. She needed to get off her leg for a bit.

She got an idea for an easy lunch and got the butter jars settled on the pantry shelf, and grabbed up a large jar of chicken broth that she had put up the week before. So happy that Edith taught her how to make a good tasty chicken broth for soups. She grabbed a cup full of rice and went to the kitchen. She pulled out a big pot and poured in the broth. Then stoked the fire in the wood stove. She chopped up a few of the green onions, and then wandered back into the pantry for a few stalks of celery Ted had gotten at the grocers. She chopped those up and scooped them into the water too.

She went to the back door and rang the small hand bell for Ted, who was probably in the barn. He knew that when she rang the bell in a short burst that she just needed something or it was mealtime. If she kept on ringing, then there was something urgent.

Angela sat and rested at the kitchen table, she rubbed her sore leg and tried to quiet her mind from the small amount of worry that was sneaking in. She was suddenly so very tired and she fought off the urge to lay down on the bed. She knew she would need to keep an eye on the lunch that was bubbling on the stove, but she was definitely weary.

Ted interrupted her thoughts when she heard the back door open. His head peeked around the corner of the doorway.

"Hello, wife." He said with his usual cheeriness.

"Hello, husband." She replied in her usual way. He took a few steps in and she could see that he was dirty from the hard work he was doing. She felt a momentary pang of guilt when she thought of all the work of boiling water and juggling heavy pots later to prepare a bath. She shook off the thought with a frown.

"I started a soup for lunch, but I think a chicken would make it that much better." Angela said wearily. She tried to smile and hide how she was feeling.

Ted nodded. "Our flock is growing, and we have a hen that hasn't been producing." Ted frowned pathetically, knowing she despised killing any of her chickens.

She appreciated that he understood. "I know just the one. The smallest white hen will do." She sighed and then added. "If you have time for it that is." Angela didn't want to come across as a bossy wife after all.

"I can use a break from the barn. I can get it cleaned up for you in two shakes." Ted smiled and gave her a wink.

Angela watched him leave and then stood back up to check her broth, she moved the pot to a cooler part of the stove so it would simmer as she waited.

Ted was back with a headless chicken with a majority of its feathers gone. She teased him as she picked off the few tiny feathers that he had missed.

She made quick work of butchering the chicken, removing all the bones and she had a hot pan with a little lard ready to sear the chicken already on the stove. A sprinkle of salt and pepper and she was pleased when the chicken sizzled as it hit the pan.

"It is getting mighty hot in here." Ted waved a hand in front of his face dramatically.

"Indeed it is, I might be forced to think about a summer kitchen one day. Just like Edith's." Angela smiled and lifted her eyebrows in Ted's direction.

"It is sad, as hot as it is outside that it is probably warmer in here." He agreed. "A summer kitchen may be added to my lengthy list of projects."

She leaned into Ted for a hug and then teased him for his wet shirt. She made a face. He got her to laugh when he pulled her closer for a sweaty kiss.

She pushed him away and giggled.

"You get back to work. I will get lunch ready and let you know when Sean arrives." She blew him a kiss and took two steps backwards to keep away from him. His eyes showed that he thought about playing chase but instead he nodded and gave her a wave.

The chicken was soon done and cut up and added to the soup. She tidied up and let herself rest in a chair for a few minutes as she waited. The wind gusts outside were fierce and she heard the rattle and creak of the house as it protested the onslaught.

Angela worried about her brother being safe on the road. She fretted for a few minutes and watched the windows for any sign of him. It wasn't even a minute later that she heard the thumping feet on her front porch and saw his shape coming through the windows and glass of her front door.

She stood up quickly and felt her leg tighten up and try to give way. She caught herself and sighed before she continued to walk.

She opened the door just as he knocked. Sean's smile was broad and his eyes were bright.

"Hello brother." Angela said wistfully. Feeling fully happy to see him, without any lingering doubt or dread. Her heart was relieved.

She welcomed him in and shut the door behind him quickly for the wind was trying to steal the door from her fingertips.

"Oh my, it sure is gusty." Angela said with a laugh.

"It was blowing me and my horse around the roadway." Sean shoved his hands through his unruly black hair. "Shipley, my horse, was more than mildly annoyed with me." He chuckled.

"Let me ring the bell out back and call in Ted, and we can eat. Sorry if it is so warm in here. I opened a window for a bit to let the heat out but the gusty wind knocked over too many things." Angela felt silly for all her talking but took a few slow steps toward the back room. She almost jumped out of her wits when she heard a loud creak and a snapping noise outside, a moment later the ground shook with a huge crash.

She ran to the back and Sean was instantly by her side as she pulled the back door open. The largest pine by the barn was down. She could instantly tell it hadn't hit the barn but she could not see if it had hit anything, or anyone. She felt Sean's hand on her shoulder, it was comforting and she was relieved by his presence.

Ted ran around the back of the barn and gave Angela a wave, to let her know he was fine. Her heart was drumming in her chest but seeing him safe was just the thing she needed to allow it to slow.

Ted ran up the hill to the back door, the dark blue shirt was billowing, the edges flapping.

"The goats have all escaped... and are running about... willy-nilly. The cows and horses... are now shut up in the barn." Ted was panting in between his words.

"Let's go find them then." Sean offered.

Angela followed them and Ted gave a look. "You can stay dear. I saw your leg was bugging you, I saw you walking toward the creak earlier." Ted said, his tone sounded final.

Angela felt herself bristle. "I can decide for myself, Mr. Greaves." She said with just as much firmness.

The wind whipped around Angela's face as she stubbornly walked in the opposite direction of the men. She would look over by the chicken coop to see if any of the goats went that way.

Her hair was waving in the wind again and the dark clouds rolled by in the sky. As she neared the chicken coop, the ground was soft from the rain the day before. Her black boot-heels sunk into the ground.

She slowed her pace and peeked through some of the bushes to see if there was any sign of movement. She passed the chicken coop. All of her precious darlings were snug inside the coop, avoiding the weather.

She walked around the edge of the fence, she had a windbreak for a while but once she was past the edge of the barn the gusts had free reign to handle her with its full force. Her leg stiffened again. She reached down and rubbed at it angrily.

She saw some movement as she neared the compost pile. A few scrubby bushes were next to the large pile of manure and leaves that were piled up next to the northern edge of the fence. A few branches and twigs were flying about and Angela squealed a bit when a flying leaf smacked her in the face. Her red hair was flying about her face but she saw from the corner of her eye some movement. She turned on her heel and saw Cookie, the goat, behind a bush. She smiled to the goat, took her hair with a free hand and tried to keep it in control.

"Cookie, you little rascal. You are coming with me." He was tannish-brown, with white flecks on his back and a devilish glint in his eye. He was a stubborn little cuss. She thought to herself as he edged away from her. He had gotten his name from stealing a cookie from Ted when he was smaller.

The smell of the manure was strong and Angela cringed as she stepped nearer to the pile to coax the goat from his free wandering state.

"Come here, little guy." She tried a different tactic. She could be sweet to draw him in. She smiled and blew some hair out of her mouth that was blown about despite her attempts to control it.

Cookie, obviously wise on the strategy of Angela's intentions, took a few steps further toward the manure pile and then jumped up in a playful leap when the wind gusted with a forceful wail.

Angela took a few faster steps toward him, she ignored her pain and reached out with both of her hands.

"You little brat..." She said and tried to ignore the pain that shot down her leg. The ground was uneven and she took her eyes off the goat and finally paid closer attention to her surroundings.

Cookie took that moment to make his escape. He took off with a dart.

Angela yelled out and took several fast steps, a protruding rock tripped her slightly. Her leg protested and locked up again. She corrected herself but her balance was thrown. She stepped into a hole a few feet from the dreaded manure pile, pain shot through her ankle as it twisted unnaturally and again threw out her hand as she tried to catch her fall. She was down.

She was laying on the ground crying, again. It seemed like a recurring nightmare, but here she was. Lying a few feet from a stinky manure pile, covered in muck and hurting in several places.

She called out a few times, but the gusty wind was stealing her words the moment they left her mouth. She tried to move her wrist and knew that somehow it was broken in some way. Her ankle was probably just as bad. The deep bruise that had never healed properly was screaming for attention as well.

Cookie was back, he was standing nearby, nibbling on a weed. He was not the best company, certainly, but at least she wasn't alone.

Angela wondered absently how long she was going to be here. She turned her head side to side, surveying the area, certain that a brown clod of a mysterious nature was only an inch away from her head. She tried to push herself up to a sitting position but gave up and cried a little more.

She cried herself out after a few more minutes. She watched cookie eat whatever struck his fancy and pondered Ted's words before she had stomped off to prove she wasn't a weakling.

If he says, 'I told you so' he can sleep this month with the chickens! She thought with a grimace. She tried to push herself up again. She was able to sit up, she pulled up a corner of her skirt to look at the ankle that was throbbing already. She could tell, even through her stockings that her ankle was discolored and swollen to at least double its normal size.

"Oh, Lord," She muttered aloud miserably. "Why does this keep happening to me?" The first time she knew had not been her fault. But this time, a sneaking sensation was creeping through her. She had brought this upon herself. She pushed the thought away and focused a bit more energy so she could let out a yell for help with all of her lungs strength. It felt pitiful and shallow sounding in the wail and whistle of the wind, but it was the best she could do.

"At least it is in the light of day." Angela muttered to herself. She held the hurt wrist protectively in front of herself. Her hair flew uncontrolled around her face as she waited for someone to find her. She was certain that she was perhaps the most wretched creature alive.

<hr>

Lucas & Corinne Grant

Lucas and Corinne settled their bags into the Portland Grand Hotel by noon. The place was indeed as beautiful as Olivia had said. The architecture was modern and elegant. Pillars and fancy carved woodwork in the grand hall, and each room was delightful.

Lucas talked with the man at the front desk and got directions to the boarding house where Megan was staying. They both agreed to get the business started with Megan as soon as possible.

Corinne reminded herself to use the name Rosie Green when they reached the boarding house. Her nerves were on edge as they walked up to the building.

Lucas held her hand and squeezed it every minute or so. She was so glad to have him with her.

"I'm certain she is still here." Lucas said as they reached the front porch. He looked her in the eyes. "Just a gut feeling, but I have an inkling that she was oblivious to Clive and Olivia."

Corinne smiled to keep her spirits up, but she was starting to dread the confrontation.

"Let's go forward. We cannot know until we see her if this was worthwhile or not." Corinne said. Wishing it was over already.

The proprietor was kind when they walked inside. The place was well kept and Corinne gave praise.

"My cousin, Rosie Green, is staying here. We have come to see her." Corinne said, her voice extra polite.

The woman brightened up. "Oh I am so glad she will have family with her. She is up with the doctor now."

Corinne's eyes grew wide.

"Doctor?" She asked.

"Oh yes, she gave birth to a baby boy yesterday morning."

Megan Capron

Megan heard the soft knock on the door. Doctor McKinnon held a hand up for her to stay where she was. She gladly obliged. She was still so very tired and achy everywhere.

Her birth had been truly the most painful and horrific thing she had ever experienced. It was all night with the doctor and his wife. His wife was kind and spoke soothing words as Megan struggled and did what she needed to do for hour after hour.

She was hoping to never experience that again.

The doctor had announced that she had a son. She had looked at his red face for a long while as the doctor did what he had to do for her... Something about an afterbirth. She wondered a few times through that long night if she should have had her mother with her. She felt a strange pity for every woman in the history of the world.

Once they had a child, why would they ever do that again? Megan wondered.

Her baby boy was quiet, beyond the first little cry when the doctor had patted his bottom.

The doctor's wife had helped her through the first attempt at nursing. It was painful and awkward. Megan didn't enjoy the process and grew extremely angry when pushed to do it again and again.

The doctor's wife was patient for most of the day. Allowing Megan to catch up on her sleep. Megan was grumpy and irritable, she knew it, but she had seen a few exasperated looks pass between the doctor and wife when he had come back to check on her.

241

They had both been very surprised that she had not arranged for anyone to help her with delivery or the next few days.

Megan felt a bit foolish when they questioned her. She hadn't prepared well for this whole thing. She had nothing for the baby, not even a blanket. They looked at her like she had sprouted horns a few times.

She had tried again to feed the boy. It had been a failure with tears and a few muttered curses by Megan. *Why would anyone do this?* She wondered.

When the knock came, she had just been given a lecture by the doctor again about making some kind of preparations for the child. Telling her all the things that she would need. Nappies, blankets, and a safe place for the baby to sleep. She grumbled under her breath and endured the lecture. *Why was it everyone's job to lecture her?*

She was glad for the reprieve. The doctor's wife was rocking the baby in the rocking chair borrowed from the parlor of the boarding house rooms down below.

Megan figured the door was the proprietor's wife, Sadie Landers, pestering her again. She just knew that she would have to part with some of her hard-earned savings to get things for this baby. She closed her eyes to try to get back to sleep.

"Hello Megan." Her cousin's voice brought her out of her sleepy haze.

"Oh grand..." She said as she saw Lucas and Corinne, standing there beside her bed.

She was discovered.

<hr/>

Angela Greaves

Angela Fahey had lain in that dirty heap for a lot longer than she expected. It was probably less than an hour, but it felt like an eternity. Her brother spotted her first.

"I will go get Ted. Hold tight Angela." Sean said and Angela felt a rush of relief.

It was a long minute waiting for her husband. Her tears had dried on her cheeks from the gusty wind but the pain made fresh tears form every few moments. What could she say to her husband? She was at a loss. She was positive now that this incident was her own fault. Why had she not listened to all the warnings she had received today?

242

Ted came around the corner, his curly hair blowing crazily in the wind, his forehead creased in concern for her. She began to cry in earnest just seeing her husband, feeling relieved and ashamed in the same instant.

"I'm here Angel. I'm here." He was at her side. Touching her cheek with such gentleness.

"I have manure... in my... hair." Angela said and hiccupped from her hard crying.

Ted frowned and kissed her. "Where are you hurt?"

Pointed with her good hand to her right wrist, and then down to her ankle.

"I should have listened to you..." Angela sobbed again. Closing her eyes to his gaze. Not wanting to see his disappointment.

She could hear Ted talking to Sean over the howl of the wind. The rain started in earnest, the large drops splattering on her forehead with loud slaps.

They lifted her and carried her around the edge of the fence. She was hurting but she had tried so hard to stop her tears. She felt so pathetic and disgusting.

"Don't put me on the bed like this!" She said with a hoarse and desperate tone. "The brown blanket..." She turned her head as they walked through the back door.

Ted and Sean leaned her gently against the wall in a sitting position. She held her hurt wrist against herself protectively.

Ted looked around for a frantic second, turning in circles before he found the brown wool blanket on the trunk behind the large washing tub. He ran ahead through the hallway and to their bedroom. She was thankful that he understood her simple request. She didn't want the mud and manure to get on the quilt or her bedding. She thought ahead of how she would ever clean that if it had gotten soiled. How was she going to do anything? Her emotions were in a frenzy and she had to force the tears back again. Wishing she could just surrender to it and sob again. She had only a shred of pride left at this point. She would not look like a weepy child any more.

It took a few minutes of painful shuffling and moving but Ted and Sean got her settled on the bed.

Ted sent Sean on an errand and Angela was laying more comfortably at least.

Ted touched her cheek again.

"I am here for you. My Angel." Ted said, still using the pet name he always had for her. It was overwhelming to see the love he had in those blue eyes. She was a mess, covered in mud and manure, and he could still love her.

"I am so sorry..." Angela croaked out. She had yelled so much in the wind that her throat was raw.

He shushed her and kissed her. Something broke inside her heart... in a way that she never understood before. Ted truly did love her. Not just attraction, or companionship... but a love that would last a lifetime.

———◆•❂•◆———◆•❂•◆———

Corinne Grant

Matthew 10:26
...for there is nothing covered, that shall not be revealed; and hid, that shall not be known.

Corinne saw the look that passed over Megan's face. She was not pleased. Corinne glanced around the room, the two windows were open, a nice breeze was fluttering the lace curtains. A dark wood table had an elegant pitcher and basin. A woman was watching them from a rocking chair across the room.

Megan was under a pretty floral quilt; a dark wood headboard was tall behind her. Megan's cheeks were a bit red. Her blue eyes flashed angrily when Corinne had said hello.

"Congratulations on the birth of a son." Corinne said and cast a glance to the woman who was rocking the baby.

"Thank you." Megan said. Her tone was flat. She smirked a little. Not a happy smile but one filled with her venom.

Corinne knew this wasn't going to go smoothly.

"We are here to help." Corinne said to Megan, and loud enough for the woman to hear.

"Oh goodness, thank you. I need to get back home. My own children have probably torn the house down looking for supper. My husband is a great doctor." She said conversationally. "But his cooking skills are not what I would say as edible. I've been here since yesterday."

The woman stood and brought the child to Corinne.

"Such a quiet little fellow." She smiled up to Corinne and handed over the tiny bundle. "You may keep the blanket dear." The woman looked to Megan and gave her a tired grin. It didn't seem very friendly between the two.

The woman looked to Corinne. "She will need some guidance through the nursing. She is not handling it well. She also needs a lot of things for the child." The woman gave Corinne a look that was serious and pursed her lips. It was obvious by that brief exchange that Megan was being difficult.

The woman left with the doctor and the room remained quiet for a minute. Corinne held the sleeping child against her chest. He was so fresh and new. A gift.

"Well, you got rid of them, thank goodness." Megan uttered.

Corinne looked to Megan and was pushing herself to seated position. She winced.

"Are you in pain?" Corinne asked, she wanted to make sure she was well. Even if she had a wicked tone to her voice.

"Yes, but my doctor said that is normal after delivery." Megan said flatly. She gave Corinne and Lucas a long look. "So, how was I discovered?"

Corinne sighed. "Clive and Olivia went on their honeymoon to the Portland Grand Hotel a few days ago."

Megan nodded and sighed. "May I have some water?" She looked up to Lucas and pointed to the pitcher on the counter across the room.

"No problem." Lucas said and went to fetch her some.

"He is the quiet one today." Megan chuckled to herself.

"Well this *is* a bit awkward." Corinne felt defensive. She wasn't enjoying this at all, and they hadn't gotten to the hard conversations yet.

Lucas handed her a mug of water. Corinne patted the head of the sleeping boy.

"Does he have a name?" Corinne asked, to stick to a lighter subject.

"No," Megan said.

Corinne felt that frustration rise within her.

"I can send Lucas out to get a few things. Do you have a list?" Corinne asked. Just trying to get somewhere with this woman.

"That would be kind." Megan said. "The doctor was just lecturing me on this very subject. I was not very well prepared." Megan said, and the smirk came over her face again.

"Well, even when we try to be prepared there is always a surprise or two with a newborn in the house." Corinne said to sooth the troubled waters. It did help and Megan's face relaxed.

"I don't have a list, but the doctor mentioned nappies and blankets. He would probably need a few clothing articles." Megan said. "I was saving my money, to travel back east. I didn't think of these things."

"If you talk to the proprietor you could probably find a good store for a few of those things. If you go to the fancy goods store, Clive's grandson is there. They may have some baby clothes." Corinne suggested.

"I will get going then." He kissed Corinne's cheek and gave a smile and nod to Megan.

"That is very kind of you both." Megan said. "You are nicer than I expected you to be."

Corinne smiled a little. Glad for the humbler tone from her cousin.

The door closed and Corinne handed the boy to Megan.

"Let me pull the chair over." Corinne said. Megan seemed a bit awkward with the boy but Corinne remembered her first few days with Trudie. She was so nervous that she would harm her in some way.

The chair moved with a few squeaks and shuffling noises.

She pulled the chair beside the bed. She took the boy again.

"You can lay back. You have some resting to do." Corinne said and rocked a little. The boy never woke. "He is a good little sleeper."

Megan's face was neutral, she snuggled back under the covers.

"I see your ring. Is the father somewhere traveling?" Corinne asked.

Megan sighed and pulled the hand up to look at the ring in question.

"I bought the ring myself." She said. She was daring Corinne to say something by the way one eyebrow was raised.

"The father is not in the picture." Megan said and sighed. "He actually doesn't even know about it. I am probably never going to tell him."

Megan spilled the whole story. The boy that stole her money after she ran away from Corinne and Lucas's home. The married man who had hired her on as the singer and made her his mistress.

Corinne was shocked but tried to keep her face calm, not showing anything. She was listening until Megan shared the whole thing.

"I know what you must be thinking. Mrs. Perfect." Megan huffed.

Corinne shifted the boy a little before she replied.

"No one is perfect, Megan." Corinne stated. She was going to think over her words carefully.

"It is strange to be called Megan again. I have been Rosie Green for a little too long." Megan said, her mood calmer.

Corinne wondered at the young woman in front of her, her moods as changing as the wind. How would she manage this new responsibility?

"When Clive came to my house, just two days ago, I was concerned for your welfare. I want to be a help to you." Corinne said. Megan was watching her expectantly. "Knowing you were expecting... I wanted to make sure you were safe. Knowing how much..." Corinne stopped, not certain how Megan would respond to her mentioning Megan's parents.

"What?" Megan prodded when the pause grew longer.

"Well... I definitely don't want to upset you. I get a letter from your parents every month or so. They are still looking for you." Corinne said gently.

Megan nodded. "I thought of my mother yesterday. Wishing she was here with me." Megan said.

Corinne wanted to celebrate. Megan was showing the smallest of signs that she was willing to listen.

"Childbirth is hard work." Corinne laughed.

"Yes, I never knew. How my mother did that twice is beyond my reckoning." Megan laughed. She held a hand to her belly. "Ugh, it hurts to laugh." Which made her smile and grimace at the same time.

"That will fade in a few days, hopefully." Corinne said.

"Do you have a child now?" Megan asked.

Corinne smiled broadly. "Yes, a daughter, Trudie." Corinne felt the rush of warmth, just thinking of her. "She is almost six months old."

Megan smiled a little, she was looking tired.

"You should rest." Corinne suggested again. "If he needs fed I will wake you. I'll be right here."

Megan nodded. She closed her eyes for a moment then opened them again. "I am glad for you cousin. I know that you really wanted to be a mother." Megan looked so young at that moment. Her blue eyes sleepy and her hair in simple braids.

"Thank you dear. You get some sleep." Corinne said. Remembering why she had come. This girl was still so young, she was going to need some help through this whole situation.

Chapter 21

Portland, Oregon
Corinne Grant

"Megan," Corinne nudged, somewhat in disbelief, that Megan could sleep through the crying so near her.

The boy was clearly hungry, squirming with an angry red face.

Megan finally stirred, her face awash in the same kind of annoyance that her son exhibited.

"What is it?" Megan said with an annoyed tone.

"It is feeding time." Corinne said loud enough to be heard over the consistent cry of the newborn.

Megan sighed and sat up.

Corinne was extremely uncomfortable. Having missed a feeding with Trudie, her body was responding to the baby's cries.

Megan accepted her child and gave a shocked look to Corinne. Corinne looked down and the front of her blouse. It was soaked.

"What in the heavens happened?" Megan said, ignoring her child.

"It is a response to the crying. My body is producing milk." Corinne explained simply. Megan would find out on her own the realities of having a child.

"I don't do this well. You feed him then." She shoved the baby forward towards Corinne.

Corinne pulled her head back. "No! You have to learn this Megan. It is for your child."

"There it is... I was waiting for it." Megan sat back, her child still wailing. She had yelled and the fervor of her son's cries grew in intensity. She settled her son in her lap and unbuttoned the front of her nightgown.

"Waiting for what?" Corinne asked as Megan attempted to do her mothering duty. The child stopped crying and tried to suckle.

"I was waiting for your lectures and judgement." Megan said in a quieter tone but her glare was just as angry as before.

Corinne sighed, wondering when this young woman was going to realize how childish she sounded.

"It is not judgement or a lecture when people are trying to help you learn a vital skill. Do you want to be a good mother and provide

249

food for your child?" Corinne asked after a minute of watching the mother and child struggle forward.

Megan glared at her again, saying nothing. She winced loudly a few times and pulled the boy away from her body.

"This is hopeless." She said right before the child began his pitiful crying again.

Corinne tried to give her instructions, to relax and let the process happen. After two more attempts Megan growled in frustration.

"To answer your question," Megan huffed and pushed the baby down her lap. "No, I do not want to feed my child."

Corinne felt her heart break, saw the pitiful child, so upset. She knew it was a mistake, a tragic decision in a moment of weakness. She took the child and fed him. Hot tears escaped her eyes as she saw the victorious smile cross Megan's face. The girl had won this battle. Her son and Corinne had lost this round.

The boy was ravenous and drank his full. Megan buttoned up and watched. Corinne kept her words to a minimum for a few minutes. Letting her anger at her cousin calm while she prayed for the words to say.

Once she trusted herself to speak, she gave simple instructions.

"See how I hold him...." Corinne asked calmly then continued to teach Megan, whether she was listening or not. "It is nothing to fear. Your body will grow used to it." Megan said nothing while Corinne instructed, she just nodded with her usual annoyance.

After the feeding was done, the boy fell into a blissful sleep. Megan wordlessly crawled back under the covers and did the same.

Corinne waited in the quiet, trying to solve the dilemma until she heard Lucas at the door. She grabbed her light shawl, to cover the wet spots on her blouse and walked to the door, tucking the shawl gently under the baby. Since there was no place to lay the child down safely, she carried the sleeping boy, so small and precious to the door to open it.

Lucas and another man was there.

"We come bearing gifts." Lucas had a large linen sack over his shoulder and a young broad shouldered man helped carry in a small cradle.

They quietly entered and set up everything. Corinne settled the boy into the cradle and wrapped him snugly. His face was so peaceful after the trying few hours she had spent with him.

She followed Lucas and the young man out into the hall with the door cracked so she could hear the child.

"This is Gabriel Quackenbush." Lucas introduced with a low voice.

Corinne skipped the formality of shaking hands and gave the man an unexpected hug. He chuckled softly.

"Your grandfather is a dear friend and Angela speaks of you and Amber often, she has read snippets of your letters in our visits." She said and grinned from ear to ear.

"I have heard some praise of your name from letter reading as well." The young man said.

Corinne looked over his features, seeing the resemblance of Clive, JQ and even Millie Quackenbush around the eyes.

"Gabe here had a few clothes to share, and the cradle was not in use." Lucas said.

"Oh, thank you so much." Corinne said softly. Wishing she could say more. Knowing anything she said in the moment could be harsh in her judgement of her ill-prepared cousin. Wisdom dictated in the back of her mind to stay quiet.

"I'll get back to the store, but I want you both to come for a family meal before you return to Oregon City. I would love to hear all the news and catch up."

Lucas and Corinne promised to do that very thing. Corinne felt a rush of warmth, knowing how much Angela would love to hear about Amber and Gabe's family.

Lucas and Corinne remained in the hallway and Corinne filled Lucas in on all that Megan had shared about how she had ended up back in Oregon, who the father was, and the unfortunate choice Corinne had made to feed the child when Megan refused.

"If she hadn't just given birth…" Lucas muttered, leaving the rest of the sentence unsaid. He was a patient man, but Megan got under his skin so easily.

Corinne soothed him with a hand on his arm, smiling as she felt the same way. Megan still needed a parent's discipline and guidance.

They talked over a few plans and thoughts as they leaned against the wall in the boarding house hallway. Trying to think of a way that this situation could benefit everyone involved.

They decided together on a course of action. They would wait for Megan to rest completely before they spoke to her.

After a few hours and a lot of fussing from Edith, the doctor, her brother Sean and her husband, Angela was clean and settled into her bed.

Her wrist had been declared fractured or broken by Doc Williams, her ankle was sprained. Both extremities were extremely swollen and unhappy. Angela was proud that she had not yelled out when he examined her, bending her hand this way and that. She gasped a few times, but she kept the scream inside.

The ankle had been the worst somehow. He judged by the bruising that she would be unable to put any weight on it for quite some time.

"You really did a thorough job." Doc Williams had said after her examination.

Angela felt hot tears as she told him how the whole incident had been her fault. She was ashamed and was ready to confess. Ted had reached for her good hand while she spoke.

"Every time, Doctor, as you told me to be careful with overexerting myself I always felt that twinge of stubbornness creep in." Angela took a deep breath and sought for any ability within herself to calm down. She couldn't stop but she wanted to continue... She needed to confess. "What is wrong with me Doctor?"

Doc Williams was a patient man, he sat in the chair next to the bed and let her cry. She felt so pathetic, vulnerable and foolish.

"What you are so upset about is called human frailty, my dear Mrs. Greaves. There is no human upon earth that is born without a flaw, excepting for our Lord Jesus." He waited for her to wipe her face with a handkerchief that Ted had handed to her. "You have survived some harsh things, especially for a woman that is still so young. The stubborn streak you have has helped you get through some hard times. That strength can always turn to a weakness for any person; man, woman or child alike. The greatest gift that God offers us is Wisdom. Lean into God and he will guide you into all truth. We each are on a journey to grow each day into the person God has made us to be."

Angela nodded, thankful that his words were not harsh.

252

"I am praying for you. Do not chastise yourself too long over this. But lean into God's word and let God show you, in His gentle way how to live." Doc William's eyes were warm, like a father lovingly guiding his own child. Angela took a few deep breaths and then thanked him.

"I will leave you in the gentle hands of Edith Sparks to get you cleaned up and then we will set that wrist of yours. I am sorry to say that crutches are out of the question for you. I will go into town and get an invalid chair for you to get around with. I'll bring it 'round tomorrow when I come back to check in on you."

Edith was indeed gentle and with a lot of shuffling and a bit of a mess, Angela was thoroughly cleaned head to toe. Angela was glad to have Edith Sparks nearby. It felt like a return to a former time, when Edith had cared for her so well back at Fort Kearney. Now Angela could admit that her injuries were mild in comparison to back then, but reliving the experience of being a bit helpless and hurt was not something she wanted to repeat.

Angela was dressed in a light nightgown and settled back into her bed, the messy brown blanket removed and the cool sheets were clean and soft on her skin.

Doc Williams had quickly wrapped her wrist tightly and got her into a sling. She had to have her ankle elevated with a pillow under it.

He gave instructions to Edith and Ted to give her Willow bark tea and fetch some ice from the ice cellar in town to handle the swelling and pain as much as they could for a few days.

Angela prayed and rested after the Doctor left. She was relieved for the quiet to reflect. Sean and Ted visited for a time in the other room. She said goodbyes to Sean a few hours later, wondering what his thoughts were about the strange day but she had to let it go.

She had some healing to do, not only in her body, but her heart as well.

Corinne Grant

Megan had listened to the speech that Lucas and Corinne had given her. It was not harsh or judgmental in Corinne's mind, but she knew that Megan was particularly sensitive to any kind of instructions.

Corinne had explained that if she was unwilling to try to nurse her child he could die. It was simple and blunt but Megan took it well. She had even shed a tear or two.

"I can try again." She said finally, her voice was low and humble. Corinne wondered if the rest had done her the most good. She was a little more reasonable than before.

The next feeding session had started with more than a few frustrated tears, a growl, and an exasperated utterance or two, but it had succeeded. The child was fed, and Megan had accepted her defeat. This was *her* responsibility.

The child fell asleep after Megan successfully burped him and Corinne helped with a nappy change thanks to the pile of cloth nappies that Lucas had bought in town. Megan struggled with the clumsy pins and stabbed her finger twice before the job was done, but Corinne could almost see a sense of pride in Megan's eyes when she had accomplished the task.

"It is good that the diaper was full." Corinne stated and placed the dirty laundry in a bucket, also purchased by the practical Lucas, by the front door.

Megan grimaced at the smell but Corinne explained how Megan would need to watch her son's health and be certain his little body was absorbing the food and how even his elimination was so very important.

"Things to look forward to." Megan made another face and shook her head. "All he does now is sleep and eat."

Lucas chuckled and Corinne gave him a knowing smile. He had said something similar when Trudie was only a few days old. 'I want to see her with her eyes open, she sleeps and eats.' He had said.

"That will fade soon enough. He is only a newborn." Lucas said quietly, he took charge and wrapped up the boy in the blanket, having had a few months practice, and settled the boy into the rocker.

Corinne sent Lucas back to the hotel for a few hours and helped Megan get cleaned up and they took care of a few necessities. Megan was moving slow, but Corinne could tell that the birth, though a challenge, had not done much damage to Megan's young body. She would be sore for a few days.

Megan was clean and settled back into her bed.

"I need to get changed out of my soiled dress. It would only be about an hour and I could be right back to help you." Corinne said.

She was uncomfortable in her dress, the cloth was tacky and chafed against her skin from the earlier mishap.

"If you speak to Sadie Landers downstairs she can send up the maid who has been hired to help me sometimes. I'm sure she wouldn't mind sitting with me. I am finally feeling hungry again. Could you ask her to bring up a plate of food?" Megan asked practically. "You can take some time to eat and visit with Lucas." Megan smiled a little. Corinne was relieved to see it.

Corinne was hungry herself and was relieved at the thought of getting a chance to rest.

Angela Greaves

Ted smiled down to Angela, his face handsome and caring as he checked on her. She was in pain, but if she stayed very still it was manageable, mostly.

"You get the goats rounded up?" Angela asked softly.

"Warren and Earl got the rest of them back to the barn. We will have to get the fence repaired double quick." Ted said. "You don't need to worry about that." He gave her a once over. Noticing that she had pushed the blankets down, away from her.

"You warm enough?" He asked.

"It is the end of May... it is stifling in here. Once the wind settles down I want the window open... if possible." She added the 'if possible' because she felt herself sounding snappish. *Pain never brings out the best in anyone.* Angela was certain.

Thunder boomed outside and they both glanced to the windows. The dark clouds were angry and the wind was blowing the rain on a slant. Angela frowned.

"I am glad you aren't still out there, lying in the mud." Ted said and gave her a loving look.

"You said what I was just thinking." Angela said, feeling relieved to be safe and sound.

"This bring up bad memories?" Ted asked.

Angela nodded. She was thoughtful for a moment. "But I know this was my fault." Her throat was tightening from emotion again. "I hope you forgive me." Her voice sounded high and almost squeaky.

Ted grabbed her good hand. "You are too hard on yourself." He touched her fingers with his, soothing and calming her. But she had things to say so she tried not to be distracted.

"I want to be certain that I am learning something from all this. I..." She sighed, feeling like the hard pit in her tummy was ready to come out. She would just have to say what was on her heart to feel any kind of peace. "I feel like I have been a little girl playing a game. I got a handsome, sweet husband, a new house with all the money I got from my inheritance. I was in a happy little world where everything gets to be my way, all the time." She admitted. "You deserve more than that. You deserve a wife that will start acting like a woman, not a child..." She winced as she shifted and her ankle sent a stabbing, throbbing pain through her.

Ted settled and soothed her. "I don't feel that way."

Angela held up her good hand. She needed to finish her speech.

"I have talked with God a lot lately, not just about this incident but also the way I handled Sean's reunion." Angela took in a deep breath and sighed. "I missed out on a lot, my life was hard for a long time. Perhaps I expect things to be perfect and easy now that my situation has changed. The doctor said something earlier that is settling inside me. He talked about my strength. How I needed it to survive." She looked up to Ted's eyes. Eyes that have always seen the good in her, from the very first days of their acquaintance. "I need to remember that strength. I am not a child anymore, I cannot pretend away the injuries I had from the ravine, and I cannot pretend away my life, wanting everything to be the way it should be. I need to learn to accept what is, and stop being so stubborn when something challenges my idyllic world." She had said it. She felt better. She hoped beyond all hope that he understood her.

Ted took a moment. Staring into her eyes.

"Well, I can say from my experience, that you are on a good path. We all struggle with those things, Angie. I have enjoyed this first year of our marriage. Getting to love you and this house and everything we have. It has been more than enjoyable. We have created something beautiful here. But I do understand when God gives us that little nudge, when the Holy Spirit is asking a bit more of us then just coasting along." Ted took her hand firmly, no more playing in his eyes. "Today I saw you hurting and broken again. My first thought was that it was my fault, I allowed this to happen to my Angel. It was not a good feeling."

"I want to give you permission Ted, because perhaps I never have before. I need to know when my stubbornness is out of line." She was hurting again but she wanted to communicate this so desperately. "I need you to help me be that strong woman again. I know we are both young. But..." Angela sighed, she had lost her train of thought in the throbbing pain in both her wrist and her ankle.

"I can see that maybe we have been trying to be sweet so much that we don't say the hard things." Ted offered.

Angela closed her eyes in relief and violently nodded. He understood. She needed to grow up, and she needed his help to do that.

She felt tears escape her eyes and she looked up to her husband. Ted held her hand. He bowed his head.

"Dear Heavenly Father, we come to you. We know you give Wisdom, as a free gift, without judgement or a harsh reprimand. I thank you for my wife, that she is safe. I pray for her healing. Lord I ask you to help me to be the man she needs. Lord help her to be the woman I need. Help us to always look to You for guidance. As we grow old together Lord, you teach us to speak truth to each other, to love each other the way You would have us do. Lord, please never allow us to take each other for granted, but to lift each other up in the hard times, to find peace in the life we have, and lean on each other. We thank you for your Grace and Mercy..." Ted squeezed her hand.

Angela felt the moment heavily on her heart, so very thankful for this man in front of her.

"Dear Lord," She spoke, feeling the hot tears roll down her cheeks. "Thank you for helping me find Ted. Please Lord, help me to be a good wife to him. I need your guidance so much Lord. I ask your forgiveness for my stubbornness. Teach me to be a woman, to chase away all of my foolish desires. Help me to continue to forgive those that have hurt me in the past. Please remind me every day to come to your word, to remember my limitations and teach me to be content when I just don't understand everything that is happening around me. I now know that You have a plan for me. Help me to follow the path to becoming a strong woman of faith." She felt a peace fill her, so overwhelming and comforting. Like an all-encompassing embrace around her.

She was out of words. Ted held her hand and they sat in the silence. Both supporting each other without speaking until Ted whispered. "Amen..."

Angela spoke it as well. The rain pounded outside, and the wind wailed around their house on the hill. But her heart was at peace.

Chapter 22

Galina Varushkin

Galina walked back to the Grant's home with a light step, glad that Angela was in good spirits after the visit. Galina had been so worried when she had heard about the accident but she was glad that Angela was handling the pain better than expected. She would be healing for a long while.

Galina felt sympathy course through her, having been on her own healing journey so recently. Her ribs still were tender and Galina had to be careful to take care of herself, but she felt whole again.

Galina had visited with Edith, once Angela was tired and in need of some rest, Edith and Heidi were tidying up Angela's kitchen. Edith was so warm and friendly and Galina watched how patient she was with Heidi, who was a few years younger than her.

Galina felt an urge to do something foolish... well foolish was not the exact perfect word. She was looking for a change. She stopped mid-step and looked up. Wondering if this excited feeling was her own heart, or something else guiding her feet, but she turned around to walk back up the hill. She needed to find Ted Greaves.

That evening she walked back to the Grant cabin, she felt an enormous sense of relief. She had spoken to Ted first, and waited for Angela to awaken from her nap. They had agreed to her plan, and she felt certain that she was doing the right thing.

She walked into the cabin, seeing Violet fuss over Trudie. Debbie Travis gave Galina a friendly nod. In a few ways, Debbie reminded her of her own mother. She couldn't exactly say all the reasons, for they were hidden in her heart, with no clear definition, but something in her strength, and the sad eyes but the ever-present smile.

"How is your friend?" Debbie asked. She was settled at the dining table. Galina assumed they had just eaten dinner.

"She has a broken wrist and her ankle is the size of a summer melon." Galina grimaced.

Violet frowned. "Oh no..."

Galina filled them in on Angela's condition, but shared how well Angela was handling it.

"She said she struggled at first. But that God was getting her through it." Galina said, knowing how much she had prayed through the hardest days of her own struggles.

"Well, I will be going to visit tomorrow, Lord willing." Violet said, her face still showing concern over her friend.

"Is Reynaldo coming tonight to take you out on a walk again?" Galina asked, giving Violet a sly smile.

"Yes, I do believe so." Violet gave her a glare then laughed.

"Good, Angela is sleeping again. I am glad she is getting some rest." Galina sat at the table.

"I was going to wait but I cannot hold in my news." Galina settled her hands on the table, they were shaking from her jitters.

"I am going to move in with Angela and Ted." Galina announced.

Violet stood and gave Galina a wide-eyed stare.

"I want to learn how to be a housekeeper. I know I can do the work, I cared for my brothers this past year. Edith has promised to help me, and I was hoping you would continue to teach me recipes and things. While Angela is healing I can lift a burden for her, and Edith will not have to do so much once I am able to handle everything on my own." Galina looked up to Violet, hoping to see acceptance.

Violet smiled. "You have a generous heart Galina. You will do a good job." She had some misty tears in her eyes. Was it pride? Galina wondered.

"Ah, girl, that is a grand plan." Debbie said and placed her hands together. Her and Debbie had spent the last few evenings talking. Debbie was a good listener and now knew Galina's story. "Having a skill makes a woman able to survive through the hard times."

Both Violet and Debbie shared a look, both having a certain understanding of things not always working the way they expected.

"You think that Corinne will be vexed, if I just move without waiting for them to come home first?" Galina asked, the last thing she wanted to do was to offend Corinne and Lucas, they had given her so much.

"I think they would understand, Corinne especially. Corinne would turn the world inside out to help a friend in need." Violet said to comfort her.

Galina nodded. "As soon as I hear that they have come back I will run right back over. I want them to know how much I truly love them for all they have done for me."

Debbie chuckled. "If I was Corinne I would know it already. But I want to say, young woman..." Debbie gave Galina a serious look. Making her heart jump, wondering if something harsh was about to be said. "You are brave and strong, and even at a young age you know how to pick yourself back up and pull yourself together." Debbie smiled broadly in that way that was so sincere and it sunk into Galina's bones.

Galina smiled and fought off tears. She couldn't speak, but she knew that Debbie knew how much those words meant.

Galina packed up her few things, and walked next door, where Edith was waiting for her. She was settled in a room upstairs, across the hallway from Dolly's bedroom, when she was staying there. She remembered the last time she was in that room it was empty, and Angela and Galina had hung up laundry to dry on a wet and rainy day.

So much had changed since then. Now the room had a nice bed with a brass headboard. A few small floral paintings were on the wall, a small wood stove, a tall dresser with brass knobs to pull them open. Little by little, Angela and Ted had made a beautiful home.

Galina wondered if she would be able to add to the joy of this home, the way Violet did for Corinne and Lucas. Even Debbie Travis, in the few days that Galina had known her, was now considered a friend. Galina sat on the bed, and bowed her head. Praying to God that she would be a blessing in this house.

She went downstairs to see if Angela was still awake, her new job would begin now. She would care for people; it would give her life meaning.

❖❖❖

Corinne Grant

The next two days were busy, living out a strange new reality of long talks with Megan, getting through feedings and nappy changes and frustrations.

Lucas was there, every step of the way to give Corinne and Megan the support they needed, but allowing Corinne to take the lead.

Megan had fought like a tiger at the suggestion that she send a telegram to her parents.

"I believe that is none of your concern." Megan had fumed.

261

It had been exhausting for Corinne, the mental part more than the workload.

Megan was moving better the second day, and was getting more spunk in her arguments on the third day.

Corinne was nearly ready to throw in the towel when Megan began a conversation on the third evening.

Her son was sleeping again, after a bath and feeding. Lucas had pulled up a chair and they had been sitting quietly for a while.

"I am willing to consider the telegram to my parents." Megan said with a frown. "It was not something I ever was willing to do... but I may be needing their help. Now that I have a child."

Corinne nodded. She wasn't sure what else she could say to Megan that hadn't already been said. Lucas spoke for her.

"I think that is wise." He offered simply. There was no tone or harshness. Corinne was relieved. She said an inward prayer. Thanking God for Lucas.

"I would like to think on it for a day or so." Megan said. She looked to Corinne, solemnly. Perhaps the most serious she had looked on this entire adventure.

"That is reasonable." Corinne said. She was missing her home. She was wondering how much longer she would have to stay here in Portland.

"I think you should both enjoy your evening together. I can take care of my son tonight. If you could send up the maid with a plate again. I have been taking advantage of both of you too much the last few days. I need to learn to be alone with my son." She let out a deep breath.

Corinne and Lucas both thanked her, Lucas took the bucket of dirty nappies downstairs for the proprietor, Sadie Landers, to add to the laundry. Corinne gave Megan some praise for all of her hard work.

"You have learned so very much, Megan, I know it is a vast change for you, as it was for me when Trudie was still a few days old. You will grow accustomed to it and he will grow faster than you can ever imagine." She smiled and placed a hand on Megan's.

"Thank you cousin. You both enjoy your evening off. Perhaps you can hear the orchestra." She smiled. "You will miss out on my singing though. I am sad for that." She grinned a little.

"Perhaps tomorrow when we come you could sing a song for me." Corinne smiled broadly. Seeing a more playful side to her cousin was good for her heart.

"I could do that." Megan offered and gave Corinne's hand a squeeze.

She left feeling a bit lighter, her prayer for Megan's future was easier to pray, seeing that small glimpse of Megan's cooperation.

Corinne and Lucas paid a visit to the fancy goods store and Gabe and Amber were more than thrilled to invite them to dinner. Their home above the store was elegant and the company charming. Their son and daughter were entertaining and made Corinne miss her daughter more and more with each passing hour.

Lucas and Gabe got along well and they talked well past dark in the welcoming home of new friends. Corinne and Lucas walked back to the Grand Hotel in high spirits after being refreshed with good company.

The next morning Corinne woke up early, dressed in a simple dark blue skirt and white blouse, her last clean one. She had had too many incidents and would need to use the hotel laundry services.

She packed a linen bag full of her soiled clothes, Lucas helped and gathered up a few of his to add to the pile and carried them and placed them outside the door as they were instructed by the hotel.

It was nearly 8 a.m. by the time, they were finished with breakfast in the hotel dining room.

They walked across the main street, the morning hustle and bustle was starting as wagons and buggies passed through the muddy streets. The wind and rain of the days before were gone and the sun was shining brightly.

Lucas held Corinne's hand as they passed a few shops. Corinne admired a small dresser in front of a woodworking shop. The early morning ferry whistled shrilly as they walked.

"I am hoping to be on that ferry soon." Corinne said wistfully.

"Our thoughts are aligned on that. I miss our home, and our daughter." Lucas smiled at her and then gave her a wink to make her laugh.

Corinne swung her arm a little, enjoying his company and the morning sunshine.

The boarding house was tucked behind a few trees and the leaves gave the front porch some pleasant shade. An older man was sitting on the front porch reading a newspaper and gave them both a friendly nod as they walked up the steps.

Corinne thought Portland was just as charming as her own small town. It was good to see a new place sometimes. Gives you a glimpse of the world and makes you appreciate your home even more.

They walked in and Sadie Landers was cleaning up some plates at the large dining table.

She glanced around at them, her normal smile dropped.

"I thought you were gone this mornin'." She said and settled the dirty dishes back onto the table with a clatter of silverware.

"Not at all. Just here to be with my cousin." Corinne said with a smile.

"Your cousin Rosie left this morning. She had all her trunks delivered down to the docks." Sadie Landers said. "She was in a rush, I was not even able to kiss the sweet boy's head before she was out the door."

Corinne's eyes were wide and her heart was thumping irritably in her chest.

What in the world was that girl up to now? She wanted to throttle the woman.

Corinne and Lucas followed Sadie up the stairs to Megan's room.

There was no preparing her for what they found in the room. Megan's bed was in disarray, nappies and blankets piled haphazardly around the room. A woman's nightgown thrown on the floor.

It wasn't until the baby's cry was heard that everyone finally gasped at once.

"Oh merciful Lord!" Corinne exclaimed as she ran across the room. The boy was lying there, in his cradle, his mouth open in a frustrated cry. Corinne scooped him up, knowing he was probably soiled and hungry.

Oh dear Lord... Corinne prayed without any more words. She held the boy close and looked to Lucas.

"Where is she?" Corinne asked, but knowing the answer. The morning ferry had just left. The whistle had sounded, announcing it just a few minutes ago.

"I could have sworn she had her son." The woman spoke. Her eyes glistened with tears. She sat on the unmade bed. Her face looked haunted and sad.

She reached behind her. She pulled out a piece of paper. She took a glance and handed it to Lucas.

Corinne sat in the rocker, dumb-founded that she could be experiencing another betrayal by her cousin... again.

She looked to Lucas, trying to find any words.

Lucas coughed to clear his throat, his forehead creased.

Dear Cousin Corinne,

I am sorry I deceived you. I have tried to behave myself these past few days, and do what you told me to do. But I cannot continue on with the facade of being the woman you expect me to be. I am too young and talented to be tied down to a life of feedings and babies. Perhaps that is a fine life for you but I will not allow it to continue.

I am giving you full guardianship of my son. You can decide to do whatever you like with him. He certainly is safe in your and Lucas's care. If my parents want him, or you find him a safe home that is all I can ask of you.

I am taking my hard earned savings and going far from here. Please do not search for me or seek me out in the future. Please tell my parents the same.

I am a different person than all of you.

I am off to see the world. I hope you can respect my decision.

Please thank the Hotel for treating me so well, and Mrs. Landers for her excellent service.

Megan Capron

(Rosie Green)

Lucas finished and set the letter down on the bed.

"What will we do?" Corinne asked. Her heart was broken. This boy was just left here. *How could anyone do that?*

Lucas walked to Corinne and knelt down next to her, stared into her eyes.

"We love him." Lucas said and placed a hand on his tiny head. "That is what we do."

———◆••◆———◆••◆———

It had taken all day to get everything settled. The letter was taken down to the courthouse and Lucas spent most of the day fetching people who knew Megan, alias Rosie Green, and her handwriting, acknowledged by her boss at the hotel, and Mrs. Landers, because Sadie Landers had seen Megan just that morning with a bundle, acting as if she had a child with her. The doctor and his wife were very convincing as well, describing Rosie, aka Megan, as an unwilling and negligent mother. All the history of Corinne and Lucas's experience were explained to the judge in his office. It was rather informal compared to courts back east.

Baby Boy Capron was officially given into the guardianship of Lucas and Corinne Grant. Corinne held the boy, watching his face as he slept. She could never imagine being capable of leaving him behind. Lucas was handed a paper declaring them the legal guardians, and handed them back the letter that Megan had written.

"Her parents may wish to see this with their own eyes." The judge, a wise sturdy man in his fifty's. "I am glad you were here for the lad."

Lucas had shaken his hand, for Corinne he gave her a smile and that warm look of concern.

Suddenly Corinne was so very tired, an inner sadness that just overwhelmed her. She wanted to push all these negative thoughts away. Her anger growing for her cousin's actions was like a weight on her shoulders.

Corinne and Lucas promised the judge that the child would be cared for and Megan's grandparents would be notified of the birth and allowed to take custody if they wished it.

Corinne bathed and cared for the child, calmed him with a feeding, and packed up the few belongings while he napped in his cradle. By evening everything was taken care of, Lucas had moved their things, gathered the clean laundry, and checked out of the hotel and they stayed at the boarding house one night.

Corinne held the boy to her chest as Lucas held her arm and they walked up the gangplank to the morning ferry the next day.

The world had changed in such a short time. She was not certain how everything would work, but she was sad and heart-broken for this little boy, who may never know his own mother.

A few hours later, they arrived back in Oregon City. She had no idea what they would say to everyone here but her mind and heart were tangled in emotions as they found a wagon ride home.

Chapter 23

Grant Cabin

The Grant cabin was full to the brim.

Once Corinne and Lucas arrived, there was a flurry of questions and activity.

Violet and Debbie instantly latched on to the little boy, taking turns to kiss on his sweet face.

Corinne and Lucas, both exhausted from the mental stress of the last few days were open with them about what had happened.

"I have no idea what to say to everyone else though." Corinne exclaimed. "I know just showing up with a newborn will not go unnoticed." Lucas had taken her hand.

Trudie was cuddled into mama's lap and content to have her parents back.

"I feel a bit lost." Corinne said. She was feeling emotional again.

The little boy let out a wail.

Debbie held up a hand.

"I can feed him if you wish." She offered.

Lucas looked to Corinne and without a word passed between them, he turned back to Debbie. "Can you stay?"

Debbie nodded, it was as simple as that.

"I'll help with the children while you do your work." Debbie said as she held the boy close.

Corinne smiled and then burst into tears. So relieved and worn out and sad over everything that had happened.

Lucas comforted his wife and let Debbie go sit in Trudie's room for privacy.

Once Corinne had cried herself out Lucas took Trudie into his lap for some daughter time.

"We can handle all this, can't we?" She asked.

"With God, all things are possible." He smiled a silly smile at his daughter. They were rewarded with a chuckle out of Trudie.

That made Corinne smile again. It was a much-needed comfort.

"We are going to need a bigger cabin." Lucas said practically, with a bit of laughter behind his eyes.

"We are not building a brand new home!" Corinne said seriously, knowing how much Lucas loved to plan things.

"How about we add a nice front porch, and a few more rooms that way. He pointed to the south wall." Lucas smiled at her and tried to bat his eyelashes.

Corinne just laughed. "I could see that happening."

"I will order a big piece of glass for a lovely big window. I was thinking to make a new parlor too. Ours is too small." Lucas offered. He was bouncing Trudie on his knee.

Corinne knew that Lucas was already getting grand ideas. Once things settled down, he would have his papers out and begin drawing out a design.

Corrine sat there for a moment quietly, in a half prayer about her fast growing family when a thought came to her.

"Do we name him? Or wait to contact my Uncle?" Corinne felt that pang of sadness. The boy needed a name, certainly.

"We should name him." Trudie wanted down so he set her at his feet. She was happy to play with his bootlaces.

Corinne was quiet for a minute. Nothing was coming to mind.

"I had a thought yesterday, while waiting for the judge to sign the papers." Lucas picked Trudie back up, who was a bit fickle about whether she wanted to be cuddled or roam free. "I had a friend at Yale, a quiet and thoughtful fellow. His name was Caleb. Just a random memory, but I thought it was something. Our boy is sweet tempered and quiet so far." Lucas shrugged.

"I like how you said 'our boy.'" Corinne said.

Lucas let out a heavy sigh. "He is ours for now. We will have to trust God with the rest of it."

"We should call him Caleb." She said it and it felt peaceful.

There were many changes to cope with but to have a name, was a relief. While Debbie Travis and Corinne were fussing over Caleb and Trudie, Violet was getting started on preparations for supper.

Lucas took a walk to talk with the Harpole's next door, filling them in on the news. Everyone so far had agreed to keep the story to themselves, but Corinne and Lucas would have to decide soon how they wanted the news to spread. Because it was not a secret that could be kept for long.

Corinne had a quiet moment, as everyone else in her busy house was scattered around while she held Caleb. Absorbing every feature and feeling the soft down on the top of his head.

"Lord, please bless this child. You, above all are Caleb's heavenly father. Give us wisdom to move forward. Please give me the strength to love him, and if I do not get to keep him Lord, give me the strength to let him go." Corinne let a few more tears slip down her cheeks that night. But she was resigned to know that God was with them all.

The next day dawned, Corinne had worked out a plan with Debbie. Corinne was feeding Trudie, and Debbie was taking Caleb. At one point in the night, they were both in the parlor, one lantern casting a glow over them as the two babies were fed. Corinne and Debbie shared a bond quickly. The still and quiet felt sacred and the friendship and companionship was started.

Debbie went to town at first light to gather her things. She would get out of her rented room and live full time with the Grants. It seemed meant to be.

The news in the valley had spread that Corinne was home from Portland and the visitors started arriving.

Galina had come first thing after breakfast and they had a good long talk. Corinne was pleased to let Galina go with her blessing. Galina was on a path to find her purpose, and though her heart stung for a few moments, knowing she would miss her. She knew that everyone had to follow the plan that God had for them.

Clive and Olivia were the second visitors, eager to find out what had happened in Portland. Shocked to see a new child there.

"Well, dear, I heard in town that someone saw you with a baby. I thought nothing of it." Olivia declared and shook her head. "Ya know, I have too much to do in my day to watch every single person that passes by. How do any of these people accomplish anything?"

Clive and Corinne chuckled.

They hadn't stayed long, since they could see that Corinne and Lucas had their hands full with a lot of new challenges.

"I'll bring you a crib tomorrow. I'm sure that Amos Dreys has some in his shop downtown." Clive offered.

Lucas pulled out his billfold to give Clive money.

"Nah..." Clive said with a familiar shake of his head. "This one is a gift to God. Caleb deserves all the love we all can give him."

Lucas gave Clive a meaningful embrace. Corinne could see that her husband had been touched by Clive's gesture. She had been so focused on her own confusion and emotions that she hadn't given too much thought of her husband. She told herself to make a remedy to that, and promised herself to find a minute, sometime that day to talk with him.

Marie arrived near to lunchtime, with a jar of berry preserves and a full bag of newborn clothes.

"I need to kiss a few babies!" She said and her smile was all dimples and joy.

Corinne laughed and accepted the gifts with much gratitude.

Debbie handed over the newborn, and Marie was in ecstasy over every inch of him.

"Some of those items will be as he grows, but a few should fit him now." She smiled and cooed. "Oh, he opened his eyes." She gushed. "I think they are blue."

Corinne sat and went through all the small treasures that Marie had given her.

"Well his mother has blue eyes. They may just stay." Corinne said, she was still trying to forgive Megan for the betrayal, but she had to acknowledge that Megan was his mother, even if she hadn't wanted the responsibility.

Marie gave the little one back to Debbie after a few minutes and then scooped up Trudie for more cuddles.

Marie and Corinne chatted with Violet and Debbie joining in when they had a chance.

Caleb was still so young that he slept a good portion of the day. Trudie was more of a challenge, and her hands reached for everything. She wanted to touch and taste the world it seemed.

"I am so glad you have Debbie to help now." Marie offered when Debbie had gone to check on Caleb again.

Corinne agreed. "All the way home I wondered how everything would work. I even pondered closing up my lab. But, we have the crop of lavender growing, it seemed a waste to let the plants not be used. I was talking to God the whole day while we settled things in Portland. God has found a way. I know better to trust Him. None of this was a shock to him."

Marie laughed. "I have had some days like that myself, wondering and worrying. When God had a plan the whole time."

Corinne was so thankful for Marie, a sweet and generous heart.

271

"Today I kept having this feeling sneak up on me... What if we hadn't shown up in Portland? What if I hadn't been there?" Corinne put a hand to her heart. "Caleb may have not survived. Would she have left him in that room, alone if no one was coming?" The thought had revisited her in her dreams too. The fear that the boy would have starved.

"Well, I wondered that a bit myself. Perhaps it is human nature to wonder about the what ifs... but I am thankful today for God sending us all out. To save the lost children that he puts in our path." Marie sniffled and dabbed with a lace handkerchief at her glistening eyes.

Corinne knew how much they loved their adopted child Lila. She couldn't imagine life now without having her as a younger sister. Whether blood or not, love covers the space between them.

The evening was spent learning new patterns and routines. Debbie settled into her room. Happy to have a job with a good family.

Corinne was pleased that they all got along so well. She finally got some alone time after the sun went down to talk things out with Lucas. He was generally quiet about his feelings, but she was pleased when he shared some deeper thoughts about Caleb, and how they had obtained him.

"I think my biggest fear now, is how much we will love him." He said. They were cuddled together in the parlor. She was leaned against his chest and enjoying some closeness.

"I am afraid that I will have to let him go. How silly is that?" She shook her head. "We have only had him such a short time. But the thought of my Aunt and Uncle swooping in just makes me want to cry."

They talked for a time, letting the day settle over them. Corinne finally let out a huge yawn and after Lucas teased her, they headed for bed. Early morning feedings were waiting, and Lucas was watching out for his wife.

Angela Greaves

Angela was seated in her invalid chair; it was nearly identical to the one she had used when she had been living at Fort Kearney a few years ago. She had come to accept it. Grateful that she had a way to get around a little bit. She was still very uncomfortable and in pain. But she told people often. "I've had worse."

She watched Galina work, seeing Edith Sparks teach her, like she had taught Angela, the simple tips and ways to get things done. Galina looked happy.

It had been a challenge to allow the girl to come and work for her. Her past had been as 'the help'. But Galina had been so persistent, and Ted had been sincere in his arguments for it.

"You know that Edith has her own home. She would gladly come every day, but this way, Galina gets to learn a trade. You get plenty of time to heal, and slowly get back to your former self. Having someone help with the harder tasks will be a Godsend." Ted had been right of course.

Her friend Corinne had the perfect example of a happy home with the help from Violet.

Corinne came by earlier, bringing Trudie, and telling her all about baby Caleb.

The valley would be buzzing with news certainly.

Angela felt a little foolish. She had let the afternoon fly by without sharing her news but she thought to hold on to it for just a few more days. She still had to tell Ted after all.

The doctor and Edith had been chatting, and Edith had a suspicion.

Angela hadn't believed the doctor at first, but once she had thought it through, and realized in all the time since Sean had arrived, she had not once had her monthly courses. He had just come that morning, so Angela had only a few hours to think on the change of her circumstances.

It seemed that the valley was going to be full of children. Suddenly an invalid chair did not quite matter so much, and the pain in her wrist was a little less. Her ankle was pretty mean and swollen, but she had a pleasant thing to think on.

She suddenly could not wait for Ted to come inside for supper. She bit her lip and let the feeling rush over her. So filled with love and hope.

Edith gave her a look from across the kitchen. Angela grinned, because she couldn't hold it in. Edith smiled and gave her a wink. It was only going to be a secret between them for just a little while more.

Ted shook the whole table a few hours later when he jumped out of his seat and let out a whoop.

Angela had laughed, and Galina looked nearly ready to flee.

He had kissed Angela and then whooped again.

Galina had finally figured it out that Ted was excited and not enraged.

"I'm gonna be a papa." He kissed the tip of Angela's nose. She had no other words but she did start to cry. Just so very happy to see him so overjoyed. He knelt down beside her chair.

Ted kissed her again. Angela was starting to feel embarrassed when she realized that Galina had excused herself and was trotting up the stairs with a plate in her hand.

"You scared Galina away." Angela laughed. Ted wiped at her tears.

He ignored her and kissed her again. "You are gonna be a mama."

Angela nodded happily.

So much heartache and joy in such a short amount of time. It may have seemed too much to handle.

Somehow, Angela knew that God would show them how to get by, day by day, miracle my miracle.

———◆◦◆◦◆—— ——◆◦◆◦◆———

Dolly Bouchard

Dolly wore her new moccasins and the ground was soft beneath her feet, the moss was thick and the bed of last year's leaves made her steps soft. The sound of the leaves crunching was hard to avoid but she had learned as a child to step lightly. She felt every rock and tree root beneath her. It was very different from walking in shoes from the stores now. They were stiff and inflexible, but in many ways warmer in the winter months. In the warmer weather, she much preferred making her own shoes again.

Outside the forest the sun shone brightly, the breeze was fine. Inside the dense woods near the mountain bluffs the air was thick. The canopy overhead was well grown with dark green treetops. The sound of the breeze was barely heard in the stillness. A dragonfly buzzed by, charming Dolly and causing her to smile wistfully.

Dolly had been practicing her shot with her bow and she knew she needed to test herself with living prey to prove to herself that she was still able to hunt. She knew a few families that would benefit greatly with a meal or two. It was a part of her, her childhood and now in her adulthood, to bless those that were in need was part of life.

Her mind flowed as she made her way through the great woods. She felt alive and still within herself. She thought of the verse she had read that morning at the breakfast table at Chelsea's house.

Psalm 41 verse 1. Blessed is he that considereth the poor: the Lord will deliver him in time of trouble.

She felt a bit silly but when she thought of the verse again. *'Blessed is **she** that considereth the poor...'*

She heard the smallest of noises, a chittering of a small creature, perhaps a chipmunk or a squirrel. She stopped walking and let her breathing fall shallow and silent.

She stood still, her eyes capturing the details around. The large mushroom growing sideways from the trunk of the tree near her. She knew from a glance it was poisonous to eat. She looked up to the closest branch and saw a small black and white finch, he skittered forward a few steps and peeped out a call then shook his feathers out, then took flight with amazing speed. He swooped and dipped away from Dolly with a few more peeps.

She saw from the corner of her eye a wild turkey, she moved her head slowly. She heard it clucking softly. She watched its head bob and take a few steps, a few smaller heads peaked from around the tree. It was a mother with her young. Dolly let her bow stay on her back and watched the progress of the mother and chicks, the little ones following their mother. There were three young turkeys. Dolly couldn't help but smile at the site. She would not hunt the turkey today, though it would make a grand meal for a hungry family. Instead, she will let this mother raise her young.

Dolly heard no other sounds so she went forward and walked toward the creek that she knew was nearby. She watched the brush as she moved, she pulled out her bow to be ready if she scared out anything.

She stepped gingerly and heard the trickle of the small creek. Her eyes were sharp as she settled herself. The cover of small plants rustled the tiniest bit near the water. She saw a rock near her foot and reached for it, she placed it on the top of her foot, she readied her bow with an arrow.

She got her breathing slow and her arrow notched then she kicked the small stone forward and two birds burst out of the brush, feathers flying and furiously flapping. Her movements were smooth, in an instant her arrow flew, and she watched one bird fall. The other flew away.

Dolly took a few steps to retrieve her fallen bird. The feathers were a blue gray; a red spot was near the head. It was definitely a male, perhaps a grouse or pheasant, she wasn't certain. It was a clean shot and the bird was dead. She was pleased. She plopped the bird in her leather pouch on her back and continued along the creek bed. She wanted a full pouch if possible.

A few hours later the warmth of the woods was growing thicker. She drank from her canteen and refilled it in the creek. She was feeling satisfied with five birds in her pouch. She had nibbled on a leftover roll from breakfast, she had put it in her pocket to snack on.

She stood and walked back toward the way she had come, she hoped for one more bird or even bigger game on her trip back. It was always a good feeling to know that her hunting skills were as sharp as ever.

She walked along the creek bed, still keeping her steps soft, when she saw movement ahead. A young buck was nearby, nibbling on a berry bush. The berries were too green for Dolly to pick but the deer didn't seem to mind them.

The buck had four points, only a few years old. He looked healthy and Dolly pulled out her bow, trying to make no sound. Bucks were extremely skittish and will bound away if any noise was made. She considered the size of the deer. It wasn't a large buck, so she certainly could handle carrying it out of the woods. But it would be a challenge. She weighed the pros and cons for the kill as she watched the buck eat. The amount of meat was the greatest determination and she let the arrow fly a moment later. It went down within a second.

She heard a whistle and whipped her head around.

"That was a great shot!" The voice was familiar but she saw nothing. Dolly turned and notched another arrow, uncertain if she was safe.

Sean Fahey waved and she finally saw him some ways off. She was surprised she hadn't heard him. Her first thought had been that white people usually tramped loudly through the woods, scaring off every creature for a mile. She instantly felt chagrinned for her thoughts though. She knew Clive and many men had learned the skill of being quiet with their steps. She felt foolish and put her bow down. She smiled softly to Sean as he moved toward her. He was dressed in dark browns with mud on his cheeks.

"I was going to march up the bluff to do some hunting tonight. Clive said he saw a few rams up there yesterday. A few elk were around as well." Sean smiled broadly.

"You look ready for a good hunt." Dolly said with her tone calmed. She felt an inner tension around Sean sometimes. He got under her skin. Perhaps she compared him a little too much with her friend Reggie, who had left last year after trying to court her, then changing his mind.

Dolly settled her bow on her back and walked to her kill. Sean whistled again.

"I saw your shot, it was a beautiful smooth kill. You have built a fine bow." Sean praised. She could not help but enjoy his words.

"I spent much of the spring practicing with it. My arms had to grow stronger to be able to pull it back." Dolly said. She knelt to the ground and Sean knelt with her. They flipped the buck and positioned him for cleaning.

"If you like I could clean it for you." Sean offered.

Dolly gave him a look that silenced him for a moment. He laughed a second later.

"You are quite a woman, I do forget myself. I know that you can handle just about anything here in the woods." Sean laughed again. The sound was pleasant and Dolly relaxed her glare and smiled softly as she began her work.

"If you wish to help then you watch for bears or mountain lions. My arrows are not as strong against those creatures here. Your gun would be better." Dolly said simply.

She had sharpened her blade that morning with a stone and she made smooth cuts to the animal. She pulled out the unnecessary innards and laid them aside.

Sean pulled out the arrow and gave it a good once over. "You do fine work." He smiled at her again.

Her hands were covered in blood, she was sweating and her hair was sticking to the sweat on her forehead, and yet, now she blushed over this man's words and the soft gaze.

She thought again of Reggie, how he had looked at her that way before. The appreciation and respect was shining through Sean's eyes. Dolly resumed her work, calling herself every kind of fool in two languages. Sean was not the kind of man that would stay for long. Perhaps only men that wander were attracted to her.

She lifted the buck to test its weight. It was going to be a long walk.

"Let me help you get to the road." Sean said and stood firm when she glared again at him. "Don't get so agitated. I know you are capable. But I do remember some chivalry from my upbringing. It is a mile to get back to the road. I saw your mount tied alongside. Let me do this for you and I will feel better."

Dolly pressed her lips together to think.

Sean handed the arrow he had retrieved from the buck. She accepted and nodded.

"As long as you know that I could carry the burden myself." She said and placed the arrow in the quiver on her back.

"I am certain Dolly, there is nothing you cannot do." Sean said. Her name on his lips made her stomach turn and she looked away. She helped Sean to get the buck on his shoulders and she walked with him. They weaved around the heavy brush and obstacles and found the road in an hour.

Her mount, Clover, was waiting, nibbling on green grass. Dolly gave Clover a pat on her nose.

Sean placed the old blanket that Dolly had left behind in a pack and tied the buck behind the saddle expertly. Dolly saw that Sean's clothes were covered in blood.

"Oh, you cannot hunt in those clothes. You will draw every bear within two miles." Dolly exclaimed in earnest.

"My house is just there. I can clean up and change. I may just stay in tonight anyhow. I was avoiding repairing a section of fence, my conscience is weighing heavily on me. I am not nearly as motivated to do repairs as I am to get back into the woods." Sean smiled sheepishly. "But seeing you hunt with your bow was quite invigorating, I can do mundane repairs with a lighter heart."

Dolly tilted her head and grinned at his silliness. "You are like me then, more alive in the woods?" She asked.

He nodded slowly and his smile faded to a quieter look, his eyes were locked in on hers. The moment stood between them heavy and silent. He was trying to tell her something but her brain was slow and she wasn't certain what his intense look was about.

"Thank you for your chivalry." Dolly said finally.

He nodded. "You are most welcome... Dolly." His voice was low. She grinned foolishly and looked away.

"I will get going. You have a pleasant day... evening." Dolly stumbled over her words.

Sean took her bow, arrows and pouch of game birds as she mounted Clover. He handed them up to her. He seemed amused by something and was smirking as he untied Clover. He handed the reins to her.

"You have a nice day...evening too." He smiled again as Dolly felt her cheeks blush. She was nearly a mile down the road before the English word came to her. Sean was 'flirting'. That was the word.

She rode slowly, letting the idea settle into her fluttering stomach. She thought of Reggie, his face was fading from her mind, but those feelings were harder to let go. She had received a few letters from him. He was happy where he was. She wondered if there was any kind of disloyalty within her heart if she allowed herself to think of Sean now.

Dolly felt that feeling again though, the doubt about Sean, how he had treated his own sister in the past. Would he ever do that again? Could she trust him that he had truly grown roots here in Oregon? She rode the long way home wondering if she had crossed that invisible barrier already in her heart, letting his eyes and praising words in to soften her resolve. She needed to pray and find some peace, she mused. Until then she had good work to do and friends to feed.

Chapter 24

Corinne Grant

It had taken two weeks but Corinne finally welcomed Arnold Capron into her home. Her heart was a tangled mess again, full of worry and heartache. She wasn't certain she had slept a wink the night before.

The mirror above her dresser had shown the dark circles under her eyes.

Her Uncle's dark traveling suit was a little rumpled and he had a look of the travel weary on his brow.

Lucas invited him in. Violet and Debbie took Trudie into the parlor, Corinne held Caleb. Wishing she knew how this day would end.

"Let me see the little tyke." Arnold had said. Corinne took the boy over. His dark blue eyes were open and seeing the world more now than the first few days he had been with them. His small pink lips were smacking against his fisted hand. The most interesting thing in the world to him, unless it was feeding time.

Arnold smiled wearily at the boy. "He has the look of her."

Lucas offered him a place at the table and he took a seat. He gave Corinne a nod to say he had seen enough for now.

"Thank you for sending the telegram. It must have cost a pretty penny to send such a long one." He huffed out a large sigh. Corinne thought his eyes looked sad.

"It was no trouble." Lucas offered him coffee, but he declined.

"Could I see the letter she left behind?" He asked.

Lucas had been prepared for that and had the letter on the table, waiting for that very moment.

Arnold Capron read through the letter several times, it seemed to Corinne. His frown deepened and his hand worried the edge of his chin.

"Well, that is that." He sighed again. He closed his eyes and shook his head.

It was interesting to Corinne, watching the play of emotions on his face. She was so very numb when Lucas had read the letter the first time. It was odd getting to experience the shock and pain of it through Megan's father's eyes.

"We have all the paperwork necessary to do whatever you wish." Lucas said, once Arnold seemed ready to listen.

He nodded and glanced at the guardianship papers. He frowned again.

"My wife and I discussed this as much as she could handle it. I'm afraid all of my daughter's drama have affected her very deeply. She has barely left her room since the day we received your telegram.

Corinne could not imagine how she was feeling.

Corinne felt at a loss to say anything to comfort him. She said the only thing she could think of.

"He is a good boy..." She said, trying to keep the conversation going. "We named him Caleb, but if you wish..."

"No need for another name, Caleb is a good solid name." He interrupted then smiled in apology. She could tell he felt uncomfortable.

"We need to know what you and your wife would like to do going forward." Lucas finally said.

Corinne felt her heart drop. Here it was. The truth of Caleb's fate was going to be decided now. She could not let her own wishes cloud the moment. She would have to accept whatever Arnold decided.

"Well, that is a hard thing to say aloud." Arnold grasped ahold of his chin again. "My wife and I are not certain we should take on the child." He said.

Corinne felt her heart begin to beat again. Perhaps she wasn't going to lose the boy. Perhaps, she could continue to love him.

"Are you certain?" Lucas asked.

"I want to be certain of course, that you and my niece are willing to raise the child." Arnold said, he looked up hopefully.

Corinne kept silent. Allowing her uncle and Lucas to talk. She was afraid that she might just burst into hysterical talking and make everything worse.

"We are willing. But I want to be certain that is what you both want. It would be even more difficult in the long term to fall even more in love with the child, only to let him go." Lucas had said it perfectly. Everything she feared, but in a way, a man would understand.

"I would never want to do that to either of you." Arnold said. He sat up a bit straighter. "I do not think my wife is handling Megan's betrayal so very well. Raising the boy may just be that daily reminder to her...." Arnold frowned then continued. "She feels somehow that she had failed Megan. Even though I saw no lack of discipline in our home. Our son, who was raised in the same home, has none of the same rebellious tendencies."

Arnold placed his hand on the letter from his daughter. His eyes dark and searching, looking beyond the letter, perhaps recalling a memory.

"She has always had a wild spirit. She was sometimes impossible to reign in." He looked up.

Corinne watched him work through his pain.

"God knows we all do our best." Lucas said, trying to help ease the man's suffering.

"We can raise Caleb. We would be happy to. You and your family need not ever worry about him being loved and taken care of here." Lucas reached to Arnold's side and gave him a pat on the shoulder.

Corinne watched in curiosity how men soothed each other, so very different from the ways of women. Certainly, by now there would have been a torrent of tears and deep embraces, maybe even some sobbing. This exchange between them was heartwarming in a different way.

"I want to provide a trust fund for his education. If you would allow me." Arnold offered.

Corinne was certain that they could afford to send Caleb off to University on their own but she saw that Lucas nodded in acceptance. Allowing this was a way to ease them, and Corinne wouldn't want to take that away.

"I know a certain time will need to pass, but Corinne and I would like to formally adopt Caleb eventually." Lucas said.

Arnold looked brighter, a little more relief lifted the burden off his shoulders.

"I would be happy to come back and sign any papers that need to be signed. I may just have to come by every so often... See my grandson." Arnold gave Caleb a glance and a hint of a smile played upon his lips.

"You will tell him about her one day?" He asked.

Corinne and Lucas looked at each other, the moment was bittersweet.

"When the time is right." Corinne said. She looked down to Caleb, knowing that someday the news could break his heart. But it would have to be done.

"I will get going for now. I want to see John before I head back to the boarding house in town. I haven't slept well in days. Perhaps now I can sleep easier." Arnold stood. "I will come back tomorrow probably. I want to see the land and get a glimpse of the boy's future. It will keep me going on the hard days." He gave Lucas a clap on the back.

Corinne stood and walked up to him. Letting him get one more glimpse.

"He is a good quiet boy." He ran a finger down the soft cheek of his grandson.

He said his name, "Caleb," with such a soft tone.

He gave Corinne a warm look and was gone a minute later.

Lucas was there in a moment embracing her so perfectly and gently. Caleb nestled between them safely.

They would be able to keep their little Angel. Somehow, the struggles and sleepless nights would all be worth every ounce of effort.

Their family was growing in a way they never expected, but Corinne wouldn't change a single moment.

<hr>

Galina Varushkin

Galina had spent a few weeks working for Ted and Angela, helping in every way she could think of. Making Angela comfortable, doing the laundry, helping with the meals they enjoyed. It was growing easier.

Ted was kind, she knew Angela well, from her years of helping with the laundry. But knowing Ted was a new experience, he was as different as night and day from her own father. Ted was affectionate with Angela, even more so than Lucas with Corinne. Ted was more out-going. Galina wouldn't say that Lucas was too serious, but perhaps a bit more shy about showing his affection in front of others.

Galina enjoyed the camaraderie between them.

Angela was starting to do a little better, her ankle swelling was less, but she was still bound to the rolling chair, which Angela tried not to despise.

The doctor came by to check on Angela every few days, and he was always asking her a few questions too. Making sure that she wasn't doing too much. Galina promised everyone, Ted, Angela and the Doctor that if she was hurting she would take breaks. So far, she had only had one issue, carrying the heavy and wet laundry to the line. A few days before she had filled the basket far too full and after making it down the hill half way, she felt a stabbing pain shoot through her side.

She hadn't even known that she yelled out. She was sitting on the hill, staring at the basket that had miraculously not spilled on the ground. The young strapping Warren was bounding up the hill.

"Miss Galina!" He said, he puffed out a few breaths. He could run faster than she expected.

"I am well enough." She grimaced a bit and stretched while sitting. "The basket was a bit too heavy for my poor ribcage."

"Are you sure you are healed enough for that?" He asked. The sun was high in the sky, nearly noon, and he had an eye squinted as he sized her up.

"No, I am not." She laughed. "But I have learned my lesson, and will make smaller loads to carry." She smiled, feeling foolish. "At least the basket hadn't spilled. I would've had to wash them all again."

She was trying to stand and he reached a hand down to give her a boost.

She felt a spark when she took his hand. Perhaps she was reading too many novels, but she was pleased to see his smile when she held his hand for just a moment longer than she needed too.

"You let me carry this down to the line for you." He offered.

She nodded and followed Warren, watching him carry the load that had been so heavy for her. It seemed to be a bit too easy with his broad shoulders.

She was trying not to notice those shoulders more than she should.

Every day it became a habit, they would get to greet each other each morning, when Galina decided to get up just a few minutes early. With the excuse to make coffee before Ted got up in the morning. But she enjoyed seeing Warren every morning at dawn when he delivered the pail of milk.

After a week of seeing him every morning they had an easy friendship. She was enjoying herself, and was glad that Angela was healing. She had a few hours off one afternoon and with Angela resting Galina took a walk to Spring Creek. She sat on a large rock and watched the water go by. She was thinking about the day when her and Violet had dunked themselves in the river last year. A sort of baptism. She remembered the feeling, being washed clean of her anger.

She dunked her hands into the water, scooped out some water, and drank from her cupped hands. The water was refreshing and she smiled at her memories.

"You have a lovely smile, Miss Galina." She heard Warren's voice say.

She turned, he was carrying two large buckets, swinging them easily.

"Thank you." She said simply, feeling giddy and blushing.

He kneeled down and filled the buckets full.

"You are fifteen?" He asked and pursed his lips together in thought.

Galina nodded.

"When is your birthday?" He asked.

"In September..." She raised an eyebrow, wondering at his line of questioning.

He nodded and looked a little smug.

He picked up the buckets and made to turn around and leave.

She stared at him.

"Well?" She asked him.

Warren smiled, just a little one.

"I plan on stealing a kiss on your birthday." He said.

Her eyes flew open wide, utterly shocked.

"Just giving you fair warning, if you tell me not to I won't." He gave a look that said he meant it.

She didn't say a word. Warren gave her a nod and turned away, with a self-satisfied smirk.

Galina sat in wonder for quite a while on that rock, just wondering about life, gentlemen, and the mysteries of the world. She was content.

✦•◦•◆━━◆•◦•✦

Violet Griffen

Violet watched the morning sun peek over the eastern mountains. She had a smelly and unpleasant job to do, but she could still enjoy the morning. She shaved off a piece of the handmade soap that Corinne and Dolly had made in the lab, it smelled of mint and pine. She scrubbed at the dirty nappies with a bristle brush. They had soaked overnight and came clean easily.

She got through the job efficiently, glad it was done. Certainly not her favorite task, but she was glad to help out. Debbie and Corinne had been up a few times during the night for feedings. Violet had heard the cries even from her own room in the other wing of the cabin. Two young babies in the house was going to be a challenge.

She pulled some wooden pegs from her apron, walked around the back of the cabin, and hung the clean nappies on the line. The ones from last night were dry so she swapped them out.

For a while, it would be this way, one revolution or routine to be replaced by another.

The lives of everyone around her were changing, in small ways and large ones. It was that way... Life would not hold steady for long for you to catch a breath before something new would take your breath away again.

Reynaldo was like that for her. She was taking it slow. She enjoyed their walks together. Knowing he wished for more. But he also knew that she was content as things were for now. There were no promises made, just enjoying his company, but she knew someday, that would not be enough. There was a secret thrill, realizing she was on a new path, towards something that others had found, but had eluded her before.

Her husband Eddie was a glimpse, but he was not meant for her for always. That was what she wanted, not today, but someday.

For now, she would enjoy her mornings, care for a family that she loved, and spend a few nights a week walking along a road that led to her future.

THE END

Please look for the next book **A Kiss in Winter**... coming soon.

Wildflower Series – Character list

Corinne Grant – (nee Harpole) Married to Lucas Grant. Born 1832. Started a business making medicinal oils from plants. Also has built a greenhouse for the cultivating of plants and herbs. She was married to Andrew Temple for a few months before he died of Cholera on the Oregon Trail.

Lucas Grant - Graduate of Yale agricultural school, thrives on farming technology and making improvements in the agricultural field. Married to Corinne.

Chelsea Grant - Married to Russell Grant. Granddaughter of Clive Quackenbush. Mother of Brody and Sarah Grant.

Russell Grant - Lucas Grant's brother, owns a farm nearby. They help each other often on each other's land.

John & Marie Harpole - Corinne's father, first wife Lily (Corinne's mother) - deceased - 2nd wife Marie Harpole - Mother to Cooper and Abigail.

Megan Capron -17-year-old - daughter of Arnold Capron - granddaughter to Rose Capron. She enjoys painting, singing and flirting. She ran away from the Grant's cabin in the summer of 1851 with a ranch hand.

Clive Quakenbush – Born 1782 - Mountain man, fur trapper, Hudson Bay store owner, Government liaison for Indian Affairs, hunter and business man. First wife Christina – they had three children, Jedediah, Thomas and Greta. Second wife- Martha. He currently owns two fancy goods stores in Oregon Territory and a Hudson Bay store in San Francisco. He is also a business partner with Angela Fahey with a family legacy project.

Jedediah Quackenbush - (nickname JQ) son of Clive, works at Oregon City store.

Millicent Quackenbush - (nickname Millie) married to JQ. Works the counter in the store but is active in her community and church.

Dolly Bluebird Bouchard - (Indian name is Bluebird) half-Indian, half-white. Mother was Hopi and father was a French fur trapper. She was sent by her adoptive tribe to learn from Corinne about plants and medicines to bring back and teach the tribe. Her father's name was Joseph Bouchard.

Angela Fahey Greaves - Irish immigrant orphaned and sold into a workhouse at a young age with her brother. She became a maid in Corinne's Aunt's home and they were fast friends. She attempted to cross the Oregon Trail and was injured early on and had to recover before continuing her journey. She bought land outside of Oregon City and the boarding house in town. She is Corinne Grant's neighbor. She received an inheritance from her deceased parents after Corinne found a Boston lawyer. Married to Ted (Thaddeus) Greaves

Sean Fahey - Irish Immigrant who ran away from a Boston work orphanage. Older brother to Angela Fahey. Last known whereabouts, fur trapping along the Snake River in the company of Ol' Willie. He sent Angela away from San Francisco when she crossed the country to find him.

Thaddeus Greaves - (nicknamed Ted) – married to Angela Fahey. They met in San Francisco, he traveled back to upstate New York and retrieved his family. He traveled back by boat with his family to the west and settled in Oregon City to reunite with Angela.

Amelia Greaves – Mother to Ted, widow. She is a skilled lace maker. She joined her son to get a fresh start and a guaranteed business. They live in a townhouse in Oregon City with a storefront in their home. She also has a daughter, Sophia.

Olivia Greaves – Sister to Amelia. She is also a skilled lace maker and has a yearning for adventure.

Warren Martin Jr. - Hired as a spare hand, does milking and odd jobs. Stays with Earl in his cabin during the week.

Earl Burgess – Works as the land manager for Angela Fahey. Also does maintenance for the Orchard House, the boarding house that Angela owns. Lost a hand in an accident years before, but is a hard worker with a lot of farm knowledge.

Henry & Edith Sparks - Henry is the Captain at Fort Kearney, they took Angela in after an unfortunate accident. Edith and Henry nursed her back to health. They adopted three orphan children from a wagon train passing through Fort Kearney. When Henry's post as Captain was completed they left the fort to travel west on the Oregon Trail. Living on Ted and Angela Greaves property.

Galina Varushkin – age 15 – lives outside of Oregon City in a small cabin for her family. Not allowed to finish school she works at different homes throughout the week to earn money by doing laundry.

Slava Varushkin – Russian Immigrant Married to Magdalena (deceased)-Father of Galina, Miloslava (age 11), Pavel (age 9), and Radimir (deceased). He was injured while working for a logging camp and left for the Gold Rush the year before, leaving his family starving and with no resources. He came back with nothing to find that his family had been given a cabin by the Spring Creek Church. He is currently working for Lucas Grant, clearing lumber for more crops.

Magdalena Varushkin – (deceased) Polish immigrant. Married Slava when she was 16. Mother to all the Varushkin children.

Violet Smithers Griffen – Housekeeper for Corinne and Lucas. Married to Edward Griffen, left for gold fields. (Deceased)

Tim Smithers Jr. –brother to Violet, five years younger.
Harold Smithers – youngest brother to Violet.

Oregon City

Doctor Vincent Williams – Oregon City doctor. He works with Corinne and the apothecary to take care of the Oregon City citizens.
Persephone Willliams- the Doctor's wife and friend to Corinne. She helps with birthing and assists her husband in his duties.
Mr. Higgins - runs the local apothecary.
Gomer Hynes – Runs the Oregon gazette, a weekly newspaper.
Pastor Darrell Whittlan & wife Helen – run the Spring Creek Fellowship church outside of Oregon City on Spring Creek road. They adopted orphans and minister to the rural community.
Marshall Crispin - Schoolteacher outside of town.
Reynaldo Legales – Ranch Manager at Harpole Ranch. His father owns a ranch in California territory. Hard worker and right hand man

for John Harpole

Amos Drays - local carpenter in town,

Mrs. Gemma Caplan- former owner of Oregon City boarding house, hired on as manager and head housekeeper.

Sherriff Nigel Tudor – Sherriff of Oregon City. Acts as Judge, Sherriff and county law.

Governor John Pritchlan – resident of Oregon City, governor of Oregon Territory.

Jedidiah Prince – head of the town Council in Oregon City.

Effie Prince – wife of Jedediah Prince. Head of the Christian women's group in town, headstrong and advocate for the poor - Mother of Sydney Prince.

Meredith & Timotheus Smithers – Parents of Violet, Tim and Harold. Timotheus Smithers was hung, by decision of Oregon City after finding him guilty of abuse to Violet Smithers Griffen as a child. Meredith had sided with her husband and believed him instead of her children.

Tim and Harold Smithers – Brothers to Violet, currently running the watermill in Oregon City.

Portland, Oregon Territory

Gabriel Quackenbush - Son of JQ and grandson of Clive, runs the Hudson Bay store in San Francisco, California territory, they moved to Portland when San Francisco became a dangerous boomtown.

Amber Quakenbush - Married to Gabriel, Irish immigrant came over as a child with her parents. Helps her husband run the fancy goods store in Portland.

Kevin & Sadie Landers – proprietors of Portland Boarding House.

San Francisco, California Territory

Brian Murphy - Manager of Q & F Distillery, runs the distillery for the Irish whiskey recipe that Angela found in an old family diary.

Wildflower Series

Book 1 – Finding Her Way
(previously released as Seeing the Elephant)

Book 2 – Angela's Hope

Book 3 – Daughters of the Valley

Book 4 – The Watermill

Released ... Book 5 – Love In Full Bloom

Writing in Progress... Book 6 – A Kiss in Winter

Also by Leah Banicki

Runner Up – A Contemporary love story,
Set in the world of reality TV.

Also Coming Soon:

IMPARATOS Series:

Book 1 – Aurora

This is a young adult contemporary series,
full of action and adventure.

Connect with me online:

https://www.facebook.com/Leah.Banicki.Novelist

Please share your thoughts with me. leahsvoice@me.com

The self-publishing world is very rewarding but has its marketing challenges. Please remember to spread the word about my books if you like them. By using word-of-mouth!
You can help to bless an author.
Like – Share - Leave a review

Thank you, Leah Banicki

My Biography -

I am a writer, wife and mother. I live in SW lower Michigan near the banks of Brandywine Creek. I adore writing historical and contemporary stories, facing the challenges that life throws at you with characters that are relatable. I love finding humor in the ridiculous things that are in the everyday comings and goings of life. For me a good book is when you get to step into the character's shoes and join them on their journey. So climb aboard, let us share the adventure!

My writing buddy is my miniature poodle Mr. Darcy, who snuggles at my feet while I write until he must climb onto my chest for dancing or snuggles. My beagle Oliver is more concerned with protecting the yard from trespassers — squirrels and pesky robins.

I love hearing from my readers and try to answer every email personally.

I am always on Facebook and let my readers know about how the next books are coming along.

I have a slew of books in the works and plan on releasing a new series soon. Keep your eyes peeled for news!
My health does not always allow me to work as fast as I would always like but I am so thankful for every day that God lets me continue to do this work that I love so very much.

I am in the last year of homeschooling my high school daughter. (My sweet girl!)
After that, Lord willing, will allow for more books and research trips.

I plan on continuing the Wildflower Series for many more years.

https://www.facebook.com/Leah.Banicki.Novelist

Please share your thoughts with me.
leahsvoice@me.com

Mr. Darcy – my writing buddy!

Printed in Great Britain
by Amazon

37714260R00169